PENGUIN BOOKS

RUMPOLE AND THE ANGEL OF DEATH

John Mortimer is a playwright, novelist and former practising barrister. During the war he worked with the Crown Film Unit and published a number of novels, before turning to theatre. He has written many film scripts, and plays for both radio and televison, including *A Voyage Round My Father*, the Rumpole plays, which won him the British Academy Writer of the Year Award, and the adaptation of Evelyn Waugh's *Brideshead Revisited*. His many collections of Rumpole stories are published by Penguin, as well as a volume of his plays, two volumes of his acclaimed autobiography, *Clinging to the Wreckage* and *Murderers and Other Friends*, and *In Character* and *Character Parts*, which contain interviews with some of the most famous men and women of our time. His novels include *Summer's Lease*, *Paradise Postponed*, *Titmuss Regained* (its sequel), *Under the Hammer*, all of which have been made into successful television series, *Charade* and *Dunster*.

John Mortimer lives with his wife and their two daughters in what was once his father's house in the Chilterns.

JOHN MORTIMER IN PENGUIN

Fiction
Paradise Postponed   Charade
Like Men Betrayed   The Narrowing Stream
Summer's Lease   Titmuss Regained
Dunster   The Rapstone Chronicles
Under the Hammer

The Rumpole Series
Rumpole of the Bailey   The Trials of Rumpole
Rumpole's Return   Rumpole for the Defence
Rumpole and the Golden Thread   Rumpole's Last Case
Rumpole and the Age of Miracles
Rumpole à la Carte   Rumpole on Trial
The Best of Rumpole
The First Rumpole Omnibus   The Second Rumpole Omnibus
Rumpole and the Angel of Death

Autobiography
Clinging to the Wreckage   Murderers and Other Friends

Interviews
In Character   Character Parts

Plays
A Voyage Round My Father/The Dock Brief/What Shall We Tell
Caroline?

John Mortimer

Rumpole and the Angel of Death

PENGUIN BOOKS

Published by the Penguin Group
Penguin Books Ltd, 27 Wrights Lane, London W8 5TZ, England
Penguin Books USA Inc., 375 Hudson Street, New York, New York 10014, USA
Penguin Books Australia Ltd, Ringwood, Victoria, Australia
Penguin Books Canada Ltd, 10 Alcorn Avenue, Toronto, Ontario, Canada M4V 3B2
Penguin Books (NZ) Ltd, 182–190 Wairau Road, Auckland 10, New Zealand

Penguin Books Ltd, Registered Offices: Harmondsworth, Middlesex, England

First published by Viking 1995
Published in Penguin Books 1996
3 5 7 9 10 8 6 4 2

Copyright © Advanpress Ltd, 1995
All rights reserved

The moral right of the author has been asserted

Printed in England by Clays Ltd, St Ives plc

Except in the United States of America, this book is sold subject
to the condition that it shall not, by way of trade or otherwise, be lent,
re-sold, hired out, or otherwise circulated without the publisher's
prior consent in any form of binding or cover other than that in
which it is published and without a similar condition including this
condition being imposed on the subsequent purchaser

For Stephen Tumin
'So shines a good deed in a naughty world'

Contents

Rumpole and the Model Prisoner

Quintus Blake, O.B.E. and the staff cordially invite

Horace Rumpole Esq.

to a performance of *A Midsummer Night's Dream* by
William Shakespeare
15th September at 7 p.m. sharp.

Entry by invitation only. Proof of identity will be required.

RSVP
The Governor's Office
Worsfield Prison
Worsfield, Berks

I had been to Worsfield gaol regularly over the years and never without breathing a sigh of relief, and gulping in all the fresh air available, after the last screw had turned the last lock and released me from custody. I never thought of going there to explore the magical charm of a wood near Athens.

'Hilda,' I said, taking a swig of rapidly cooling coffee and lining myself up for a quick dash to the Underground, 'can you prove your identity?'

'Is that meant to be funny, Rumpole?' Hilda was deep in the *Daily Telegraph* and unamused.

'I mean, if you can satisfy the authorities you're really She – I mean (here I corrected myself hastily) that you're my wife, I'll try for another ticket and we can go to the theatre together.'

'What's come over you, Rumpole? We haven't been to the theatre together for three years – or whenever Claude last dragged you to the opera.'

'Then it's about time,' I said, 'we went to the *Dream*.'

'Which dream?'

'The *Midsummer Night*'s one.'

'Where is it?' Hilda seemed prepared to put her toe in the water. 'The Royal Shakespeare?'

'Not exactly. It's in Her Majesty's Prison, Worsfield. Fifteenth September. Seven p.m. sharp.'

'You mean you want to take me to Shakespeare done by criminals?'

'Done, but not done in, I hope.'

'Anyway' – She Who Must Be Obeyed found a cast-iron alibi – 'that's my evening at the bridge school with Marigold Featherstone.'

Hilda, I thought, like most of the non-criminal classes, likes to think that those sentenced simply disappear off the face of the earth. Very few of us wonder about their wasted lives, or worry about the slums in which they are confined, or, indeed, remember them at all.

'You'll have to go on your own, Rumpole,' she said. 'I'm sure you'll have lots of friends there, and they'll all be delighted to see you.'

'Plenty of your mates in here, eh, Mr Rumpole? They'll all be glad to see you, I don't doubt.' I thought it remarkable that both She Who Must Be Obeyed and the screw who was slowly and carefully going over my body with some form of metal detector should have the same heavy-handed and not particularly diverting sense of humour.

'I have come for William Shakespeare,' I said with all the dignity I could muster. 'I don't believe he's an inmate here. Nor have I ever been called upon to defend him.'

Worsfield gaol was built in the 1850s for far fewer than the number of prisoners it now contains. What the Victorian forces of law and order required was a granite-faced castle of despair whose outer appearance was thought likely to deter the passers-by from any thoughts of evil-doing. Inside, five large cellular blocks formed the prison for men, with a smaller block set aside for the few women prisoners. In its early days all within was secrecy and silence, with prisoners, forbidden to speak to each other, plodding round the exercise yard and the treadmill – the cat o' nine tails and the rope for ever lurking in the shadows. When it was built it was on the outskirts of a small industrial town, a place to be pointed out as a warning to shuddering children being brought back home late on winter evenings from school. Now the town has spread over the green fields of the countryside and the prison is almost part of the city centre. This, I thought, as my taxi passed it on the way from the station, looked in itself, with its concrete office blocks, grim shopping malls and multi-storey carparks, as if it were built like the headquarters of a secret police force or a group of houses of correction.

Inside the prison there were some attempts at cheerfulness. Walls were painted lime green and buttercup yellow. There was a dusty rubber plant, and posters for seaside holidays, in the office by the gate where I filled in a visitor's form and did my best to establish my identity. But the scented disinfectant was fighting a losing battle with the prevailing smell of stale air, unemptied chamber-pots and greasy cooking.

The screw who escorted me down the blindingly lit passages, with his keys jangling at his hip, told me he'd been a school teacher but became a prison warder for the sake of more pay and free membership of the local golf club. He was a tall, ginger-haired man, running to fat, with that prison pallor which can best be described as halfway between sliced bread and underdone potato chips. On one of his pale cheeks I noticed a recent scar.

The ex-teacher led me across a yard, a dark concrete area lined with borders of black earth in which a few meagre plants didn't seem to be doing well. A small crowd of visitors from the outer world – youngish people whom I took to be social workers and probation officers with their partners, grey-haired governors of other prisons with their wives, enlightened magistrates and a well-known professor of criminology – was waiting. Their voices were muted, serious and respectful, as though, instead of having been invited to a comedy, they were expecting a cremation. They stood in front of the chapel, a gaunt Gothic building no doubt intended to put us all in mind of the terrible severity of the Last Judgement. There, convicted murderers had prayed while their few days of life ticked away towards the

3

last breakfast. 'Puts the wretch that lies in woe / In remembrance of the shroud' – I remembered the lines at the end of the play we were about to see. Then the locked doors of the chapel opened and we were shepherded in to the entertainment.

'I have a device to make all well. Write me a prologue; and let the prologue seem to say, we will do no harm with our swords, and that Pyramus is not kill'd indeed; and for the more better assurance, tell them that I Pyramus, am not Pyramus but Bottom the weaver. This will put them out of fear!' The odd thing was – I had discovered by a glance at my programme before the chapel lights dimmed and the cold, marble-paved area in front of the altar was bathed in sunlight and became an enchanted forest – the prisoner playing Nick Bottom was called Bob Weaver. What he was in for I had no idea, but this weaver seemed to be less of a natural actor than a natural Bottom. There was no hint of an actor playing a part. The simple pomposity, the huge self-satisfaction, and the like-ability of the man were entirely real. When the audience laughed, and they laughed a good deal, the prisoner didn't seem pleased, as an actor would be, but as hurt, puzzled and resentful as bully Bottom mocked. And, when he came to the play scene, he acted Pyramus with intense seriousness which, of course, made it funnier than ever.

We were a segregated audience, divided by the aisle. On one side, like friends of the groom, sat the inmates in grey prison clothes and striped shirts – and trainers (which I used to call sand-shoes when I was a boy) were apparently allowed. On the other side, the friends of the bride were the great and the good, the professional carers and concerned operators of a curious and notoriously unsuccessful system. Of the two sides, it was the friends of the groom who coughed and fidgeted less, laughed more loudly and seemed more deeply involved in the magic that unfolded before them:

> 'But we are spirits of another sort.
> I with the morning's love have oft made sport,
> And like a forester the groves may tread
> Even till the eastern gate, all fiery red,
> Opening on Neptune with fair blessèd beams
> Turns into yellow gold his salt green streams.'

I hadn't realized how handsome Tony Timson would look without his glasses. His association, however peripheral, with an armed robbery (not the sort of thing the Timson family had any experience of, nor indeed talent for) had led him to be ruler of a fairy kingdom. Puck, small, energetic and Irish, I remembered from a far more serious case as a junior member of the clan Molloy. All too soon, for me anyway, he was alone on the stage, smiling a farewell:

> 'If we shadows have offended,
> Think but this, and all is mended:
> That you have but slumbered here,
> While these visions did appear . . .'

Then the house lights went up and I remembered that all the lovers, fairies and Rude Mechanicals (with the exception of the actresses) were robbers, housebreakers, manslaughterers and murderers, there because of their crimes and somebody's – perhaps my – unsuccessful defence.

'I think you'll all agree that that was a pretty good effort.' The Governor was on the stage, a man with a ramrod back, cropped grey hair and pink cheeks, who spoke like some commanding officer congratulating his men after a particularly dangerous foray into enemy territory. 'We owe a great deal to those splendid performers and all those who helped with the costumes. I suggest we might give a hand to our director who is mainly responsible for getting these awkward fellows acting.'

A small, middle-aged man with steel-rimmed spectacles rose up from the front row of the inmates and lifted a hand to acknowledge the applause. This the Governor silenced with a brisk mutter of words of command. 'Now will all those of you who live in, please go out. And those of you who live out, please stay in. You'll be escorted to the boardroom for drinks and light refreshments.'

The screws who had been waiting, stationed round the walls like sentries, reclaimed their charges. I saw the director who had been applauded walking towards them with his knees slightly bent, moving with a curious hopping motion, as though he were a puppet on a string. I hadn't seen his face clearly but something in the way he moved seemed familiar, although I

5

couldn't remember where I'd met him before, or what crime he might, or might not, have committed.

'Never went much for Shakespeare when I was at school,' Quintus Blake, the Governor, told me. He was holding a flabby sausage-roll in one hand and, in the other, a glass of warmish white wine which, for sheer undrinkability, had Pommeroy's house blanc beaten by a short head. 'Thought the chap was a bit long-winded and couldn't make his meaning clear at times. But, by God, doesn't he come into his own in the prison service?'

'You mean, you use him as a form of punishment?'

'That's what I'd've thought when I was at school. That's what I'll tell Ken Fry if he complains we're giving the chaps too good a time. If they misbehave, I'll tell him we put them on Shakespeare for twenty-eight days.' Ken Fry is our new, abrasive, young Home Secretary who lives for the delighted cheers of the hangers and floggers at party conferences. Given time, he'll reintroduce the rack as a useful adjunct to police questioning.

'The truth of the matter' – Quintus bit bravely into the tepid flannel of his sausage-roll – 'is that none of the fellows on Shakespeare duty have committed a single offence since rehearsals began.'

'Is that really true?'

'Well, with one exception.' He took a swig at the alleged Entre Deux Mers, decided that one was enough and put his glass down on the boardroom table. 'Ken Fry says prison is such a brilliant idea because no one commits crimes here. Well, of course, they do. They bully each other and get up to sexual shenanigans which put me in mind of the spot behind the fives court at Coldsands. I don't know what it is about prison that always reminds me of my school-days. Anyway, as soon as they landed parts in the *Dream*, they were as good as gold, nearly all of them. And for that I've got to hand it to Gribble.'

'Gribble?'

'Matthew Gribble. Inmate in charge of Shakespeare. Just about due for release as he's got all the remission possible.'

'He produced the play?'

'And even got a performance out of that human bulldozer who played bully Bottom. One-time boxer who'd had his brains turned into mashed potatoes quite early in his career.'

'Gribble was the man who stood up at the end?'

'I thought I'd get this lot to give him a round of applause.' The Governor looked at the well-meaning elderly guests, the puzzled but hopeful social workers, who were taking their refreshments, as they took all the difficulties in their lives, with grim determination. It was then I remembered Matthew Gribble, an English teacher at a Berkshire polytechnic, who had killed his wife.

'I think,' I said, 'I defended him once.'

'I know you did!' The Governor smiled. 'And he wants you to do the trick again before the Board of Visitors. I said I'd try and arrange it because, so far as I'm concerned, he's an absolutely model prisoner.'

All this happened at a time when Claude Erskine-Brown (who had not yet become a Q.C. – I call them Queer Customers) took to himself a young lady pupil named Wendy Crump. Mizz Crump was a person with high legal qualifications but no oil painting – as Uncle Tom, of blessed memory, would have been likely to say. She had, I believe, been hand-picked by Claude's wife, the Portia of our Chambers, who had not yet got her shapely bottom on to the Bench and been elevated to the title of Mrs Justice Phillida Erskine-Brown, a puisne judge of the High Court.

'Your Mizz Crump,' I told Claude, when we met at breakfast time in the Tastee-Bite eatery a little to the west of our Chambers, 'seems a bit of an all-round asset.'

'All round, Rumpole. You've said it. Wendy Crump is very all round indeed.' He gave a mirthless laugh and spoke as a man who might have preferred a slimline pupil.

'Hope you don't mind,' I told him, 'but I asked her to look up the effect of self-induced drunkenness on crimes of violence. She came up with the answer in a couple of shakes, with reference to all the leading cases.'

'I'll agree she's a dab hand at the law.'

'Well, isn't that what you need a pupil for?' I knew it was a

7

silly question as soon as I'd asked it. An ability to mug up cases on manslaughter was not at all what Claude required of a pupil. He wanted someone willing, husky-voiced and alluring. He wanted a heartshaped face and swooping eyelashes which could drive the poor fellow insane when they were topped by a wig. He wanted to fall in love and make elaborate plans for satisfying his cravings, which would be doomed to disaster. What the poor old darling wanted was yet another opportunity to make a complete ass of himself, and these longings were unlikely to be fulfilled by Wendy Crump.

'What a barrister needs, Rumpole, in a busy life with heavy responsibilities and a great deal of nervous tension is, well, a little warmth, a little adoration.'

'I shouldn't be in the least surprised if Mizz Crump didn't adore you, Claude.'

'Don't even suggest it!' The clever Crump's pupil master gave a shudder.

'Anyway, don't you get plenty of warmth and affection from Philly?'

'Philly's been on circuit for weeks.' Claude took a quick swig of the coffee from the Old Bailey machine and didn't seem to enjoy it. 'And when she's here she spends all her time criticizing me.'

'How extraordinary.' I simulated amazement.

'Yes, isn't it? Philly's away and I have to spend my days stuck here with Wendy Crump. But not my nights, Rumpole. Never, ever, my nights.'

I lost his attention as Nick Davenant from King's Bench Walk passed us, followed by his pupil Jenny Attienzer. She was tall, blonde, willowy and carrying his coffee. Poor old Claude looked as sick as a dog.

That afternoon I was seated at my desk, smoking a small cigar and gazing into space – the way I often spend my time when not engaged in Court – when there was a brisk knock at the door and Wendy Crump entered and asked if I had a set of Cox's Criminal Reports. 'Not in here,' I told her. 'Try upstairs. Cox's Reports are Soapy Sam Ballard's constant reading.' And then, because she looked disappointed at not finding these alluring volumes at once, I did my best to cheer her up.

'Claude thinks you're a wonderful pupil.' I exaggerated, of course. 'I told him you were a dab hand at the law. He's very lucky.'

It's rare nowadays that you see anyone blush, but Wendy's usually pale cheeks were glowing. 'I'm the lucky one,' she said, and added, to my amazement, 'to be doing my pupillage with Erskine-Brown. Everyone I know is green with envy.' Everyone she knew, I thought, must be strangely ignorant of life at the Bailey, where prosecution by Claude has come to be regarded as the key to the gaolhouse door.

Wendy ended her testimonial with 'I honestly do regard it as an enormous privilege.' I supposed the inmates of Worsfield would consider basketball or macramé a privilege if it got them out of solitary confinement. Looking at the enthusiastic Mizz Crump I thought that Claude had been unfair about her appearance. It was just that she had acquired the look of an intelligent and cheerful middle-aged person whilst still in her twenties. She was, I suppose, what would be called considerably overweight, but there was nothing wrong with that. With her wiry hair scraped back, her spectacles and her willing expression, she looked like the photographs of the late Dorothy L. Sayers, a perfectly pleasant sight.

'I just hope I can be a help to him.'

'I'm sure you can.' Although not, I thought, the sort of help the ever-hopeful Claude was after.

'I could never rise to be a barrister like that.'

'Perhaps it's just as well,' I encouraged her.

'I mean I could never stand up and speak with such command – and in such a beautiful voice too. Of course he's handsome, which means he can absolutely dominate a courtroom. You need to be handsome to do that, don't you?'

'Well,' I said, 'thank you very much.'

'Oh, I didn't mean that. Of course *you* dominate all sorts of courtrooms. And it doesn't matter what you look like.' She gave a little gasp to emphasize her point. 'It doesn't matter in the least!'

'The extraordinary thing is that his name is Weaver. He was on the same floor as me, a couple of cell doors away.' Matthew

9

Gribble spoke as if he were describing a neighbour in a country village. 'Bob Weaver. He used to laugh at me because I kept getting books from the library. He was sure I got all the ones with dirty bits in because I knew where to look for them. Of course, in those days, he couldn't tell the difference between soft porn and *Mansfield Park*. He was hardly literate.'

'You say he *was*.'

'Until I taught him to read, that is.'

'You taught him?'

'Oh, yes. I honestly don't know how I'd've got through the years here if I hadn't had that to do.' He gave a small, timid smile. 'As a matter of fact, I enjoyed the chance to teach again.'

'How did you manage it?'

'Oh, I read to him at first. I read all the stories I'd liked when I was a child. We started with *Winnie-the-Pooh* and got on to *Treasure Island* and *Kidnapped*. Then he began to want to read for himself.'

'So you decided to cast him?'

'If we ever did the *Dream*. He looked absolutely right. A huge mountain of a man with the outlook of a child. And kind, too. He *even* had the right name for it.'

'You mean, to play Nick, the weaver?'

'Exactly! I asked him to do it a long time ago. Two years at least. I asked him if he'd like to play Bottom.'

'And he agreed?'

'No.' The timid smile returned. 'He looked profoundly shocked. He thought I'd made some sort of obscene suggestion.'

We had been in the Worsfield interview room four and a bit years before, sitting on either side of the same table, with the bright blue paint and the solitary cactus, and the walls and door half glass so the screws could look in and see what we were up to. Then, we had been talking about his teaching, his production with the Cowshott drama group, the performances which he got out of secretaries and teachers and a particularly dramatic district nurse – and of his wife who apparently hated him and his amateur theatricals. When she flew at him and tore at his face with her fingernails during one of their nightly quarrels over the washing up, he had stabbed her through the heart. I thought I had done the case with my usual brilliance and got the jury to find provocation and reduce the crime to manslaughter, for which the Judge, taking the view that a kitchen knife is not the proper reply to an attack with finger-nails, had given him seven years. As the Governor told me, he was a model prisoner. With full remission he'd be out by the end of the month. That is, unless he was convicted on the charge I was now concerned with. If the Board of Visitors did him for dangerous assault on a prison warden, he'd forfeit a large chunk of his remission.

'The incident we have to talk about,' I said, 'happened in the carpenter's shop.'

'Yes,' he sighed, 'I suppose we have to talk about it.'

All subjects seemed to him, I guessed, flat, stale and unprofit-able after the miracle of getting an illiterate East End prize-fighter to enjoy acting Shakespeare. I remembered his account of the last quarrel with his wife. She had told him he was universally despised. She had mocked him for his pathetic sexual attainments while, at the same time, accusing him, quite without foundation, of abusing his child by a previous marriage. He had heard it all many, many times before. It was only when she told him that he had produced *Hamlet* as though it were a television situation comedy that their quarrel ended in violence.

'Yes, the carpenter's shop.' Matthew Gribble sighed. Then he cheered up slightly and said, 'We were building the set for the *Dream*.'

I had a note of the case given to me by the Governor. There were only four members of the cast working on the scenery, one civilian carpenter and a prison officer in overall charge. His name was Steve Barrington.

'Do you know' – my client's voice was full of wonder – 'Barrington gave up a job as a teacher to become a screw? Isn't that extraordinary?'

'Do you think he regrets it? He may not have got chisels thrown at him in class, with any luck.'

What was thrown was undoubtedly the tool which Matthew had been using. The screw was talking to one of the carpenters and didn't see the missile before it struck his cheek. The other cast members, except for one, said they were busy and didn't see who launched the attack.

'I put the chisel on the bench and I was just turning round to tack the false turf on to the mound we'd built. I didn't see who threw it. I only know that I didn't. I told you the truth in the other case. Why should I lie to you about this?'

Because you don't want to spend another unnecessary minute as a guest of Her Majesty, I thought of saying, but resisted the temptation. It was not for me to pass judgement, not at any stage of the proceedings. My problem was that there was a witness who said he'd seen Matthew Gribble throw the chisel. A witness who seemed to have no reason to tell lies about his friend and educator. It was Bob Weaver who had made the journey from illiteracy to Shakespeare, and been rewarded with the part of bully Bottom.

'Rumpole, a terrible thing has happened in Chambers!' Mizz Liz Probert sat on the edge of my client's chair, her face pale but determined, her hands locked as though in prayer, her voice low and doom-laden. It was as though she were announcing, to waiting relations on the quayside, the fact that the *Titanic* had struck an iceberg.

'Not the nailbrush disappeared again?'

'Rumpole, can't you ever be serious?'

'Hardly ever when it comes to things that have happened in Chambers.'

'Well, this time, perhaps your attitude will be more helpful.'

'It depends on whether I want to be helpful. What is it? Don't tell me. Henry blew the coffee money on a dud horse?'

'Claude has committed the unforgivable sin.'

'You mean, adultery? Well, that's something of an achievement. His attempts usually end in all-round frustration.'

'That too, most probably. No. This is what he said in the clerk's room.'

'Go on. Shock me.'

'Kate Inglefield, who's an assistant solicitor in Damiens, heard him say it. And, of course, she was tremendously distressed.'

'Can you tell me what he said?' I wondered. 'Or are you too embarrassed? Would you prefer to write it down?'

'Don't be silly, Rumpole. He asked Henry if he'd seen his fat pupil about recently.'

There followed a heavy silence, during which I thought I was meant to say something. So I said, 'Go on.'

'What do you mean?'

'Go on till you get to the bit that caused Kate Inglefield – not, I would have thought, a girl who distresses easily – such pain.'

'Rumpole, I've said it. Do I have to say it again?'

'Perhaps if you do, I'll be able to follow your argument.'

'Erskine-Brown said to Henry, "Have you seen my fat pupil?"'

'Recently?'

'What?'

'He said recently.'

'Really, Rumpole. Recently is hardly the point.'

'So the point is my fat pupil?'

'Of course it is!'

I took out a small cigar and placed it between the lips. Sorting out the precise nature of the charge against Claude would require a whiff of nicotine. 'And he was referring – I merely ask for clarification – to his pupil Mizz Crump?'

'Of course he meant Wendy, yes.'

'And he called her fat?'

'It was' – Liz Probert described it as though murder had been committed – 'an act of supreme chauvinism. It's daring to assume that women should alter the shape of their bodies just for the sake of pleasing men. Disgusting!'

'But isn't it' – I was prepared, as usual, to put forward the argument for the Defence – 'a bit like saying the sky's blue?'

'It's not at all like that. It's judging a woman by her appearance.'

'And isn't the other judging the sky by its appearance?'

'I suppose I should have known!' Mizz Probert stood up, all her sorrow turned to anger. 'There's no crime so contemptible that you won't say a few ill-chosen words in its favour. And, don't you dare light that thing until I'm out of the room.'

'I'm sure you're busy.'

'I certainly am. We're having a special meeting tonight of the Sisterhood of Radical Lawyers. We aim to blacklist anyone who sends Claude briefs or appears in Court with him. We're going to petition the Judges not to listen to his arguments and Ballard's got to give him notice to quit.'

'Mizz Liz,' I said, 'how would you describe me?'

'As a defender of hopeless causes.'

'No, I mean my personal appearance.'

'Well, you're fairly short.' The Prosecutor gave me the once over. 'Your nose is slightly purple, and your hair – what's left of it – is curly and you're . . .'

'Go on, say it.'

'Well, Rumpole. Let's face it. You're fat.'

'You said it.'

'Yes.'

'So should I get you blackballed in Court?'

'Of course not.'

'Why not?'

'Because you're a man.'

'I see.'

'I shouldn't think you do. I shouldn't think you do for a moment.'

Mizz Probert left me then. Full of thought, I applied the match to the end of the small cigar.

It was some weeks later that Fred Timson, undisputed head of the Timson clan, was charged with receiving a stolen video recorder. The charge was, in itself, something of an insult to a person of Fred's standing and sensitivity. It was rather as if I had been offered a brief in a case of a non-renewed television licence, or, indeed, of receiving a stolen video recorder. I only took the case because Fred is a valued client and, in many respects, an old family friend. I never tire of telling Hilda that a portion of our family beef, bread, marmalade and washing-up liquid depends on the long life of Fred Timson and his talent for getting caught on the windy side of the law. I can't say that this home truth finds much favour with She Who Must Be Obeyed, who treats me, on these occasions, as though I were only a moderately successful petty thief working in Streatham and its immediate environs.

The Defence was elaborate, having to do with a repair job delivered to the wrong address, an alibi, and the fact that the chief prosecution witness was a distant relative of a member of the Molloy family – all bitter rivals and enemies of the Timsons. While Fred and I were drinking coffee in the Snaresbrook canteen, having left the Jury to sort out the complexities of this minor crime, I told him that I'd seen Tony Timson playing the King of the Fairies.

'No, Mr Rumpole, you're mistaken about that, I can assure you, sir. Our Tony is not that way inclined.'

'No, in *Midsummer Night's Dream*. An entirely heterosexual fairy. Married to the Fairy Queen.'

Fred Timson said nothing, but shook his head in anxious disbelief. I decided to change the subject. 'I don't know if you've heard of one of Tony's fellow prisoners. Bob Weaver, a huge fellow. Started off as a boxer?'

'Battering Bob Weaver!' Fred seemed to find the memory amusing. 'That's how he was known. Used to do bare-knuckle fights on an old airfield near Colchester. And my cousin Percy Timson's young Mavis married Battering Bob's brother, Billy Weaver, as was wrongly fingered for the brains behind the Dagenham dairy-depot job. To be quite candid with you, Mr Rumpole, Billy Weaver is not equipped to be the brains behind anything. Pity about Battering Bob, though.'

'You mean the way he went down for the Deptford minicab murder?'

'Not that exactly. That's over and done with. No. The way he's deteriorated in the nick.'

'Deteriorated?'

'According as Mavis tells Percy, he has. Can't hold a decent conversation when they visits. It's all about books and that.'

'I heard he's learnt to read.'

'Mavis says the family's worried desperate. Bob spent all her visit telling her a poem about a nightingale. Well, what's the point of that? I mean, there can't be all that many nightingales round Worsfield Prison. Course, it's the other bloke they put it down to.'

'Matthew Gribble?'

'Is that the name? Anyway, seems Bob thinks the world of this chap. Says he's changed his life and that he worships him, Mr Rumpole. But Mavis reckons he's been a bad influence on Bob. I mean that Gribble's got terrible form. Didn't he kill his wife? No one in our family ever did that.'

'Of course not. Although Tony Timson was rumoured to have attempted it.'

'Between the attempt and the deed, as you well know, Mr Rumpole, there is a great gulf fixed. Isn't that true?'

'Very true, Fred.'

'And Mavis says Bob's been worse for the last three months. Nervous and depressed like as though he was dreading something.' What, I wondered, had been bugging Battering Bob? It couldn't have been the fact that his friend was in trouble for attacking a warden; that had only happened a month before. 'I suppose,' I suggested, 'it was stage-fright. They started rehearsing *Midsummer Night's Dream* around three months ago.'

'You mean like he was scared of being in a play?'

'He might have been.'

'I hardly think a bloke what went single-handed against six Molloys during the minicab war would be scared of a bit of a play.'

It was then that the tireless Bernard came to tell me that the Jury were back with a verdict. Fred stood up, gave his jacket a tug, and strolled off as though he'd just been called in to dinner at the local Rotary Club. And I was left wondering again why Battering Bob Weaver should decide to be the sole witness against a man he had worshipped.

I got back to Chambers in a reasonably cheerful mood, the Jury having decided to give Uncle Fred the generous benefit of a rather small supply of doubt, and there waiting in my client's chair was another bundle of trouble. None other than Wendy Crump, Claude's pupil, clearly in considerable distress. 'I had to talk to you,' she said, 'because it's all so terribly unfair!'

Was unfair the right word, I wondered. Unkind, perhaps, but not unfair, unless she meant it as a general rebuke to the Almighty who handed out sylphlike beauty to the undiscerning few with absolutely no regard for academic attainment or moral worth. 'Of course,' I said, '*I* think you look very attractive.'

'What?' She looked at me surprised and, I thought, a little shocked.

'In the days of Sir Peter Paul Rubens,' I assured her, 'a girl with your dimensions would have been on page three of the *Sun*, if not on the ceiling of the Banqueting Hall.'

'Please, Rumpole,' she said, 'there are more important things to talk about.'

'Well, exactly,' I assured her. 'People have suggested that *I'm* a little overweight. They have hinted that from time to time, but do I let it worry me? Do I decline the mashed spuds or the fried slice with my breakfast bacon? I do not. I let such remarks slide off me like water off a duck's back.'

'Rumpole!' she said, a little sharply, I thought. 'I don't think your physical appearance is anything to do with all this trouble.'

'Is it not? I just thought that we're birds of a feather.'

'I doubt it!' This Mizz Crump could be very positive at times. 'I came to see you about Erskine-Brown.'

'Of course, he shouldn't have said it.' I was prepared, as I have said, to accept the brief for the Defence. 'It was just one of those unfortunate slips of the tongue.'

'You mean he shouldn't have told me about Kate Inglefield?'

'What's he told you about Mizz Inglefield? You mean that rather bright young solicitor from Damiens? She's quite skinny, as far as I can remember.'

'Rumpole, why do you keep harping on people's personal appearances?'

'Well, didn't Claude say . . .?'

'Claude told me that Kate Inglefield had decided never to brief him again. And she's taken his VAT fraud away from him. And Christine Dewsbury, who's meant to be his junior in a long robbery, has said she'll never work with him again, and Mr Ballard . . .'

'The whited sepulchre who is Head of our Chambers?'

'Mr Ballard has been giving him some quite poisonous looks.'

'Those aren't poisonous looks. That's Soapy Sam's usual happy expression.'

'He's hinted that Erskine-Brown may have to look for other Chambers. He's such a wonderful advocate, Rumpole!'

'Well now, let's say he's an advocate of sorts.'

'And a fine man! A man with very high principles.' I listened in some surprise. Was this the Claude I had seen stumbling into trouble and lying his way out of it over the last twenty years? 'And he has absolutely no idea why he is being victimized.'

'Has he not?'

'None whatever.'

'But *you* know?'

'No, really. I have no idea.'

'Well' – I breathed a sigh of relief – 'that's all right then.'

'No, it's not all right.' She stood up, her cheeks flushed, her voice clear and determined. Mizz Crump might be no oil painting, but I thought I saw in her the makings of a fighter. 'We've got to find out why all this is happening. And we've got to save him. Will you help me get him out of trouble? *Whatever* it is.'

'Helping people in trouble,' I assured her, 'has been my job for almost half a century.'

'So you're with me, Rumpole?' She was, I was glad to see, a determined young woman who might go far in the law.

'Of course I am. We fat people should stick together.' Naturally, I regretted it the moment I had said it.

'The Governor says you're a model prisoner.'

'Yes.'

'Well, that's a kind of tribute.'

'Not exactly what I wanted to be when I was at university. I'd just done my first *Twelfth Night*. I suppose I wanted to be a great director. I saw myself at the National or the R.S.C. If I couldn't do that, I wanted to be an unforgettable teacher of English and open the eyes of generations to Shakespeare. I never thought I'd end up as a model prisoner.'

'Life is full of surprises.' That didn't seem too much of a comfort to Matthew Gribble as we sat together, back in the prison interview room. Spring sunshine was fighting its way through windows that needed cleaning. I had sat in the train, trees with leaves just turning green, sunlight on the grass. A good time to think of freedom, starting a new life and forgetting the past. 'If we can get you off this little bit of trouble, you should be out of here by the end of the month.'

'Out. To do what?' He was smiling gently, but I thought quite without amusement, as he stared into the future. 'I shouldn't think they'll ever ask me to direct a play for the Cowshott amateurs. "You'd better watch out for this one, darling," I can just hear them whispering at the read through. "He stabbed his wife to death with a kitchen knife."'

'There may be other drama groups.'

'Not for me. Do you think they'd have me back at the poly? Not a hope.'

'Anyway' – I tried to cheer him up – 'you did a pretty good job with *A Midsummer Night's Dream.*'

'Shakespeare with violent criminals, deputy-governors' wives and wardens' daughters. Not the R.S.C. exactly, but I can put on a good show in Worsfield gaol. Wasn't Bob Weaver marvellous?'

'Extraordinary.'

'And you know what I discovered? He responds to the sound of poetry. He's got to know it by heart. Great chunks of it.' From Battering Bob to Babbling Bob, I thought, treating his bewildered visitors to great chunks of John Keats. It was funny, of course, but in its way a huge achievement. Matthew Gribble appeared to agree. 'I suppose I'm proud of that.' He thought about it and seemed satisfied. I turned back to the business in hand.

'Those other cast members in the carpenter's helping make the scenery – Tony Timson, the young Molloy? Do you think either of them saw who threw the chisel?'

'If they did, they're not saying. Grassing's a sin in prison.'

'But your protégé Babbling Bob is prepared to grass on you?'

'Seems like it.' He was, I thought, resigned and strangely unconcerned.

'Have you talked to him about it?'

'Yes. Once.'

'What did you say?'

'I told him to always be truthful. That's the secret of acting, to tell the truth about the character. I told him that.'

'Forget about acting for a moment. Did you ask him why he said you attacked the screw?'

There was a silence. Matthew Gribble seemed to be looking past me, at something far away. At last he said, 'Yes, I asked him that.'

'And what did he say?'

'He said' – my client gave a small, not particularly happy smile – 'he said we'd always be friends, wouldn't we?'

The master–pupil relationship – the instructing of a younger, less experienced person in the mysteries of some art, theatrical or legal – seemed a situation fraught with danger. While Matthew Gribble's devoted pupil was turning on his master with damaging allegations, Wendy Crump's pupil master was in increasing trouble, being treated by the Sisterhood of Radical Lawyers as a male pariah. As yet, neither Erskine-Brown, nor his alleged victim, had been informed of the charges against him, although Mizz Probert and her supporters were about to raise the matter before the Bar Council as a serious piece of professional misconduct by the unfortunate Claude, who sat, brooding and unemployed in his room, wondering what it was that his best friend wouldn't tell him which had led to him being shunned by female lawyers. I learnt about the proposed petitioning of the Bar Council when I visited the Soapy Head of our Chambers in order to scotch any plan to drive the unfortunate sinner from that paradise which is 4 Equity Court.

'There is no doubt whatever' – here Ballard put on his carefully modulated tone of sorrowful condemnation – 'that Erskine-Brown has erred grievously.'

'Which one of the Ten Commandments is it exactly, if I may be so bold as to ask, which forbids us to call our neighbour fat?'

'There is such a thing, Rumpole' – Ballard gave me the look with which a missionary might reprove a cannibal – 'as gender awareness.'

'Is there, really? And who told you about that then? I'll lay you a hundred to one it was Mizz Liz Probert.'

'Lady lawyers take it extremely seriously, Rumpole. Which is why we're in danger of losing all our work from Damiens.'

'The all-female solicitors? Not a man in the whole of the firm. Is that being gender aware?'

'However the firm is composed, Rumpole, they provide a great deal of valuable work for all of us.'

'Well, I'm aware of gender,' I told Soapy Sam, 'at least I think I am. You're a man from what I can remember.'

'That remark would be taken very much amiss, Rumpole. If made to a woman.'

'But it's not made to a woman, it's made to you, Ballard. Are you going to stand for this religious persecution of the unfortunate Claude?'

'What he said about Wendy Crump was extremely wounding.'

'Nonsense! She wasn't wounded in the least. None of these avenging angels has bothered to tell her what her pupil master said.'

'Did you tell her?'

'Well, no, I didn't, actually.'

'Did you tell Wendy Crump that Erskine-Brown had called her fat?' For about the first time in his life Soapy Sam had asked a good question in cross-examination. I was reduced, for a moment at least, to silence. 'Why didn't you repeat those highly offensive words to her?'

I knew the answer, but I wasn't going to give him the pleasure of hearing it from me.

'It was because you didn't want to hurt her feelings, did you, Rumpole? And you knew how much it would wound her.' Ballard was triumphant. 'You showed a rare flash of gender awareness and I congratulate you for it!'

Although a potential outcast from the gender-aware society, Claude hadn't been entirely deprived of his practice. New briefs were slow in arriving, but he still had some of his old cases to finish off. One of these was a complex and not particularly fascinating fraud on a bookmaker in which Claude and I were briefed for two of the alleged fraudsters. I needn't go into the details of the case except to say that the Prosecution was in the hands of the dashing and handsome Nick Davenant who had a large and shapely nose, brown hair billowing from under his wig, and knowing and melting eyes. It was Nick's slimline pupil, Jenny Attienzer, whom Claude had hopelessly coveted. This fragile beauty was not in Court on the day in question; whether she thought the place out of bounds because of the gender-unaware Claude, I'm unable to say. But Claude was being assisted by the able but comfortably furnished (slenderly challenged) Wendy Crump and I was on my own.

The case was being tried by her Honour Judge Emma MacNaught, Q.C., sitting as an Old Bailey judge, who had treated Claude, from the start of the case, to a number of withering looks and, when addressing him in person became inevitable, to a tone of icy contempt. This circus judge turned out to have been the author of a slender handbook entitled 'Sexual Harassment in the Legal Profession'. (Wendy Crump told me, some time later, that she would challenge anyone to know whether they had been sexually harassed or not unless they'd read the book.)

Nick Davenant called the alleged victim of our clients' fraud – a panting and sweating bookmaker whose physical attributes I am too gender aware to refer to – and his last question was, 'Mr Aldworth, have you ever been in trouble with the police?'

'No. Certainly not. Not with the police.' On which note of honesty Nick sat down and Claude rose to cross-examine. Before he could open his mouth, however, Wendy was half standing, pulling at his gown and commanding, in a penetrating whisper, that he ask Aldworth if he'd ever been in trouble with anyone else.

'Are you intending to ask any question, Mr Erskine-Brown?' Judge MacNaught had closed her eyes to avoid the pain of looking at the learned chauvinist pig.

'Have you been in trouble with anyone else?' Claude plunged in, clay in the hands of the gown-tugger behind him.

'Only with my wife. On Derby night.' For this, Mr Aldworth was rewarded by a laugh from the Jury, and Claude by a look of contempt from the Judge.

'Ask him if he's ever been reported to Tattersall's.' The insistent pupil behind Claude gave another helping tug. Claude clearly didn't think things could get any worse.

'Have you ever been reported to Tattersall's?' he asked, adding 'the racing authority' by way of an unnecessary explanation.

'Well, yes. As far as I can remember,' Mr Aldworth admitted in a fluster, and the Jury stopped laughing.

'Ask him how many times!'

'How many times?' Wendy Crump was now Claude's pupil master.

'I don't know I can rightly remember.'

'Do your best,' Wendy suggested.

'Well, do your best,' Claude asked.

'Ten or a dozen times . . . Perhaps twenty.'

I sat back in gratitude. The chief prosecution witness had been holed below the waterline, without my speaking a word, and our co-defendants might well be home and dry.

At the end of the cross-examination, the learned Judge subjected Claude to the sort of scrutiny she might have given a greenish slice of haddock on a slab, long past its sell-by date. 'Mr Erskine-Brown!'

'Yes, my Lady.'

'You are indeed fortunate to have a pupil who is so skilled in the art of cross-examination.'

'Indeed, I am, my Lady.'

'Then you must be very grateful that she remains to help you. For the time being.' The last words were uttered in the voice of a prison governor outlining the arrangements, temporary of course, for life in the condemned cell. Hearing them, even my blood, I have to confess, ran a little chill.

When the lunch adjournment came Claude shot off about some private business and I strolled out of Court with the model pupil. I told her she'd done very well.

'Thank you, Rumpole.' Wendy took my praise as a matter of course. 'I thought the Judge was absolutely outrageous to poor old Claude. Going at him like that simply because he's a man. I can't stand that sort of sexist behaviour!' And then she was off in search of refreshment and I was left wondering at the rapidity with which her revered pupil master had become 'poor old Claude'.

And then I saw, at the end of the wide corridor and at the head of the staircase, Nick Davenant, the glamorous Prosecutor, in close and apparently friendly consultation with the leader of the militant sisterhood, Mizz Liz Probert of our Chambers. I made towards them but, as she noticed my approach, Mizz Liz melted away like snow in the sunshine and, being left alone with young Nick, I invited him to join me for a pint of Guinness and a plateful of steak and kidney pie in the pub across the road.

'I saw you were talking to Liz Probert?' I asked him when we were settled at the trough.

'Great girl, Liz. In your Chambers, isn't she?'

'I brought her up, you might say. She was my pupil in her time. Did she question your gender awareness?'

'Good heavens, no!' Nick Davenant laughed, giving me a ringside view of a set of impeccable teeth. 'I think she knows that I'm tremendously gender aware the whole time. No. She's just a marvellous girl. She does all sorts of little things for me.'

'Does she indeed?' The pie crust, as usual, tasted of cardboard, the beef was stringy and the kidneys as hard to find as beggars in the Ritz, but they couldn't ruin the mustard or the Guinness. 'I suppose I shouldn't ask what sort of things.'

'Well, I wasn't talking about that in particular.' The learned Prosecutor gave the impression that he *could* talk about that if he wasn't such a decent and discreet young Davenant. 'But I mean little things like work.'

'Mizz Liz works for you?'

'Well, if I've got a difficult opinion to write, or a big case to note up, then Liz will volunteer.'

'But you've got Miss Slenderlegs, the blonde barrister, as your pupil.'

'Liz says she can't trust Jenny to get things right, so she takes jobs on for me.'

'And you pay her lavishly of course.'

'Not at all.' Still smiling in a blinding fashion, Nick Davenant shook his head. 'I don't pay her a thing. She does it for the sake of friendship.'

'Friendship with you, of course?'

'Friendship with me, yes. I think Liz is really a nice girl. And I don't see anything wrong with her bum.'

'Wrong with what?'

'Her bum.'

'That's what I thought you said.'

'Do you think there's anything wrong with it, Rumpole?' A dreamy look had come over young Davenant's face.

'I hadn't really thought about it very much. But I suppose not.'

'I don't know why she has to go through all that performance about it, really.'

'Performance?'

'At Monte's beauty parlour, she told me. In Ken High Street. Takes hours, she told me. While she has to sit there and read *Hello!* magazine.'

'You don't mean that she reads this – whatever publication you mentioned – while changing the shape of her body for the sake of pleasing men?'

'I suppose,' Davenant had to admit reluctantly, 'it's in a good cause.'

'Have the other half of this black Liffey water, why don't you?' I felt nothing but affection for Counsel for the Prosecution, for suddenly, at long last, I saw a chink of daylight at the end of poor old Claude's long, black tunnel. 'And tell me all you know about Monte's beauty parlour.'

The day's work done, I was walking back from Ludgate Circus and the well-known Palais de Justice, when I saw, alone and palely loitering, the woman of the match, Wendy Crump. I hailed her gladly, caught her up and she turned to me a face on which gloom was written large. I couldn't even swear that her spectacles hadn't become misted with tears.

'You don't look particularly cheered up,' I told her, 'after your day of triumph.'

'No. As a matter of fact I feel tremendously depressed.'

'What about?'

'About Claude. I've been thinking about it so much and it's made me sad.'

'Someone told you?' I was sorry for her.

'Told me what?'

'Well' – I thought, of course, that the damage had been done by the sisterhood over the lunch adjournment – 'what Claude had said about you that caused all the trouble.'

'All what trouble?'

'Being blackballed, blacklisted, outlawed, outcast, dismissed from the human race. Why Liz Probert and the gender-aware radical lawyers have decided to hound him.'

'Because of what he said about me?'

'They haven't told you?'

'Not a word. But *you* know what it was?'

'Perhaps.' I was playing for time.

'Then tell me, for God's sake.'

'Quite honestly, I'd rather not.'

'What on earth's the matter?'

'I'd really rather not say it.'

'Why?'

'You'd probably find it offensive.'

'Rumpole, I'm going to be a barrister. I'll have to sit through rape, indecent assault, sex and sodomy. Just spit it out.'

'He was probably joking.'

'He doesn't joke much.'

'Well, then. He called you, and I don't suppose he meant it, fat.'

She looked at me and, in a magical moment, the gloom lifted. I thought there was even the possibility of a laugh. And then it came, a light giggle, just as we passed Pommeroy's.

'Of course I'm fat. Fatty Crump, that set me apart from all the other anorexic little darlings at school. That and the fact that I usually got an A-plus. It was my trademark. Well, I never thought Claude looked at me long enough to notice.'

When this had sunk in, I asked her why, if she hadn't heard from Liz Probert and her Amazonians, she was so shaken and wan with care.

'Because' – and here the note of sadness returned – 'I used to hero-worship Claude. I thought he was a marvellous barrister. And now I know he can't really do it, can he?'

She looked at me, hoping, perhaps, for some contradiction. I was afraid I couldn't oblige. 'All the same,' I said, 'you don't want him cast into outer darkness and totally deprived of briefs, do you?'

'Good heavens, no. I wouldn't wish that on anyone.'

'Then, in the fullness of time,' I told her, 'I may have a little strategy to suggest.'

'Hilda,' I said, having managed to ingest most of a bottle of Château Fleet Street Ordinaire over our cutlets, and with it taken courage, 'what would you do if I called you fat?' I awaited the blast of thunder, or at least a drop in the temperature to freezing, to be followed by a week's eerie silence.

To my surprise she answered with a brisk 'I'd call you fatter!'

'A sensible answer, Hilda.' I had been brave enough for one evening. 'You and Mizz Wendy Crump are obviously alike in tolerance and common sense. The only trouble is, she couldn't say that to Claude because he has a lean and hungry look. Like yon Cassius.'

'Like yon *who*?'

'No matter.'

'Rumpole, I have absolutely no idea what you're talking about.'

So I told her the whole story of Wendy and Claude and Mizz Probert, with her Sisterhood, ready to tear poor Erskine-Brown apart as the Bacchantes rent Orestes, and the frightened Ballard. She listened with an occasional click of the tongue and shake of her head, which led me to believe that she didn't entirely approve. 'Those girls,' she said, 'should be a little less belligerent and learn to use their charm.'

'Perhaps they haven't got as much charm as you have, Hilda,' I flannelled, and she looked at me with deep suspicion.

'But you say this Wendy Crump doesn't mind particularly?'

'She seems not to. Only one thing seems to upset her.'

'What's that?'

'She's disillusioned about Claude not because of the fat chat, but because she's found out he's not the brilliant advocate she once thought him.'

'Hero-worship! That's always dangerous.'

'I suppose so.'

'I remember when Dodo and I were at school together, we had an art mistress called Helena Lampos and Dodo absolutely hero-worshipped her. She said Lampos revealed to her the true use of watercolours. Well, then we heard that this Lampos person was going to leave to get married. I can't think who'd agreed to marry her because she wasn't much of a catch, at least not in my opinion. Anyway, Dodo was heartbroken and couldn't bear the idea of being separated from her heroine so, on the morning she was leaving, Lampos could not find the blue silky coat that she was always so proud of.'

When she starts on her schooldays I feel an irresistible urge to apply the corkscrew to the second bottle of the Ordinaire. I was engaged in this task as Hilda's story wound to a conclusion. 'So, anyway, the coat in question was finally found in Dodo's locker. She thought if she hid it, she'd keep Miss Lampos. Of course, she didn't. The Lampos left and Dodo had to do a huge impot and miss the staff concert. And, by the way, Rumpole, there's absolutely no need for you to open another bottle of that stuff. It's high time you were in bed.'

At the Temple station next morning I bought a copy of *Hello!*, a mysterious publication devoted to the happy lives of people I had never heard of. When I arrived in Chambers my first port of call was to the room where Liz Probert carried on her now flourishing practice. She was, as the saying is, at her desk, and I noticed a new scarlet telephone had settled in beside her regulation black instrument.

'Business booming, I'm glad to see. You've had to install another telephone.'

'It's a hotline, Rumpole.'

'Hot?' I gave it a tentative touch.

'I mean it's private. For the use of women in Chambers only.'

'It doesn't respond to the touch of the male finger.'

'It's so we can report harassment, discrimination and verbally aggressive male barrister or clerk conduct direct to the S.R.L. office.'

The S –?'

'Sisterhood of Radical Lawyers.'

'And what will they do? Send for the police? Call the fire brigade to douse masculine ardour?'

'They will record the episode fully. Then we shall meet the victim and decide on action.'

'I thought you decided on action before you met Wendy Crump.'

'Her case was particularly clear. Now she's coming to the meeting of the Sisterhood at five-thirty.'

'Ah, yes. She told me about that. I think she's got quite a lot to say.'

'I'm sure she has. Now what do you want, Rumpole? I'm before the Divisional Court at ten-thirty.'

'Good for you! I just came in to ask you a favour.'

'Not self-induced drunkenness as a defence? Crump told me she had to look that up for you.'

'It's not the law. Although I do hear you work for other barristers for nothing, and so deprive their lady pupils of the beginnings of a practice.'

Mizz Probert looked, I thought, a little shaken, but she picked up a pencil, underlined something in her brief and prepared to ignore me.

'Is that what you came to complain about?' she asked without looking at me.

'No. I've come to tell you I bought *Hello!* magazine.'

'Why on earth did you do that?' She looked up and was surprised to see me holding out the publication in question.

'I heard you read it during long stretches of intense boredom. I thought I might do the same when Mr Injustice Graves sums up to the Jury.'

'I don't have long moments of boredom.' Mizz Liz sounded businesslike.

'Don't you really? Not when you have to sit for hours in Monte's beauty parlour in Ken High Street?'

'I don't know what you're talking about . . .' The protest came faintly. Mizz Probert was visibly shaken.

'It must be awfully uncomfortable. I mean, I don't think I'd want to sit for hours in a solution of couscous and assorted stewed herbs with the whole thing wrapped up in tinfoil. I suppose *Hello!* magazine is a bit of a comfort in those circumstances. But is it worth it? I mean, all that trouble to change what a bountiful nature gave you – for the sake of pleasing men?'

I didn't enjoy asking this fatal question. I brought Mizz Liz up in the law and I still have respect and affection for her. On a good day she can be an excellent ally. But I was acting for the underdog, an undernourished hound by the name of Claude Erskine-Brown. And the question had its effect. As the old-fashioned crime writers used to say in their ghoulish way, the shadow of the noose seemed to fall across the witness-box.

'No one's mentioned that to the S.R.L.?'

'I thought I could pick up the hotline, but then it might be more appropriate if Wendy Crump raised it at your meeting this afternoon. That would give you an opportunity to reply. And I suppose Jenny Attienzer might want to raise the complaint about her pupil work.'

'What *are* you up to, Rumpole?'

'Just doing my best to protect the rights of lady barristers.'

'Anyone else's rights?'

'Well, I suppose, looking at the matter from an entirely detached point of view, the rights of one unfortunate male.'

'The case against Erskine-Brown has raised strong feelings in the Sisterhood. I'm not sure I can persuade them to drop it.'

'Of course you can persuade them, Liz. With your talent for advocacy, I bet you've got the Sisterhood eating out of your hand.'

'I'll do my best. I can't promise anything. By the way, it may not be necessary for Crump to attend. I suppose Kate Inglefield may have got hold of the wrong end of the stick.'

'Exactly. Claude said "that pupil". Not "fat pupil". Try it anyway, if you can't think of anything better.'

And so, with the case of the *Sisterhood* v. *Erskine-Brown* settled, I was back in the gloomy prison boardroom. When I'd first seen it, members of the caring, custodial and sentencing professions were feasting on sausage-rolls and white wine after *A Midsummer Night's Dream*. Now it was dressed not for a party but for a trial, and had taken on the appearance of a peculiarly unfriendly Magistrates Court.

Behind the table at the far end of the room sat the three members of the prisoners' Board of Visitors who were entitled to try Matthew Gribble. The Chairwoman centre stage was a certain Lady Bullwood, whose hair was piled up in a jet-black mushroom on top of her head and who went in for a good deal of costume jewellery, including a glittering chain round her neck from which her spectacles swung. Her look varied between the starkly judicial and the instantly confused, as when she suddenly lost control of a piece of paper, or forgot which part of her her glasses were tied to.

Beside her, wearing an expression of universal tolerance and the sort of gentle smile which can, in my experience, precede an unexpectedly stiff sentence, sat the Bishop of Worsfield, who had a high aquiline nose, neatly brushed grey hair and the thinnest strip of a dog-collar.

The third judge was an elderly schoolboy called Major Oxborrow, who looked as though he couldn't wait for the whole tedious business to be over, and for the offer of a large gin-and-tonic in the Governor's quarters. Beside them, in what I understood was a purely advisory capacity, sat my old friend the Governor, Quintus Blake, who looked as if he would rather be anywhere else and deeply regretted the need for these proceedings. He had, I remembered with gratitude, been so anxious to see Matthew Gribble properly defended that he had sent for Horace Rumpole, clearly the best man for the job. There was a clerk at a small table in front of the Visitors, whose job was, I imagined, to keep them informed as to such crumbs of law as were still available in prison. The Prosecution was in the nervous hands of a young Mr Fraplington, a solicitor from some government department. He was a tall, gangling person who looked as though he had shot up in the last six months and his jacket and trousers were too short for him.

What I didn't like was the grim squadron of screws who lined the walls as though expecting an outbreak of violence, and the fact that my client was brought in handcuffed and sat between two of the largest, beefiest prison officers available. After Matthew had been charged with committing an assault, obstructing an officer in the course of his duty, and offending against good order and discipline, he pleaded not guilty on my express instructions. Then I rose to my feet. 'Haven't you forgotten something?'

'Do you wish to address the Court, Mr Rumpole?' The clerk, a little ferret of a man, was clearly anxious to make his presence felt.

'I certainly do. Have you forgotten to read out the charges of mass murder, war crimes, rioting, burning down E-wing and inciting to mutiny?'

The ferret looked puzzled. The Chairwoman sorted hopelessly through her papers and Mr Fraplington for the Prosecution said helpfully, 'This prisoner is charged with none of those offences.'

'Then if he is not,' I asked, with perhaps rather overplayed amazement, 'why is he brought in here shackled? Why is this room lined with prison officers clearly expecting a dreadful scene of violence? Why is he being treated as though he were some hated dictator guilty of waging aggressive war? My client, Mr Gribble, is a gentle academic and student of Shakespeare. And there is no reason for him to attend these proceedings in irons.'

'Your client, as I remember, was found guilty of the manslaughter of his wife.' The handsome bishop was clearly the one to look out for.

'For that,' I said, 'he has almost paid his debt to society. Next week, subject to the dismissal of these unnecessary charges, that debt will be fully and finally settled and, as I'm sure the Governor will tell you, during his time in Worsfield he has been a model prisoner.'

Quintus did his stuff and whispered to the Chairwoman. She found her glasses, yanked them on to her nose and said that, in all the circumstances, my client's handcuffs might be removed.

After that the proceedings settled down like an ordinary trial in a Magistrates Court, except for the fact that we were all in gaol already. Mr Fraplington nervously opened the simple facts. Then Steve Barrington, the screw who received the flying chisel, clumped his way to the witness stand and gave the evidence which might keep Matthew Gribble behind bars for a good deal longer. He hadn't seen the chisel thrown. The first he knew about it was when he was struck on the cheek. Gribble had been the only prisoner working with a chisel and he had seen him using it immediately before he turned away to answer a request from prisoner D41 Molloy. Later he took statements from the prisoners, and in particular from B19 Weaver. What Weaver told him led to the present charges against A13 Gribble. What Weaver told him, I rose to point out, had better come from Weaver himself.

'Mr Barrington' – I began my cross-examination – 'you were a teacher once?'

'Yes, I was.'

'And you gave it up to become a prison officer?'

'I did.'

'Is that because you found teaching too difficult?'

'I wonder if this is a relevant question?' Young Fraplington had obviously been told to make his presence felt and interrupt the Defence whenever possible.

'Mr Fraplington, perchance you wonder at this question? But wonder on, till truth make all things plain.'

'Mr Rumpole, I'm not exactly sure what you mean.' The Chairwoman's glasses were pulled off and swung gently.

'Then you didn't see *A Midsummer Night's Dream*? You missed a treat, Madam. Produced brilliantly by my client and starring Prisoner Weaver as bully Bottom. You enjoyed it, didn't you, Mr Barrington?'

'I thought they did rather well, yes.'

'And I don't suppose, as a teacher who gave up the struggle, you could have taught a group of hard-boiled villains to play Shakespeare?'

'Mr Rumpole, I *must* agree with Mr Fraplington. How is this in the least relevant to the charge of assault?' The Bishop came in on the act.

'Because I think we may find, Bishop, that this isn't a case about assault, it's a case about teaching. Mr Barrington, you would agree that my client took Weaver and taught him to read, taught him about poetry and finally taught him to act?'

'To my knowledge, yes, he did.'

'And since this pupillage and this friendship began, Weaver, too, has been a model prisoner?'

'We haven't had any trouble from him lately. No.'

'Whereas before the pupillage, he was a general nuisance?'

'He was a handful. Yes. That's fair enough. He's a big man and . . .'

'Alarming when out of control?'

'I'd have to agree with you.'

'Good. I'm glad we see eye to eye, Mr Barrington. So before Matthew Gribble took him on, so to speak, there'd been several cases of assault, three of breaking up furniture, disobeying reasonable orders, throwing food. An endless list?'

'He was constantly in trouble. Yes.'

'And since he and Gribble became friends, nothing?'

'I believe that's right.'

'So you believe Matthew Gribble's influence on Weaver has been entirely for the good.'

'I said, so far as I know.'

'So far as you know. Well, we'll see if anyone knows better. Now, you questioned the other prisoners, Timson and Molloy, about this incident in the carpenter's shop?'

'Yes, I did.'

'And what did they tell you?'

'They said they hadn't seen anything.'

'And did you believe them?'

'Do I have to answer that question?'

'I have asked the question, and I'll trouble you to answer it.'

'No, I didn't altogether believe it.'

'Because prisoners don't grass.'

'What was that, Rumpole?' The Chairwoman asked for an explanation.

'Prisoners don't tell tales. They don't give evidence against each other. On the whole. Isn't that true, Mr Barrington?'

'I thought they might have seen something, but they were sheltering the culprit. Yes.'

'So Timson might have seen Molloy do it. Or Molloy might have seen Timson do it. Or either of them might have seen Weaver do it. But they weren't telling. Is that possible?'

'I suppose it's possible. Yes.'

'Or Weaver might have seen Timson or Molloy do it and blamed it on Gribble to protect them?'

'He wouldn't have done that.' There was an agitated whisper from my client and I stooped to give him an ear.

'What?'

'He wouldn't have blamed it on me. I know Bob wouldn't do that.'

'Matthew,' I whispered sternly, 'your time to give evidence will come later. Until it does, I'd be much obliged if you'd take a temporary vow of silence.' I went back to work. 'Yes, officer. What was your answer to my question?'

'B19 Weaver had a particular admiration for A13 Gribble, sir. I don't think he'd have blamed him. Not just to protect the other two.'

'He wouldn't have blamed him just to protect the other two, eh?' The Bishop, who seemed to have cast himself as the avenging angel, dictated a note to himself with resonant authority.

Bottom the Weaver towered over the small witness table and the screws that stood behind him. He looked at the Visitors, his head slightly on one side, his nose broken and never properly set, and smiled nervously, as he had stood before the court of Duke Theseus, awkward, on his best behaviour, likely to be a bore, but somehow endearing. He didn't look at A13 Gribble, but my client looked constantly at him, not particularly in anger but with curiosity and as if prepared to be amused. That was the way, I thought, he might have watched Bob Weaver rehearsing the play.

Mr Fraplington had no trouble in getting the witness to tell his story. He was in the carpenter's shop in the morning in question. They were making the scenery. He was enjoying himself as he enjoyed everything about the play. Although he was dead nervous about doing it, it was the best time he'd ever had in his life. A13 Gribble was a fantastic producer, absolutely brilliant, and had changed his life for him. 'Made me see a new world', was the way he put it. Well, that morning when all the others were busy working and Mr Barrington was turned away, he'd seen A13 Gribble pick up the chisel and throw it. It struck the prison officer on the cheek, causing bleeding which he fully believed was later seen to by the hospital matron. He kept quiet for a week, because he was reluctant to get the best friend he ever had into trouble. But then he'd told the investigating officer exactly what he saw. He felt he had to do it. Doing the play was the best day in his life. Standing there, telling the tale against his friend, was the worst. Sometimes he thought he'd rather be dead than do it. That was the honest truth. To say that Battering Bob was a good witness is an understatement. He was as good a witness as he was a Bottom; he didn't seem to be acting at all.

'The first question, of course, is why?'

'Pardon me?'

'Why do you think your friend Matthew threw a chisel at the officer? Can you help me about that?' It would have been no use trying to batter the batterer – he had clearly won the hearts of the Visitors – so I came at him gently and full of smiles. 'He's always been a model prisoner. Not a hint of violence.'

'Perhaps' – Bob Weaver closed one eye, giving me his careful consideration – 'he kind of had it bottled up, his resentment against Mr Barrington.'

'We haven't heard he resented Mr Barrington?'

'Well, we all did to an extent. All of us actors.'

'Why was that?'

'He put Jimmy Molloy on a charge, so he lost two weeks' rehearsal with Puck.'

The Visitors smiled. I had gone and provided my client with a motive. Up to now this cross-examination seemed a likely candidate for the worst in my career so I tried another tack.

'All right. Another why.'

'Yes, sir.'

'If you feel you'd rather be dead than do it, why did you decide to grass against your friend?'

'I don't know why you have adopted the phrase "grass" from prison argot, Mr Rumpole.' The Bishop was clearly a circus judge manqué. 'This inmate has come here to give evidence.'

'Evidence which may or may not turn out to be the truth. Very well then. The Bishop has told us to forget the argot.'

'Forget the what?' Bob looked amicably confused and the Bishop smiled tolerantly. 'Slang,' he translated. 'I should have called it slang.'

'Why did you decide to give evidence against your friend?'

'Let me tell you this quite honestly.' The Batterer turned from me and faced the Visitors. 'Years ago, I might not have done it. In fact, I wouldn't. Grass on a fellow inmate. Never. Might have given him a bit of a hiding like. If I'd felt the need of it. But never told the tale. Rather have had me tongue cut out. But then . . . Well, then I got to know Matthew. I'd still like to call him that. With all respect. And he taught me . . . Well, he taught me everything. He taught me to read. Yes. He taught me to like poetry, which I'd thought worse than a punch in the kidneys. Then he taught me to act and to enjoy myself like I never did even in the old days of the minicab battles, which now seem a complete waste of time, quite honestly. But Matthew taught me more than that. "You have to be truthful, Bob", those were his words to me. Well, that's what I remembered. So, when it came to it, I remembered his words. That's all I've got to say.'

'You took his advice and told the truth.' The Bishop was clearly delighted, but I was looking at Bob. It had never happened before. It certainly didn't happen when he performed in the *Dream*, but now I knew that he was an actor playing a part.

And then something clicked in my mind. A picture of Dodo Mackintosh at school, not wanting to let her heroine go, and I knew what the truth really was.

'You've told us Matthew Gribble is the friend who meant most to you.'

'Meant everything to me.'

'The only real friend you've ever had. Would you go as far as to say that?'

'I would agree with that, sir. Every word of it.'

'And one who has let you into a new world.'

'He's already told us that, Mr Rumpole.' I prayed for the Bishop to address himself to God and leave me alone.

'It's too true. Too very true.'

'I don't suppose life in Worsfield Category A Prison could

ever be compared to a holiday in the Seychelles, but he has made your life here bearable?'

'More than that, Mr Rumpole. I wouldn't have missed it.'

'And in a week, if he is acquitted on this charge, Matthew Gribble will be free.'

It was as if I had got in a sudden, unexpectedly powerful blow in the ring. Bob closed his eyes and almost seemed to stop breathing. When he shook his head and answered, he had come back, it seemed to me, to the truth.

'I don't want to think about it.'

'Because you may never see him again?'

'Visits. There might be visits.'

'Are you afraid there might not be?' Matthew appeared to be about to say something, or utter some protest. I shot some *sotto voce* advice into his earhole to the effect that if he uttered another sound, I would walk off the case. Then I looked back at the Batterer. He seemed not to have recovered from the punch and was still breathless.

'It crossed my mind.'

'And did it cross your mind that he might move away, to another part of England, get a new job, work with a new drama group and put on new plays with no parts in them for you? Did you think he might forget the friend he'd made in prison?'

There was a long silence. Bob was getting his breath back, preparing to get up for the last round, but with defeat staring him in the face.

He said, 'Things like that do happen, don't they?'

'Oh yes, Bob Weaver. They happen very often. If a man wants to make a new life, he doesn't care to be reminded of the people he met inside. Did that thought occur to you?'

'I did worry about that, I suppose. I did worry.'

'And did you worry that all that rich, fascinating new world might vanish into thin air? And you'd be left with only a few old lags and failed boxers for company?'

There was silence then. Bob didn't answer. He was saved by the bell. Rung, of course, by the Bishop.

'Where's all this leading up to, Mr Rumpole?'

'Let me suggest where it led you, Bob.' I ignored the cleric and concentrated on the witness. 'It led you to think of the one way you could stop Matthew Gribble leaving you.'

'How was I going to do that?'

'Quite a simple idea but it seems to have worked. Up to now. The way to do it was to get him into trouble.'

'Trouble?'

'Serious trouble. So he'd lose his remission. I expect you thought of that some time ago and you waited for an opportunity. It came, didn't it, in the carpenter's shop?'

'Did it?'

'Matthew turned away to fix the grass covering on the mound. No one else was looking when you picked up his chisel. No one saw you throw it. Like all successful crimes it was helped by a good deal of luck.'

'Crime? Me? What are you talking about? I done no crime.' Bob looked at the Visitors. For once even the Bishop was silent.

'I suppose I'm talking about perverting the course of justice. Of assaulting a prison officer. I've got to hand it to you, Bob. You did it for the best of motives. You did it to keep a friend.'

Bob's head was lowered, but now he made an effort to raise it and looked at the Visitors. 'I didn't do it. I swear to God I didn't. Matthew did it and he's got to stay here. You can't let him go.' By then I think even they thought he was acting. But that wasn't the end of the story.

'Why did you do it?' The trial, if you could call it a trial, was over. Matthew and I were together for the last time in the interview room. We were there to say goodbye.

'I told you. What've I got outside? Schools that won't employ me. Actors and actresses who wouldn't want to work with me. What would they think? If I didn't like their performances, I might stab them. They'd be talking about me, whispering, laughing perhaps. And I'd come in the room and they'd be silent or look afraid. Here, they all want to be in my plays. They want to work with me, and I want to work with them. I thought of *Much Ado* next. Won't Bob make a marvellous Dogberry? Then, I don't know, do you think he could possibly do a Falstaff?'

'Become an old English gent? Who knows. You've got plenty of time. They knocked a year and a half off your remission.'

'Yes. A long time together. You were asking me why I threw the chisel?'

He knew I wasn't asking him that. At the end of Battering Bob's evidence I had to decide whether or not to call my client. Matthew had kept quiet when I'd told him to, and I knew he'd make a good impression. He walked to the witness table, took the oath and looked at me with patient expectation.

'Matthew Gribble. We've heard you were a model prisoner.'

'I've never been in trouble here, if that's what you mean.'

'And of all you've done for Bob Weaver.'

'I think it's been a rewarding experience for both of us.'

'And you are due to be released next week.'

'I believe I am.'

I drew in a deep breath and asked the question to which I felt sure I knew the answer. 'Matthew, did you ever throw that chisel at Prison Officer Barrington?'

The answer, when it came, was another punch in the stomach, this time for me. 'Yes, I did. I threw it.' Matthew looked at the Visitors and said it as though he was talking about a not very interesting part of the prison routine. 'I did it because I couldn't forgive him for putting Puck on a charge.' After that, the case was over and Matthew's exit from Worsfield inevitably postponed.

'You know I wasn't asking you why you threw the chisel because you didn't throw it. I'm asking you why you said you did.'

'I told you. I've decided to stay on.'

'You knew Battering Bob did it and he blamed you to keep you here because he thought he needed you.'

'Don't you think that's rather an extraordinary tribute to a friendship?'

There seemed no answer to that. I didn't know whether to curse Matthew Gribble or to praise him. I didn't know if he was the best or the worst client I ever had. I knew I had lost a case unnecessarily, and that is something I don't like to happen.

'You can't win them all, Mr Rumpole, can you?' Steve

Barrington looked gratified at the result. He took me to the gate and, as he waited for the long unlocking process to finish, he said, 'I don't think I'll ever go back to teaching. They seem half barmy, some of them.'

At last the gates and the small door in the big one were open. I was out and I went out. Matthew was in and he stayed in. Damiens sent a brief in a long case to Claude and I told him he had a brilliant pupil.

'I suppose she'll be wanting a place in Chambers soon?' Claude didn't seem to welcome the idea.

'So far as I'm concerned she can have one now.'

'Young Jenny Attienzer is apparently not happy with Nick Davenant over in King's Bench Walk. Do you think I might take her on as a pupil?'

'I think,' I told him, 'that it would be a very bad idea indeed. I'm sure Philly wouldn't like it, and I'd have to start charging for defending you.'

'Rumpole' – Claude was thoughtful – 'do you know why everyone went off me in that peculiar way?'

'Not really.'

But Claude had his own solution. 'It never ceases to amaze me,' the poor old darling said, 'how jealous everyone is of success.'

Six months later I saw a production of *Much Ado About Nothing* in Worsfield gaol with Bob Weaver as Dogberry. I enjoyed it very much indeed.

Rumpole and the Way through the Woods

There are times, I have to admit, when even the glowing flame of Rumpole sinks to a mere flicker. It had been a bad day. I had finished a case before old Gravestone, a long slog against a hostile judge, an officer in charge of the case who seemed to regard the truth as an inconvenient obstacle to the smooth and efficient running of the Criminal Investigation Department, and a client whose unendurable cockiness and self-regard rapidly lost all hearts in the Jury. It had been a hard slog which would have seemed as nothing if it had ended in an acquittal. It had not been so rewarded and, when I said goodbye to my client in the cells, carefully failing to remind him that he might be away for a long time, he said, 'What's the matter with you, Mr Rumpole? Losing your touch, are you? They was saying in the Scrubs, isn't it about time you hung up the old wig and took retirement?' Every bone in my body seemed to ache as I stumbled into Pommeroy's where the Château Thames Embankment tasted more than ever of mildew and Claude Erskine-Brown cornered me in order to describe, at interminable length, the triumph he had enjoyed in a rent application. Leaving for home early, I had to stand up in the tube all the way back. Returning to the world from the bowels of Gloucester Road station, I struggled towards Froxbury Mansions with the faltering determination of a dying Bedouin crawling towards an oasis. All I wanted was my armchair beside the gas fire, a better bottle of the very ordinary claret, and a little peace in which to watch other people in trouble on the television. It was not to be.

When I entered the living-room the lights were off and I heard the sound of heavy and laboured breathing. My first thought was that She had fallen asleep by the gas fire, but I could hear the clatter of saucepans from the kitchen. I sniffed the air and received the usual whiff of furniture polish and cabbage being boiled into submission. But, added to this brew, was a not particularly exotic perfume, acrid and pervasive, which might, if bottled extravagantly, have been marketed as wet dog. Then the heavy breathing turned into the sort of dark and distant rumble which precedes the arrival of an Underground train. I snapped on the light and there it was: long legged, overweight and sprawled in my armchair. It was awake now, staring at me with wide-open, moist black eyes. I put out a hand to shift the intruder and the sound of the approaching train increased in volume until it became a snarl, and the animal revealed sharp and unexpectedly white pointed teeth. 'Hilda,' I called for help from a usually reliable source, 'there's a stray dog in the living-room.'

'That's not a stray dog. That's Sir Lancelot.' I turned round and She was standing in the doorway, looking with disapproval not at the trespasser but at me.

'What on earth do you mean, Sir Lancelot?'

'That's your name, isn't it, darling?' She approached the animal with a broad smile. 'Although sometimes we call you Lance for short, don't we?' To these eager questions the dog returned no answer at all, although it did, I was relieved to see, put away its teeth.

'Whatever its name is, shall we call the police?'

'Why?'

'To have it removed.'

'Have you *removed*, Sir Lancelot? What a silly husband I've got, haven't I?' In this, the dog and my wife seemed to be of the same mind. It settled itself into my chair and she tickled it, in a familiar fashion, under the chin.

'Better be careful. It's got a nasty snarl.'

'He only snarls if you do something to annoy him. Was Rumpole doing something to annoy you, Lance?'

'I was trying to budge it off my chair,' I told her quickly, before the dog could get a word in.

'You like Rumpole's chair, don't you, Lance? You feel at home there, don't you, darling?' I was starting to feel left out of the conversation until she said, 'I think we might

43

make that his chair, don't you, Rumpole? Just until he settles in.'

'Settles in? What do you mean, settles in? What's this, a home of rest for stray animals?'

'Lance isn't a stray. Didn't I tell you? I meant to tell you. Sir Lancelot is Dodo Mackintosh's knight in shining armour. Aren't you, darling?' Darling was, of course, the dog.

'You mean he's come up from Cornwall?' I looked at the hound with new respect. Perhaps he was one of those animals they make films about, that set off on their own to travel vast distances. 'Hadn't we better ring Dodo to come and fetch him?'

'Don't be silly, Rumpole.' Hilda had put on one of her heroically patient voices. 'Dodo brought Lancelot up here this afternoon. She left him on her way to the airport.'

'And what time's she getting back from the airport? I suppose I can wait until after supper to sit in my chair.'

'She's going to Brittany to stay with Pegsy Throng who was jolly good at dancing and used to be at school with us. Of course, she couldn't take Sir Lancelot because of the quarantine business.'

'And how long is Pegsy Throng entertaining Dodo?' I could feel my heart sinking.

'Just the three weeks, Rumpole. Not long enough, really. Dodo did ask if I thought you'd mind and I told her, of course not, Lance will be company for both of us. Come and have supper now, and after that you can take him out on the lead to do his little bit of business. It'll be a chance for you two to get to know each other.'

Sleep was postponed that night as I stood in the rain beside a lamp-post with the intruder. Sir Lancelot leapt to the extent of his lead, as though determined to choke himself, wrenching my arm almost out of its socket, as he barked savagely at every passing dog. Looking down at him, I decided that I never saw a hound I hated more, and yet it was Sir Lancelot that brought me a case which was one of the most curious and sensational of my career.

'What on earth are we doing here, Hilda?' Here was a stretch of countryside, blurred by a sifting March rain so, looking towards the horizon, it was hard to tell at which precise point the soggy earth became the sodden sky.

'Breathe in the country air, Rumpole. Besides which, Sir Lancelot couldn't spend all his time cooped up in a flat. He had to have a couple of days' breather in the Cotswolds. It'll do you both good.'

'Couldn't Sir Lancelot have gone for a run in the Cotswolds on his own?'

'Try not to be silly, Rumpole.'

The dog was behaving in an eccentric manner, making wild forays into the undergrowth as though it had found something to chase and, ending up with nothing, it came trotting back to the path quite unconscious of its own stupidity. It was, I thought, an animal with absolutely no sense of humour.

'Why on earth does your friend Dodo Mackintosh call that gloomy hound Sir Lancelot?'

'After Sir Lancelot of the Lake, of course. One of the knights of the Table Round. Dodo's got a very romantic nature. Come along, Lance. *There's* a good boy. Enjoying your run in the country, are you?'

'Lance,' I told her firmly, 'or, rather, *Launce* is the chap who had a dog called Crab in *Two Gentlemen of Verona*. Crab got under the duke's table with some "gentlemanlike dogs" and after "a pissing while" a terrible smell emerged. Launce took responsibility for it and was whipped.'

'Do be quiet, Rumpole! You always look for the seamy side of everything.' At which point, Lance, in another senseless burst of energy, leapt a stile and started chasing sheep.

'Can't you keep that dog under control?' The voice came from a man in a cap, crossing the field towards us, with a golden labrador trotting in an obedient manner at his side. Hilda and I, having climbed the stile and called Lance, with increasing hopelessness, were set out on a course towards him.

'I'm afraid we can't,' I apologized from a distance. 'The animal won't listen to reason.'

'What did you say its name was?'

'Sir Lancelot,' Hilda boasted.

'Of the Lake. To give him his full title,' I added, trying to make the best of our lamentable attachment.

'Sir Lancelot! Here, boy!' the man in the cap called in a commanding tone and gave a piercing whistle. Whereupon Dodo's dog stood still, shook itself, came to its senses and, much to the relief of the sheep, joined our group. At which, the man in the cap turned, looked me in the face for the first time and said, 'By God, it's Horace Rumpole!'

'Rollo Eyles!'

'And this is your good lady?''

I resisted the temptation to say, 'No, it's my wife.' Rollo was telling Hilda about our roots in history. He had been the Prosecution junior in the Penge Bungalow affair, arguably the classic murder of our time and undoubtedly the greatest moment of triumph in the Rumpole career.

Until they heard my first devastating cross-examination of the police surgeon, legal hacks in the Penge Bungalow case treated me as an inexperienced white-wig who shouldn't be allowed out on a careless driving. A notable exception was young Rollo Eyles, the Prosecution junior, then a jovial, school-boyish young man, born, like me, without any feelings of reverence. He was a mimic, and we would meet after Court in Pommeroy's to drown our anxiety, and Rollo would do his impressions of the Judge, the prosecuting silk and the dry, charnel-house voice of Professor Ackerman, master of the morgues. In the middle of his legal career Rollo inherited an estate, and a good deal of money, from an uncle, and left the busy world of the Old Bailey for, it appeared, these damp fields where he was a farmer, Master of Foxhounds and Chairman of the Bench.

For a while he wrote to me at Christmas, letters in neat handwriting, full of jokes. After a while, I forgot to answer them and our friendship waned. Now he said, 'Why don't you come up to the house and we'll all have a strong drink.' Rollo Eyles always had a sensible solution to the most desperate case. Sir Lancelot, realizing he had met a man he couldn't trifle with, came and joined us with unusual docility.

It was over a large whisky in front of a log fire that I told Rollo where we were staying. Our hotel was a plastic and

concrete nightmare of a building conveniently situated for the
trading estate outside the nearest town. It had all the joys of
piped music in the coffee shop, towels in a thinness contest
with the lavatory paper, and waitresses who'd undergone
lengthy training in the art of not allowing their eyes to be
caught. It was the only place we could find where we were
allowed, after slipping a bribe larger than the legal aid fee for a
guilty plea to the hall porter, to secretly have Sir Lancelot in
the bathroom. There, he was due to spend a restless night on a
couple of wafer-thin blankets. Having heard this sad story,
Rollo offered us dinner and a bed for the night; Lancelot could
be kennelled with the gentlemanlike dogs. Our host said he was
looking forward to hearing the latest gossip from the Old
Bailey and, in return, we could have the pleasure of seeing the
hunt move off from his front drive before we went back to
London.

The rain had stopped during the night and the March morning
was cold and sunny. Sir Lancelot was shivering with excitement, as if delightedly aware that something, at some time, was
going to be killed; although I doubted if, during his peaceful
cohabitation with Dodo Mackintosh in Lamorna Cove, he had
ever met foxhunters before. However, he leapt into the air,
pirouetted at the end of his lead, barked at the horses and did
his best to give the impression that he was entirely used to the
country sports of gentlemanlike dogs. So there I was, eating
small slices of pork pie and drinking port which tasted, on that
crisp morning, delicious. Hilda, wearing an old mac and a
tweed hat which she'd apparently bought for just such an
occasion, was doing her best to look as though, if her horse
hadn't gone lame or suffered some such technical fault, she'd've
been up and mounted among our dinner companions of the
night before.

I looked up with my mouth full of pork pie to join in Hilda's
smiles at these new acquaintances who had merged with the children on ponies, the overweight farmers, the smart garage owners
and the followers on foot. Rollo was there, sitting in the saddle
as though it was his favourite armchair, talking to a whipper-
in, or hunt servant, or whatever the red-coated officials

may be called. Mrs Rollo – Dorothea – was there, the relic of a great beauty, still slim and upright, her calm face cracked with lines like the earth on a dried-up river bed, her auburn hair streaked with grey, bundled into a hairnet and covered with a peaked velvet cap. I also recognized Tricia Fothergill, who had clung on to the childish way she mispronounced her name, together with the good looks of an attractive child, into her thirties. She was involved in a lengthy divorce and had, during dinner, bombarded me with questions about family law for which I had no ready answer. And there, raising his glass of port to me from the immense height of a yellow-eyed horse, sitting with his legs stuck out like wings, was the old fellow who had been introduced to us as Johnny Logan and who knew the most intimate details of the private lives of all sporting persons living in the Cotswolds. Rollo Eyles, in the absence of any interesting anecdotes from the Central Criminal Court, clearly relied on him for entertaining gossip. 'Roll 'em in the aisles, that's what I call him,' Logan whispered to me at dinner. 'Our host's extremely attractive to women. Of course, he'll never leave Dorothea.'

Now, at the meet in front of Wayleave Manor, Logan said, 'Seen our charming visitors at the end of the drive? You might go and have a look at them, Horace. They're the antis.'

Dorothea Eyles was leaning down from her horse to chat to Hilda in the nicest possible way, so I took Lancelot for a stroll so I could see all sides of the hunting experience. A van was parked just where the driveway met the road. On it there were placards posted with such messages as STOP ANIMAL MURDER, HUNT THE FOXHUNTERS, and so on. There was a small group standing drinking coffee. At that time they seemed as cheerful and excited as the foxhunters, looking forward as eagerly to a day's sport. There was a man with a shaven head and earrings, but also a woman in a tweed skirt who looked like a middle-aged schoolmistress. There was a girl whose hair was clipped like a sergeant-major back and sides, with one long, purple lock left in the middle. The others were less colourful – ordinary people such as I would have seen shopping in Safeway's and there, I thought, probably buying cellophane-packed joints and pounds of bacon. The tallest was a young man who remained profoundly serious in spite of the excited laughter around him. He was wearing jeans and a crimson shirt which made him stand out as clearly, against the green fields, as the huntsmen he had come to revile.

There was the sound of a horn. The dogs poured down the drive with their tails waving like flags. Then came Rollo, followed by the riders. The antis put down their sandwiches, lowered their mugs of coffee and shouted out such complimentary remarks as 'Murdering bastards,', 'Get your rocks off watching little furry animals pulled to pieces, do you?' and 'How would you like to be hunted and thrown to the dogs this afternoon, darling?' – an invitation to Tricia.

Then Dorothea came riding slowly, to find the Crimson Shirt was barring her path, his arms spread out as though prepared to meet his death under a ton of horseflesh. A dialogue then took place which I was to have occasion to remember.

'You love killing things, don't you?' from the Crimson Shirt.

'Not particularly. Mostly, I enjoy the ride.'

'Why do you kill animals?'

'Perhaps because they kill other animals.'

'Do you ever think that something might kill you one fine afternoon?'

'Quite often.' Dorothea looked down at him. 'A lot of people die, out hunting. A nice quick death. I hope I'll be so lucky.'

'You might get killed this afternoon.'

'Anyone might.'

'It doesn't worry you?'

'Not in the least.'

'It's only what you deserve.'

'Do you think so?' Looking down from her horse, I thought she suddenly seemed thin and insubstantial as a ghost, her lined face very pale. Then she pulled a silver flask from her jacket pocket, unscrewed it and leant down to offer the Crimson Shirt a drink.

'What have you got in there?' he asked her.

'Fox's blood, of course.'

He looked up at her and said, 'You cruel bitch!'

'It's only whisky. You're very welcome.' He shook his head and the cobweb-faced lady took a long pull at the flask. Other

49

riders had come up beside her and were listening, amused at first and then angry. There were shouts, conflicting protests, and the Crimson Shirt called out in the voice of doom, 'One of you is going to die for all the dead animals. Justice is sure to be done!'

I saw a whip raised at the back of the cavalcade but the Crimson Shirt had dropped his arm and moved to join his party by the van. Dorothea Eyles put away her flask, kicked her horse's sides and trotted with the posse after her. They were chattering together cheerfully, after what had then seemed no more than a routine confrontation between the hunters and the sabs – rather enjoyed by both sides.

The sound of the horn, the baying of the dogs and the clattering of horses had died away. The van, after a number of ineffectual coughs and splutters, started its engine and went. It was very quiet as Lancelot and I walked back down the drive to join Hilda who was enjoying a final glass of port. We went into the house to wait for the taxi which would take us back to the station.

That evening we were at home at the mansion flat and I had been restored to my armchair. Lancelot, exhausted by the day's excitement, was asleep on the sofa, breathing heavily and, no doubt, dreaming of imaginary hunts. The news item was on the television after a war in Africa and an earthquake in Japan. There were stock pictures of hunters and sabs. Then came the news that Dorothea Eyles, out hunting and galloping down a woodland track, had ridden into a high wire stretched tight between two trees. Her neck was broken and she was dead when some ramblers found her. An anti-hunt demonstrator named Dennis Pearson was helping the local police with their inquiries.

Rollo Eyles had returned to my life, suffered a terrible tragedy and immediately disappeared again. Of course I telephoned but his recorded voice always told me he was not available. I left messages of sorrow and concern but the calls were never answered, and neither were the letters I wrote to him. Tragedy too often causes embarrassment and we didn't visit Rollo in the Cotswolds. Tragedy vanishes quickly, swept on by the tide of horrible events in the world, and I began to think less often of Dorothea Eyles and her ghastly ride to death. Rollo joined the unseen battalion of people whom I liked but never saw.

'Rumpole! I have heard reports of your extraordinary behaviour!'

'Don't believe everything you hear in reports.'

'Erskine-Brown has told me that Henry told him . . .'

'I object! Hearsay evidence! Totally inadmissible.'

'Well well. I have had a direct account from Henry himself.'

'Not under oath, and certainly not subject to cross-examination!'

'You were seen entering the downstairs toilet facility with a bowl.'

'What's *that* meant to prove? I might have been rinsing out my dentures. Or uttering prayers to a water god to whose rites I have been recently converted. What on earth's it got to do with Henry, anyway? Or you, for that matter, Bollard?'

'Having filled your bowl with water, you were seen to carry it to your room.'

'It would be inappropriate to say prayers to the water god in the downstairs toilet facilities.'

'Come now, Rumpole, don't fence with me.' Soapy Sam Ballard was using one of the oldest and corniest of legal phrases, long fallen into disuse in the noble art of cross-examination, and I allowed myself a dismissive yawn. It wasn't the brightest period of my long and eventful practice at the bar. Since our visit to the Cotswolds, and its terrible outcome, briefs had been notable by their absence. I came into Chambers every day and searched my mantelpiece in vain for a new murder, or at least a taking away without the owner's consent. My wig gathered dust in my locker down the Bailey; the ushers must have forgotten me and I looked back with nostalgia on the days when I had laboured long and lost before Mr Injustice Gravestone. At least something was happening then. Now the suffocating boredom of inactivity was made worse by the arrival of an outraged Head of Chambers in my room, complaining of my conduct with something so totally inoffensive as a bowl of water.

'You might as well confess, Rumpole.' Ballard's eye was lit

with a gleam of triumph. 'There was one single word written in large letters on that chipped enamel bowl.'

'Water?'

'No, Rumpole. Henry's evidence was quite clear on this point. What was written was the word DOG.'

'So what?'

'What do you mean, so what?'

'Plenty of people wash their socks in bowls with DOG written on them.'

Before Ballard could meet this point, there was that low but threatening murmur, like the sound heralding the dark and distant approach of a tube train, from behind my desk.

'What was that noise, Rumpole?'

'Low-flying aircraft?' I suggested, hopefully. But at this point the accused, like so many of my clients, ruined his chances by putting in a public appearance. Sir Lancelot, looking extra large, black and threatening, emerged like his more famous namesake – with lips curled, dog teeth bared – eager to do battle in the lists. There was no contest. At the sight of the champion, even before the first snarl, Sir Soapy Sam, well-known coward and poltroon of the Table Round, started an ignominious retreat towards the door, crying in terror, 'Get that animal out of here at once!'

'No!' I relied on my constitutional rights. 'Not until the matter has been properly decided by a full Chambers' meeting.'

'I shall call one,' Ballard piped in desperation, 'as a matter of urgency.' And then he scooted out and slammed the door behind him.

The fact of the matter was that Hilda had been out a lot recently at bridge lessons and coffee mornings, and I, lonely and unoccupied in Chambers, started in a curious way to relish the company of a hound who looked as gloomy as I felt. On the whole, the dog was not demanding. Like many judges, Lancelot fought, nearly all the time, a losing battle against approaching sleep. Water from the downstairs loo, and the dog biscuits I brought in my briefcase, satisfied his simple wants. The sound of regular breathing from somewhere by my feet was company for me as I spent the day with *The Times* crossword.

★

The Chambers' meeting was long and tense. At first the case for the Prosecution looked strong. Henry sent a message to say that he undertook to clerk for a barristers' chambers and not a kennel. He added that the sight of Sir Lancelot peering round my open door and baring his teeth had frightened away old Tim Daker of Daker, Winterbotham & Guildenstern, before he'd even delivered a brief. Erskine-Brown questioned the paternity of Sir Lancelot and when I said labrador loudly, he replied, 'Possibly a labrador who'd had hankypanky with a dubious Jack Russell.' He ended up by asking in a dramatic fashion if we really wanted a mongrel taking up residence in 4 Equity Court. This brought a fiery reply from Mizz Liz Probert who said that animals had the same rights to our light, heat, comforts, and presumably law reports, as male barristers. She personally could remember the days, not long past, when she, as a practising woman, was treated as though she were a so-called labrador of doubtful parentage. Gender awareness was no longer enough. In Mizz Probert's considered opinion we needed species awareness as well. She saw no reason, in the interests of open government and tolerance of minorities, why a living being should be denied entrance to our Chambers simply because it had four legs instead of two. 'Of course,' Mizz Probert concluded, looking at Erskine-Brown in a way which forced him to reconsider his position, 'if we were to support the pin-striped chauvinists who hated mongrels and women, we should be alienating the Sisterhood of Radical Lawyers, devoted to animal rights.'

I took up her last point in my speech for the Defence and did so in a way calculated to make Soapy Sam's flesh creep. I had seen something of animal rights enthusiasts. Did we really want their van parked outside Chambers all day and most of the night? Did Ballard want a shorn-headed enthusiast with earrings shouting, 'Get your rocks off shutting out innocent dogs, do you?' Could we risk a platoon of grey-haired, middle-class dog-lovers staging a sit-in outside our front door every time we wanted to go to Court? After this, the evidence of a Member of Chambers, to the effect that dogs made him sneeze, seemed to carry very little weight. The result of our deliberations was, of course, leaked and a paragraph appeared in next day's Londoner's Diary in the *Evening Standard*:

Should dogs be called to the Bar? The present showing of the legal profession might suggest that they could only be an improvement on the human intake. Indeed, a few Rottweilers on the Bench might help reduce the crime rate. The question was hotly debated in the Chambers of Samuel Ballard, Q.C. when claret-tippling Old Bailey character Horace Rumpole argued for the admittance of a pooch, extravagantly named Sir Lancelot. Rumpole won his case but then he's long been known as a champion of the underdog.

It was a pyrrhic victory. Dodo came back from holiday a week later and reclaimed Sir Lancelot. She was delighted he had been mentioned in the newspapers but furious he was called a pooch.

Sir Lancelot's trial had a more important result, however. Henry told me that a Mr Garfield of Garfield, Thornley & Strumm had telephoned and, having heard that I was a stalwart battler for animal rights, was going to brief me for a hunt saboteur charged with murder. I was relieved that my period of inactivity was over, but filled with alarm at the thought of having to tell Hilda that I had agreed to appear for the man accused of killing Dorothea Eyles.

Mr Garfield, my instructing solicitor, was a thin, colourless man with a pronounced Adam's apple. He had the rough, slightly muddy skin of the dedicated vegetarian. The case was to be tried at Gloucester Crown Court and we sat in the interview room in the prison, a Victorian erection much rebuilt, on the outskirts of the town. Across the plastic table-top our client sat smiling in a way which seemed to show that he was either sublimely self-confident or drugged. He was a young man, perhaps in his late twenties, with a long nose, prominent eyes and neat brown hair. The last time I had seen him he was wearing a crimson shirt and telling the hunt in general, and Dorothea Eyles in particular, that one of them was going to die for all the dead animals. Garfield introduced him to me as Den; my instructing solicitor was Gavin to my client. I had the feeling they had known each other for some time and later discovered that they sat together on a committee concerned with animal rights.

'Gavin tells me you fought for a dog and won?' Den looked at me with approval. Was that to be my work in the future, I wondered. Not white-collar crime but leather-collar crime, perhaps?

'More than that,' I told him. 'I'm ready to fight for you and win the case.'

'I'm not important. It's the cause that's important.'

'The cause?'

'Den feels deeply about animals,' Gavin interpreted.

'I understand that. I was there, you know. Watching the hunt move off. I'd better warn you I heard what you said, so it's going to be a little difficult if you deny it.'

'I said it,' Den told me proudly. 'I said every word of it. We're going to win, you know.'

'Win the case?'

'I meant the war against the animal murderers. Did you see the looks on their faces? They were going out to enjoy themselves.'

I remembered the words of the historian Lord Macaulay: 'The Puritan hated bear-baiting, not because it gave pain to the bear, but because it gave pleasure to the spectators.' But I wasn't going to be drawn into a debate about fox-hunting when I was there to deal with my first murder case for a long time, too long a time, and I fully intended to win it. I rummaged in my papers and produced the first, the most important witness statement, the evidence to be given by Patricia Fothergill of Cherry Trees near Wayleave in the county of Gloucester.

'I'd better warn you that I met this lady at dinner.'

'I don't mind where you met her, Mr Rumpole.'

'I'm glad you take that view but I had to tell you. All right, Tricia — that's what she calls herself — Tricia is going to say that she saw a man in a red shirt in the driveway of the Eyles's house, Wayleave Manor. She heard you shout at Mrs Eyles. Well, we all know about that. Now comes the interesting bit. At about one o'clock in the afternoon of the day before the meet she'd been out for a hack and was riding home past Fallows Wood — that's where Dorothea Eyles met her death.

She says she saw a man in a red shirt coming out of the wood, carrying what looked like a coil of wire: "I didn't think much of it at the time. I suppose I thought he had to do with the telephone or the electricity or something. There was a moment when I saw him quite clearly and I'm sure he was the same man I saw at the meet, shouting at Dorothea." We can challenge that identification. It was far away, she was on a horse, how many men wear red shirts – all that sort of thing . . .'

'I'm sure you will destroy her, Mr Rumpole.' Gavin was trying to be helpful.

'I'll do my best.' I hunted for another statement. 'I'm just looking . . . Here it is! Detective Constable Armstead searched the van you came in and found part of a coil of wire of exactly the same make and thickness as that which was stretched across the path and between the trees in Fallows Wood.' I looked at my client and my solicitor. Neither had, apparently, anything to say. 'Who drives the van?'

'Roy Netherborn. It's his van,' Gavin volunteered.

'Is he the hairless gentleman with the earrings?'

'That's the one.'

'And did Mr Netherborn pack the things in the van? The tools and so on?'

'He did, didn't he, Den?' Gavin had been answering the questions. When he was asked one, Dennis Pearson was silent.

'Had you taken wire with you before?'

'We'd discussed it,' Den admitted. 'There'd been some talk of using it to trip up the horses.'

'Did you know there was wire in the van that day?' I asked Den the question direct, but Gavin intervened, 'I don't think you did, did you?'

Den said nothing but shook his head.

'Did you know that exactly the same wire was used as a death-trap in Fallows Wood?'

'Den didn't know that. No.' Gavin was positive.

'When did you arrive in Wayleave village? And *that's* a question for Mr Dennis Pearson,' I invited.

'We came up the morning before. We were staying with Janet Freebody who lives in the village. Janet's a schoolteacher.'

'And chair of our activist committee.' Gavin was finding it difficult to keep quiet.

'Where was the van parked?'

'In front of Janet's house.'

'From what time?'

'About midday.'

'You hadn't taken a trip in it to Fallows Wood before then?'

'Den tells me he hadn't.' Once again, Gavin took on the answering.

'Was the van kept locked?'

'Supposed to be. Roy's a bit careless about this, isn't he, Den?'

'Roy's careless about everything,' Den agreed.

There were a lot more questions that required answering, but I didn't want them all answered by way of the protective Gavin Garfield.

'There's one other thing I should tell you,' I said as I gathered up my papers. 'I know Rollo Eyles. I met him when he was at the Bar. And I was staying with him the night before ... Well, the night before the fatal accident. I'll have to tell him I'm defending the man accused of murdering his wife. If you don't want me to defend you, you know that, of course, I shall understand.' I was giving them a chance to sack me even before my precious murder case had begun. I kept my fingers crossed under the table.

'I'd like you to carry on with the case, Mr Rumpole,' Den was now speaking for himself. 'Seeing what you did for that dog, I don't think I'll cause you much trouble.'

'Oh, why's that?'

'Well, you see ...' Dennis Pearson was still smiling pleasantly, imperturbably.

Gavin looked at him anxiously and started off, 'Den ...'

But my client interrupted him, 'You see, I did it.'

'You knew he was going to do that?' Gavin was driving me from the prison to Gloucester station in a car littered with bits of comics, old toys, empty crisp packets and crumpled orange juice cartons with the straws still stuck in them. I supposed that, in his pale, vegetarian way, he had fathered many children.

'I had an idea. Yes,' Gavin admitted it. 'What do we do now?'

'We're entitled to cross-examine the prosecution witnesses and see if they prove the case. We can't call Dennis to deny the charge, so, if the Prosecution holds up, we'll have to plead guilty at half-time.'

'Is that what you'd advise him to do?'

'I'd advise him to tell us the truth.'

'Why do you say that?'

'Because I don't believe he is.'

I wanted to work on the case away from the garrulous Gavin and the uncommunicative Den. I thought that they lurked somewhere between the world of human communication and the secret and silent kingdom of animals, and I didn't feel either of them would be much help down the Bailey. The case seemed to me to raise certain awkward and interesting questions, not to say a matter of legal ethics and private morality which was, not to put too fine a point upon it, devilishly tricky to cope with.

As I sat in Chambers I decided it was better for a legal hack like me to stop worrying about such things as ideas of proper or improper behaviour and concentrate on the facts. I lit a small cigar and opened a volume of police photographs. As I did so, I stooped for a moment to pat the head of the gloomy Lancelot, who had become my close companion, and then realized he was gone, ferreting for disgusting morsels, no doubt, at the edge of the sea while Dodo Mackintosh sat at her easel and perpetrated a feeble watercolour. I felt completely alone in the defence of Den Pearson, who didn't even want to be defended.

I hurried past the mortuary shots of Dorothea and her fatal injuries, and got to a picture of a path through trees. It was a narrow strip hardly wide enough for two people to pass in comfort, so the beech trees on either side were not much more than six feet apart. A closer shot showed the wire, then still stretched between nails driven into the trees. The track was muddy, with patches of grass and the bare earth. I picked up a magnifying glass and looked at the photo carefully. Then I rang little Marcus Pitcher, who, I had discovered, was to be in charge of the Prosecution. 'Listen, old darling,' I said, when I got his chirrup on the line, 'what about you and me organizing a visit to the *locus in quo*?' When he asked me what I meant, I said, 'There was once a road through the woods.'

'A day out in the country?' Marcus sounded agreeable. 'Whyever not. I'll drive you.'

My learned friend was a small man with a round face, slightly protruding teeth and large, horn-rimmed glasses, so that he looked like an agreeable mouse, although he could be a cunning little performer in Court. Marcus owned a bulky old Jaguar and had to sit up very straight to peer out of the windscreen. In the back seat a white bull-terrier sat, pink-eyed and asthmatic, looking at me as though she wondered why I'd come to ruin the day out.

'Meet Bernadette,' Marcus introduced us. 'As soon as she heard about the trip to the Cotswolds, she had to come. Hope you don't mind.'

'Not at all. In fact I might have brought my own dog, but Lancelot's away at the moment.'

At the scene of the crime Bernadette went bounding off into the undergrowth, while Marcus, his solicitor from the D.P.P.'s office, and I stood with the Detective Inspector in charge of the case. D. J. Palmer was a courteous officer who lacked the tendency of the Metropolitan force to imitate the coppers they've seen on television. He led us to the spot where death had taken place. The wire and nails had been removed to be exhibited in the case, and the hoof marks had been rubbed out by the rain.

'"There was once a road through the woods,"' I told the Inspector, '"Before they planted the trees./It is underneath the coppice and heath,/And the thin anemones . . ."' But this one isn't, is it, Inspector?'

'I'm not quite sure that I follow you, Mr Rumpole.'

'This road hasn't disappeared so that

> Only the keeper sees
> That, where the ring-dove broods,
> And the badgers roll at ease,
> There was once a road through the woods.'

'It's a footpath here as I understand it, Mr Rumpole.' The D.I. was ever helpful. 'Mr Eyles is very good about keeping open the footpaths on his land.' It did seem that the edges of the path had been trimmed and the brambles cut back.

'Is the footpath used a lot? Did you ever find that out, Inspector?'

'Ramblers use it. It was ramblers that found Mrs Eyles. A shocking experience for them.'

'It must have been. Don't know why they call it rambling, do you? We used to call it going for a walk. So people don't ride down here much?'

'I wouldn't think a lot. You'd have to be a good horseman to jump that.'

We had come to a stile at the end of the narrow track. Beside it there was a green signpost showing that the footpath continued across the middle of a broad field dotted with sheep. The stile had a single pole to hold on to and a wide step set at right angles to the top bar. I supposed it would have been a difficult jump but I saw a scar in the wood. Could that have been the mark of a hoof that had just managed it?

Marcus Pitcher called Bernadette and she came lolloping over the brambles and started to root about in the long grass at the side of the stile.

'You gents seen all you want?' the D.I. asked us.

Marcus was satisfied. I wasn't. I thought that if we waited we might learn something else about that cold, sunny day in March when Dorothea died as quickly as she'd said she'd always wanted to. And then I was rewarded. Bernadette pulled some weighty object out of the grass, carried it in her mouth and laid it, as a tribute, at the feet of Marcus Pitcher. I said I'd like a note made of exactly where we found the horseshoe.

'I don't see what it can possibly prove.' Marcus was doubtful. 'It might have been dropped from any horse at any time.'

'Let's just make a note,' I asked. 'We'll think about what it proves later.'

So the polite Inspector took charge of the horseshoe and he, Marcus and Bernadette moved on across the field on their way back to the road. I sat on the stile to recover my breath and looked into the darkness of the wood. What was it at night? A

sort of killing field – owls swooping on mice, foxes after small
birds – a place of unexpected noises and sudden death? Was it
a site for killing people or killing animals? I remembered
Dorothea, old and elegant, handing down with a smile to Den
what she said was a flask of fox's blood. I thought about the
hunters and the antis shouting at each other and Den's yell:
'One of you is going to die for all the dead animals.' And I
tried to see Dorothea, elated, excited, galloping down the
narrow path and her sudden, unlooked-for near-decapitation.
From somewhere in the shadows under the trees, I seemed to
hear the sound of hoofs and I remembered more of Kipling, a
grumpy old darling but with a marvellous sense of rhythm. I
chanted to myself:

> 'You will hear the beat of a horse's feet,
> And the swish of a skirt in the dew,
> Steadily cantering through
> The misty solitudes,
> As though they perfectly knew
> The old lost road through the woods.
> But there is no road through the woods.'

But there was no swish of a skirt. It was Rollo Eyles who came
cantering down the track, reined in his horse and sat looking
down on me as I sat on his stile.

'Horace! *You* here? I heard the police were in the wood.'

I looked up at him. He was getting near my age but
healthier and certainly thinner than me. He was not a tall
man, but he sat up very straight in the saddle. His reins
were loose and his hands relaxed; his horse snorted but
hardly moved. He wore a cap instead of a hard riding-hat,
regardless of danger, and an old tweed jacket. His voice was
surprisingly deep and there was little grey in the hair that
showed.

'I was having a look at the scene of the crime.' Then I told
him, as I had to, 'I'm defending the man who's supposed to
have killed your wife.'

'Not the man who killed her?'

'We won't know that until the Jury get back. Do you mind?'

'That he killed Dorothea?'

'No. That I'm defending him.'

'You have to defend even the most disgusting clients, don't you?' His voice never lost its friendliness and there was no hint of anger. 'It's in the best traditions of the Bar.'

'That's right. I'm an old taxi.'

'Well, I wish you luck. Who's your judge?'

'We're likely to get stuck with Jamie MacBain.'

'"I was not born yesterday, y'know, Mr Rumpole. I think I'm astute enough to see through *that* argument!"' Rollo had lost none of his talents as a mimic and did a very creditable imitation of Mr Justice MacBain's carefully preserved Scottish accent. 'Why don't you come down to the house for a whisky and splash?' he asked in his own voice.

'I can't. They'll be waiting for me in the car. You're sure you don't mind me taking on the case?'

'Why should I mind? You've got to do your job. I've no doubt justice will be done.'

I climbed over the stile then walked away. When I looked back, he wasn't going to jump but turned the horse and trotted back the way he had come. He had said justice would be done but I wasn't entirely sure of it.

I kept all of this to myself and said nothing to She Who Must Be Obeyed, although I knew well enough that the time would come when I'd certainly have to tell her. As the trial of Dennis Pearson drew nearer, I decided that the truth could no longer be avoided and chose breakfast time as, when the expected hostilities broke out, I could retreat hastily down the tube and off to Chambers and so escape prolonged exposure to the cannonade.

'By the way,' I said casually over the last piece of toast, 'I'll probably be staying down in the Gloucester direction before the end of the month.'

'Has Rollo Eyles invited us again?'

'Well, not exactly.'

'Why exactly, then?' With Hilda you can never get away with leaving uncomfortable facts in a comforting blur.

'I've got a trial.'

'What sort of a trial?'

'A rather important murder as it so happens. You'll be glad to know, Hilda, that when it comes to the big stuff, the questions of life and death, the cry is still "Send for Rumpole".'

'Who got murdered?'

The question had been asked casually, but I knew the moment of truth had come. 'Well, someone you've met, as a matter of fact.'

'Who?'

My toast was finished. I took a last gulp of coffee, ready for the off.

'Dorothea Eyles.'

'You're defending that horrible little hunt saboteur?'

'Well, he's not so little. Quite tall actually.'

'You're defending the man who murdered the wife of your friend?'

'I suppose someone has to.'

'Well! It's no wonder you haven't got any friends, Rumpole.'

Was it true? Hadn't I any friends? Enemies, yes. Acquaintances. Opponents down the Bailey. Fellow Members of Chambers. But *friends*? Bonny Bernard? Fred Timson? Well, I suppose we only met for work. Who was my real friend? I could only think of one. 'I got on fairly well with the dog Lancelot. Of course he's no longer with us.'

'Just as well. If you defend people who kill your friends' wives, you're hardly fit company for a decent dog.' You have to admit that when Hilda comes to a view she doesn't mince words on the matter.

'We don't know if he killed her. He's only accused of killing her.'

'No hair and earrings? You only had to take a look at him to know he was capable of anything!'

'They didn't arrest the one with no hair,' I told her. 'I'm defending another one.'

'It doesn't matter. I expect they're all much of a muchness. Can you imagine what Rollo's going to say when he finds out what you're doing?'

'I know what he thinks.'

'What?'

'That it's in the best tradition of the Bar to defend anyone, however revolting.'

'How do you know that's what he thinks?'

'Because that's what he said when I told him.'

'You told him?'

'Yes.'

'I must say, Rumpole, you've got a nerve!'

'Courage is the essential quality of an advocate.'

'And I suppose it's the essential quality of an advocate to be on the side of the lowest, most contemptible of human beings?'

'To put their case for them? Yes.'

'Even if they're guilty?'

'That hasn't been proved.'

'But you don't know he's not.'

'I think I do.'

'Why?'

'Because of what he told me.'

'He told you he wasn't guilty?'

'No, he told me he *was*. But, you see, I didn't believe him.'

'He told you he was guilty and you're still defending him? Is that in the best traditions of the Bar?'

'Only just,' I had to admit.

'Rumpole!' She Who Must Be Obeyed gave me one of her unbending looks and delivered judgement. 'I suppose that, if someone murdered *me*, you would defend them?'

There was no answer to that so I looked at my watch. 'Must go. Urgent conference in Chambers. I won't be late home. Is it one of your bridge evenings?' I asked the question, but answer came there none. I knew that for that day, and for many days to come, as far as She Who Must Be Obeyed was concerned, the mansion flat in Froxbury Mansions would be locked in the icy silence of the tomb.

During the last weeks before the trial Hilda was true to her vow of silence and the mansion flat offered all the light-hearted badinage of life in a Trappist order. Luckily I was busy and even welcomed the chance of a chat with Gavin Garfield whom, although I had excluded him from my visit to the Cotswolds, I now set to work. I told him his first job was to get statements from the other saboteurs in the van, and when he protested that we'd never get so far as calling evidence in view of what Den had told us, I said we must be prepared for all eventualities. So Gavin took statements, not hurriedly, but with a surprising thoroughness, and in time certain hard facts emerged.

What surprised me was the age and respectability of the saboteurs. Shaven-headed Roy Netherborn was forty and worked in the accounts department of a paper cup factory. He had toyed with the idea of being a schoolmaster and had met Janet Freebody, who was a couple of years older, at a teacher training college. Janet owned the cottage in Wayleave where the platoon of fearless saboteurs had put up for the night. She taught at a comprehensive school in the nearby town where we had fled from the dreaded hotel. Angela Ridgeway, the girl with the purple lock, was a researcher for BBC Wales. Sebastian Fells and Judy Caspar were live-in partners and worked together in a Kensington bookshop, and Dennis Pearson, thirty-five, taught sociology at a university which had risen from the ashes of a polytechnic. They all, except Janet, lived in London and were on the committee of a society of animal rights activists.

Janet had kept Roy informed about the meet at Rollo Eyles's house, and they had taken days off during her half-term when the meet was at Wayleave. The sabbing was to be made the occasion of a holiday outing and a night spent in the country. When they had got their rucksacks and sleeping-bags out of the van, Roy, Angela, Sebastian and Judy retired to the pub in Wayleave where real ale was obtainable and they used it to wash down vegetable pasties and salads until closing-time at three. Janet Freebody had things to do in the cottage, exercise books to correct and dinner to think about, so she didn't join the party in the pub. Neither did Den. He said he wanted to go for a walk and so set off, according to Roy, apparently to commune, in a solitary fashion, with nature. This meant that he was alone and unaccounted for at one o'clock when Tricia was going to swear on her oath that she saw him coming out of Fallows Wood with a coil of wire.

Other facts of interest: Fallows Wood was only about ten

minutes from Wayleave. Roy couldn't remember there being any wire in the van when they set out from London; it was true that they had discussed using wire to trip up horses, but he had never bought any and was surprised when the police searched the van and found the coil there. It was also true that the van was always in a mess, and probably the hammer found in it was his. Den had brought a kitbag with his stuff in it and Roy couldn't swear it didn't contain wire. Den was usually a quiet sort of bloke, Roy said, but he did go mad when he saw people out to kill animals: 'Dennis always said that the movement was too milk and watery towards hunting, and that what was needed was some great gesture which would really bring us into the news and prove our sincerity – like when the girl fell under a lorry that was taking sheep to the airport.' I made a mental note not to ask any sort of question likely to produce that last piece of evidence and came to the conclusion that Roy, despite his willingness to give Gavin a statement, wasn't entirely friendly to my client, Dennis Pearson.

The placards, a small plantation at the meet, had become a forest outside the Court in Gloucester. Buses, bicycles, vans, cars in varying degrees of disrepair, had brought them, held up now by a crowd which burst, as I elbowed my way towards the courthouse door, into a resounding cheer for Rumpole. I didn't remember any such ovation when I entered the Old Bailey on other occasions. In the robing-room I found Bernadette asleep in a chair and little Marcus Pitcher tying a pair of white bands around his neck in front of a mirror. 'See you've got your friends from rent-a-crowd here this morning, Rumpole.' He was not in the best of tempers, our demonstrators having apparently booed Bernadette for having thrown in her lot with a barrister who prosecuted the friends of animals.

I wondered how long their cheers for me would last when I went into Court, only to put my hands up and plead guilty. My client, however, remained singularly determined: 'When we plead guilty, they'll cheer. It'll be a triumph for the movement. Can't you understand that, Mr Rumpole? We shall be seen to have condemned a murderer to death!'

The approach of life imprisonment seemed to have concentrated Den's mind wonderfully. He was no longer the silent and enigmatic sufferer. His eyes were lit up and he was as excited as when he'd shouted his threats at the faded beauty on the horse. 'I want you to tell them I'm guilty, first thing. As soon as we get in there. I want you to tell them that I punished her.'

'No, you don't want that. Does he, Mr Garfield?' Gavin, sitting beside me in the cell under the Court, looked like a man who had entirely lost control of the situation. 'I suppose if that's what Den has decided . . .' His voice, never strong, died away and he shrugged hopelessly.

'I *have* decided finally' – Den was standing, elated by his decision – 'in the interests of our movement.' For a moment he reminded me of an actor I had seen in an old film, appearing as Sydney Carton on his way to the guillotine, saying, 'It's a far, far better thing I do, than I have ever done.'

'You're not going to do the movement much good by pleading guilty straight away,' I told him.

'What do you mean?'

'A guilty plea at the outset? The whole thing'll be over in twenty minutes. The animal murderers, as you call them, won't even have to go into the witness-box, let alone face cross-examination by Rumpole. Will anyone know the details of the hunt? Certainly not. Do you want publicity for your cause? Plead guilty now and you will be lucky to get a single paragraph on page two. At least, let's get the front page for a day or so.' I wasn't being entirely frank with my client. The murder was serious and horrible enough to get the front pages in a world hungry for bad news at breakfast, even if we were to plead guilty without delay. But I needed time. In time, I still hoped, I would get Den to tell me the truth.

'I don't know.' My client sat down then as though suddenly tired. 'What would you do, Gavin?'

'I think' – Gavin shrugged off all responsibility – 'you should be guided by Mr Rumpole.'

'All right' – Den was prepared to compromise – 'we'll go for the publicity.'

'Dennis Pearson, you are accused in this indictment of the murder of Dorothea Eyles on the sixteenth of March at Fallows

Wood, Wayleave, in the county of Gloucester. Do you plead guilty or not guilty?'

'My Lord, Members of the Jury' – Den, as I had feared, was about to orate. 'This woman, Dorothea Eyles, was guilty of the murder of countless living creatures, not for her gain but simply for sadistic pleasure and idle enjoyment. My Lord, if anything killed her, it was natural justice!'

'Now then, Mr –' Mr Justice James MacBain consulted his papers to make sure who he was trying. 'Mr Pearson. You've got a gentleman in a wig sitting there, a Mr Rumpole, who's paid to make the speeches for you. It's not your business to make speeches now or at any time during this case. Now, you've been asked a simple question: Are you guilty or not guilty?'

'She is the guilty one, my Lord. This woman who revelled in the death of innocent creatures.'

'Mr Rumpole, are you not astute enough to control your client?'

'It's not an easy task, my Lord.' I staggered to my feet.

'Your first job is to control your client. That's what I learnt as a pupil. Make the client keep it short.'

'Well, if you don't want a long speech from the dock, my Lord, I suggest you enter a plea of not guilty and then my learned friend, Mr Marcus Pitcher, can get on with opening his case.'

'Mr Rumpole, I was not born yesterday!' Jamie MacBain was stating the obvious. It was many years since he had first seen the light in some remote corner of the Highlands. He was a large man whose hair, once ginger, had turned to grey, and who sat slumped in his chair like one of those colourless beanbags people use to sit on in their Hampstead homes. He had small, pursed lips and a perpetually discontented expression. 'And when I want your advice on how to conduct these proceedings, I shall ask you for it. Mr Moberly!' This was a whispered summons to the clerk of the court, who rose obediently and, after a brief *sotto voce* conversation, sat down again as the Judge turned to the Jury.

'Members of the Jury, you and I weren't born yesterday and I think we're astute enough to get over this little technical difficulty. Now we don't want Mr Pearson, the accused man here, to start giving us a lecture, do we? So what we're going to do is to take it he's pleading not guilty and then ask Mr Marcus Pitcher to get on with it and open the prosecution case. You see, there's no great mystery about the law. We can solve most of the problems if we apply a wee bit of worldly wisdom.'

I suppose I could have got up on my hind legs and said, 'Delighted to have been of service to your Lordship,' or, 'If you're ever in a hole, send for me.' But I didn't want to start a quarrel so early in the case. I sat quietly while little Marcus went through most of the facts. The Jury of twelve honest Gloucestershire citizens looked stolid, middle-aged and not particularly friendly to the animal rights protesters who filled the public gallery to overflowing. I imagined they had grown up with the hunt and felt no particular hostility to the Boxing Day meet and horses streaming across the frosty countryside. They had looked embarrassed by Dennis's speech from the dock, and flattered when Jamie MacBain shared his lifetime's experience with them. Like him, they hadn't been born yesterday, and worldly wisdom, together with their dogs and their rose gardens, was no doubt among their proudest possessions. As I listened to my little learned friend's opening, I thought he was talking to a jury which, whatever plea had been entered, was beginning to feel sure that Den was as guilty as he was anxious to appear.

The first witness was the rambler, a cashier from a local bank who, out for a walk with his wife and daughter, had been met with the ghastly spectacle of an elderly woman almost decapitated and fallen among the brambles of Fallows Wood.

'Where was the horse?' was all I asked him in cross-examination.

'The horse?'

'Yes. Did you see her horse by any chance?'

'I think there was a horse there, some distance away, and all saddled up. I think it was just eating grass or something. I didn't stay long. I wanted to get my wife and Sandra away and phone the police.'

'Of course. I understand. Thank you very much, Mr Ovington.'

'Is that all you want to ask, Mr Rumpole?' Jamie MacBain looked at me in an unfriendly fashion.

'Yes, my Lord.'

'I don't think that question and answer has added much to our understanding of this case, Members of the Jury. I'd be glad if the Defence would not waste the time of the Court. Yes. Who is your next witness, Mr Marcus Pitcher?'

I restrained myself and sat down in silence 'like patience on a monument'. But my question *had* added something: Dorothea's riderless horse hadn't galloped on and jumped the stile. We learnt more from Bob Andrews, a hunt servant who, when the hunt was stopped, went back to the wood to recover Dorothea's horse which had been detained by the police. I risked Jamie's displeasure by questioning Andrews for a little longer.

'When you got to the wood, had Mrs Eyles's body been removed?'

'It was covered. I think it was just being taken away on a stretcher. I knew the ambulance was in the road. The police were taking photographs.'

'The police were taking photographs – and where was Mrs Eyles's horse?'

'I think a police officer was holding her.'

'Can you remember, had Mrs Eyles's horse lost a shoe?'

'Not that I noticed. I looked her over when I took her from the policeman. He seemed a bit scared, holding her.'

'I'm not surprised. Horses can be a little alarming.'

'Can be. If you're not used to them.'

There were a few smiles from the Jury at this; not because it was funny but as a relief from the agony of hearing the details of Dorothea Eyles's injuries. The Jury, I thought, rather liked Bob Andrews, while the animal rights enthusiasts in the public gallery looked down on him with unmitigated hatred and contempt.

'Mr Andrews,' I went on, while Mr Justice MacPain (as I had come to think of him) gave a somewhat exaggerated performance of a long-suffering judge, bravely enduring terminal boredom, 'tell me a little about the hunt that day. You were riding near to Mr Eyles?'

'Up with the master. Yes.'

'Did your hunt go near Fallows Wood?'

'Not really. No.'

'What was the nearest you got to that wood?'

'Well, they found in Plashy Bottom. Down there they got a scent. Then we were off in the other direction entirely.'

'How far is Plashy Bottom from Fallows Wood?'

'About half a mile . . . I'd think about that.'

'Did you see Mrs Eyles leave the hunt and ride up towards the wood?'

'Well, they'd got going then. I wouldn't have looked round to see the riders behind me.'

'Did you see anyone else – Miss Tricia Fothergill, for in-stance – leave the hunt and ride up towards Fallows Wood?'

'I didn't, no.'

'He's told us he wasn't looking at the riders behind him, Mr Rumpole.' Jamie managed to sound like a saint holding on to his patience by the skin of his teeth.

'Then let me ask you a question you *can* answer. It's clear, isn't it, that the hunt never went through Fallows Wood that day?'

'That's right.'

'So, it follows that in order to come into collision with that wire, Mrs Eyles had to make a considerable detour?'

'That's surely a matter for argument, Mr Rumpole.' Jamie MacBain did his best to scupper the question so I asked another one, very quickly.

'Do you know why she should make such a detour?'

'I haven't got any idea, no.'

'Thank you, Mr Andrews.' And I sat down before the Judge could recover his breath.

Johnny Logan replaced the whipper-in. He was wearing a dark suit and some sort of regimental tie; his creased and brown walnut face grinned over a collar which seemed several sizes too large for him. He treated the Judge with a mixture of amusement and contempt, as though Jamie were some alien being who could never understand the hunting community of the Cotswolds. Logan said he had heard most of the dialogue between the sabs and the hunters in the driveway of Wayleave

Manor. He also told the Jury that he had seen the saboteurs' van at various points during the day, and heard similar abuse from them as he rode by.

'You never saw the saboteurs' van near Fallows Wood?' I asked when it was my turn.

'We never went near Fallows Wood as far as I can remember.'

'Then let you and I agree about that. Now, will you tell me this? Did you ever see Mrs Eyles leave the hunt and ride off in a different direction?'

'No, I never saw that. I'm not saying she didn't do it. We were pretty spread out. I'd seen a couple of jumps I didn't like the look of, so I'd gone round and I was behind quite a lot of the others.'

'Gone round, had you?' Jamie MacBain, about to make a note, looked confused.

'Quite a lot of barbed wire about. I don't think you'd have fancied jumping that, my Lord,' Johnny Logan added with a certain amount of mock servility.

'Never mind what I'd've fancied. Just answer the questions you get asked. That's all you're required to do.' It was clear that the Judge and the witness had struck up an immediate lack of rapport.

'Did you see anyone else leave the hunt?'

'I don't think so. Well, you mean at *any* time?'

'At any time when you were out hunting, yes.'

'Well, I think Tricia Fothergill left. But that was at the very end, just before the police arrived and told us that Mrs Eyles had been – well, had met with an accident.'

'So that must have been after Mrs Eyles's death?' The Judge made the deduction.

'You've got it, my Lord,' Johnny Logan congratulated him in such a patronizing fashion that I almost felt sorry for the astute Scot.

'Why did she leave then, do you remember?'

'I'm not sure. Her horse was wrong in some way, I think.'

'Just one more thing, Mr Logan.'

'Oh, anything you like.' Johnny showed his contempt for us all.

'It would be right to say, wouldn't it, that Mr Rollo Eyles was devoted to his wife?'

'He would certainly never have left her. Is that what you mean?'

'That's exactly what I mean. Thank you very much.'

As I was about to sit down, the Judge said, 'And what were the Jury meant to make of that last question and answer?'

'They may make of it what they will, my Lord, when they are in full possession of the facts of this interesting but tragic case.' At which point I lowered my head in an ornate eighteenth-century bow and sat down with as much dignity as I could muster.

'Work at the Bar!' little Marcus said. 'Sometimes I think I'd rather be digging roads.'

'Only one thing to be said for work at the Bar,' I tended to agree, 'is that it's better than no work at the Bar.'

It was the lunch adjournment and the three of us – Marcus, Bernadette and I – were in a dark corner of the Carpenters Arms, not far from the Court. There they did a perfectly reasonable bangers and mash. Marcus and I had big glasses of Guinness and Bernadette took hers from a bowl on the floor. The little prosecutor said he was looking forward to going for a holiday with a Chancery barrister called Clarissa Clavering on the Isle of Elba. 'I'd been living for the day, but now it seems likely I'll have to cancel.'

'Why on earth?'

'I can't find anyone to leave Bernadette with. Clarissa only likes cats. And I do love her, Rumpole! Love Clarissa, I mean. She has a lot of sheer animal magnetism for a girl in the Chancery Division.'

'Couldn't you put her in a kennel? Bernadette, I mean.'

'I couldn't do that.' Marcus looked as though I'd invited him to murder his mother. 'Much as I fancy Clarissa, I couldn't possibly do that.'

'Then, there's nothing else for it . . .'

'Nothing else for it.' His little mouselike face was creased with lines of sorrow. My heart went out to the fellow. 'Except cancel the holiday. I won't blame Bernadette, of course. It's not *her* fault. But . . .'

'It's a pity to miss so much animal magnetism?'

'You've said it, Rumpole. You've said it exactly.'

When we arrived back at the Court, there was a certain amount of confusion among the demonstrators. They started with the clear intention of cheering me and Bernadette, who, even if she was part of the prosecution team, was, after all, an animal. They knew they should boo and revile young Marcus, the disappointed lover. Finally, when they saw that I, as well as Bernadette, was on friendly terms with the forces of evil and the prosecutors of sabs, they decided to boo us all.

In the entrance hall the prospective witnesses sat waiting. I saw Tricia Fothergill as smartly turned out as a pony at a show, with gleaming hair, shiny shoes and glistening legs. She was prepared for Court in a black suit and her hands were folded in her lap. On the other side of the hall sat the prospective witnesses for the Defence: purple-haired Angela Ridgeway, Sebastian and Judy from the bookshop, and shaven-headed Roy Netherborn. Janet, the schoolteacher, sat next to Roy, but I noticed that they didn't speak to each other but sat gazing, as though hypnotized, silently into space. Then, as I was wigged and gowned by now, I crossed the entrance hall towards the Court. Roy got up and walked towards me slowly, heavily and with something very like menace. 'What the hell's the idea,' he muttered in a low voice, full of hate, 'of you getting into bed with the prosecution barrister?'

'Little Marcus and I are learned friends,' I told him, 'against each other one day and on the same side the next. We went out to lunch because his dog Bernadette felt in need of a drink. And I didn't get into bed with him. I left that to his girlfriend Clarissa of the Chancery Division. Any more questions?'

'Yes. Haven't you got any genuine beliefs?'

'As few as possible. Genuine beliefs seem to end up in death threats and stopping other people living as they choose. I do have one genuine belief, however.'

'Oh, do you? And what's that when it's at home?'

'Preventing the conviction of the innocent. So, if you will allow me to get on with my job . . .' I moved away from him then, and he stood watching me go, his fists clenched and his knuckles whitening.

Tricia had given her evidence-in-chief clearly, with a nice mixture of sadness, brightness and an eagerness to help. The Jury had taken to her and Jamie MacBain seemed no less smitten than little Marcus was with Clarissa, although there was a great gulf fixed between them and she called him my Lord, and he called her Miss Fothergill in a voice which can best be described as a caressing, although still judicial, purr. She looked, as she stood in the witness-box and answered vivaciously, prettier than I had remembered. Her nose was a little turned up, her front teeth a little protruding, but her eyes were bright and her smile beguiling.

'Tricia Fothergill, you say your name is?' I rose, after Marcus had finished with her, doing my best to break the spell woven by the most damaging prosecution witness. 'Why not Patricia?'

'Because I couldn't say Patricia when I was a little girl. So I stayed Tricia, even when I went away to school.'

'Which, I'm sure, wasn't long ago. Don't you agree, Members of the Jury?' the judge purred and a few weaker spirits in the jury box gave a mild giggle. Tricia Fothergill, in Jamie's view, it seemed, *had* been born yesterday.

'I'll call you Miss Fothergill, if I may, if that's your grown-up name. Or is it? Were you once married?'

'Yes.'

'And your husband's name is . . .?'

'Charing.'

'Cheering, did you say?'

'No, Charing.'

'Are you going deaf, Mr Rumpole?' the Judge raised his voice to me as though at the severely afflicted.

'Not quite yet, my Lord.' I turned to this witness. 'Are you divorced from this Mr Charing?'

'Not quite yet, Mr Rumpole,' the witness answered with a smile and won a laugh from the Jury. The Judge's pursed lips were stretched into a smile, and the inert beanbag was shaken up and repositioned in his chair. 'The divorce hasn't gone through,' Tricia explained when order was restored.

'Yet you call yourself Miss Fothergill?'

'It was such an unhappy relationship. I wanted to make a clean break.'

'Surely you can understand that, Mr Rumpole?' Jamie was giving the witness his full and unqualified support.

'And have you now found a new and happier relationship?'

Little Marcus, the mouse that roared, rose to object, but the learned Judge needed no persuading. 'That was an entirely irrelevant and embarrassing question, Mr Rumpole. Please be more careful in the future.'

'I hope we shall all be careful,' I said, 'in our efforts to discover the truth. So I understand you live alone, Miss Fothergill, in Cherry Trees in the village of Wayleave?'

'That is another entirely improper question. What does it matter whether this young lady lives alone or not?' This time the Judge was doing Marcus's objections for him. 'We'd be greatly obliged, Mr Rumpole, if you'd move on to something relevant.'

'I'll move on to something very relevant. Do you say you saw a man coming out of Fallows Wood carrying wire on the day before the hunt?'

'That's right.'

'What time was it?'

'One o'clock.'

'How do you know?'

'I'd just looked at my watch. I was out for a hack and had to be home before two because my lawyer was ringing me. I saw it was only one and I decided to do the long round through Plashy Bottom. Then I saw the man coming out of the wood, with the coil of wire.'

'When you saw the man with the wire, you were alone?'

'Yes.'

'No one else saw him at that time?'

'Not so far as I know.'

'You say you thought he might have been working for Telecom or the electricity company? Did you see a van from any of those companies?'

'No.'

'Or the van the saboteurs came in?'

'I didn't see the van then, no. Of course it might have been parked on the road.'

'Or it might still have been parked in the village. As far as you know.'

'As far as I know.'

'You saw a man the next day, shouting at Mrs Eyles?'

'That was the same man. Yes.'

'Why didn't you warn everyone in the hunt that you'd seen that man coming out of the wood, carrying wire?'

'I suppose I just didn't put two and two together at the time. It was only when I heard Dorothea had been killed by a wire . . .'

'You put two and two together then?' The Judge was ever helpful to his favourite witness.

'Yes, my Lord. And I was going to say that, in all the excitement of starting out with the hunt, I may have forgotten what I saw, just for a little while.'

'I don't suppose Mr Rumpole knows much about the excitement of the hunt.' Jamie MacBain was wreathed in smiles and seemed almost on the point of laying a finger alongside his nose.

I didn't join in the obedient titters from the Jury, or the shocked intake of breath from the faces in the public gallery. I started the long and unrewarding task of chipping away at Tricia's identification. How far had she been away from the wood? Was the sun in her eyes? How fast was her horse moving at the time? As is the way with such questioning, the more the witness was attacked the more positive she became.

'On your way back to your house in Wayleave, on the day before the hunt, did you pass Janet Freebody's cottage?'

'Yes, I had to pass that way.' Tricia made it clear that she wouldn't go near anything of Janet Freebody's unless it were absolutely necessary.

'Did you see the sabs' van parked outside Miss Freebody's cottage?'

'I think I did. I can't honestly remember.'

'Was it locked?'

'How would she know that, Mr Rumpole?' Jamie put his oar in.

'Perhaps you tried the door.'

'I certainly didn't! I was just riding past.'

'Let me ask you something else. Mr Logan has told us that you left the hunt shortly before the police arrived with the news of Mrs Eyles's death. There was something wrong with your horse. What was it?'

'Oh, Trumpeter had lost a shoe,' Tricia said as casually as possible. 'It must have happened earlier, but I hadn't noticed it. I noticed it then and I had to take him home.'

It was a moment when I felt a tingle of excitement, as though, after a long search in deep and muddy waters, we had struck some hard edge of the truth. 'Miss Fothergill,' I asked her, 'were you riding with Mrs Eyles in Fallows Wood on the day she met her death?'

The Jury were looking at Tricia, suddenly interested. Even Jamie MacBain didn't rush to her assistance.

'No, of course I wasn't.' She turned to the Judge with a small, incredulous giggle which meant 'What a silly question'.

'My Lord. I call on my learned friend to admit that a horseshoe was found by Inspector Palmer near to the stile in Fallows Wood.'

'Perfectly true, my Lord,' Marcus admitted. 'It was found some weeks after Mrs Eyles died.'

'So it might have been dropped by one of any number of horses at any unknown time?' Jamie was delighted to point out. 'Isn't that so, Miss Fothergill?' Tricia was pleased to agree and repeated that she had never ridden through Fallows Wood that day. I was coming to the end of my questions.

'When your divorce proceedings are over, Miss Fothergill, are you going to embark on another marriage?' I asked and waited for the protest. It came. Little Marcus drew himself up to his full height and objected. Jamie agreed entirely and said that he wouldn't allow any question about the witness's private life. So my conversation with Tricia ended, finally silenced by the Judge's ruling.

At the end of the afternoon I came out of Court frustrated, despondent, seeing nothing in front of me but a pathetic guilty plea. Gavin hurried away to see Den in the cells and I heard an urgent voice saying, 'Mr Rumpole! I've got to talk to you.' I looked around and there was Janet Freebody, showing every sign of desperation. I saw Roy and a representative group of the sabs watching us, as well as the hunters who were leaving the Court. I said I'd meet her in the Carpenters Arms round the corner in half an hour.

'It's kind of you to see me. So kind.' I realized I had never looked closely at Janet Freebody before, but just filed her away in my mind as a grey-haired schoolmistress in a tweed skirt. It was true that her hair was grey and her skirt was tweed but her eyes were blue, her eyelids finely moulded and her long, serious face beautiful as the faces on grave madonnas or serious angels in old paintings. At that moment her cheeks were pink and her hands, caressing her glass of gin-and-tonic, were long-fingered and elegant.

'What is it you want to tell me?'

She didn't answer directly, but asked me a question. 'Wasn't it at one o'clock that Dennis was meant to be coming out of that wood, carrying wire?'

'That's what Tricia said.'

'Well, he wasn't. I know where he was.'

'Where?'

'In bed with me.'

I looked at her and said, 'Thank you for telling me.'

'I know I've got to tell that in Court. Den's going to be furious.' And then it all came out, shyly at first, nervously, and then with increasing confidence. She'd had an affair with shaven-headed Roy, who was jealous of Den and now in a perpetually bad temper. She and Dennis had waited until the others went out to the pub to go upstairs, where, it seemed, the solemn Den forgot his duty to the animals in his love for the schoolmistress. Meanwhile, the saboteurs' van was unlocked and unattended outside Janet's front gate.

'You can't go on pretending.'

'Pretending what?'

'Pretending you're guilty, just to help animals. I doubt very much whether the animals are going to be grateful to you. In

79

fact they'll hardly notice. Like Launce's dog, Crab. Do you know *The Two Gentlemen of Verona*?'

'How do they come into the case?'

'They don't. They're in a play. So is Launce. And so is his dog, Crab. When Crab farts at the Duke's dinner party, Launce takes the blame for it and is whipped out of the room. Launce also sat in the stocks for puddings Crab stole and stood in the pillory for geese Crab killed. How did Crab reward him? Simply by lifting his leg and peeing against Madam Silvia's skirt. That's how much Crab appreciated Launce's extraordinary sacrifice.'

There was a silence and then Dennis said, 'Mr Rumpole.'

'Yes, Den.'

'I am not quite following the drift of your argument.'

'It's just that Launce led an unrewarding life trying to take the blame for other people's crimes. Don't be a martyr! And don't pretend to be a murderer.'

'I'm not.'

'Of course you are. And what do you think it's going to get you? A vote of thanks from all the foxes in Gloucestershire?'

'I don't know what you're saying, Mr Rumpole.'

'I'm saying, come out of some fairy-story world full of kind little furry animals and horrible humans and tell the truth for a change.'

'What's the truth?'

'That you didn't kill anyone. All right, you can shout bloodthirsty threats and work yourself into a fury against toffs on horses. But I don't believe you'd really hurt a fly. Particularly not a fly.'

It was early in the morning, before Jamie MacBain had disposed of bacon and eggs in his lodgings, and I was alone with my client in the cells. I hadn't bothered to tell Gavin about this dawn meeting, and he would have been distressed, I'm sure, at Dennis's look of pain.

'I'm thinking of the cause.'

'The cause that can't accept that we're all hunters, more or less?'

'And I told you I was guilty.'

'You told me a lie. That was always obvious.'

'Why? Why was it obvious?'

'Because you had no way of knowing that Dorothea Eyles was going to leave the hunt and gallop between the trees in Fallows Wood.'

'You can't prove it.' For a moment Den was lit up with the light of battle.

'Prove what?'

'That I'm innocent.'

'Really! Of all the cockeyed clients. I've had some dotty ones but never one that didn't want to be proved innocent before.' It was early in the morning and the hotel had only been serving the continental breakfast. I'm afraid that my temper was short and I didn't mince my words. 'I can prove you didn't carry wire out of the wood at one o'clock on the day before the murder.'

'How?'

'Because you were doing something far more sensible. You were making love to Janet Freebody.'

There was a silence. Den looked down at his large hands, folded on his lap. Then he looked up again and said, 'Janet's not going to say that, surely?'

'Yes, she is. She's going to brave the story in the *Sun* and the giggles in her class at the comprehensive, and she's going to say it loud and clear.'

'I'm not going to let her.'

'You can't stop her.'

'Why not?'

'Because you're going to tell the truth also. And because you're going to fight this case to the bitter end. With a little help from me, you might even win.'

'Why should I fight it?' Den looked back at his hands, avoiding my eye. 'You give me one good reason.'

So then I gave him one very good reason indeed. 'You can't tell the story,' I warned Den. 'It can't be proved and you'd be sued for libel. But I promise to tell them what I know.' Later, when I had finished with Den, I went into the robing-room to slip into the fancy dress and there I confronted little Marcus, combing his mouse-coloured hair. 'My learned friend,' I told him, 'I'm serving an alibi notice on you. Only one witness.

You'll be a sweetheart and tell darling old Jamie that you don't want an adjournment or anything awkward like that. I can rely on you, can't I, Marcus?'

'Why on earth' – Marcus looked like a very determined mouse that morning – 'should you think that you can rely on me?'

'Because,' I told him, with some confidence, 'if you behave well, Hilda and my good self might see our way to looking after Bernadette while you're away in the Chancery Division.'

'That' – little Marcus turned back to the mirror and the careful arrangement of his hair – 'puts an entirely different complexion on the matter.'

'What is the single most important fact about this case, Members of the Jury? The fact which I ask you to take with you into your room and put first and last in your deliberations. It's just this: Mrs Eyles met her death half a mile from any point where the hunt had been. If Dennis Pearson intended to kill her, how did he lure her away to that remote woodland path? Did he offer her a date or an assignation? Did he promise to give her the winner of the two-thirty at Cheltenham? Or did he say, "Just gallop along the track in Fallows Wood and you'll probably be killed by a bit of tight wire I stretched there yesterday lunchtime"? How did he organize not only that she should be killed, but that she should go so far out of her way to meet her death? It was impossible to organize it, was it not, Members of the Jury? Doesn't that mean that you must have doubts about Dennis Pearson's guilt?

'Remember, he was seen at various places during the hunt, with the other saboteurs, shouting his usual abuse at the riders. So whoever went off and lured Dorothea Eyles to her death, it certainly wasn't him. And remember this, if he's guilty, the whole hunt would have had to come down that track, and the first to be killed wouldn't have been Mrs Eyles but the Master of Foxhounds himself, or one of the hunt servants. The Prosecution haven't even tried to explain these mysteries and, unless they can explain them, you cannot be certain of guilt.'

Little Marcus was reading a guidebook on Elba and Jamie MacBean was feigning sleep, but the Jury was listening, attentive and, I thought, even interested. The abrupt manner in which the Judge had put an end to my cross-examination of Tricia had, I suspected, aroused their curiosity. What was it that the Judge didn't wish them to know? There are moments when an objection sustained can be almost as good as evidence.

And then Janet Freebody turned out to be a dream witness. When Jamie asked her, in what he hoped were withering tones, if she was in the habit of having sexual intercourse with men at lunch time, she answered, with the smallest of smiles, 'Only when my feelings overcome me, my Lord. And I am dreadfully in love.' The Judge was silent, the Jury liked her, and little Marcus closed his eyes and no doubt thought of Clarissa. I needn't go through all the points I made in my final speech, brilliant as they were. They will have become obvious to my readers who have studied my cross-examination. Jamie summed up for a conviction which, as the Jury were not entirely on his side, was a considerable help to us. They were out for an hour and a half, but when they came back they looked straight at my client and said not guilty. The Judge then threatened to have those cheering in the gallery committed to prison for contempt; however astute he was, and however long ago he'd been born, he had failed to achieve a conviction.

When I said goodbye to Dennis he was hardly overcome with gratitude. He said, 'You prevented me from striking a real blow for animal rights, Mr Rumpole. I came prepared to suffer.'

'I'm sorry,' I said, 'Janet Freebody ruined your suffering for you. And I think she's prepared to give you something a good deal more valuable than a martyr's crown.'

Months later, on the occasion of a long-suffering member of our Chambers becoming a Metropolitan magistrate, he gave his fellow legal hacks dinner at the Sheridan Club. She Who Must was not of the party, having gone off on yet another visit to Dodo and the dog Lancelot on the Cornish Riviera. As I sat trying not to drop off during one of Ballard's lively discussions of the Chambers' telephone bill, I saw, softly lit by candlelight, Rollo Eyles and Tricia Fothergill dining together at a distant table. I remembered a promise unfulfilled, a duty yet undone. I excused myself and went over to join them.

'Horace! Have a seat. What's going on over there? A Chambers dinner? This is the claret we choose on the wine committee. Not too bad.' Rollo was almost too welcoming. Tricia, on the other hand, looked studiously at her plate.

'So' – Rollo was signalling to the waiter to bring me a glass – 'you won another murder?'

'Yes.'

'I suppose the Jury thought another of those revolting antis did it.'

'I don't suppose we'll ever know exactly what they thought.'

'By the way, Horace' – Rollo looked at me, one eyebrow raised quizzically – 'I thought you'd like to know. Tricia and I are going to get married.'

'I thought you would be.'

For the first time Tricia raised her eyes from her plate. 'Did you?'

'Oh, yes. Rollo would never have left his wife, while she was alive. Thank you.' The waiter had brought a glass and Rollo filled it. 'You know my client, Dennis Pearson, was going to take the blame for the crime. He thought, in some strange way, that it might help the animals. He only agreed to fight because, if he was acquitted, the real murderer might still be discovered.'

'The real murderer?' I still didn't believe that Rollo knew the truth. Tricia knew it and I wanted Tricia to be sure I knew it too.

'What made Dorothea ride through Fallows Wood?' I looked at Tricia. 'I think you were riding with her in the hunt and you said something, probably something about Rollo, which made her want to know more. But you rode away and she followed you. When you got on to the track between the trees, you knew where the wire was and you ducked. Dorothea was galloping behind and knew nothing. It was a very quick death. You carried on and jumped the stile, where your horse lost a shoe.'

'You're drunk!' Rollo had stopped smiling.

'Not yet!' I took a gulp of his wine.

Tricia said, 'But I saw the man with the wire.'

'At least we proved you were lying about that. The only person who went into the wood with wire was you. And when you'd done the job, you dumped the coil in the sabs' van. You knew one of them could be relied on to threaten the riders. Dennis said exactly what was required of him.'

'Tricia?' Rollo looked at her, expecting her furious denial. He was disappointed.

'You repeat one word of that ridiculous story, Rumpole' – he was angry now – 'and I'll bloody sue you.'

'I don't think you will. I don't think she'll let you.'

'What are you going to do?' Tricia was suddenly businesslike, matter of fact.

'Do? I'm not going to do anything. I don't know who could prove it. Anyway, I'm not the police, or the prosecuting authority. What you do is for you two to decide. But I promised the man you wanted to convict that I'd let you know I knew. And now I've kept my promise.'

I drained my glass, got up and left their table. As I went, I saw Rollo put his hand on Tricia's and hold it there. Did he not believe in her crime, or was he prepared to live with it? I don't know and I can't possibly guess. I had left the world of the hunters and those who hunted them, and I never saw Rollo or his new wife again, although Hilda did tell me that their wedding had been recorded in the *Daily Telegraph*.

When I got back to our table I sat in silence for a while beside Mrs Justice Erskine-Brown, Phillida Trant that was, the Portia of our Chambers.

'What are you thinking about, Rumpole?' Portia asked me.

'With all due respect to your Ladyship, I was thinking that a criminal trial is a very blunt implement for digging out the truth.'

Some weeks later Ballard entered my room when I was busy noting up an affray in Streatham High Street.

'I'm sending you a memo about the telephone bill, Rumpole.'

'Good. I shall look forward to that.'

'Very well. I'll send it to you then.' Apparently in search of another topic of conversation, the man sniffed the air. 'No dogs in here now, are there?'

'Certainly not.'

'I well remember the time when you had a dog in here.'

'No longer.'

'And we had to call a Chambers' meeting on the subject!'

'That was some while ago.'

'And you assure me you now have got no dog here, of any sort?'

'Close the door behind you, Bollard, when you go.'

As he left, the volume was turned up on the sound of heavy breathing. Bernadette was sleeping peacefully behind my desk.

Hilda's Story

MRS HILDA RUMPOLE TO DOROTHY (DODO) MACKINTOSH

My dear Dodo

This is the story Rumpole will never tell. It's not at all how he would wish to present himself to his audience, his readers, his ladies and gentlemen of the Jury, in the many accounts he has written of his brilliance down at the Old Bailey, and his particular cleverness at enabling assorted scamps and scally-wags to escape their just deserts. Such work Rumpole sees as protecting the liberty of the subject, Magna Carta and the presumption of innocence, and he assumes a look of injured nobility when I tell him that he has become little more than an honorary uncle to the Timson family – that infamous clan of South London villains, whom Rumpole, when under attack, says I have to rely on for my scanty housekeeping allowance. Rumpole also prides himself on his worldly wisdom and the fact that he can see further through a brick wall than anyone else in the legal profession, the entire Bench of Judges, includ-ing the Lord Chancellor, the Master of the Rolls and the Lords of Appeal in Ordinary. My reason for writing this account, entirely for my own consumption – and yours, Dodo, as my oldest schoolfriend and one who has seen the best and the worst of Rumpole at quarters which may have been, from time to time, uncomfortably close – is to show that in the case of *R*. v. *Skelton*, I certainly saw further through a brick wall than he could without having passed a single Bar exam. I pulled off a coup to equal his in that case which he never tires of telling us about, the Penge Bungalow murders.

Rumpole is, I have to tell you, Dodo, a bit of an actor. I don't think you've ever seen him in Court, with his grey wig askew (dirty when he bought it secondhand from the ex-Attorney-General of the Windward Islands, and now even dirtier after fifty years of contact with Rumpole's glistening forehead), his gown tattered (he never asks me to mend it), and his waistcoat gravy-stained (he seldom allows me to take it to the Smarty Pants cleaners, who give a pretty reliable service in the Gloucester Road). He is, of course, acting the part of an inadequately paid and outspoken rebel against authority. And when he's at home, and you've seen this, my dear old Dodo, many times, he is acting the part of a free spirit imprisoned, through no fault of his own, in marriage, just as the clients in his less successful cases are banged up in Wormwood Scrubs.

Dodo, I don't know if you remember the case of Michael Skelton? There was a good deal about it in the *Daily Telegraph* at the time, but I know you object to the amount of quite gratuitous violence there is in crime-reporting these days, and perhaps you were too busy with your splendid watercolours to notice it! Your 'Lamorna Cove on a Wet Afternoon' hangs over the gas fire as I write and I can *feel* the dampness rising. We all know that young people have got quite difficult lately. Since our Nick went off to teach in Florida and married his Erica we have hardly been close but, quite honestly, Dodo, families have got to learn to live together and, although no one knows better than you how completely maddening Rumpole can be at times, it's impossible to imagine Nick ever being tempted to beat his father to death with a golf club, the crime which the Skelton boy was up for. I mean, it simply isn't the way youngsters from nice homes carry on.

You can imagine the poorer sort of people doing it – people on drugs and income support and such like – although I can't really imagine them having golf clubs available in their entrance halls. But young Michael Skelton seemed to have nothing in the world to complain about. His father, Dimitri Skelton, was a very successful surgeon. (I believe there was Russian blood in the family somewhere and, although I can connect the Russians with violence, they don't seem, in the course of history, to have played much golf . . . Just a passing thought, Dodo.) Anyway, the father did cosmetic surgery, I think they call it, which means giving other rich people better bosoms or more youthful faces. I don't know, you and I have lived quite comfortably with our faces since we were a couple of new bugs, all wet around the ears, at Chippenham. And, as for Rumpole's face, it seems to me, it is quite beyond repair – only fit for demolition, I might think sometimes – but I wouldn't say it aloud, Dodo. Apart from the various acts he puts on, he can be quite a sensitive soul at times and I don't wish to cause him pain – unless it's absolutely necessary.

Well, as I was saying, this business of yanking up people's bosoms and tightening their cheeks had provided the Skeltons with an extremely nice converted farmhouse in Sussex, with a marble swimming-pool (there were colour pictures in the *Weekend Telegraph*), a jacuzzi, four cars in the garage, and all the trimmings, which we tell each other we wouldn't want but might quite like if we found them provided for us. Having been sent to Lancing, and then to Cambridge to study medicine and follow in his father's footsteps (or should I say his father's wrinkles, Dodo, if you will forgive a small joke on a serious subject) the boy should have been grateful or, if he couldn't have managed that, at least not beaten his father about the head with a favourite driver.

Late one afternoon – could it have been last July? Anyway, I know it was still light – I came home from my bridge lesson with Marigold Featherstone. She's Lady Featherstone, you know, the Judge's wife, and we both suffer from extremely irritating husbands. Of course she's not an *old* friend like you, Dodo. Marigold and I were never together as new bugs at Chippenham. She is a somewhat younger person but actually not as silly as she quite often sounds. Well, when I got back to Froxbury Mansions, I found Rumpole home surprisingly early. An urgent conference in Pommeroy's Wine Bar over a bottle of Château Fleet Street usually takes up at least two hours at the end of his working day. He had his jacket and waistcoat off and sat in his braces and shirtsleeves in a flat with closed windows, where you might have roasted a chicken without the help of the gas oven.

'You seem to be enjoying that brief, Rumpole,' I said as I

forced open a reluctant window, 'even more than a bottle of your usual third-rate red wine.'

'Are you planning to freeze me to death before I can pull off what promises to be one of my most sensational defences?' he asked in a plaintive sort of voice.

'If you're cold' – when dealing with Rumpole, you have to be merciless – 'there's always your cardigan. Don't tell me you've found another Penge Bungalow murder?'

'Penge Bungalow? What was that exactly? I tell you, *R*. v. *Skelton* is going to outdo the fame of all my previous triumphs. This is a case which will go down in history. I envisage a final speech lasting at least a day.'

'Why will you be giving the final speech, Rumpole?'

'Because, needless to say, I am doing this case – as I did that rather more trivial affair of the Penge Bungalow – alone and without a leader!'

'Is that because all the leaders realize that Michael Skelton has simply got no defence?'

'It's because my instructing solicitor knows that I am a far greater defender than all those self-important amateurs who wrap themselves in silk gowns and flaunt the initials Q.C. after their names.'

'And who is your instructing solicitor?' I asked to put an end to a speech which, after a lengthy marriage to a permanent non-Q.C., I could repeat by heart. 'Some owner of a South London bucket-shop? Cut-price defences in hopeless murder cases offered to close friends of the Timson family?'

'What nonsense you do talk, Hilda.' Rumpole sighed heavily. 'My instructing solicitor happens to be Daniel Newcombe. To those of us who know him well, and undertake his more difficult cases, he will always be Danny Newcombe.'

'And who is this Danny, anyway?' It seems extraordinary to me now, Dodo, that there was ever a time when I had to ask such a question.

'Hilda, I know you are a complete innocent when it comes to the law, but Newcombe, Pouncefort & Delaney are quite the grandest firm dealing in criminal matters. Danny is the senior partner. I believe that, with me in command, his firm may pull off something sensational.'

'You mean, get a boy off who murdered his father.'

'Who is *alleged* to have murdered his father. Young Michael is as innocent as you are until he's proved guilty.'

'I don't suppose you'd get Nick off if he'd beaten you to death with a golf club.'

'If he'd beaten me to death I'd scarcely be in a position to stand up and defend him.' Rumpole had the intolerable expression he puts on when he thinks he's said something clever, so I ignored this and opened another window.

'And, by the way, Danny's invited me to dine with him at the Sheridan Club next Thursday. He said he wanted to get to know me better.'

'If that's what he wants, he'd be better off talking to me. At least he'd get an unbiased opinion.'

'Oh, you're coming too.'

'You mean, he's invited me?'

'"And do bring your lovely wife." I assume it was you he had in mind.'

'But, Rumpole! You hate going to dinner at the Sheridan Club. You say it is full of pompous bores and . . .'

'Hilda! We all have to make sacrifices if we are to rise to the top in the legal profession, and for the sake of a brief from Newcombe, Pouncefort & Delaney, I would willingly rent a dog-collar and go to dinner with the Archbishop of Canterbury. My God! There's a wind whistling round my knees that must have come straight from the Ural Mountains.'

'I told you, Rumpole. If you're feeling cold, then go and put on warm clothing.'

He left me then, his lips forming those syllables which, I had come to understand, spelt out She Who Must Be Obeyed.

'I'm sorry to drag you to my club, which I'm afraid you'll find desperately dull, Hilda. My excuse is, we need girls like you to lighten the old place up occasionally. Don't we, Horace?' Danny fished the bottle of Chablis out of the ice-bucket and considerately refilled my glass when I was only halfway through the potted shrimps.

'I really don't know.' I think it was the first time I'd known

Rumpole short of an answer to a question. 'I'm not a member here.'

'Not a member here?' Danny seemed genuinely surprised. 'We must do something about that. Or are you against Horace joining the Sheridan, Hilda? Do you want to keep an eye on him at home?'

'I wouldn't mind in the least. Life at home's far more peaceful without him. That's provided he can spare time from his other port of call.'

'What's that?'

'Pommeroy's Wine Bar.'

'I don't know it, I'm afraid,' Danny smiled. 'But it sounds interesting.' I felt a sudden affection for a lawyer who'd never heard of Pommeroy's. 'Is that white Burgundy all right for you?' he was asking Rumpole with what I thought was admirable consideration. To which my husband replied, if you can believe this, Dodo, 'Thanks. If you're asking, I'd rather have a slurp of the red. A couple of slurps, if that's at all possible.' I suppose I should count myself lucky that Rumpole and I don't go out to dinner very much.

When the red wine came Rumpole said thoughtfully, 'From the photographs it's obvious there'd been a hell of a fight in the hall. The grandfather clock was knocked over and stopped at ten forty-five. You noticed that, of course?'

'Horace, please! We didn't come here to talk shop.' Danny put a hand on his Counsel's sleeve and I noticed how clean and well-manicured his fingernails were, something you could hardly say for Rumpole. 'We came here to get to know each other. Thee are some pretty dusty old members here, Hilda. But we do boast of quite decent pictures. There' – he turned to look at the portrait of a man in a wig, smiling in what I thought rather a condescending way, over the mantelpiece – 'Richard Brinsley himself, a true wit like you, Horace, and a man of many love affairs.' Not like Horace, I thought. I began to wonder about Danny ... I must confess, Dodo, he seemed a great deal more interesting than any other lawyer I'd met. He had come alone, and there had been no mention of a Mrs Newcombe. Later I remember him saying that he dreaded going back to his empty flat. 'Since I lost Deirdre it's been lonely. I mean, you can't have much of a conversation with the television. Television is full of discussion programmes, but you can't discuss anything with it. It's not like a wife. It never answers back.' When Danny said this, I had to fight a curious impulse to put my arm round his shoulder to cheer him up. But, of course, I couldn't do that. Not in the Sheridan Club, not with Rumpole sitting there slurping his claret and asking a really charming Indian waiter if he had anything remotely resembling a toothpick about him.

'And over there,' Danny said, 'is the portrait of Elizabeth Linley, whom Sheridan loved. There's a difference in years, of course, but don't you think, Horace, she has a distinct look of Hilda about her?' Rumpole looked surprised and said, 'No.'

At the weekend Rumpole and I went shopping in Safeway's. I'd honestly rather he'd stayed at home but he'd become strangely attentive since our dinner at the Sheridan and had insisted on coming with me 'to help lug the heavy stuff'. As I wandered round the shelves – I have to tell you, Dodo, I wasn't even comparing prices, I was shopping in a kind of dream – I couldn't help thinking of Danny (whom I no longer thought of as Mr Newcombe). I wondered how old he might be and thought he was timeless, anything from the late fifties to the early seventies. His skin was a healthy pink and as free from wrinkles, apart from laugh lines around the eyes, as it would've been if Michael Skelton's father had been at it, which I was quite sure he hadn't. His eyes had a strange brilliance, an almost unearthly blue, I remembered as I reached for a tin of pineapple chunks which turned out to be Japanese bean shoots when I got them home. Danny's eyes were as blue as the clearest of seas on the sunniest of days. No reflection, Dodo, on the wonderful way you painted a wet afternoon in Lamorna. I thought about the well-cut tweed suit, the highly polished brogues, the silk handkerchief in the breast pocket and the slight whiff of some completely masculine eau de cologne. And I thought of the way he leant towards me, one ear always turned in my direction, seriously interested in anything I might have to say.

And then I saw Rumpole come padding towards me down

the long alleyway between the fancy breads and the pet food, wearing his weekend uniform of a woollen shirt and cardigan, tubular grey flannels and battered Hush Puppies, worn with the feet turned distinctively outwards. He shouted at me from some distance, 'Blood, Hilda! I've been thinking about blood.'

'Stop making an exhibition of yourself, Rumpole! Everyone can hear you,' I rebuked him in my most penetrating whisper as soon as he was in earshot.

'You know why Michael Skelton didn't want to be a doctor like his father?'

'Young people nowadays are always trying to be different from their parents.'

'It was the blood. He couldn't stand the sight of blood.'

'Well, some people *are* squeamish, Rumpole. We all know you're not squeamish about anything. Now, have you achieved that simple little list I gave you?'

'Of course I have. Perfectly painless business, shopping – *if* you've got a system. I can't imagine why women make such a song and dance about it.' At the checkout he returned to his favourite subject. 'The hallway was covered in blood. Splashes on the walls, pictures, everything in sight.'

'I see you forgot the washing powder, Rumpole, and I said frozen potato chips not potato *cakes*. Is that the result of your wonderful system?' The girl at the till was looking a little green and I wanted to shut my husband up. Bloodstains are not the thing to talk about on a Saturday morning in Safeway's.

'How would a boy who couldn't stand the sight of blood commit a murder? Poison, perhaps. An electric fire dropped in the bath, even. Hire a contract killer and he wouldn't have had the embarrassment of taking any part in it. Surely the last thing he'd choose is the way they deal with pigs in an abattoir?'

'Rage, Rumpole,' I told him, 'can drive people to forget squeamishness. Now, give me the list and I'll finish off the shopping properly.'

How would you react, Dodo, to being called a girl? I'm quite sure Mizz Liz Probert, the young radical lawyer in Rumpole's Chambers, would have found it patronizing at best and probably deeply insulting. And yet we *were* girls, weren't we, Dodo, when we passed notes to each other in the back row during Gertie Green's French lesson, or when we used watercolours as experimental make-up in the art room? I don't know how it is with you, but I don't feel that we've changed much over the years. A little stiffer when I wake up perhaps, a lot more weight to push up off the sofa, and a few hopes dashed. Do you remember when I made a desperate plan to marry Stewart Granger – I was going to bump into him, one morning, quite casually, during the Christmas holidays in Cornwall Gardens, where that awful little show-off Dorothy Bliss told us, quite erroneously, he lived at the time. So far as I remember, Dodo, you were after James Mason? So you've ended up unmarried and I'm landed with Rumpole, and sometimes I find myself wondering which of us is more lonely. But I think we're still girls at heart, time has never robbed us of that, and when Danny called me one in the Sheridan, I felt, to be quite honest with you, nothing but pleasure.

All the same, it was a huge surprise as the telephone rang one morning, when I was looking forward to keeping myself company in Froxbury Mansions, and some secretary's voice said, 'Mrs Rumpole? I've got Mr Daniel Newcombe on the line.'

'It must be some mistake. Mr Rumpole's in Court and . . .'

She told me there was no mistake. He'd asked for Mrs Rumpole particularly. I was surprised, Dodo, and even more surprised when I found myself alone with Danny at a corner table at the Brasserie San Quentin, and Danny, who had a meeting with clients in Knightsbridge – a millionaire from Kuwait, who, he told me, was accused of pinching nighties from Harrods – was pouring out Beaujolais for me. He had a double-breasted suit on this time, and gleaming black brogues instead of brown, and some regimental or old school tie, and the same bright blue eyes glittered at me.

'Bit of luck,' he said, 'you happened to be free.'

'It wasn't luck at all. I'm free nearly always.'

'And your husband's in Court?'

'Luckily. When he isn't, you'd think there'd been a death in the family.'

'And when he's busy, it's because there's been a death in

someone else's family?' This was rather neatly phrased, don't you think, Dodo?

'Oh, he doesn't always do murders. It's usually thieving, or something or other indecent. Murder is a rare treat for Rumpole. Of course, he's full of himself because you decided to let him do Skelton alone and without a leader.'

'I didn't want the Jury to think Michael's a poor little rich boy.' Danny looked at me and I saw the wrinkles at the corner of his blue eyes. 'If I'd had a top Q.C., they'd've said, "That's what he does with his father's money!" Your husband, with his gravy stains and torn gown, might make the good citizens of East Sussex feel quite sorry for the lad.'

'Is that the reason?'

'I'm sure I can be honest with you, Hilda.'

'I'm sure you can but I don't think I'll tell Rumpole.'

'It might be more tactful not to.' I don't know why I felt a sort of excitement then, Dodo. It wasn't only because I was drinking wine in the middle of the day – something I never do. It was, I'd better admit it, because Danny and I were sharing a secret, something which Rumpole would never know. I mean, to put it far more bluntly than he'd have liked, it seemed he had been chosen because of the state of his waistcoat.

'Rumpole seems to have found a defence.'

'Good for him. I've been racking my brains.'

'Apparently Dimitri Skelton was desperate for Michael to become a surgeon.'

'Naturally the father wanted his only son to follow in his footsteps. Didn't Rumpole's son . . .?'

'Oh, Nick had seen quite enough of the law to put him off it for ever. It seems that Michael Skelton almost fainted at the sight of blood.'

'So he told me.'

'So how, Rumpole's going to ask, could he have committed such a blood-stained murder?'

Danny didn't answer my question, or Rumpole's question, for a while, but when he did, he was still smiling. 'I suppose money overcomes a lot of finer feelings. A terrible lot of money.'

'You mean . . .?'

'About three million in the estate. New faces can be expensive. And the profits from the beauty treatment had been cleverly invested.'

'So it wasn't just a quarrel about the boy's career?'

'More serious than that. Dimitri's wife died of cancer five years ago. It seems he never got on with her family. Michael was his sole heir. He stood to gain a huge amount of money from his father's death. That's the big hurdle Rumpole's got to get over. I don't envy him that, however much I envy him other things.'

'I can't imagine what sort of other things.'

'Like your companionship.' I have to say, Dodo, I found Danny's answer strangely disturbing. 'By the way, Hilda,' he went on, in quite a businesslike way, to cover my confusion, 'I've got seats at Covent Garden next Thursday. If you happen to have a free evening?'

> *'Underneath these granite crosses*
> *No one counts their gains and losses –*
> *But they whisper underground*
> *All the answers they have found.*
>
> *How else can our quarrels end?*
> *Our enemy become our friend?*
> *The dead around us all reply*
> *Peace be with you – you must die.'*

'What's that, Rumpole? Poetry?'

'Hardly. Not really poetry. Not the sort of stuff that gets into *The Oxford Book of English Verse*, the Quiller-Couch edition.'

'I thought it was quite good. At least it rhymes. Who wrote it?'

'It's called "In a Sussex Graveyard" by Michael Skelton.'

'He's a poet?'

'He wants to be. His father wanted him to be a plastic surgeon. Personally, I don't believe he was suited to either profession. If you're going to be a poet you've got to be able to stand the sight of blood.' This was one of Rumpole's epigrams – or *bons mots*, as Gertie Green used to call them, Dodo. So, as you may imagine, I ignored it. I was more than a little irritated by him. He had a load of new instructions open on the kitchen table so I could hardly get at my chops and mash, and he was slightly above himself, as he always is after he's been to see a customer in prison in an important case, and he seemed to regard his day trip to Sussex as something of a day out.

'A strange young man, Hilda. He seems to think that because he writes poetry he exists in a world of his own, rather above ordinary mortals. Can you believe it, he hardly bothered to answer my questions? He didn't seem nervous or frightened or even especially concerned about the case. Just bored by it. But he's wrong, you know. In my opinion poetry is written by people who live quite ordinary lives and have a way with words:

> "Golden lads and girls all must,
> As chimney-sweepers, come to dust."

The man who wrote that went to the pub and worried about his bank account.'

'You must be a poet then, Rumpole. You spend enough time in Pommeroy's Wine Bar. Was that another bit of young Skelton?'

'No, another bit of old Shakespeare.' You know, Dodo, Eng. Lit. was never my strongest subject, but Rumpole needn't have sounded so patronizing.

'You're not telling me this boy killed his father because he wanted to be a poet, are you, Rumpole?'

'I'm not telling you he killed his father full stop. That is a fact which still has to be decided by twelve honest citizens of East Sussex.'

I gave a heavy sigh, signalling that I'd heard quite enough of Rumpole on the burden of proof to last a lifetime. Then I said, 'I should think he probably killed his father for the money.'

'Hilda, have you accepted a brief for the Prosecution?'

'Well, he was his father's sole heir, wasn't he? And I don't suppose cosmetic surgery comes cheap.' In my anxiety to put Rumpole down I had said rather more than I intended.

'How did you know that?' Rumpole gave me his sharp cross-examiner's look.

'I really can't remember. Hadn't the mother died and Michael was the only child? It said that in the *Daily Telegraph*.'

'It's not quite true that he's the sole heir.' Rumpole ferreted about among his papers for a copy of the will. 'Skelton left £100,000 to his secretary – an attractive girl, Michael tells me: "And all the rest and residue of my estate to my son, Michael Lymington Skelton, or if he should predecease me to my cousin Ivan Lymington Skelton, now resident in Sydney, Australia."'

'Well, Michael didn't predecease him, did he? Otherwise you wouldn't be defending him.'

'Oh, Hilda, what a wonderful grasp of legal principles you have!' It was at moments like these that I was strongly tempted to tell Rumpole why he'd been chosen to defend young Skelton alone and without a leader. However, I contented myself with saying, 'I don't really know what kind of defence you've got.'

'The grandfather clock' – Rumpole produced the photograph of the bloodstained hall – 'stopped at ten forty-five. I told you that was important.'

'Why?'

'Michael's got an alibi for ten forty-five.'

'Really. What is it?'

'That poem. He was walking in the beechwoods, about half a mile from the house. Composing it.'

'But you said it wasn't even a good poem.'

'Or convincing evidence. In itself. But there were witnesses.'

'Who?'

'New Age travellers. That's what they call themselves. Sort of politically correct gypsies. They were camping in the woods and Michael stopped to talk to them. He even recited his poem to them, so they might remember him.'

'So have you found these gypsies?'

'Not yet. But today, after we'd seen Michael in Lewes gaol, old Turnbull took me for a walk to the beechwoods near Long Acre, the Skeltons' home.'

'Who's Turnbull?'

'Newcombe's clerk or legal executive – I think that's what they call themselves now. I really don't know what you find so funny, Hilda.'

'Just the thought of you, going for a walk in any sort of wood.'

'One has to make sacrifices – for all-important murders. We found some tyre marks, the remains of a sort of camp-fire and an old shirt bearing the legend LESBIANS WITH ATTITUDE.'

'Talking of Danny Newcombe, Rumpole.'

'I wasn't. I was talking of his clerk.'

'Danny's invited me to Covent Garden next Thursday. He didn't think you'd care for the opera.'

'Opera? Isn't that the stuff Claude Erskine-Brown takes young legal ladies to when he's trying to get off with them? No, Danny's damned right, I wouldn't care for it. I'd rather be stuck before Mr Injustice Graves on a six months' post office fraud. But why on earth has he asked *you*, Hilda?'

'I think, Rumpole' – the time had come to take his mind off his murder case and give him something serious to worry about – 'that Danny Newcombe has taken a bit of a shine to me.'

There was a short silence and then Rumpole said, 'The first thing Danny Newcombe's got to do is to find those New Age travellers.' At that moment he didn't seem to give a hoot whether his instructing solicitor had taken a shine to me or not, and, quite honestly, Dodo, I decided to proceed accordingly.

Well, there I was in the Crush Bar at Covent Garden Opera House, which I had often heard about, but never been crushed in before. It was the first interval and I had sat for an hour and a half in the great gold and plush of the place, letting the music wash over me and getting little clue about the story from the words which occasionally flickered on a screen over the stage. I couldn't really understand what the fuss over Don Giovanni was all about. He was a shortish, stout person, who sweated a good deal, and I would be prepared to say that, as a lady-killer, he didn't rank far ahead of Rumpole. I had bought something new and blue for the occasion from Debenham's and, by an amazing coincidence, Danny was also wearing a dark blue suit with a cornflower-coloured tie which made him look younger and went stunningly with his eyes. There at least, I thought, as he came towards me with two glasses of champagne, was a man who might have made a thousand and three conquests in Spain.

'This is a great treat for me,' he said, as he handed me a glass clouded by the iced wine. 'My favourite opera with a truly sympathetic companion!'

'A treat for me,' I told him, 'to be in a theatre without having to give Rumpole a quick dig with my elbow every time his eyes start to close and the snores threatens to begin.'

'I hope he doesn't mind our going out together?'

'Not at all. He's perfectly happy to be left at home with your murder.'

'Oh, dear. Is he boring you to death with that?'

'I do get rather a lot of the Skeltons. When I was trying to eat my supper the other night he insisted on reading out the father's will . . .'

'Was that interesting?'

'Not really. Rumpole seemed surprised to discover that Michael wasn't the only person to benefit.'

'Oh, you mean the Aussie secretary. We checked up on her. She had gone to a girlfriend's birthday party in Wimbledon and spent the night there. She was celebrating until she went to bed around two in the morning. Anyway, I doubt if she'd be much of a hand with a golf club. You know, looking round this bar, I can see a good many people I've acted for when they were charged with various offences. They all look extremely prosperous and, of course . . .'

'And what?' I asked when he hesitated, smiling.

'Envious. That I'm with such a charming companion. Oh, good evening, Judge.' We were joined, not by one of Danny's clients, but by a woman sent to try them, Mrs Justice Phillida Erskine-Brown, always known to Rumpole (who, for many years, had had the softest of spots for her) as the Portia of his Chambers. In her wake trailed her husband Claude Erskine-Brown, now a Q.C. You will remember, Dodo, that he only achieved what Rumpole calls Queer Customer status when his wife was made up to a scarlet judge, adding beauty and an unexpected degree of serenity to the Bench. 'Hilda Rumpole and Mr Newcombe. Good heavens!' her ladyship delivered judgement. 'It *is* a surprise seeing you two here together.'

'Hilda had a free evening and I was happy to introduce her to my favourite opera.'

'I'm afraid it's not my favourite Leporello.' Claude Erskine-Brown looked as though he'd been invited to a feast and offered a damp sausage-roll. 'Quite the worst "Non voglio piu servire" I've ever heard at the Garden.'

'But, of course, you're not usually listening so carefully, are you, Claude? You're usually far more interested in whomever you happen to have invited. Isn't that true?' The Judge accompanied her question with a sort of humourless laugh, and I remembered that she'd learnt the art of cross-examination from Rumpole.

'How's the Skelton case going?' Claude asked Danny with, I thought, ill-concealed anxiety. 'I only ask because my diary's getting pretty full since I took silk.'

'Oh, I think Danny's going to leave *R. v. Skelton* to Rumpole.' I spoke as a person with inside knowledge. 'He's not taking in a leader.'

'Can that be right?' Claude looked seriously concerned, but his wife said, 'Not a bad idea, that. Rumpole's always at his best in a hopeless case.'

'But he'll start attacking the police. He'll try to destroy all the prosecution witnesses. They won't like that sort of thing in East Sussex.' Claude moved closer to Danny in a vain attempt to sell his forensic talents as though they were double-glazing, and Phillida leant forward and asked for a word in my ear. They were a few words and they came as a question, 'Don't tell me you're going out with Danny Newcombe?'

'Well, isn't it obvious?'

'Is it?'

'We're not exactly sitting at home watching television, are we?'

'But, you mean . . . you're actually going *out* with him.'

'Yes, of course. Well, we've only actually done it twice.'

There was what I believe is known as a pregnant pause, and then Phillida said, 'And Rumpole doesn't know?'

'Well, he knows about the opera. I haven't told him about

the other thing.' I had, you will remember, Dodo, kept quiet about the Brasserie San Quentin.

The Judge gave me a long look of deep concern and said, 'I promise you, Hilda, your secret is absolutely safe with me. And if Claude starts blabbering, I'll do him for contempt of Court!'

Before she could explain this urgent but mysterious message, the interval was over and the bell called us to the further adventures of the Don, who, in my honest opinion, Dodo, couldn't hold a candle to Danny Newcombe in the lady-killing department.

In the second interval we saw Phillida and Claude together in the distance, talking to each other with unusual vivacity and studiously avoiding looking in our direction, as though we were tedious relations they hoped they need have nothing further to do with, or people suffering from a contagious disease. I might have taken some offence at this, Dodo, but I was too busy listening to what Danny was saying to me. Although his eyes were still bright and smiling, his voice had become low and unusually serious. He looked at me, Dodo, in what I can only describe as a yearning sort of way and said, 'Sometimes I long for a complete change in my life.'

'I'm sure we all do.'

'I'd love to give up the legal treadmill. Go away to the sunshine. Perhaps with new companions, or a new companion. You know what, Hilda?'

'No, what?' Quite honestly, Dodo, I was feeling quite weak at the knees, and I'm quite sure it wasn't the champagne when he said, '"'Tis not too late to seek a newer world."'

I couldn't look at him, Dodo. I glanced across at the Judge and her husband, and caught them turning hurriedly away. Then I stared down into my glass of champagne and knocked the rest of it back. My mouth was full of air bubbles which made me suddenly speechless, which may have been just as well.

'"Push off, and sitting well in order smite / The sounding furrows;"' Danny went on and I realized that he was reciting poetry, as Rumpole does at important moments. I don't know what you'd've thought, Dodo, but I was quite sure that the words contained some sort of an invitation. Then we were summoned to see the last bit of the opera, where the General's statue comes to supper, and the unfortunate lady's man is sent down to hell.

Some nights later the scene was far less exciting. Rumpole and I were sitting either side of the gas fire in Froxbury Mansions, and I thought I'd discover whether he was noticing me or not, so I asked, 'What are those photographs, Rumpole?'

'Oh, nothing very sensational.' His brief in Skelton was spread out on the floor around him. 'Pictures I got Turnbull to take in the woods. The remains of the gypsy encampment. I'm getting Newcombe to advertise: ANY NEW AGE TRAVELLERS WHO MET A YOUNG MAN WHO READ POETRY TO THEM ABOUT 10.45 ON THE NIGHT OF 12TH MAY ... I thought he should put it in *Time Out*, the *Big Issue* and the *East Sussex Gazette*. Can you think of anything else politically correct gypsies might read?'

'I have no idea *what* gypsies read.' I went back to the *Daily Telegraph* crossword, but Rumpole was in an unusually communicative mood. 'I had the most extraordinary conversation with Claude Erskine-Brown,' he told me. 'By the way, he's prosecuting me in Skelton. Graves is coming down to try it.'

'I thought Claude was busy angling to lead you.'

'Did you hear that at your bridge lesson?'

'Yes.' It was very strange, Dodo, how quickly I took to telling Rumpole some untruths.

'Well, Danny wouldn't brief him, but Ambrose Clough, who was prosecuting, went off with jaundice and Claude got the brief. Oh, yes, and he's leading Mizz Liz Probert. She'll know what paper New Age travellers take in, I'll have to ask her. Anyway, Claude and I were chatting about the case and he suddenly said, "Philly and I are tremendously sorry for you, Rumpole."'

'Why on earth did he say that?' I asked, knowing the answer.

'That's what I asked him. I told him I'd done far more hopeless cases than Michael Skelton, and I thought I'd been able to put up with the funereal Graves in the past and the old Death's Head had no further terrors for me. Furthermore, having Claude for the Prosecution was always a distinct plus for the Defence . . .'

'How very kind of you, Rumpole, to tell him that.'

'And then he said the reason he felt sorry for me had got nothing to do with the case.'

'Well, what on earth had it got to do with?'

'"If you don't want to talk about it, of course, I understand perfectly," Claude said, in a most mysterious way.

'"Have you been taking lessons from the Sphinx, old thing?" I ventured to ask Claude. "You're speaking in riddles."

'"It must have come" – the chump Claude looked at me extremely seriously – "like a dagger through the heart."

'"If you're speaking of my occasional fits of indiscretion I find a quick brandy works wonders," I told him, and then he asked how long you and I had been married.'

'And what did you tell him?'

'That I couldn't remember.'

'Typical, Rumpole. Entirely typical. Well, it's getting along for forty-seven years.' Nearly half a century, and, I wondered, Dodo, if that made it too late to seek a newer world?

'And then Claude said the most extraordinary thing,' Rumpole said, quite seriously. '"It might make it a lot easier if you were thinner."'

'What did he mean?'

'I asked him that and he said, "Positions and all that sort of thing." Can you understand what he meant?'

'No.' That was true, at least, Dodo. Quite honestly I couldn't.

'Do you think anything would be easier if I were thinner?' Rumpole was puzzled.

'Putting on your socks, perhaps.'

'Perhaps *that's* what he meant.' Rumpole thought it over. 'Claude said that a simple diet might make all the difference. Then he gave me a long, sorrowful look and buggered off.' I turned my own long, sorrowful look back to the *Daily Telegraph* crossword, which had managed to defeat me, and silence reigned in Froxbury Mansions until Rumpole said, 'Skelton's fixed for the fourth of next month. It'll be quite an occasion. Danny Newcombe's attending the trial in person. He'll be staying in the same hotel. Rather a drawback, really. I don't want to spend every dinner time getting unhelpful advice from my instructing solicitor.'

'Rumpole . . .' I started, not after I'd thought things over, but after I'd given way to a sudden, irresistible temptation, 'can I come too?'

'Come where?'

'To East Sussex Assizes. To stay in the . . .'

'The Old Bear hotel?'

'Yes.'

'Why on earth would you want to do that?'

'Because it's a long time since I've seen you in action, Rumpole.'

'What *do* you mean, Hilda?'

'I mean, it's a long time since I've seen you in Court.'

'Well, if you really want to. I'll be working most evenings. I mean, I don't suppose it'll be much fun for you.'

'Oh, I think I might like it quite a lot.' And then, after we had sat in silence for another five minutes, I said, 'Rumpole . . .'

'Yes, Hilda.'

'You know the poem you're always reciting: "'Tis not too late to seek a newer world . . . / We are not now that strength which in old days / Moved earth and heaven;"?'

Rumpole's brief was folded and in his lap with his hands over it. He sat back in his chair, his eyes shut and recited:

> 'We are not now that strength which in old days
> Moved earth and heaven; that which we are, we are;
> One equal temper of heroic hearts,
> Made weak by time and fate, but strong in will
> To strive, to seek, to find, and not to yield.'

'"And not to yield,"' I repeated. 'I'm not quite sure about that.'

It was true, Dodo, I hadn't seen Rumpole in Court for a long time, and I had to admit, reluctantly, that as soon as he took his seat in the second row (the front one is reserved for the

Queer Customers), he was a man in his element. Mr Justice
Graves looked just like Rumpole's description – a man on his
deathbed about to make a will, cutting out almost everyone he
could think of. Claude, opening the case, looked nervous and
not always in complete control of his voice, which trilled up
into a high note of indignation as he described the peculiar
horror of the crime. Liz Probert, sitting behind him, was
frowning as though she feared some terrible insult to women
was about to be offered in evidence, although I couldn't for the
life of me see how the case concerned women at all. Michael
Skelton, in the dock, was small, dark, pale and neat, looking
absurdly young, like a schoolboy at some important event such
as a prizegiving, and not like a murderer at all; although I
wondered if there was any particular way of recognizing a
murderer, and how many of those old clients Danny recognized
in the Crush Bar might have done someone in. Only Rumpole,
spreading out his papers, dropping them on the floor, pushing
back his wig to scratch his head, or pushing it forward as he
yawned heavily and closed his eyes, seemed likely to dominate
the courtroom. He looked, I thought, far more at home than he
ever does in Froxbury Mansions; and I was in no doubt he
would continue his real life in Court whether I was there or
not.

I sat with the solicitors, next to Danny. The Court was so
full that we had to sit close together and, from time to time,
when he moved to look for a statement or pass a note, his arm
brushed mine. I could feel the roughness of his sleeve and
smell his discreet eau de cologne. On Danny's other side sat
Mr Turnbull, a squat, red-faced man with a bull neck who
called me madam and already seemed to regard me as attached
to his employer rather than to Rumpole.

Well, Dodo, I don't know how much you remember of the
Skelton murder trial, and I'm certainly not going to bore you
by going through all the evidence that took up one of the
strangest and most unnerving weeks of my life. Of course *I*
remember every moment of it. But it's difficult for me to write
about it without cold shivers and flushes of embarrassment
but, as we used to say long ago, if you can live through Gertie's
French lessons, you can live through anything, so here goes.

First came the Beazleys who worked for Skelton and lived in a cottage about fifty yards from the back door of Long Acre. Mrs Beazley, a wobbling, panting woman, with a look of perpetual discontent, was the cook–housekeeper, and Mr Beazley, a short, weaselly sort of person, who spoke as though he was always apologizing for something – perhaps working for the deceased plastic surgeon meant always having to say you're sorry – was the driver and handyman.

'I'm afraid Mrs Beazley has quite a taste for old war films, my Lord,' Beazley apologized from the witness stand. 'And we had the one on again about the Yankees fighting over a Pacific island . . .'

'Iwojima,' Claude was helping him, as Rumpole growled, 'Don't lead . . .'

'Iwojima. Thank you, sir. Well. The guns were firing and the bombs dropping and my wife, sir, was thoroughly enjoying herself, and that was it until the film finished. I doubt very much if we'd've heard anything from the house before then.'

'And what time did the film end?' Claude asked.

'I think it was about eleven o'clock time.'

'And what happened after that?'

'Well, I heard someone calling from the house. It was a sort of call for help.' And then Beazley described how he went across to the house and found a scene of bloodstained confusion, and saw Michael Skelton holding a golf club beside the battered body of his father, who appeared to be already dead.

'Now then, Beasley.' Rumpole, it seemed, was prepared to sail into the first prosecution witness with his guns blazing. 'You heard a cry for help and you crossed the yard and went into the house. How long did it take you to get into the hallway from the moment you heard the cry?'

'I might venture to suggest . . . a matter of seconds, sir.'

'You might venture to suggest it, Beazley. And you might well be correct. And when you first saw Mr Skelton Senior, he appeared to you to be dead?'

'He appeared to me to be very dead, sir.'

'So if he was dead, then he's unlikely to have been able to call out for help a few seconds before?'

'That would seem to follow, Mr Rumpole.' A weary and

sepulchral voice came from the Bench, apparently inviting Rumpole to get on with it and not waste time. At which my husband, with elaborate courtesy, said, 'Thank you, my Lord. Thank you for that helpful interruption in favour of the Defence. Now, Beazley, you say you and your wife were watching a war film at ten forty-five?'

'He has already told us that, Mr Rumpole.' Graves was making it clear that he hadn't joined the defence team.

'Any rumpus in the hallway which took place at that time would have been drowned by the battle of Iwojima?'

'Yes, sir.'

'So you heard no voices from the house at that time?'

'No, sir.'

'But when you did hear a voice, we are agreed it could hardly have been that of Mr Skelton Senior?'

'No, sir.'

'It might very well have been the voice of my client, young Michael Skelton?'

'It might have been.'

'Calling for help for the man he's accused of murdering? Is *that* your evidence?'

And without waiting for a reply, Rumpole swathed himself in his gown and sat down in triumph. This gesture had the unfortunate effect of tempting Graves (Mr Injustice Gravestone, I've heard Rumpole call him) to restore the balance by asking the witness if it were also possible that the young man was calling for help because he didn't realize how seriously he had injured his father, a proposition with which the obedient Beazley was delighted to agree.

'The Judge is against us,' Danny turned to whisper to Rumpole.

'So much the better.' Rumpole was indestructibly cheerful. 'We'll make the Jury realize how highly prejudiced the old Death's Head is. That might get us a sympathy verdict.'

But all looks of sympathy seemed to me to drain out of the Jury's faces when Mrs Beazley struggled into the witness-box and described what had happened when she served dinner on that fatal evening. From the first course ('a nice roast beef done with my own horseradish sauce and all the trimmings,' she panted), she'd heard father and son arguing, and the son getting more and more agitated, as Mr Skelton stayed calm and determined. Michael would have to finish his medical course or he wouldn't get another penny, his father told him. And, if he thought he could live on poetry, he was welcome to try it, eked out with a bit of National Assistance, but he wasn't going to live for nothing in his father's house. I thought it was strange of Mr Skelton to tell his son all that with a heavily breathing cook in the room, but perhaps he was one of those people who think their workers are deaf and blind, and probably have no real existence at all.

The evidence was at its worst when Mrs Beazley came back with the treacle tart and cream. 'Mr Skelton always had a sweet tooth, bless him, and I make treacle tart according to my own recipe which, he said, couldn't be beaten.' She had no doubt about what she heard. Michael was standing up and shouting at his father, 'I've got a whole long life to lead and you might die quite soon.' There was a sudden, awful silence and then Mrs Beazley went on. 'They just looked at each other and neither of them said anything. I set the plates for their dessert and just got out as quick as I could.' When she came back to clear away at about nine o'clock, the dining-room was empty and she thought they had probably gone into the drawing-room. (Mr Skelton always liked the coffee served *with* the pudding.) Then she settled down to watch her favourite war film and knew no more until her husband told her that he'd telephoned for the police and an ambulance was on its way.

Rumpole always told me that if a witness was telling the truth you should keep the cross-examination short. I don't know why he told me that, Dodo. He could hardly have thought that I'd ever be in a position to cross-examine anybody. So he was clearly anxious to get Mrs Beazley out of the witness-box as quickly as possible. He established the fact that Michael might have left the house after dinner and not returned until after eleven, and then he let her go. Danny turned his head and whispered in my ear, 'He hasn't even challenged her evidence about Michael saying his father might die quite soon. The strongest evidence against us and Rumpole hasn't even contradicted it!' It seemed to me he spoke more in sorrow than in anger.

I'll spare you all the gory details, Dodo. Rumpole particularly enjoyed himself with the forensic evidence. He seems to regard himself as the greatest living authority on bloodstains. There was blood of his father's group on Michael's hands, his shirt cuffs, on one of his sleeves and on the head of the golf club. Rumpole seemed to be suggesting that the blood got on Michael's clothes when he knelt down to examine his father's wounds, and I thought that he had made a bit of headway with this theory, in spite of the gloomy interventions of the learned Judge. 'I thought your client didn't want to be a doctor, Mr Rumpole,' was one of them. 'I don't know why he would have been so anxious to examine the wounds.' Rumpole also got the scene of the crime officer to agree that the grandfather clock in the hall had fallen over and stopped at ten forty-five, which probably would have been the time of the attack. He also established that it was a Saturday, and that Skelton had been playing golf and had left his bag of clubs in the hall, so his assailant wouldn't have had far to look for a weapon.

At four o'clock Claude got to his feet and asked to raise a matter. He told the Judge that the Defence had filed an alibi notice stating that Michael Skelton was in the woods reading a poem he had written to some New Age travellers. However, Mr Rumpole had failed to give the Prosecution the names of the witnesses they intended to call to support this so-called alibi.

'Well, Mr Rumpole?' Graves asked in a voice as near to doom as he could make it. 'Why has the Defence not supplied the names of their alibi witnesses?'

'Simply because we haven't traced them yet, my Lord.' Rumpole can, when hard pressed to it, manage a disarming smile.

'And what steps have you taken?'

'We have advertised, my Lord, in several publications.'

'Aren't these travellers committing an offence under the new Criminal Justice Act? I imagine they were camping without permission in Mr Skelton's woodland.'

'Even those who commit offences read newspapers, my Lord. We shall produce the advertisements we placed in *Time Out*.'

'Time *what*, Mr Rumpole?' His Lordship was making a note.

'*Out*, my Lord. The *Big Issue* and the *East Sussex Gazette* – have you got them there?' Rumpole leant forward to whisper to Danny who, in close consultation with Turnbull, was going through the file.

'I'm afraid we didn't.'

'You didn't what?'

'I'm sorry, Mr Rumpole.' The red-faced clerk was looking extremely flustered. 'Pressure of work. I'm afraid the advertising got overlooked.'

'Overlooked! This is a charge of murder, you know, not an unrenewed dog licence.' I saw Claude and Liz Probert smiling, enjoying Rumpole's discomfiture, and Danny, as shocked as he was, told Rumpole, 'I'm afraid there's no excuse for Turnbull. Of course, I can't deal with every detail personally. I've told him that.'

Well, Rumpole managed to wipe the anger off his face and stood up and smiled again. He asked Graves to adjourn the case so that the advertisements might be published. After lengthy argument, his Lordship refused to grant an adjournment. The case could take several more days and would be fully reported in the press. When he left Court, Rumpole said, 'Thank God, he's given us a ground for appeal!' But I could tell that he was still very angry indeed.

Rumpole was late getting back to the hotel that night, so Danny and I decided to go in to dinner without him. It was hardly cheerful in the dining-room, distinctly cold, hung with sporting prints and heavy with the smell of furniture polish and overcooked lamb. Whilst we were waiting for the soup, Danny said, 'I'm seriously worried about your husband, Hilda.'

'Why?' At that moment I wasn't worrying about Rumpole particularly.

'He's started off badly, getting on the wrong side of the

Judge. And I'm not at all sure the Jury like the way he's handling our case. Do you honestly think he wants to win?'

'I honestly think Rumpole wants to win every case he does. The only thing is . . .'

'What, Hilda?'

'I think he was cross because the advertisements hadn't gone in the papers.'

'I tore Turnbull off a most terrific strip about that. Not that I believe it was a particularly hopeful line of country. Can you imagine any of these travellers turning up? Let's face it, Hilda, those sort of free spirits spend their time keeping away from the law.'

The soup came then, beige in colour and not particularly hot. In spite of these drawbacks, I was enjoying my stay at the Old Bear, particularly when Danny gave me one of his most twinkling looks and said, in a confidential sort of way, 'Hilda?'

'Yes.'

'Will you do something for me?'

I don't know why it was, Dodo, that I felt suddenly breathless when he asked me that, but I tried to answer him as calmly as possible. 'It depends what it is. But I'll try . . .'

'Keep an eye on Rumpole, will you? I know he's not pleased with me, and he may not tell me what he's got in mind. So if he's planning to take any sort of peculiar line . . .'

'What sort of peculiar line?'

'I don't know. But if he gets any really strange ideas you will let me know, won't you?'

'I suppose so,' I found myself saying. 'Well, all right.'

'Thank you, Hilda dear. I knew I could trust you.' And then he put his hand on mine.

I can see it now in my mind's eye, Dodo. My hand was on the table and his, slightly suntanned, with the carefully tended nails and heavy gold signet ring on the little finger was on top of it, and then I looked up and there was Rumpole standing in the doorway. I think he must have seen where Danny's hand was but he never mentioned it; and as for me, well you may be sure, Dodo, I never asked him whether he had seen it or not.

'I hope you don't mind. We've started without you.' Danny gave my husband his most dazzling smile.

'Apparently.' Rumpole was far from friendly.

'You haven't been working?' I wanted to sound sympathetic.

'Someone has to. I've been down the cells with Michael.'

'I don't suppose you learnt anything new?'

'As a matter of fact I did. Something he hadn't the sense to tell us before. He said he didn't, out of respect for his father's memory. He's a strange lad. It's almost as though he wants to get himself convicted. Anyway, he gave me the name of the doctor.'

'Which doctor, Rumpole?'

'Fellow called Christie-Vickers. Minds a shop somewhere in Harley Street. Michael isn't sure where. About two weeks before the quarrel . . .'

'You mean the quarrel when Skelton got killed?' Danny interrupted.

'No, I mean the quarrel Mrs Beazley heard at dinner . . . His father told him that Christie-Vickers had diagnosed cancer of the prostate. That's why he said the skin doctor might die soon, and he couldn't expect Michael to live on doing a job he hated.'

'He's only just thought of that?' Danny looked doubtful.

'He's only just decided to tell us. Perhaps he's beginning to realize that even poets can't ignore the evidence against them.'

'It wasn't a particularly nice thing for the boy to say to his father.' I was feeling as sceptical as Danny did about young Skelton.

'He's not accused of not being particularly nice, Hilda.' Rumpole was quite sharp with me, Dodo. 'He's on trial for murder.'

'So you want me to get on to this Christie-Vickers?' Danny got out a little pad in a leather case and made a note with a gold pencil.

'Now would hardly be soon enough.' So Danny went off to telephone and, when the waitress came to take his order, Rumpole astonished me. 'Just a green salad if you can manage it,' he said. 'And perhaps a hunk of cheese. A smallish hunk, I suppose.'

'Rumpole' – I looked at him – 'are you sickening for something?'

'I don't think so,' he said. 'Are you?' We didn't say much more until Danny came back and said he'd found Dr Christie-Vickers in the telephone book and tried his house number but got no reply. He'd ring the Harley Street consulting room in the morning.

That night I honestly thought I must tell Rumpole. Tell him what, you may say after reading this far, which, as a story of illicit love and infidelity, would be considered too uneventful for your average parish magazine and would certainly not get a line in the *Daily Telegraph*. But Danny had invited me, hadn't he, not only to the opera but to share his life? What else was all that stuff about it not being too late to seek a newer world and pushing off and smiting the sounding furrows? I was sitting up in my twin bed in the Old Bear as these thoughts flickered through my mind, looking at the yellowing walls and repeated patterns of daisies on the curtains and bed covers, the elecric kettle and assorted tea bags on a rather unsteady shelf, and hearing the sound, like a whale rising up through the waves and spouting, which was Rumpole cleaning his teeth in the *en suite* bathroom. When he came back with his hair standing on end, in his old camel-hair dressing-gown and striped pyjamas, he looked, I thought, like a small boy to whom something unexpectedly outrageous has suddenly happened. I really don't know why it was, perhaps I wanted to put off telling him for as long as possible, or did I want to justify myself by putting Rumpole in the wrong? Quite honestly, Dodo, I can't be sure why I did it, but I said, 'Danny's worried about the way you're doing the case.'

'Danny? Why do you call him Danny?'

'You said everyone did.'

'Perhaps *everyone* hasn't got a special reason. Have you, Hilda?'

'I told you. He's worried about the case.'

'I expect he has other worries on his mind also. What was that wretched opera you saw? *Don Giovanni*? That bed-hopping Spaniard had a few worries on his plate from what I remember. And didn't he come to a sticky end?'

'Rumpole!' I didn't like the turn the conversation was taking. 'You're going to lose Skelton, aren't you?'

'Why? Am I in the habit of losing cases?'

'It has been known. Danny . . .'

'Let's call him Mr Newcombe, shall we? Now that you've really got to know him.'

'All right. Mr Newcombe says it's obvious Michael did it for the money. Even if you lose and he goes away for ten years, he'll come out and collect three million.'

'Did Newcombe tell you that?'

'He didn't say he couldn't.'

At this point, Rumpole sat down on the edge of my bed and began to talk in a slow and patient sort of way, as though to a child. 'A murderer can't profit as a result of his crime, Hilda. If Michael's convicted of murder he won't be able to benefit from his father's estate. Newcombe knows that as well as I do.'

'Did Michael know?'

'He said he did, when I pointed it out to him.'

'Then he must be an extremely stupid young man.'

'Not at all. He got a scholarship to King's. And he writes poetry, of a sort.'

'So he does the murder in a way which is almost certain to be discovered, hangs about by the corpse and calls for help so that a witness can see him with a bloodstained golf club in his hand – all so that he won't get the money from his father's will. Does that really sound likely?'

Rumpole, who had been looking at me with a mixture of resentment and grief, now spoke with unusual respect. 'Hilda,' he said, 'I don't know how you managed it but you seem to have hit on a better argument than a little queasiness at the sight of blood.'

'Thank you.' I was able to look dignified and aloof. 'You're perfectly at liberty to use it, Rumpole.'

He couldn't quite decide how to reply to that and, instead of raising the difficult subject of Danny Newcombe again, he took off his dressing-gown, hung it up, as usual, on the floor and climbed into his twin bed.

'Perhaps we should go to sleep now. You've got the police interviews tomorrow, remember?' I switched off my light and he switched off his.

'Hilda?' His voice came out of the darkness. 'Have you got anything else to tell me?'

'No, Rumpole. Not now, anyway. Let's go to sleep.'

But I didn't. I lay awake for a long time. And I was surprised to find that I was no longer thinking about pushing off and smiting the sounding furrows. I was remembering the pale, calm face of Michael Skelton and asking myself questions which became more unnerving as I stared into the darkness where familiar objects, such as Rumpole's fallen dressing-gown and the electric kettle, seemed to take on new and surprising shapes.

The next morning, I have to confess, Dodo, was boring. I was sitting in Court, turning over the photographs bound together in a slim volume and marked Prosecution I (you see how used I'm getting to courtroom expressions). Before the Judge sat, Mr Turnbull told us that he'd rung Christie-Vickers's secretary, and the doctor was driving through France with his wife but they'd do their best to find him. Rumpole had received the news fairly calmly, for him, and when the police were reading accounts of their interviews with Michael from their notebooks, he closed his eyes and acted the part of someone enjoying a light doze, in order to show the Jury how unimportant the evidence was. Turnbull had gone off on some errand and I was alone in the front row with Danny, who was also finding it hard to keep his eyes open.

I'm not as squeamish as young Michael, Dodo. You know how we used to open up a frog in biology lessons? And I had no qualms about cutting up a rabbit when we used to eat them after the war. But, I must confess, I flicked over the photos taken on the mortuary slab and the colour close-ups of the head wounds. I enjoyed the exterior views of Long Acre and thought that such a spread would be a step up from Froxbury Mansions. And then I got to the most recent photograph of the beauty doctor when he was alive – the picture the police used for the purposes of identification. He was as handsome as his son, with the same high arched nose, full lips and large, dark eyes and black hair. Only, the surgeon's good looks were more arrogant, more supercilious, and his hair was just starting to turn grey over the ears. I thought it odd that the victim looked more dangerous and even brutal than his killer.

I yawned a little, bit my tongue to keep myself awake, and then looked up to the ceiling of the old courtroom. The public gallery was quite full but there, standing in a doorway at the back of it, I saw Skelton, the murdered man.

I swear to you, Dodo, I saw him clearly. There were no head wounds, of course. In fact he looked remarkably well and suntanned as though, since his death, he'd found time for a Caribbean holiday. Indeed, he looked as though he were still on holiday. His white shirt was open at the neck, he wore a blazer and, I think, fawn-coloured trousers. He seemed to be reasonably interested in the proceedings caused by his death, although I couldn't help noticing, as the police evidence droned on, that he covered his mouth with the back of his hand, politely concealing a small yawn.

I must have given a small gasp, an intake of breath, hardly a cry and certainly not loud enough to stir Rumpole from his simulated sleep. But Danny looked towards where I was staring and it seemed to me that he aged quite suddenly. I had, at my most besotted moments, given him late fifties and now he was middle seventies, without a doubt, in front of my eyes. He got to his feet and, in trying to go quietly, stumbled a little, bowed to the Judge and left the Court.

I made sure that Michael, sitting in the dock, his hands folded in his lap and his head down, couldn't see who was in the gallery immediately above his head, and so he missed the sight of his father returned from the grave and looking extremely well. I also saw that Rumpole wasn't looking. Then I turned my eyes to heaven again and there, by the gallery doorway, Danny Newcombe was whispering urgently to the ghost – for if it wasn't Dimitri Skelton's spirit I had no idea, I promise you, Dodo, what it was. But I was going to find out. I got up, did my best possible bow to the Judge who, as usual, also looked dead, and left the Court. As I left Rumpole opened one speculative eye.

I came out of the courtroom door into the entrance hall and I heard voices from the stairs which lead down from the public gallery. You know what I took into my head to do, Dodo? I hid! You might think I'm not exactly the shape for it now, not sylphlike as I was when we squeezed in behind the dormitory door to jump out and scare that ghastly little show-off, Dorothy Bliss, witless. But the hall was pretty dark and there were some thick stone pillars and I tucked behind them somehow. I was just in time to see Danny and the deceased cross to the main entrance. Danny was talking quietly but his voice echoed across the stone floor. I suppose he might have been speaking to a ghost. 'I told you to keep away,' he was saying. 'I told you to go back down under and never come near me again.' Then he pulled open one of the big glass doors and they both stepped out into the sunlight.

I tried to walk quietly across the hallway then. My footsteps seemed to clatter and echo but there was no one there to notice me. I stood by the doors and looked through to the sunlit car park. I saw the figure that seemed to be Dimitri Skelton get into a car and Danny slammed the door. The car was parked very near the Law Court steps and I could see a sticker for RUDYARD'S CARS, LEWES on the back window. I was even able to notice part of the number: ARB and I think it ended with an S. You see, at that moment, I had stopped being a discontented housewife with longings for a newer world. At that moment, Dodo, I had become a lawyer – or at least a detective.

Oh, when the man with the suntan and the open-necked shirt drove the car away, I made quite sure, Dodo, that he wasn't dead. I've had very little experience of the after-life, but I don't think dead people go driving around East Sussex in a hired car.

I didn't go back to Court that afternoon; I had too much to think about. What was that poem of Michael's? Something about 'The dead around us all reply'? Well, the dead, or someone very like the dead, had brought a message to me which I knew was important although I didn't fully understand it yet. There was a lot still to find out so I took a taxi to Long Acre, about five miles out of the town, and asked the driver to wait for me.

It had obviously been a lovely old farmhouse, Dodo, but there was something rather flashy and obviously false about it, like a woman who has had too obvious a face-lift and wears a lot of costume jewellery. Carriage lamps gleamed brassily on each side of the front door. There were white plastic lounging-chairs around the pool bar, a lot of chalky-white statues from a garden centre – cherubs and frogs and things like that – and an ostentatious burglar alarm. I walked round to the back of the house and knocked at the Beazleys' door. There was some noisy shuffling and gasping from inside and then Mrs Beazley opened it. I introduced myself, said I was just passing and there was something I wanted to ask her. When I told her that my husband, one of the lawyers in the case, doted on treacle tart, and I was never quite sure of the recipe, she invited me in. She was alone and seemed in need of company.

'Spoonful of black treacle,' she told me, 'to go with the golden syrup. Three teaspoonfuls of white breadcrumbs and the grated rind of a lemon. I'll write it out for you if you'd like.' At which, she sat down heavily at the kitchen table. 'Would you?' I said. 'That would be extremely kind.' While she made off in the direction of a pencil and paper I carried on, 'Life must seem strange to you, without Mr Skelton?'

'I don't know what's going to happen to us,' Mrs Beazley gasped. 'I don't know what he's done for us in the will. Mr Newcombe's not told us about that.'

'Mr Newcombe?'

'The gentleman what's the family solicitor.' She waddled back to the table and sat down with the pencil and paper which she forgot about as we moved away from the subject of treacle tart.

'Yes, of course.' I knew what Dimitri Skelton had done about the Beazleys in his will – nothing. He didn't seem to have been a man who cared much for the people who worked for him but I didn't say that. I said, 'Mr Skelton must have been very handsome. Such an attractive man, wasn't he?'

'To some people, I suppose.' She spoke as though she had a considerable contempt for handsome men, this scarcely mobile woman with a passion for war films. 'To that secretary of his, I suppose he *was* attractive. That's why we were going to have to leave anyway. Even if none of this had ever happened.' She spoke of 'this' – a terrible murder, Dodo – as though it had been an inconveniently leaking radiator. 'Raymond and I couldn't have stayed after *she* took over.'

'You didn't like Miss – ?'

'Miss Ashton. Miss Elizabeth Ashton. Came into my kitchen and said she'd show me how to cook. Trendy food, she said, like they got in some place up in London. Pasta – that meant spaghetti – but she *would* call it pasta. Well, you don't need much brain to boil spaghetti and I could do that, but she wanted it with scallops and squids in it, and stuff like that. If he wants fish, I told her, what about a nice fish pie? One night she decided to cook for herself and made a terrible mess of my kitchen. Clean out the saucepans? She wouldn't have considered it!'

'Wasn't she Australian?'

'That's no excuse though, is it? Yes, I think he said she'd come from Australia. Mr Skelton had some relation over there, cousin or something, and he'd said she might be suitable for the job. Far too suitable Raymond and I thought he found her. We couldn't have stayed. Not if she were permanent.'

I have to say, Dodo, I felt quite triumphant, when she told me that. You see, I was out on my own and far, far ahead of Rumpole. I thought perhaps that Mrs Beazley had still more to tell me, so I said, 'I did admire the way you gave your evidence. It must have been terrifying standing up there in front of all those people in wigs.'

'Oh, I didn't mind once I got started. And your husband was very nice to me. Nice as pie he was, though they warned me he could be a bit of a terrier with a witness. The trouble was . . .' She hesitated.

'Yes, Mrs Beazley. What was the trouble?'

'Well, you can't tell them everything, can you? You're only meant to answer *their* questions.'

'Is there anything you didn't tell them?'

She panted a little and then said, 'Yes. About Raymond.'

'What about Raymond?'

'Well, he missed a bit of the film, a really good bit he missed, when they was hand-fighting. He had to go to the toilet, if I have to be honest. And he looked out of the window, upstairs.

And in the yard between us and the big house there was a car parked.'

'A strange car?'

'Well, Ray'd never seen it before. He happened to notice the number. I know the first three letters, if you like, because they happen to be his initials.'

'What are your husband's names? Raymond Beazley?'

'Albert Raymond Beazley. We went to Mr Newcombe, you know, and asked if we should say anything about it. But he said it wasn't that important. I think it may have been, don't you?'

'Yes, Mrs Beazley, I think it may have been very important indeed. Now, do you think there's any chance of a cup of coffee while we write out that recipe?' It was a bit of cheek saying that, I knew, in someone else's kitchen. But I felt I'd earned it.

When I got back to the hotel I had some telephone calls to make: one to Rudyard's Cars and another to the house of Dr Christie-Vickers – who, I was not altogether surprised to find, had got back from his holiday trip in France. Then I have to confess, Dodo, that such was my mood that I went straight into the bar and ordered myself a small sherry, and there was the bull-necked Turnbull in conversation with a strange-looking creature. I believe she was a woman, but her hair was clipped and bristly, a sort of stubble all over her head. At first sight, her face seemed beautiful and even young. But when you looked more closely she had lines which, like you or I, Dodo, she made no attempt to conceal. She wore patched jeans and a sort of camouflage jacket over a T-shirt, and enormous earrings. She was smoking what seemed to be a homemade cigarette and talking very quietly, so I couldn't overhear what she was saying. After a while she got up and left. Turnbull finished what looked like a dark and generous whisky and said, 'Good evening, Mrs Rumpole,' on his way out.

'Was that a New Age traveller?' I asked him as though my curiosity was perfectly idle.

'How did you know?'

'I thought that was what they looked like.'

'She'd read about the case in the local paper.'

'And you're going to call her?'

'Hardly. You know what she said?'

'I've no idea.'

'That she knew we needed one of the travellers to give evidence and she'd say anything for a hundred pounds in the hand. Terrible world, isn't it, Mrs Rumpole? They live like pigs and then pervert the course of justice. Good evening to you.'

'Good evening, Mr Turnbull.' I tried my best to look as though I believed what he'd told me. Then, I'm very much afraid, I ordered another sherry. I had hardly finished it when Rumpole came into the Downlands Bar looking tired and not particularly happy. I told him to order a large red wine – a bottle of it, if that would cheer him up – and invited him to sit beside me.

'Hilda, are you feeling well?' He looked, I have to admit, apprehensive. 'Have you something to tell me?'

'A good many things. But first let me ask you something. What do you call down under?'

'Down under?' The poor man looked entirely confused and, when the first glass of wine was put in front of him, he took a quick and consoling gulp. 'What do you mean?'

'I don't mean hell, Rumpole. I don't mean where Don Giovanni ended up. Where else do you call down under?'

'Do you mean Australia?'

'Yes, Rumpole, I mean Australia.' And, of course, that was what Danny meant.

'Hilda, I asked if you were feeling well. Has this trial been too much for you?'

'Not at all. I was afraid it was too much for *you*. So I've found you a defence.'

'I thought you went out shopping.' He gave a distinctly mirthless laugh. 'Where did you get my new defence from, Marks & Sparks? You were out shopping a long time. I was surprised that Mr Daniel Newcombe had the courtesy to stay with me. When he went out of Court this morning I saw you troop after him soon enough.'

'Rumpole' – I hope I smiled tolerantly, as that would have been the most effective way – 'you're never jealous, are you?'

'Jealous? Should I be?'

'No, I really don't think you should. Mr Newcombe and I left the Court because we both saw Dimitri Skelton in the public gallery.'

'Hilda! You're joking . . .' Or delirious, I felt was what he wanted to say.

'It wasn't exactly funny.'

'You mean you saw . . .'

'The man they all say was murdered.'

'I've tried that defence before.' Rumpole was back to his usual patronizing self. 'Witnesses saying they saw the corpse alive after the date of the murder. It has a sort of biblical authority, I suppose, but it never worked particularly well down the Old Bailey. Is that your defence, Hilda?'

'No, as a matter of fact it isn't. We didn't see Dimitri Skelton.'

'Hilda, please . . . I'm tired and unusually depressed.'

'If you're tired, sit back in your chair and listen, Rumpole. I'll tell you who we did see. And then you'd better scoot down to the cells early tomorrow morning and ask your Michael Skelton some pertinent questions.'

'Such as?'

'Such as, how much he knows about Miss Elizabeth Ashton from down under?' He looked at me then and, entirely for his own good, decided to listen quietly. We talked for a while, time enough for Rumpole to get through a bottle of wine, and do you know, Dodo, it was the most serious, even enjoyable, conversation we'd had for a long time. It didn't take him long to get the hang of what I was saying and when he did he knew exactly what to do. When I had told him everything he said, 'I suppose you realize what this means?'

'What it means for Michael Skelton?'

'No. For your friend Danny boy.'

'Yes,' I said, 'I do realize.'

'And you don't mind?'

'No,' I told him, 'I don't think I mind at all.'

Rumpole left very early in the morning to go to the cells and have a further conversation with the non-talkative Michael

Skelton. Dodo, I felt strangely calm. I realized that for the last
few months, ever since that dinner in the Sheridan with Danny
Newcombe, in fact, I'd been nervous, strung up and even, if I
have to say it myself, rather silly. Now I had killed what had
been going on in my mind for a long time. Rumpole always
says that the real murderers he had met – I mean the ones who
had actually done it – were always strangely calm, as though
something had been decided for ever.

Anyway, after Rumpole had gone I had a nice bath, making
full use of the complimentary sachet of Country Garden toilet-
ries in the little wickerwork basket on the glass shelf. I have to
confess that I pinched the verbena shampoo and hollyhock skin
freshener, together with a little packet of sewing stuff. I do find
that staying in hotels brings out everyone's criminal tendencies.
Then I put on the rather nice coat and skirt I had been wearing
in Court and went down to the Sussex-by-the-Sea coffee shop
for the full English breakfast. And there was Danny Newcombe, standing at a table by the door, throwing down his
Financial Times and offering me a seat at his table. I accepted
and sat down.

'So we're going to have the pleasure of your company in
Court again today, Hilda?'

'If you think it's a pleasure, yes.'

'You must have thought it rather strange when I suddenly
bolted out yesterday.'

'I didn't think it strange at all,' I lied.

'I thought I saw someone I knew in the public gallery. Did
you see me go up there?'

'No.' I went on lying.

'It was all a mistake. I mean, it wasn't anyone I knew.'

'Well, that's all right then.'

'Yes.' And then he said, very seriously now, 'I'm afraid
there's not much hope for us.'

I looked at him and said, 'You mean you're afraid there's not
much hope for Michael Skelton?'

'That's what I mean, yes.'

'I don't think you should be so sure of that. You never know
what Rumpole's going to pull out of the bag.'

'You mean you *do* know, Hilda?' He gave me his best

twinkling smile, complete with the wrinkles at the corners of the eyes. 'And you promised to tell me if he had one of his funny ideas, didn't you?' I thought for one dreadful moment that he was going to add 'You naughty girl, Hilda'.

'If I promised that,' I told him, 'I'm afraid I'm not going to keep my promise.'

'Whyever not?'

'Because I don't think Rumpole would like it. Oh, and I'll tell you something else I'm not going to do.'

'What's that?'

'I'm not going to smite the sounding furrows. I have to tell you this, Mr Newcombe. It's far too late to seek a newer world.'

He looked at me then as though he didn't quite understand what I was talking about. I noticed he had dropped a lump of scrambled egg on what he told me was the Sheridan Club tie. I have to tell you, Dodo, that I thought it looked quite disgusting.

'Members of the Jury. Young Michael Skelton may *seem* guilty, kneeling beside the body, his father's blood on his hands, clutching that fatal golf club. But things, Members of the Jury, are not always as they seem. Let us together, you and I, set out to discover the truth behind that strange and terrible apparition. Ladies and gentlemen, look back to the time when you were but twenty years old and consider how you would have felt if you'd had to go into the witness-box and defend yourself on such a serious charge as this. It would be an ordeal for anyone.' And here Rumpole's voice sank to a tone of deep insincerity and he leaned forward and stared at the Jury. 'It must be terrible for the innocent.' Then he straightened up and trumpeted out the summons 'Call Michael Skelton'.

Michael's performance wasn't, of course, anything like as good as Rumpole's. He remained strangely aloof, but he looked pale, proud and vulnerable. He retold his story quite clearly and when Claude came to cross-examine him he seemed suddenly bored, as though he thought it quite unnecessary to go through the whole thing again, and was privately composing a poem. Claude didn't really get anywhere, but when Michael left the witness-box, the Jury probably still thought that he'd killed his father. And then Rumpole surprised everyone, and particularly Danny, by saying, 'My next witness will be my instructing solicitor, Mr Daniel Newcombe.'

Sitting next to me, but as far away as possible now, as though we were a married couple in bed after a quarrel, Danny gave a little gasp of surprise and turned round to Rumpole. 'You don't mean you're calling *me*?'

'That's the general idea. Will you just step into the witness-box?'

Danny had no choice then, but I thought he walked as grimly as a soldier crossing a minefield. When he reached the exposed little platform, he raised the Bible with a great air of confidence and, encouraged by a rare smile from the Gravestone, promised to tell the whole truth and nothing but the truth.

'Mr Newcombe' – Rumpole was quietly courteous – 'you are familiar with the late Dimitri Skelton's will?'

'I should be. I drafted it.'

'He drafted it, Mr Rumpole.' His Lordship did his best to raise a small laugh against Rumpole. Claude even obliged.

'I am aware of that, my Lord.' Rumpole gave a small bow and then turned to Danny. 'Now, in the event of this Jury finding Michael guilty, he won't be able to inherit under his father's will, will he?'

'We all know that, Mr Rumpole, don't we? A murderer can't profit from his crime.' The Judge did his best to patronize Rumpole, who replied with elaborate courtesy, 'Exactly, my Lord! I do so congratulate your Lordship. You have put your finger upon the nub, the very heart, of this case. Now, who is to benefit if my client is found guilty of murder?'

'Well, Elizabeth Ashton will still get her hundred thousand pounds legacy.' Danny looked as though he now felt that the witness-box wouldn't be so dangerous after all.

'Miss Elizabeth Ashton. Remind us. She is Dimitri Skelton's secretary, is she not?'

'That is so, my Lord.' Danny chose to give his answer to the Judge.

'And the residue of the estate?'

'That would all go to the deceased's cousin in Australia, Ivan Skelton.'

'About three million pounds, isn't it?'

'Something like that, yes.'

'Lucky old Ivan.'

The Jury giggled slightly and the Judge looked deeply pained.

'Of course, if Michael Skelton is acquitted,' Danny added in all fairness, 'Ivan doesn't get a penny.'

'So Ivan must be praying for a guilty verdict, mustn't he? This jury comes back and says Guilty, my Lord and, Bingo, the old darling's worth three million.'

'Mr Rumpole' – Graves was deeply distressed – 'is this a subject for joking?'

'Certainly not, my Lord. It is extremely serious. Mr Newcombe, Ivan Skelton is taking a considerable interest in the outcome of this case, isn't he?'

'I imagine he is concerned about it, yes,' Danny had to admit.

'You've met Ivan Skelton, haven't you?'

'Please don't lead.' It was Claude's turn to grumble.

'Very well. Mr Newcombe, have you ever met Ivan Skelton?'

'I met him when he came to England, yes.'

'What does he look like?'

'Well, it's a little difficult to describe . . .'

'It is? Is it? Doesn't he look exactly like this?' At which Rumpole held up the murdered Dimitri's photograph for all to see, and Claude stood up to whinge.

'My Lord, Mr Rumpole is cross-examining this witness.'

'No, I'm not. I'm refreshing his memory. This is a picture of the dead man, isn't it? Does his cousin look almost exactly like him?'

'They are about the same age. Yes. There is a family resemblance.'

'Thank you.' Rumpole began to rummage among his papers and Danny looked only moderately worried.

'Is that all, Mr Rumpole?' Graves sighed.

'Not quite, my Lord.'

'I'm just wondering, Mr Rumpole, how far this line is taking you in your defence?'

'It's taking me to the truth, my Lord. Never mind about the Defence. Now, Mr Newcombe' – he turned to the witness-box, looking far more pugnacious – 'you're the trusted old family solicitor?'

'I'm the family solicitor. And I suppose I'm old . . .'

'Indeed you are! This secretary, Miss Elizabeth Ashton, she comes from Australia, doesn't she?'

'I rather think so.'

'And is she engaged to be married to Ivan Skelton? So he recommended her to his cousin for the job? He's planning to come over later this year and marry her, is he not?'

'I have heard that.'

'Engaged to be married and she spent weekends with his cousin Dimitri and became his mistress?'

'Mr Rumpole' – Mr Justice Graves intruded like the dead general who came to dinner with the Don – 'I wonder what this has to do with the charge against your client?'

'Then wonder on, my Lord, till truth makes all things plain.' I suppose Rumpole was quoting poetry of some sort, as he went on quickly, 'When did you last see Ivan Skelton, Mr Newcombe?'

'I forget . . .'

'Oh, come now. Your memory's not quite as short as that. There are others in Court' – he looked down at me, and I suddenly became others – 'who can tell us, if you don't want to. When did you last see him?' Danny looked at me, I thought sadly, as though I had betrayed him.

'Yesterday.'

'Where?'

'In Court.'

'In this Court?' The Judge raised his eyebrows.

'Yes, my Lord. In the public gallery.'

'No doubt anxious to see if he was going to get his money. And you spoke to him?'

Danny looked at me again, pleadingly. I stared back and he had to answer yes.

'What did you say?'

'Mr Rumpole, that's pure hearsay.' Graves was doing Claude's job for him.

'Of course it is, my Lord. One can always trust your Lordship, with his great experience, to be right on a point of law. Mr Newcombe, I advised your firm to advertise for the New Age travellers and you have not done so?'

'That is right. I'm afraid it got overlooked.'

'You declared that the deceased's doctor couldn't be found and he has been found now, without your help?'

'I'm very glad to hear it.'

'Are you, Mr Newcombe? I shall be calling Mr Beazley to say that a strange car was parked in the yard at Long Acre on the night of the murder. Did you tell him that evidence was irrelevant?'

'My Lord' – Claude was stung into activity at last – 'Mr Rumpole is cross-examining his own witness!'

'Not at all! At the moment I'm making no attack on Mr Newcombe. He may genuinely have thought that the presence of a car hired by the murdered man's cousin was quite irrelevant. And I shall be calling Mr Beazley.'

'I may have said something . . .' Danny was about to agree but Graves did his best to save him. 'Mr Rumpole,' he said, 'I agree that this question is an attack on your own witness. It is quite improper.'

'Then let me ask you a quite proper question. Have you, Mr Daniel Newcombe, been offered a share of Ivan Skelton's winnings to make sure that this young man who stands before us in the dock is convicted of murder?'

'Mr Rumpole.' The pale judge seemed, in his indignation, to be rising in his seat, again, I thought, like some spectre arising from the tomb. He glared at Rumpole with such terrible disapproval that if you or I, Dodo, had been in his place I honestly think we'd have simply collapsed, as we felt like doing when Stalky Sullivan gave us one of her looks and said she'd have to let our unfortunate parents know we were a disgrace to the school. Rumpole just stood there, smiling in an unusually polite way and, I have to say, I rather admired him as Graves went on, 'This cross-examination is going from bad to worse.'

'Oh, I agree with every word that has fallen from your

Lordship.' Rumpole was still smiling. 'We are dealing here with something very bad indeed.'

'Mr Rumpole!' The old Gravestone unclenched his teeth in a vain attempt to call my husband to order. 'Do I understand that you are accusing your own solicitor of entering into a criminal conspiracy to get this young man falsely convicted for murder?'

'Ah, your Lordship puts the matter far more eloquently than I ever could. It is that gift for words that brought your Lordship such success at the Bar.'

In fact Graves hadn't been much of a success at the Bar. I remember Rumpole telling me that he'd got 'his bottom on the Bench thanks to his skill in winning a safe Conservative seat'. I had to admire his Lordship's self-control. The temptation to shout at Rumpole at that point is one which personally I would have found irresistible. 'At least Mr Newcombe is entitled to refuse to answer a question likely to incriminate him, is he not?'

'Of course.' Rumpole got more polite as Graves became more irate. 'As always your Lordship is perfectly right.'

'Then I fully intend to warn him.'

'Your Lordship can take no other course.'

So the Judge warned the witness that he needn't answer this incriminating question. Danny suddenly looked very old – I wondered why I had even put him in his sixties – and much smaller. He was hardly audible when he said, 'My Lord, I prefer not to answer.'

'You prefer not to? That is probably extremely wise.' And Rumpole sat down in triumph, looking meaningfully at the Jury. Danny Newcombe never returned to sit between me and Mr Turnbull but, as soon as he left the witness-box, scuttled out of Court and, to be honest with you, Dodo, I never saw him again. But when I looked up to the public gallery I saw, not Danny talking to Ivan Skelton this time, but a woman with a stubbly head, who looked quite young from a distance, and who had come to tell the truth in spite of Mr Turnbull.

The rest, of course, is history, and I'm sure you read about it in the papers. I don't know whether they gave you Rumpole's final speech or the bit which began so quietly that the Jury had to strain their ears to hear it: 'A young man is walking in the woods, making up poetry and reciting it to some modern-day gypsies when one of Rudyard's Cars drives up to Long Acre. Out of it gets the man who had hired it, Mr Ivan Skelton from Sydney, Australia. Why has he come there? Because he has heard of the love affair between Dimitri Skelton and Elizabeth Ashton whom Ivan was to marry, the girl who came over to work for his cousin and wait for him to join her.

'Nobody heard the quarrel, Members of the Jury. The Beazleys were too busy listening to ancient warfare and the house was empty. Overcome with rage and jealousy did Ivan lift this fatal weapon' – by now Rumpole had the golf club high above his head – 'and strike! And strike! And strike again in the terrible and fatal fight that followed. No one saw Ivan after that fight or gave evidence as to the bloodstains on *him*. But when young Michael came home and found his father dead, and was stained by his father's blood as he knelt beside the body, was it not natural that he should be suspected?

'And how very convenient for Ivan that he was. Because if Michael was convicted, Ivan would inherit a fortune. And remember, he was here with us the other day, Members of the Jury, the man you might think is possibly, quite, quite possibly, even probably, guilty. That man was in the public gallery making sure his inheritance was safe. And then, when he had been warned by my solicitor, did he not slink away, as he had on the night of the murder, in one of Mr Rudyard's hired cars to await the news of that young poet's wrongful conviction?

'If you think that's what *may* have happened, Members of the Jury, let us deny Ivan Skelton his final satisfaction and his undeserved wealth. Let us find young Michael Skelton not guilty of the terrible crime of murdering his father. And, remember, it is *your* decision' – here Rumpole glared at the Judge who, sitting motionless, had closed his eyes as though in pain – 'and not the decision of anyone else in the Court.'

And so the next day we were home again and sitting on either side of the gas fire at Froxbury Mansions in the evening. I'm glad to say there had been no further requests for salad.

Rumpole had done full justice to the shepherd's pie and cabbage I had cooked for him, taken with a great deal of mustard
and tomato sauce. Now he said, 'Thank you, Hilda. Thank you
for the work you put in to *R. v. Skelton*. Some of your ideas
were surprisingly helpful.'

'Only some of them?' And, when he didn't answer, I said, 'I
have to say you didn't seem able to follow up some fairly
obvious clues. At least not until I got on the case.'

'I was distracted,' Rumpole had to admit. 'I was suffering
from certain anxieties.'

'What sort of anxieties, Rumpole?'

'Matters of a domestic nature.'

'You mean, you thought it was about time we had the
kitchen redecorated? I've been thinking that too.'

'No. I was concerned . . . Well, damn it all, Hilda. I thought
you might have grown tired of life here . . . with me.'

'Life with you in Froxbury Mansions? Good heavens, how
could anyone be tired of that?'

'You said . . . Well, anyway, you told me . . .' It was the first
time in my entire life I had seen Rumpole stumped for words.
'What was all that about Newcombe having taken a shine to
you?'

'No, I was wrong about that. He hadn't taken a shine to me.
He wanted to win me over so I could be his spy.'

'His *what*?' I had surprised Rumpole.

'So I could spy on you. Tell him if you were getting too near
the truth in *R. v. Skelton*. And there was something else I
didn't like him for.'

'What was that?'

'Well, he called me a girl, which I thought was very patronizing. And I know why he gave you the brief.'

'Well, I do have a certain reputation . . . Ever since that little
problem at the Penge Bungalow.'

'He thought because you aren't a Q.C. you wouldn't do the
job properly.'

'That's ridiculous!'

'Of course it is.' There was silence for a while. Rumpole
considered my extraordinary suggestion and rejected it. Then
he said, 'I shan't include *R. v. Skelton* in my memoirs.'

'Whyever not? It was one of your greatest triumphs.'

'No, Hilda.' He picked up his brief in a little receiving job at Acton. 'The triumph was yours.'

This is the story that Rumpole will never write. So I'm writing it for you, Dodo, and for you only. It's the truth, the whole truth and nothing but the truth.

Rumpole and the Little Boy Lost

'Whoever did that,' Dot Clapton said, 'deserves burning at the stake!'

'I'm afraid they abolished that a few years ago.' I took the *Daily Trumpet* Dot was offering me across her typewriter. 'Although, given the reforming zeal of the appalling Ken Fry' – I winced as I invariably do when I mention the name of the current Home Secretary – 'we might get it back in the next Criminal Justice Act.'

What I saw was a big photograph, almost the whole tabloid front page. A young woman, wearing a T-shirt and jeans, was looking into the camera, trying to smile; a husband only a few years older, puzzled and frowning, had his arm protectively round her shoulder. Behind them was the blur of an ordinary semi-detached and a small, ordinary car, but they were the victims of an extraordinary crime. Their child had been snatched away from them, hidden among strangers and perhaps ... It was the awful perhaps which made Steve Constant put his arm round his wife and why her smile might turn so easily into a scream. SHEENA CONSTANT TALKS EXCLUSIVELY TO THE TRUMPET, the front page told the world. SEE CENTRE STORY.

'If they catch the old witch who did it, you wouldn't speak up for her in Court, would you? I mean you'd let her hang herself out of her own mouth, wouldn't you, Mr Rumpole?'

I had turned over to the central spead, entirely devoted to the little boy lost. There was an enlarged picture of little Tommy in the strangely metallic washed-out colours in which photographs appear in newspapers: an ordinary, carrot-haired three-year-old with a wide grin, no doubt a singular miracle to the Constants whose first and only child he was. There were snaps of the family at the seaside, by a swing in the garden of the semi and a picture of the huge South London hospital, gaunt and unfriendly as a nuclear power station, from which Tommy Constant had unaccountably disappeared. As I glanced over these apparently harmless records of a tragedy, I was trying to remind Dot of an Old Bailey hack's credo. 'I'm a black taxi, Dot,' I told her, 'plying for hire. I'm bound to accept anyone, however repulsive, who waves me down and asks for a lift. I do my best to take them to their destination, although the choice of route, of course, is entirely mine.'

'The destination of her who nicked that child' – Dot was unshakeable in her demand for a conviction, she was not the sort you'd want called up for jury duty – 'would be burning at the stake. If you want my honest opinion.'

I have to confess that I wasn't giving Dot my full attention. There wasn't a long story between the pictures, but what there was had been written in the simple, energetic style of the *Daily Trumpet* which, I thought, might be appreciated by a jury.

Twenty-four-year-old Sheena Constant spoke through her tears: 'After he was seen by the doctor, I put him on the kiddies' mechanical donkey in the out-patients assembly. He's been on it before, so I left him with Steve while I went to the toilet. Steve just crossed over to buy a packet of Marlboro. He was in sight of Tommy and only turned away for about a minute. It was during that minute our little son was stolen off us. He sort of vanished clutching a little yellow flop-eared rabbit which was his favourite toy!'

Police investigations continue. Who was the pale-faced woman in a black beret and black plastic mac carrying a toddler away from out-patients? Police Superintendent Greengross hadn't yet found her. Where were the social workers? Drinking carrot juice and knitting pullovers? Where were the hospital managers? Upstairs with their noses in the trough? Where was hospital security? Out to lunch? These are the questions the *Trumpet* will be asking during the coming week.

TOMORROW: WHY MY DAUGHTER'S HEART IS BROKEN. Tommy's gran talks exclusively to the *Trumpet*.

'We've got her!' Claude Erskine-Brown had entered the clerk's room in a state of high excitement. 'Got her, at last.'

'The woman who stole little Tommy?' I was still absorbing

the *Trumpet*'s simple story. I had supped full of horrors at Equity Court, but there seemed to be something peculiarly tragic about this young couple's loss.

'Of course not. She didn't steal anything. Can't you get your mind off crime for a single moment? Does the wonderful world of art mean nothing to you? We've got Katerina Regen to sing to us in the Outer Temple Hall.'

'Have you, by God?' I folded the *Daily Trumpet* neatly and put it back on Dot's typewriter. I thought I might have to forget Steve and Sheena Constant and fill my mind with other people's troubles. 'I doubt whether I shall be among those present.'

'She will give us Schubert.'

'So far as I'm concerned, she can keep him.'

'And the Bar Musical Society, of which by a strange quirk of fate I seem to have become president' – here I can only say that Erskine-Brown gave a modest simper – 'will be hosting a small champagne reception afterwards. The eighteenth of this month. Put it in your diary, Horace.'

For a moment my strong resolution wavered. Any invitation to take me to your *lieder* is one which, as a general rule, I have no difficulty in declining. But I have no such fears of a champagne reception. However, the preliminary trills seemed a highish price to pay for a glass or two of bubbles, so I sent an apology. 'I'm sorry but Hilda and I will be entertaining.'

'Entertaining who?'

'Each other. To a couple of chops in Froxbury Mansions. Awfully sorry, old darling, previous engagement.'

That night we were settled in front of the television in the mansion flat when Hilda said, 'I hope you've got the eighteenth marked down in your diary, Rumpole?'

'Yes, I have. I'm staying at home.'

'Oh no, you're not.'

Sometimes the dialogue of She Who Must Be Obeyed becomes strongly reminiscent of the pantomimes my old father used to take me to in my extreme youth. Don't I remember some such witty line having been used by the Widow Twankey?

'Hilda,' I reassured her, 'you don't want to spend a couple of hours on a hard chair in the Outer Temple Hall listening to some overweight diva trilling about departed love.'

'You know nothing, Rumpole,' she told me. (Had she forgotten my encyclopaedic knowledge of bloodstains?) 'Katerina Regen is not only Covent Garden's new Mimi but she's as slender as a bluebell.'

'Who told you that?'

'Claude Erskine-Brown, when he rang up. I told him to put us down for two tickets.'

'How much is he paying us to go?'

'Nothing, Rumpole. *We* are paying. It will be extremely good for you. You have so little art in your life.'

'I have poetry.'

'*Some* poetry. And it's like your jokes, always the same.'

'How much?'

'How much the same? Exactly.'

'No, how much are the tickets, Hilda! Erskine-Brown didn't con you out of a tenner?'

'The tickets were fifty pounds each and that includes two glasses of a really good Méthode Champenoise, which I think's a bargain considering how much you'd pay to listen to Regen at the Garden.'

And considering the happy evenings I might have had at Pommeroy's with the Méthode Fleet Streetoise for half that enormous expenditure. I might have said that but thought better of it. And then my attention was grabbed by the television on which an astonishingly young superintendent was holding a press conference. He sat between Sheena and Steve Constant – he in an ornate pullover, she in what must have been her best outfit, trying not to weep.

'I just want to say . . .' The superintendent had longish fair hair and protruding eyes. He looked as though he'd be much happier sharing jokes with his mates in the pub. However, he managed to sound both serious and sincere. '. . . to whoever's *got* Tommy, we can understand your problems. Maybe you're longing for a little boy of your own and can't have one. Perhaps you even lost a little boy in tragic circumstances. We understand and we're all sympathetic. We think you may need help and we'll see to it that you get it. So will you ring us at the number we'll put up on the screen in a minute and tell us where Tommy is? We're sure he's alive and well. (Here Sheena looked down, a hand to her forehead, covering her eyes.) We're sure you've been looking after him really well. But just tell us where he is, that's all. Give Tommy what he *really* needs: his mum and dad.'

As he talked I remembered some of the old poetry She Who Must Be Obeyed was tired of.

> 'Father! father! where are you going?
> 'O do not walk so fast.
> 'Speak father, speak to your little boy,
> 'Or else I shall be lost.'
>
> The light was dark, no father was there;
> The child was wet with dew;
> The mire was deep, & the child did weep, . . .

Sheena lowered her hand and shook her head bravely, like a diver shaking the water out of her eyes as she emerges from beneath the sea. Steve's teeth were clenched, his jaw set, his face a mask of misery.

I didn't know why I felt so concerned about the Tommy Constant case. Had I fallen a little, perhaps, in love with Sheena's face and looked forward, when the good news came, to seeing it light up with joy? I dreaded the pictures of the police with dogs crossing parkland or rubber-suited figures flopping into canals. I was even more afraid that they might find something. Whatever the reason, I found myself taking the Chambers' stairs like a two-year-old and arrived panting in the clerk's room feeling every day of seventy-four. I could hardly find enough breath to ask Dot for a quick loan of her *Daily Trumpet*.

There was a notable absence of hard news. Mrs Bellew, Sheena's mum, was reminiscing. Sheena had been a model child who did well at school and had a really lovely singing voice and was so pretty that the family hoped she might end up on television. She'd gone in for a few beauty competitions:

'Just local ones. I wouldn't have let her near the Albert Hall.'
And a schoolfriend who knew the drummer in Stolen or Strayed
(musicians whom I have to confess I'd never heard of) thought
she might get her a job singing with the group, but nothing
came of it. Tommy, it seemed, had inherited his mother's
talents and, although only three, could perform 'Ooh! Aah!
Cantona' as a solo number without prompting. Anyway Sheena
gave up her chance of becoming famous when she met Steve at
a party – a young computer salesman who was going to do very
well for himself in the fullness of time. She started going out
with him. Tommy's gran had always thought they were an
ideal little family: 'Every night in my prayers I thanked God
for their luck, until this horrible thing had to happen.' The
double-spread was filled out with pictures of Granny Bellew
stirring a cup of tea and five-year-old Sheena stumbling across
the sands carrying a bigger beach-ball than she could cope
with. We also saw Sheena singing in a school production of
Jesus Christ Superstar, heavily jewelled and wearing an unexpected sari (no doubt to keep the school play ethnically neutral).
There was a picture of Stolen or Strayed – a quartet I wouldn't
care to have met on a dark night and whose music, I felt sure,
would have made an evening of Katerina Regen's trilling sound
like the song the sirens sang – and a photograph of the Constant
wedding.

Wednesday brought a hard-hitting article entitled NUT-
CUTLET LAYABOUTS: THE SOCIAL WORKERS WHO HAVE DONE
B–ALL TO HELP FIND SHEENA'S BABY. Thursday was devoted
to Steve's family, including his aunt Brenda Constant, who had
never married but was gifted with psychic powers, practised as
a clairvoyant, and had asked for help and guidance, in finding
young Tommy, from the spirit world.

On Black Friday a man from the *Daily Trumpet* had been
out with the police and the chilling pictures of frogmen and
tracker dogs duly appeared. Young Superintendent Greengross
gave a gloomy interview: 'We still hope for the best,' he said,
'and we are pursuing every possible line of inquiry to establish
that young Tommy is still alive. But it's no use hiding the fact
that, the more the days pass by, the more reason we have to
fear the worst.'

On Saturday Chambers was shut and Dot's *Trumpet* was not available. On my way to Safeway's with She Who Must Be Obeyed for shopping duty, I read the posters and crossed the road to buy the paper. I saw a young mother with her face lit up and an apparently unharmed child in her arms. I thought the huge headline surprisingly literary: LITTLE BOY FOUND, it said. I gave a great cry of joy.

'Rumpole!' the captain of my fate called briskly from the other side of the road. 'What on earth are you doing?'

'I am whooping,' I told her, 'whooping with delight. Tommy Constant has been found and all is more or less right with the world!'

I learnt how Tommy had been discovered by reading that day's *Daily Trumpet*, and the following Sunday's papers. Next week the story was retold, in considerable detail, in a long interview with Sheena, which took up more pages of Dot's favourite publication. Later, some time later, I was to learn even more about the great kidnapping case.

It was a hot night in late summer, near midnight apparently, when the Constants got the telephone call. It was too hot, Sheena said, and anyway they were too worried to sleep. When the phone rang, Steve looked at it, frozen, expecting the worst news. Sheena took a deep breath and grabbed it. She said she felt a moment of relief when she didn't hear the voice of Superintendent Greengross. What she heard was much fainter, a woman's voice, with an attempt at disguise, as though the caller were speaking through a handkerchief. 'Nineteen Swansdown Avenue,' was all it said. 'You'd better get there quick.' Later, the call was traced to a phone box at the end of nearby Swansdown Avenue. Later still, Sheena said that she thought she recognized the mystery voice.

The street used to be quiet and well kept, the home of middle managers and owners of small businesses who cleaned their cars on Sunday mornings and decked out their back gardens with oven-ready blooms from the local garden centre. Many of the middle managers had been made redundant and the small businesses gone broke. The houses had been repossessed by the banks and the For Sale notices had grown weather-stained as the houses decayed. At one end of the avenue, a speculator was building flats – otherwise the street's sleep was more or less undisturbed, except when there was an improvised rave-up in number 19, which had been broken into so many times that the bank, which had evicted the previous owners, now hardly bothered to change the locks or mend the windows.

The Constants drove at high speed to Swansdown Avenue, less than a mile from their house. They didn't dare to hope, but couldn't help but fear. The padlock on the front gate was broken, the back door swung on its hinges. The electricity had been cut off, but a street light enhanced the moonlight and left hard shadows in the corners of the rooms. 'The place was a tip,' Sheena said in her interview. 'There were piles of discarded clothes, stained mattresses with their innards protruding, piles of bottles, half-empty Coke cans all over the place and cardboard plates of half-eaten takeaways, and needles scattered everywhere.' The couple went from room to room, Sheena said, fearing what they might see in the shadows, and for a long while they avoided the garden, terrified of signs of recent digging.

And then, sickened by the lingering smell of unwashed bodies and rotting food, Sheena pushed open a bedroom window and found herself looking down into the rank garden. She saw more bottles and syringes glistening in the moonlight, and then she heard a child cry. She had heard it often in her imagination since Tommy vanished, but now she fancied it was real and she hoped she was not mistaken. It seemed that he had been playing quite happily in the dark garden until he stung his hand on a clump of nettles. He was wearing the same red anorak and blue jeans and red boots, together with the small *Star Trek* T-shirt, which Sheena had put on him to go to the hospital. In that filthy house he was clean, well-dressed and seemed in excellent health. He greeted his mother and father without visible surprise.

A week later Superintendent Greengross told the *Daily Trumpet* that Thelma Ropner of 17 Swansdown Avenue was helping him with his inquiries. We got little further information about her, except that she was twenty-six and had recently given birth to a baby son, who died four weeks later. Later still, she was charged and hurried into the local magistrates court with a blanket over her head. Her defence was reserved and, after a good deal of argument from Mr Bernard, her solicitor, she was granted bail.

'For this song, I am a young peasant girl going to the well in my village. My lover is a soldier who has deserted me and gone away to the wars. I sing, "Oh dear, I wish I could draw my lover back to me on a rope, as easily as I draw water from this well." "Der Brunnen" is the name of this beautiful song.'

There was a polite smattering of applause from the audience assembled in the Outer Temple Hall, among which Erskine-Brown's fevered clapping sounded like a volley of rifle-fire during a church service. The gratified *chanteuse* flashed a healthy set of white teeth in Claude's direction and then leaned for a reviving moment against the grand piano, her hand spread over her chest, her eyes closed, breathing in deeply. During the pause for rest and inspiration, her perky little accompanist suspended his fingers over the keys and sat with his eyes bright and his head on one side like a hen waiting for the egg to drop. Then Miss Regen fixed her smile and the first note rang out among the oak panelling and portraits of dead judges.

She was giving us the sad story once more, but this time with plenty of trills and repetitions, and in German. She was certainly not your standard fat opera singer, but rather beautiful with blonde hair, a suntan and clear blue eyes. Everything was, however, larger than life, not only her teeth but her hands, her eyes and her mouth. She was as tall as most of the men in the audience and, I thought, any lover who tried to escape from her and join the army would have been hauled in rapidly with a rope around his neck. And then, I have to say, my attention wandered.

> He kissed the child & by the hand led
> And to his mother brought,
> Who in sorrow pale, thro the lonely dale,
> Her little boy weeping sought.

I remembered the lines and the mysterious figure of a God dressed in white who returned the child in Blake's poem. I wondered who had made the telephone call to the Constants. Was it a friend, or a contrite enemy? Then I fell into a light doze.

I was woken by the final applause, sufficiently rested to join in the scrum for the champagne-style refreshments. The clapping was renewed when Miss Regen appeared, smiling with immeasurable courage, in spite of her exhaustion, and was immediately pounced on by Claude, who greeted her with such effusive praise that she might have sung her way through the role of Brünnhilde while winning the long-distance Olympic hurdles. Our sensitive Claude seemed to be quivering with excitement, and I thought she undoubtedly had a rope round his neck if ever she wanted to haul him in.

'All through that beautiful music, Rumpole' – Hilda was in a confessional mood – 'I couldn't help thinking of something else.'

'Couldn't you? I was pretty riveted by the girl at the well, as it so happens.'

'I couldn't help thinking of that poor woman who lost her baby.'

'She's got it back now, Hilda.'

'I know. But the person who did it, can you think of a worse crime?'

'Scarcely.'

'Even you couldn't defend a woman like that, could you, Rumpole?'

'Even I might find it difficult; but she hasn't been tried yet.'

'It doesn't matter. She's clearly guilty. It sticks out a mile. And please don't start a long speech about the burden of proof. You're so childish, sometimes, Rumpole. You imagine everyone in the world's as innocent as little Tommy Constant.'

Before I could refresh the memory of She Who Must on the presumption of innocence, our ears were shattered by a yell of, 'Thank you, Fräulein Regen, for bringing sunshine into this dusty old hall. I'm so glad I persuaded my fellow benchers to invite you.' It was Barrington McTear, Q.C. (known to me as Cut Above, because he regards himself as a very superior person), who had approached the diva and, in a gesture which I thought went out with old Scarlet Pimpernel films, kissed her hand. She glowed back at him and these two immense people seemed, for a moment, like the meeting of a male and female giant in some unreadable Nordic saga. Then Cut Above straightened up, patted the hand he had been kissing, and responded to a call of 'Barrington!' from a sharp-featured woman, no doubt his wife, who looked as though she found life with Cut Above no picnic. 'Coming, Leonora.' The ex-rugby football blue of a Q.C. turned reluctantly from the singing star and went bellowing off into the distance. Claude, who had looked somewhat miffed during this encounter, moved to fill the gap left by his fellow Q.C. and started to address the Fräulein in confidential tones. On our way out I heard him mention the fatal word lunch. Whenever Claude speaks of this meal to any female, the consequences are usually dire.

But I had more to worry about than Claude's tentative and no doubt embarrassing romances. That afternoon Bonny Bernard, my trusty instructing solicitor with a thriving practice in the Timson country south of Streatham, had booked a conference in *R. v. Thelma Ropner*. I was heavily pencilled in as Counsel for the Defence, and the faggots round the stake were no doubt ready for lighting.

'She's in your room, Mr Rumpole. And she's wearing the black mac.'

That morning Dot Clapton's Botticelli face was set in anger and contempt, a young angel determined to drive the sinners out of the Garden of Eden with a flaming sword.

'It is raining, Dot, as usual.'

'So does she have to wear the *same* mac? Some sort of nerve she must have, mustn't she? But I can't stay chatting, Mr Rumpole. Some of us has got work to do.' And Dot attacked her typewriter as though it were my client's throat.

Some of us did have work – hard, unpleasant work – and the prospect, at some time in the not-too-distant future, of being treated in Court as though we were personally responsible for pinching defenceless infants from hospitals. I pushed open the door of my room and it seemed, in some curious and quite evil way, to be dominated by Miss Thelma Ropner.

Thinking back, it seems absurd to have felt so instantly chilled. Thelma was almost a caricature from a movie and I might even, in other circumstances, have found her appearance comic. She was very pale, with rust-coloured, lank hair, and her features seemed curiously misplaced: her eyes too small, her nose slightly crooked and her mouth turned downwards. She looked both unpleasant and unhappy. And she wore, as Dot had said, with what was either bravado or sheer stupidity, the black beret set at what might have been intended as a cheeky angle, and the unmistakable shiny, crackly, black plastic mac which protected her like the armour of a crustacean. One thing was absolutely certain. She could never have got out of a hospital carrying a child unnoticed.

So vivid was the effect of Miss Ropner that the rest of my room seemed to sink into shadow. Somewhere, dear old Bernard was sorting through the file on his lap and chewing peppermints. Even I, taking my place on the swing chair, felt colourless – an Old Bailey hack quite outshone by the lurid vision of evil in front of him.

'It's all a complete waste of time, Mr Rumpole. I never ever took Sheena's child.' Thelma Ropner spoke in a curiously girlish, high-pitched little voice, as though the possible child-stealer were herself a child, and added, 'I wouldn't want to.'

'You call Mrs Constant Sheena, I couldn't help noticing. Do you know her?'

'Know her. Of course I know her. We were at Cripps together.'

'Cripps?'

'Cripping Comprehensive. I'm sure it was nothing like the academy for the sons of gentlemen you attended.'

'And probably a great deal more comfortable than my draughty boarding-school. Better lunches, too, I should imagine.' She didn't smile. I never saw her smile. What I got was a mood of petulance or a sarcastic sigh. I was in for a difficult trial with a difficult client and wondered if Hilda or Dot Clapton would ever forgive me if I won.

'You mean you were close friends?' Bernard sucked his

peppermint and looked in the statement he had taken for any reference to their friendship, and didn't find it.

'We got on all right. Sheena was quite good fun until she met Steve and lost her femininity.'

'I'm not entirely sure what you mean . . .' I have kept my patience under more trying circumstances. 'She got married and had a baby. Was *that* losing her femininity?'

'Of course it was.' Thelma sighed again at my question. 'She got the one kid and the boring young man in computers, the semi and the Daf – and she was well stuck in a male-dominated rut, wasn't she?'

'Do you think Sheena felt in a rut?' I wondered.

'Of course she did. She was awfully envious of Tina Santos when she got her name in all the papers for bonking some dreadful little government minister. Sheena always wanted to be famous like a telly star or something. Well, I suppose she is now, in a way. Famous.'

'Not in the way she'd like, I'm sure.'

'Probably not.' Miss Ropner turned away from me and looked out of the window, as though she had lost interest in me and Mr Bernard, and the tedious workings of the criminal law.

I renewed my attack, to gain at least a little of her attention. 'You think everyone who has a baby gets stuck in a male-dominated rut?'

She looked at me then and said, 'You mean I had one?'

'So you say in your statement.'

'And they're going to use it against me?'

'What do you mean?'

'They're going to use it against me that Damon died. They'll say it's because my little boy died that I wanted to steal Sheena's. That's what they're going to say, aren't they?'

'I suppose it might provide a motive.'

'Well, let me tell you, Mr Legal-Eagle, that if I'd wanted to nick a child I certainly wouldn't have chosen Sheena's. I'd've found one with a far more interesting father.'

It's not often that I am to be found sitting in a stunned silence, but this was such an occasion. Bernard was also immobile. He had his tube of peppermints open, but didn't lift one to his mouth.

Then I recovered sufficiently to tell the client, 'I have known witnesses sink themselves with one unwise answer, probably more times than you've had hot dinners. But if you say anything like that in Court we might as well plead guilty and start your sentence as soon as possible.'

'I'm so sorry, Mr Lawyer.' Thelma gave a bizarre impression of a little girl's pout. 'So sorry I can't give you all the answers you'd like.'

'Don't bother about what I'd like. It's the jury who've got to like you. And they're fairly ordinary men and women stuck in various kinds of a rut.'

'Well, I'm sorry for them, that's all I've got to say. Now, is there anything you want to ask me?'

'Just a few things. You live at seventeen Swansdown Avenue?'

'That's what it says there, doesn't it?'

'If the uneven numbers are all down one side of the street, nineteen is next door.'

'I can see it from my window.'

'On that moonlit night, did you see Tommy Constant down there among the nettles?'

'Hardly. On that moonlit night I was fast asleep. Or as fast as you can get in the Edmunds's house with Classic FM always on the go and that woman getting up at all hours to feed her unattractive baby on demand.'

'Brian Edmunds is your landlord? A professor?'

'Professor! He teaches Communication Studies at some rotten poly that now calls itself the University of South-West London.'

'The Edmundses.' I picked up another statement. 'Both say that they didn't see you in their house at all during the week Tommy Constant went missing.'

'I was there every night! I've got my own key, you know. I am a grown-up, free and independent spirit, Mr Rumpole. I don't have to report to Mr Brian Edmunds every time I go out or come back. As a matter of fact I avoid them both as much as possible. I don't particularly enjoy conversation with the brain dead.'

'They say they couldn't tell if you slept in your bed during that week.' I thought the Edmundses must be cursing the day they took in Thelma as a lodger. 'Because your bed is hardly ever made, anyway.'

'I've told them not to look into my room.' Thelma clearly felt that her civil rights had been outraged. 'In fact I've expressly forbidden it!'

'What were you doing during that week?'

'I *do* work, Mr Rumpole. I have to work to live. We can't all sit around in nice comfortable rooms in the Outer Temple waiting for someone to get into trouble.'

Thelma Ropner's resentment was like a high-pitched ringing, a perpetual noise in the ear like the disease of tinnitus. I ignored it with an effort. 'Where do you work, Miss Ropner?'

'Anywhere that's interesting, and worthwhile, and exciting. I help out a lot at groups.'

'Such as?'

'The Stick-Up Theatre Company. They're based in Croydon. Friends of the Earth. Animal Rights. Outings – that's an organization for gay and lesbian groups of retired people. I organize events for them. Some of us, Mr Lawyer, think that work should have a social context.'

'Mr Rumpole's work' – my defence came, unexpectedly, from Bonny Bernard, who had sat, up till then, quietly sucking peppermints – 'is done in the interests of justice. I'm sure you understand that, Miss Ropner.'

'It's also done in the interests of meeting this quarter's gas bill and financing Saturday's trip to Safeway's.' I hastened to reassure my client that my interest in her case was not based on any abstract conception. A too fervent attachment to the interests of justice, I began to suspect, might not help me to keep the disagreeable Thelma out of chokey.

'During each night that little Tommy was missing' – I wanted to get her story entirely clear – 'you tell me you were sleeping at the Edmunds's house?'

'Entirely alone, Mr Lawyer. Without even a three-year-old in bed with me.'

'Very well.' I shuffled through the bundle of statements again. 'On the night young Tommy was found in the garden of number nineteen, Mrs Edmunds says she was up with her baby . . .'

'Surprise, surprise.' Thelma Ropner gave a small, mirthless laugh.

'She was looking out of the first-floor bedroom window. "I saw someone under the street lamp in front of number nineteen," ' I read aloud. ' "It looked like a woman in a black plastic mac and a beret. I thought it was Thelma, but she was pushing something, a pram or a pushchair, I couldn't be sure. Then my baby started crying again, and when I looked back the woman had gone." '

'Why didn't she call the police? Everyone was on the lookout for someone in a mac like mine, who'd pinched Sheena's precious little Tommy. If Polly Edmunds thought she'd seen me, why didn't she rush down, or at least call the police?' To my surprise, my client now sounded quite calm and sensible.

'That's a very good point for cross-examination. Thank you.' I was polite enough to let her think I hadn't thought of it.

'That's all right. I'm sure you need a bit of help. Anyway, why didn't she knock on my door if she thought it was me? She'd've found me tucked up with myself, wouldn't she?'

I thought I knew the answer. With a lodger like Thelma Ropner, the Edmundses must have blessed the hours when she was either out or asleep. They wouldn't have gone looking for her. I sorted through a number of police officer's statements and found the description of number nineteen's unlovely garden patch: ' "The police found wheel-marks on the wet ground which might have been made by a pushchair. There were plenty of footprints . . ." '

'And body prints too.' Thelma's smile was so chilling that I thought, for a moment, she was talking about death and not the pleasures of sexual conquests in an urban tip. 'You know they came and took my shoes away? Haven't we got any civil rights left? Haven't we?'

'Only a few. And that's because I keep on shouting about them down the Old Bailey.' My strength to be polite to Thelma seemed likely to run out before her resentment. '. . . Prints that fitted a pair of your shoes were found in the garden of number nineteen.'

'Of course they were. I was there the night before. It was pretty muddy then.'

'You went into the garden?'

'Lots of people did.'

'Why?'

'Number nineteen's the only place you meet interesting people. It was the house for free spirits.'

So was that why the three-year-old little boy lost had been dumped there, I wondered. To meet interesting people?

After a session with Thelma Ropner, there was only one place to go and I stumbled towards it as a wounded, thirsty lion might crawl to the water-hole. The first two glasses of liquid hardly banished her chilly memory, but by the third I felt some inner warmth returning. Jack Pommeroy's new and untried barmaid, who seemed a nice girl, gave me a smile of apparently genuine concern and asked unnecessarily if I would care for another. And then a strange voice said, 'Got you, Mr Rumpole. Trapped you in your lair, sir.' At the same time a card was slapped on the bar in front of me bearing the legend: JONATHAN ARGENT, *Daily Trumpet*.

I looked up, expecting to be staring at the craggy features and moist eyes of a tabloid journalist marinated in whisky, a sweat-stained trilby and a dirty mac. I saw what seemed to be an impertinent sixth former who had just, more by luck than hard work, done rather well in his A-levels – the sort of youth who would be in constant minor trouble, but usually forgiven. He had a small, upturned nose, a bang of dark hair that strayed across his forehead, and lips that were fuller and redder than might have been expected. He wore a suit with a rather long jacket and a double-breasted waistcoat, and across a stomach which hardly deserved the name a gold watchchain dangled. Young Mr Argent seemed to see himself as an Edwardian dandy. 'So, this is Fleet Street.' He looked around at the assembled legal hacks, their solicitors, whom they were flirting with energetically, and their secretaries whom they probably intended to flirt with later. 'I wasn't quite sure I'd be able to find it.'

'There was a time,' I told him, 'when your newspaper and

practically every other rag was in this street. That was before you all pushed off to some nightmare electronic city on the Isle of Dogs where you could stay safely away from the news.'

'I thought you'd talk like that,' the infant Argent said.

'Like what, exactly?'

'Like starting every sentence "There was a time".'

'Time was,' I said, rather grandly, I thought – the Château Fleet Street was loosening the throat and somewhat inflating the prose – 'is by now far the longest and most important part of my life.'

'There's an old chap at the *Trumpet* who remembers when it was in Fleet Street. They put him on to the Saturday para Down the Garden Path, but now he's been made redundant.'

Time to come, I thought, is not something I wish to sit here thinking about, taking a quick glance towards the end. Then Argent said, 'Why not ditch that ghastly-looking cough mixture and join me in a bottle of the Dom?'

'Of the what?'

'Dom Perignon? He was an old monk who had a cunning sort of a way with champagne. I don't know if you ever met him round Fleet Street?'

'Why on earth' – I was puzzled by this curious encounter – 'should you want to buy me expensive champagne?'

'Oh, it's not me, sir.' He used the word sir as though he was speaking to a schoolmaster for whom he'd long lost respect. 'The *Trumpet* wants to stand us both a drink. After that peculiar plonk you might be in the mood for a bit of blotting paper, so I'm sure the scandal sheet would run to a couple of cheese sandwiches to go with the bubbles.'

I am, I hope, a fair-minded man and I thought I should consider his offer without prejudice, and come to a fair conclusion. 'I must admit that your paper gave the Tommy Constant case very thorough coverage,' I told him.

'Oh, we want it to be much more serious than that, sir. I think there's an empty table in the corner. Shall I take your arm to steady you?'

'Certainly not' – I was quite brusque with the lad – 'I am perfectly steady, thank you very much indeed.'

Young Argent said when we landed safely at the table, 'I'm

glad you thought we told Sheena's story well, sir. Now we want to do the same for Thelma.'

'Do what?'

'Tell her story.'

'It'll be told in Court.'

'We'd like the *Trumpet* to be on the inside track with Thelma. You've got to admit she's got an even bigger circulation potential than Sheena. Thelma's story has got an added dimension.'

'Oh? What dimension's that?'

'Well, quite honestly, sir, her baby died.' He gave me his candid, boyish look, half amused, as though he had to confess that he planned to raid the tuck shop.

I did my best to suppress rage. 'Do you call that a plus? There should have been a *Daily Trumpet* around in the days of Herod the King. You might have broken all circulation records.'

'We want to do Thelma's story' – Jonathan Argent looked very serious and sincere, his eyes wide and his voice particularly quiet – 'in a way which will be a hundred per cent fair and sympathetic. We all know how women get after childbirth. We've got stuff from a psychiatrist. It's jolly understandable, really.'

Thirty-five years after childbirth, I thought, She Who Must Be Obeyed could still spring some surprises; but I didn't encourage the upper-crust young Jonno by telling him that. 'If Miss Ropner wants to tell you her story when the trial's over, that's entirely up to her.'

'I don't think Miss Ropner's going to be in much of a position to speak to anyone when the trial is over.' Jonathan Argent was smiling.

'Why? Do you assume she's going to be convicted?'

'Surprise me, then. You've got some brilliant defence tucked away under that old hat of yours? Have you, quite honestly, sir?'

How many more people would have to remind me of the burden of proof? I took a generous gulp of the old monk's recipe and said, 'Thelma Ropner is innocent and will be until the Jury down the Bailey comes back with a verdict.'

'You're expecting the thumbs up?'

'We shall see,' I said – champagne after plonk is no recipe for epigrams – 'what we shall see.'

'Quite honestly, Mr Rumpole, it's not so much Thelma we're after.'

'Who are you after, then? You seemed to have squeezed the best out of the Constant family.'

'We're after you.'

He was very young, probably quite silly and looked harmless enough. I don't know why but when he said this I felt, in some curious way, trapped; he spoke modestly, but as though he had an immense power behind him.

'I'm an old taxi' – I embarked on the much-loved speech – 'plying for hire. If the *Trumpet* wants to brief me in some lucrative action, provided it doesn't conflict with the interests of my client, well and good. I make it a rule to represent all riff-raff, underdogs and social outcasts.'

'We don't want to employ you, sir. We want to tell your story.'

'You mean the "Have you anything to say why sentence of death should not be passed against you?" And the chap in the dock says, "Bugger all, my Lord." And the Judge says to his counsel, "What did your client say, Mr Smith?"' My stories, by now, have achieved a pretty wide circulation.

'Not exactly that, sir.' Argent shook his wise young head sadly, unable to understand the wilful old. 'Your story in Tom's case: WHY I'M DEFENDING THELMA ROPNER, THE MOST HATED WOMAN IN ENGLAND. Your taxi bit can come in there: I PUT MY TALENT AT THE DISPOSAL OF THE RIFF-RAFF AND THE UNDERDOG. And then: THE LIGHT AT THE END OF THE TUNNEL. HOW I FOUND A DEFENCE IN A HOPELESS CASE.'

'What are you suggesting I do? Spill all the beans? I can't do it.'

'Whyever not? I'd write it for you.'

'It would be against all the best traditions of the Bar.'

'You might find it extremely profitable.'

'How profitable? I only ask out of idle curiosity.'

The young hack looked around conspiratorially, made sure

no one was listening and then offered me a sum of money, expressed in Ks, which I took to be thousands. I saw myself retiring, moving from icy Froxbury Mansions to a place with a small pool and a microwave on the Malaga coast, sitting in the bar with a group of accountants who had taken voluntary redundancy, drinking sangria. I stifled a huge yawn.

'No thanks,' I told him politely, 'it's too late for all that sort of thing.'

'That isn't the end of the story, sir. With syndication it might be much more.'

I drained my glass. 'In the circumstances I think it best if I pay for the Dom Perignon.'

'There's absolutely no need, sir, for that sort of gesture. It's been a pleasure and a privilege to talk to you.'

I saw the man's point. 'Then I'll be getting back to work.' I rose from the table. He smiled at me as though I had agreed to all his ridiculous propositions. As I was walking towards the door I heard him call after me, 'And we'll keep in very close touch indeed.'

I discovered later, a good deal later, that when I was being given the expensive sauce, and offered all the kingdoms of Southern Spain, by the schoolboy journalist, my learned but incautious friend Claude Erskine-Brown, Q.C., was engaged in his first romantic encounter with the statuesque Regen. The place chosen for this tryst was hardly discreet, no small spaghetti house in the purlieus of Victoria station but the glittering glass and brass 1930s Galaxy Hotel in the middle of Mayfair, where the nomadic diva was pigging it during her Covent Garden visit. By a chance which turned out to be less than happy, she arrived back from shopping just as Claude's taxi drew up and then enjoyed a notable encounter on the marble steps in front of the Galaxy's top-hatted commissionaire and revolving door.

Of course, I wasn't a spectator at this event which assumed an importance rather like Solomon's greeting to the Queen of Sheba, or King David's 'Hallo, there' to Bathsheba. I imagine that Claude was effusive and pathetically grateful that his suggestion of lunch, made at the Outer Temple concert, had been accepted and that the singing star was a little confused and perhaps unable to remember who her visitor was. Claude, however, announced himself in clear and ringing tones and swooped at her with two kisses on both cheeks, which, he imagined, would be acceptable to a jet-setting soprano. I believe Katerina Regen made a brisk movement, whether of greeting or avoidance I'm not altogether sure, and Claude stumbled on a shallow, marble step, with the result that their mouths collided in a manner which looked a great deal friendlier than it was. This mischance didn't embarrass the singer, who didn't embarrass easily. She gave a resonant laugh down the scale of C, put her arm in Claude's and dragged him in through the revolving door as though she was hauling him up from a well. And there, for a moment, and for the purpose of this narrative, we must leave the happy couple.

I decided to visit the scene, or rather the scenes, of the crime – a stretch of South London which took the place of the lonely fen in which the little boy was lost in William Blake's strange poem. We went in Bonny Bernard's unwashed Fiesta which seems to contain, in a state of unexpected chaos, all the elements of his life. Files, bulging envelopes, cardboard boxes, were piled on the back seat, together with a squash racket and a zipped-up bag of some sort of sportswear which I had never seen moved.

Our first call was the Springtide General Hospital. At my direction Bernard parked his motor in a space clearly marked RESERVED FOR HOSPITAL HEAD OF HUMAN RESOURCES and joined the throng pouring in at the main entrance, a huge space which resembled a town centre during late-night shopping when all the traffic lights are out of order and the local constabulary have gone on holiday.

Visitors sat on benches eating takeaway meals, and patients, long ago forgotten, were slumped in wheelchairs. Hospital trolleys rattled past, some heavy with sheeted figures. Other trolleys stood parked with old persons, belly upwards, staring hopelessly at the ceiling. A doctor or two, a little posse of clattering nurses, hugging their cardigans about them, were somewhere glimpsed. Otherwise, the crowd was notably civilian. The predominant smell was of rubber, disinfectant and popcorn.

We passed a row of shops selling plastic toys, girlie magazines and best-selling paperbacks. In the concourse in front of the out-patients, there was a children's corner: a broken playpen, a huge pink teddy bear and the mechanical donkey on which a small child might enjoy a stationary trip for fifty pence. At that moment, a shaven-headed, earringed nineteen-year-old was sitting astride it, swigging mineral water from a kingsize bottle. As I took in the *locus in quo*, the wonder was not how a child could be stolen there but how a small and adventurous boy could ever be kept safe.

'God protect me' – I shared my prayers with my instructing solicitor – 'from having to die in a place like this.'

'Is there anything you want me to do here?' Bernard was as anxious as I was to get out of this house of healing.

'Find out what was wrong with little Tommy. I mean, why did they take him to the out-patients that morning?' I looked towards the newspaper and tobacconist shop where Steve had turned his back on his son to buy fags, and where great piles of the *Daily Trumpet* were on sale. 'It wasn't an accident. We knew that. Sudden sickness. Sheena says that in her statement. What sort of sickness exactly? Find that out, Bonny Bernard, in the fullness of time.'

'Where to next, Mr Rumpole?'

'Up to Redwood Road, I think. Just for a glance at the matrimonial home.'

In the car park the Head of Human Resources was standing beside his unparked B.M.W. and swearing at us. I smiled sweetly and told him that we were official inspectors sent by Mrs Lavinia Lyndon, the glamorous and lethal Minister of Health, to report on his hospital's efficiency, and that shut him up effectively.

I had seen the semi-detached in Redwood Road before, faintly in that first picture in the *Trumpet*. Now it seemed bigger and brighter than I had expected. The front garden looked as though it had been recently trimmed and rhododen-drons and bright azaleas, already in flower, had been brought in from a garden centre. Parked in front of the garage was a low-lined, bright-red and sporty model with a number Mr Bernard knew to be recent. If the Constants had come into a bit of money, I saw no reason, after their week of misery, why they shouldn't enjoy it. We didn't see little Tommy, or either of his parents, although we waited for about ten minutes on the other side of the road. Then a middle-aged women in a bright yellow dress came out of the house and started to snip a bunch of early, straight-stalked and military tulips in the front garden. She had reddish hair, a pale face and a sharp nose. I thought she condemned the flowers to death in the house without mercy or regret.

On the way to Swansdown Avenue, threading our way along streets of identical pink-and-white houses (they looked, I thought, like carefully packed and identical packets of streaky bacon), round crescents and across wider roads, we stopped at traffic lights beside a row of small shops that no doubt were struggling for existence against the mass attack of the super-markets and the shopping malls. As I looked idly out of the window, I saw a shoe mender's, a dry cleaner's with a window display of wire coathangers and paper flowers, and a shop called Snappy Print: COPIES MADE AND FAXES SENT. In the window I saw a poster offering a course in computer and business studies: ONE WEEK IN A COUNTRY HOUSE NEAR TUNBRIDGE WELLS CAN PUT YOU ON THE TOP EXECUTIVE LADDER OF SUCCESS. SALESMANSHIP AND COMPETITIVE MAR-KETING THOROUGHLY TAUGHT. After the printer's came a peeling hut with blackened windows and a sign advertising THERAPEUTIC MASSAGE AND SAUNA. The door was padlocked. The next shop, so narrow it seemed to have been squashed in after the rest of the row was finished, had a surprising and half-broken neon sign. PSYCHIC it must have once said when all the letters were fully operational. ASTROLOGICAL SIGNS CHARTED AND CONSIDERED. CLAIRVOYANT ADVICE GIVEN. The shop window was empty except for a white vase which contained three wilting tulips and a photograph. It was a glimpse of that photograph that made me ask Bernard to park, and I got out and stood examining it and the window display. In the shadows of the small room behind it I was sure I saw something of importance to our case. I tried the door but it was locked and, when I got back to the car, Bernard said, 'What did you want, Mr Rumpole? To know our future in *R*. v. *Thelma Ropner?*'

'I'm afraid,' I told him, 'that we don't need a chart to tell us that the omens are against us. The star sign of the Constants, however, is definitely in the ascendant.' As we drove off towards Thelma's pad, another sporty car turned from under a sparse clump of trees. The driver seemed a very young man and I made sure he was following us.

Swansdown Avenue produced no surprises. The tip in which young Tommy had been discovered lived up to its sordid reputation, and the front garden of number seventeen next door was not much tidier. The grass was uncut, the paths weedy, and there was a pram blocking the front door. The garage doors were open and I imagined that the head of communication studies had taken the car off to the University of South-West London. There was the thin, insistent cry of a baby and I saw an upstairs window from which Mrs Edmunds would have had a clear view of the front gate of number nineteen, which was opposite a street lamp. I imagined the academic's house, and the perpetual smell of milk, vegetable soup and soaking nappies. I decided that my legal team and I couldn't go on much longer without a drink.

We found the Old Pickwick at a crossroads about half a mile from Swansdown Avenue and Dickens's fat hero would have thought it considerably less warm and welcoming than the Fleet Prison. Bernard and I sat in a cavernous bar where banks of electronic games squeaked and flashed and muttered angrily around us. The barmaid, a ferocious girl with a spiky hairdo, was heavily engaged on the telephone and avoided a glance in our direction. At long last she finished her call, switched on her favourite tape, and allowed me to yell a request for two pints of Guinness to a musical accompaniment which sounded like the outbreak of World War III. I had barely put my lips to the froth when I heard a penetrating word in my ear.

'Sherlock Rumpole? Have you brought the magnifying glass and the deerstalker?'

I turned to find young Argent of the *Trumpet* breathing

down my neck. 'I'm here,' I told him rather grandly, 'to consult with my instructing solicitor. Our conversation is, as I'm sure you'll understand, entirely privileged.'

'Kill the karaoke, sweetheart.' The reporter's voice rose high above the music, and to my amazement Miss Spiky smiled sweetly at him and plunged us into silence. 'A word in your ear if I might, a very private word.' Argent ignored Bernard and ordered himself a brandy and soda.

'I have no secrets from my instructing solicitor.'

'Oh, but the lawyer we're going to talk about probably has. And this hasn't got anything to do with little Tommy Constant. Not for the moment, anyway.' Bernard, who could take a hint almost before it was dropped, filtered off to telephone his office and the man from the *Trumpet* opened a slim leather briefcase and laid a glossy photograph on the bar. I didn't look at it.

'Are you offering me money?' I asked him.

'I've already done that. We'd pay you awfully well for the How I'm Defending Baby-snatcher story. Might even run to a new hat, Mr Rumpole. No, what we're offering now is for information.'

'What information?'

'Take a look.'

I glanced down. What I saw was the prize idiot and Queen's Counsel, Claude Erskine-Brown, locked in the sturdy embrace of Ms Katerina Regen, and apparently administering mouth-to-mouth resuscitation to her on the front step of the Galaxy Hotel.

'Top lawyer and judge's husband in afternoon bonk with German nightingale. Not a bad little story for us.'

'They are simply friends,' I hastened to assure him. 'I know he admires her voice.'

'Admires her silver tongue so much that they went up to Room 307 together and didn't emerge from the Galaxy until five-thirty in the afternoon.'

'He probably had nothing on in Court. It often happens.'

'He might try to have something on in Court if we tell him we're publishing this. You wouldn't want us to do that, would you?'

I couldn't believe that after so many disastrously fumbled and frustrated attempts, Claude had actually succeeded in consummating an extramarital romance. 'I don't see why I should care,' I told Argent. 'You're not suggesting I was bonking anyone, I sincerely hope?'

'The honour of your Chambers is at stake, sir. Its reputation for high morals and respectability. And think of the effect on her Ladyship, the learned Judge. Just about blow her wig off, wouldn't you say?'

He was right, of course. Phillida Erskine-Brown would be deeply distressed at seeing her husband splashed across the *Trumpet* as a post-prandial bonker. I will never lose a long and lingering affection for the Portia of our Chambers, now a High Court Judge, and I wanted to spare her pain.

'I can't see that this' – I pushed the photograph back towards Argent – 'is of the slightest interest to your readers.'

'You don't know our readers, sir. They love reading about the great and good bonking. Saves them all the trouble of doing it for themselves.'

'But you won't publish it?'

'That depends.'

'Depends on what?'

'On whether you're going to give us another story: How I Defended Thelma.'

There was a long silence. Miss Spiky was baring her lips to a mirror, seriously examining her teeth. I said, 'When would you want it?'

'Run the first instalment the day before the trial. No desperate hurry.'

'Can I have that picture?' I asked him. 'Of course, you've got the negative.'

'Of course.' He pushed Claude and the diva towards me. I stored them away in an inside pocket before Bernard came back.

'One thing you might do for us,' Argent said, 'if we keep your learned friend off the front page . . .'

'What's that?'

'Couldn't you just give me a little taster? Just a hint, you understand, of your approach to the defence of the wicked witch?'

'Perhaps I'd say that if I were a wicked witch I think I'd be careful not to dress as one. But you can't print that yet.'

'Understood! We'll save it for your first instalment. Anything else?'

'Just that I wonder where Thelma Ropner is meant to have kept Tommy locked up, fed, cleaned and watered for a week.'

'Have you any ideas?'

'Not yet,' I said.

'Let me know when you have. We'll be in constant touch.' Argent drained his brandy and left, leaving me, in spite of all the *Trumpet*'s promises to make my fortune, to pay for it.

'My name coupled with that of Katerina Regen?' Claude Erskine-Brown said, and I detected an unmistakable note of pride in his voice.

'Not only are your names coupled,' I assured him, 'everything about you is said to have been coupled also.'

The chump picked up the photograph and examined it closely. 'Doesn't she look beautiful?' he purred at it. 'And don't you think I'm looking rather young?'

'Positively childlike,' I told him. 'I'm sure Phillida will tell you what a spring chicken you look when she sees the front page of the *Trumpet*.'

'That would not be a good thing.' Claude put the photograph back on my desk and I saw that his hand was now trembling. 'Please put it away, Rumpole. In a sealed envelope, in case the clerk sees it. They won't really publish it, will they? Not in a *tabloid*?'

'If I let them.'

'You have some influence over the *Trumpet*, Rumpole?' Claude's voice was full of hope.

'Perhaps a little.'

'You would act for me in this matter?'

'You obviously need help.'

'On the whole,' he said, after having given the matter deep thought, 'I think it's better that the very beautiful thing Katerina and I have for each other should remain a secret. It would be better for Chambers.'

'And considerably better for you.'

'I'm not in the least ashamed of loving Katerina.'

'But Mrs Justice Phillida Erskine-Brown would condemn you to a long stretch of withering contempt if she got to hear about it.'

'I suppose you're right. Perhaps you'll let me look at this from time to time, though? Just to remember.'

'To remember what?'

'The day I had lunch with Katerina.'

'At the *Trumpet* they don't think that's all that you had.'

'Don't they?' Claude was smiling complacently. He seemed, poor chump, to be deeply flattered. 'It was a wonderful experience.'

'How wonderful exactly?'

'Well, we went into the restaurant.'

'You would do if you were having lunch.'

'And sat down.'

'You amaze me.'

'And talked about Schubert.'

'Please, Erskine-Brown, spare me the embarrassing details.'

'And then . . . Well, I touched her hand and I was about to tell her how much I really fancied her and I hadn't felt so, well, uplifted by any other woman. And then we were interrupted, rather rudely I thought.'

'By her husband?'

'Of course not. She hasn't got one. No. By the waiter who told us about that day's specials.'

'Talkative bloke, was he?'

'Honestly, Rumpole, he went on for what seemed like hours, all about sea bass grilled with aubergines and served with a light pesto and tomato coulis – and that sort of thing.'

'He broke the spell?'

'Exactly. And when I got back in my stride and said I felt my whole life in love and music was simply a prelude to that golden moment, that bloody waiter came back.'

'And interrupted?'

'He said, "Who's having the fish?"'

'Put you off your stroke again.'

'I'm afraid so. But we got very close after that. She asked me up to her room.'

'So you did . . .'

'Well, not exactly. I mean, she asked me up to give me her new CD. Strauss's last songs.' There was a lengthy pause.

'Is that the end of the story?'

'Until the next time.'

'Next time?'

'She said we must have lunch again. I knew exactly what she meant. She said, "I'll have longer for you next time." I think she had another appointment that particular afternoon.'

'The *Trumpet* thinks you strayed till five-thirty when you came out again and kissed.'

'Does it think that?' Erskine-Brown gave me another chance to study his self-satisfied smirk. 'Then it understands exactly how close we are to each other.' He made for the door and, on the way out, had another attack of anxiety. 'I say, Rumpole. About that lovely photograph . . . Of course, it would be a great deal better if Philly didn't see it in the paper.'

'I'm bound to agree with you.'

'So will you act for me in this rather delicate matter, Rumpole?'

'I suppose I'd better. I must say you seem quite incapable of acting for yourself. What time did you leave the Galaxy Hotel?'

'About two-thirty, I think. I went out of the back entrance.'

As soon as the door had closed on him, I forgot Claude and his troubles. I had other things to think of. I thought of them for a long time and then I rang Bonny Bernard and asked him to send round copies of every piece the *Trumpet* had published about Sheena Constant and the Little Boy Lost. There was something in one of them, I felt sure, which was of great importance for me to remember. And then, to complete the story, I told him to get all they had written about Tina Santos.

'Now, when I think about it again, I am sure that the voice I heard on the telephone the night we found Tommy, the voice that told us to go to nineteen Swansdown Avenue, was Thelma Ropner's. I was at school for many years with Thelma and we used to be close friends. I am prepared to give this evidence on oath in Court.' The Prosecution had served Sheena's additional statement on us and, with considerable reluctance, I had told Bernard to get Thelma in for another conference.

'Is that what Sheena says?' Miss Ropner laughed, an eerie and not very comfortable sound. 'Then Sheena is lying.'

'Why would she lie?'

'Because she doesn't like me. She's never liked me since I told her what a boring little company creep her precious Steve was.'

Another of Miss Ropner's insults had come home to roost, but there was no point in going on about it. Instead I said, 'I just hope *you've* told me the truth. If you haven't, it's going to make life very difficult for me.'

'Poor old you!' She was still laughing. 'Can't you cope with difficult cases? Anyway, it's true. I didn't take Tommy.'

'Did you tell us the truth about what you were doing during the week he went missing?'

'I told you I was sleeping at the Edmundses and working during the day.'

'Working at what exactly? Will you give Mr Bernard a list, with dates?'

'Oh, you can't expect me to remember dates.'

'I think you'd better try. And I don't suppose you'll have any difficulty in telling us where you're working now.'

'Now?' The question seemed to shock her.

'Yes. Where?' I lifted a pencil.

'I told you!' She was making an exaggerated effort to control her irritation. 'The Stick-Up Theatre Company. We've got a tour of Welsh community centres at the planning stage.'

'What do you do with a client who won't stop lying to you?' I asked Bonny Bernard when Miss Ropner had gone off with no goodbye, only a look of undying resentment. Bernard smiled sadly, as though the truth was rare and unhoped-for among his clientele. Then I told him to engage the services of a seasoned, not to say elderly, private eye to discover exactly what Thelma had been up to during the week of Tommy's captivity. Ferdinand Isaac Gerald Newton (known to his many grateful customers as Fig Newton) was well known and respected by Bernard, who doubted if the legal aid authorities would pay him and dared we ask Thelma to dig into her handbag because we seriously doubted her word? 'Try my friends on the *Trumpet*,' I told him. 'If they can afford Dom Perignon, they can afford Fig. I think it's the least they can do for us.'

'I sent for you, Rumpole, as a senior member of Chambers, because I have had some most unhappy news.'

'Then I'll be going. I've got quite enough worries at the moment.'

'Claude Erskine-Brown,' Soapy Sam Ballard rabbited on, 'has dishonoured his silk! He is likely to bring Equity Court into scandal and disrespect.' Pacing the room in a disturbed fashion, he had now blocked my passage to the door.

'He's never pinched the nailbrush from the downstairs loo?'

'These are serious matters, Rumpole. He has broken the Seventh Commandment. He has committed adultery – in the afternoon.'

'Is that so much worse than adultery in the morning?'

'He has been flagrantly unfaithful – to a High Court Judge.'

'That's not his fault.'

'Of course it's his fault.'

'Not his fault that his wife's a High Court Judge.'

'I suppose you'll say it's not his fault he's committed adultery! I suppose you'll put forward some ridiculous defence.'

'Claude's no more capable of adultery than he is of winning a difficult case. His extramarital coitus is perpetually and incurably interruptus. I ask for – no, I demand – a verdict of not guilty.'

'Rumpole! I have it from his own mouth.'

'Then he's an unreliable witness.'

'He has told me that this scandalous liaison is about to be exposed in the national press.'

'In the *Trumpet*?'

'I think that's what he said.'

'Why do you suppose he told you that?'

'I imagine because he sincerely regretted his sin and wanted to throw himself on my mercy.'

'Nonsense! He was boasting.'

'Boasting?' Soapy Sam looked entirely confused.

'Showing off. Bragging, wanting us all to think that he's a

gay young dog, when in truth he's an entirely domesticated animal that's almost never off the lead.'

'Are you saying that people would boast of breaking the Seventh Commandment?'

'They do it on practically every page of the *Trumpet*.'

Ballard sat down then, as though his legs had become weak with amazement. He gasped for breath. 'I have told Erskine-Brown that if this scandal becomes public knowledge, there will be no room for him in Chambers.'

'I thought he'd thrown himself on your mercy.'

'He did.'

'And your mercy wasn't there?'

'God may forgive Erskine-Brown. After repentance.'

'But you won't.'

'I have Chambers to consider.'

'I suggest you leave Chambers alone and get on with your practice, what there is of it.' I rose and made for the door whilst the path to it was unimpeded. 'Oh, and don't worry your pretty little head, Sam. There isn't going to be a scandal.'

'How can you be sure of that?'

'Because if Claude's Don Giovanni, I'm Tarzan of the Apes. No need for you to envy the poor blighter, Bollard. He didn't get around to bonking anybody.'

And I left before he could argue.

The Psychic Shop was open at three the next afternoon when I pushed open the door. What on earth did I think I was doing? When young Argent called me Sherlock Rumpole, had the title completely unhinged me? Was I trying to outdo the incomparable Fig Newton, or was this a mission of such delicacy that I didn't feel I could leave it to him? I had nothing in Court and for the day I was no longer a barrister; in fact I had put on the old tweed jacket, grey flannel bags and comforting Hush Puppies to prove it. I was an anonymous old man after information. If I was rumbled, I had my cover-story pat. I had just dropped in for a clairvoyant reading because I was seriously interested in the future.

A bell pinged faintly as I opened the door, but the shop was empty. I stood for a moment breathing in a smell which seemed to be a mixture of incense, Dettol and drains. There were some printed astrological charts pinned on the walls, otherwise the shop was dim and sparsely furnished. There was no sign of what I had noticed on the day when I had asked Bernard to park his car and stood looking in at the window. There was a bead curtain at the back of the shop. It rattled and a woman entered like a burst of sunlight. She had reddish hair, a bright yellow dress and the fixed, somewhat desperate smile of someone who is constantly in touch with those who have passed over and who has learnt to make the best of it. She was the woman I had seen in the Constants' front garden, snipping tulips, the woman whose photograph was in the window of the Psychic Shop. She was Steve's Aunt Brenda, who'd been in touch with the spirit world for news of the Little Boy Lost.

'Welcome, stranger,' she said. 'Have you come for a reading?'

'If you have time.'

'Perhaps you have an anxiety about your future.'

'Always. An extreme anxiety.'

'And you want your birth chart analysed?'

'That would be extremely helpful.'

'You have an interest in clairvoyancy?'

'A lifetime's interest.'

'Then, if you'll follow me, I'll see if I can fit you in.'

She led me into a sudden blaze of colour. The inner room had huge vivid green leaves on its wallpaper, and bright red, blue and yellow astrological charts. The table was covered with pink formica on which a glass ball on a bright blue stand presumably provided an entrance to a Technicolor spirit world for those with sufficient imagination to switch on to its channel. Death, I thought, in this small and lurid world was an endless soap opera in primary colours. I said, 'You are Miss Brenda Constant, aren't you?'

She was not at all surprised. 'I suppose I've got to get used to the fact that I've become famous.' She was middle-aged, but she giggled like a young girl. 'I can't complain. It's brought me a lot of customers.'

'Because of little Tommy?'

'Because the spirit people were able to tell us who'd got the baby.'

'And who had?'

'Thelma Ropner, of course. She was always jealous of Sheena. Now then, do please sit down and tell me *your* name.'

'Samuel Ballard.' I couldn't help it. It just occurred to me as I sat on a hard and shiny plastic chair and rested my elbows on the pink formica.

'Samuel. That's a very *nice* name.' She unrolled some sort of chart of the heavens and sat opposite me, ready to voyage into the unknown. 'There are plenty of Samuels in the spirit world.'

I told her that didn't surprise me in the least. I was looking past her at a narrow window which seemed to overlook a small, paved strip and a high wooden fence.

'Birth sign?' She was about to fill in a form.

'Cancer, the crab.' I thought that might be appropriate for Bollard.

'Birthdate?'

'The twenty-ninth of June 1940. It was a stormy night and there was a partial eclipse of the moon. Apparently a dead owl fell out of the sky and into my parents' garden in Waltham Cross.' From then on I was inventing and Auntie Brenda was taking copious notes. I didn't have to go on too long before the shop door pinged again. She put down her scarlet Biro, sighed heavily and said, 'Everyone wants a reading since the story came out in the *Trumpet*,' and exited through the bead curtain. I got up and crossed to the window. It was then I saw, on the strip of crazy paving, what I thought I had once seen in the shop, a child's pushchair with something on the seat which, I was sure, could be described as a yellow flop-eared rabbit, much clutched and frequently caressed.

I could hear Auntie Brenda's grand and busy greeting to a prospective customer in the shop. There was a long cupboard built against one wall of the astrological consulting room. I slid back the door as quietly as possible and was surprised, as I often am, by the casual way in which many people preserve evidence. Hanging uncertainly on a wire coat-hanger, I saw a shiny, black plastic mackintosh and, on the shelf above it, a dark beret.

I got the door shut as Auntie Brenda came back to peer into Samuel Ballard's future.

'One last question, Mrs Sheena Constant. Looking back on that telephone call in which you were told to go and look in nineteen Swansdown Avenue, can you now say who you think called you?'

'Don't let's have what she thought, my Lord.' I was up on my hind legs in no time. 'Don't let's have pure speculation.'

'The witness is fully entitled to say who she thinks telephoned her, Mr Rumpole. There is no need to delay this trial with unnecessary objections.' His Honour Judge Pick bore, in my opinion, a singular resemblance to a parakeet. He had a high colour, a small and beaky nose, a bright and malignant eye, and his usual reaction to my contributions to the proceedings was a flurried and resentful squawk.

'I'm quite sure who it was now.' Sheena smiled from the witness-box. 'It was someone I'd known from school.'

'What was her name?'

'Thelma Ropner.'

'The defendant Ropner whom we now see in the dock?' The bird on the Bench rubbed it in quite unnecessarily. My learned friend, Leonard Fanner (known to us down the Bailey as Lenny the Lion because of his extreme nervousness in Court and general lack of roaring power), appearing for the Prosecution, said, 'Thank you very much, Mrs Constant,' and sat down gratefully.

I rose to cross-examine Mrs Constant. 'You say you were at school with my client, Thelma Ropner?'

'Yes.'

'And were you also at school with a girl called Tina Santos?'

'Tina? Yes, I knew her.'

'And did she become the secretary of a local MP called David Bangor, Parliamentary Secretary to the Minister for Enterprise?'

'She worked for a politician. I think that's what Tina did.'

'You know what Tina did, don't you? She had a well-publicized love affair with the Honourable Member.'

'Mr Rumpole!'

I ignored the squawk from the Bench and continued, 'And then told the whole story to the *Trumpet* because he wouldn't leave his wife and marry her.'

Sheena frowned a little and said, 'I think I did read something about it, yes.'

'The whole nation read something about it.' I picked up a cutting: '"I shared a shower with Minister in Commons' bathroom. Skinny-dipping during the debate on Post Office privatization."'

'Mr Fanner, are you not objecting to this cross-examination?' The Judge turned to my learned friend for help.

'I'm not entirely sure where it's leading, my Lord.' Lenny the Lion stood up, magnificent in his indecision.

'Exactly where is it leading, Mr Rumpole? Perhaps you'd be good enough to explain.' The Judge was pecking away at me, but I rose above it.

'It's leading, my Lord, to a vital issue in this case.' I turned to give my full attention to the mother for whom I had felt such sympathy. 'Do you know how much Tina Santos got paid for that story?'

'Mr Rumpole!'

'I think it was quite a lot. A ridiculous lot of money, it was.'

'Exactly. For that parliamentary shower bath, Tina Santos earned thousands of pounds. Wasn't that common knowledge among the old girls of Cripping Comprehensive?'

'She told us she got a lot of money, yes.'

'Easy money, wasn't it?'

'Much too easy, I'd say, for Tina.'

'Mrs Constant, how much did the *Trumpet* pay you for the exclusive rights to the story of your Little Boy Lost?'

Up to then the witness had been quiet, composed, a young woman reliving a painful event with commendable courage. For a moment, I saw another Sheena, hard and angry. 'That's no business of yours, that isn't! I don't have to tell him that, do I?' She turned, for escape, to the Judge, who offered it to her eagerly.

'Certainly not. The question was entirely irrelevant. Members of the Jury, you will ignore Mr Rumpole's last question. I'm looking at the clock, Mr Fanner.'

'Yes, my Lord.' Lenny the Lion confirmed that that was exactly what the old bird was doing.

'I shall adjourn now. Mr Rumpole, by tomorrow morning, perhaps you will have thought of some relevant questions to ask this witness.'

'Tomorrow morning, my Lord, I shall hope to demonstrate that the question I just asked was entirely relevant.'

'I have ruled on that, Mr Rumpole. I trust that the Jury will put it completely out of their minds.'

But I knew the Jury wouldn't.

I emerged from that bout in Court panting slightly, bruised a little, but undaunted, mopping the brow and removing the wig to give the top of my head an airing. The researches of the admirable Fig Newton had allowed me to serve an alibi notice on the Prosecution, and I asked Lenny the Lionhearted if the forces of law and order had been able to check the story it contained.

'I'm not sure, Rumpole. I'll have to speak to the officer in charge of the case.'

'Screw up your courage, old darling, to the sticking point,' I encouraged him. 'And do just that.'

Then, as Lenny went off on his daring mission, I heard a voice at my elbow. 'Well, sir. You seem to know a lot about the *Trumpet*'s money. Are you going to let us pay you a slice of it?'

'I'll meet you in Pommeroy's.' I took young Argent's arm and walked him away from the assembled lawyers. 'Six o'clock convenient?'

'You'll let us in on your defence?'

'It's possible. Oh, you know that picture of Katerina Regen, the Nightingale, arriving at the Galaxy Hotel?'

'For her afternoon bonk?'

'Did your man get a snap of her leaving by any chance?'

'I'm sure he did. I told you, we've got that story sewn up.'

'Probably. But bring a copy of the leaving picture, will you? I'm curious to see it.'

'Right you are, sir.' The boy journalist seemed to be suppressing laughter, his usual problem. 'And you'll tell me what *you've* got up your sleeve?'

'My sleeve,' I promised him, 'will be entirely open to you.'

So I went back to Chambers and had a brief consultation with Bonny Bernard about the events of the day, skimmed through a forthcoming matter of warehouse-breaking by a particularly inefficient member of the Timson clan, and put on my hat for Pommeroy's. On my way out of Chambers, I passed a despondent Claude, who whispered a furtive question about his exposure in the public prints. 'I'm going to meet the journalist in question now. I have high hopes that you will emerge without a stain on your character.' As I left him I couldn't honestly tell if the fellow looked relieved or disappointed.

'You needn't invest in Dom Perignon,' I told Jonathan Argent, when we were established in a discreet table in Pommeroy's, the one under the staircase, and the furthest from the gents, 'until you're quite sure you like what I'm going to tell you.'

'You mean you still haven't thought of a defence in the case of the Little Boy Lost?'

'Not exactly. In fact, my defence is a perfectly simple one. The little boy was never lost at all.'

'You're joking!' But that was one moment when I noticed that young Argent wasn't tempted to suppress a laugh.

'Not really. Tell me how much *did* the *Trumpet* pay Sheena Constant?'

He mentioned a generous number of Ks.

'Not bad money for sending young Tommy to stay at his Great-aunt Brenda's.'

'What on earth are you talking about?'

'What on earth? Dear old Brenda doesn't want to be on earth very much, does she? She wants to be up in the stars, in the spirit world, or on the other side of the wall of death. But she is of the earth, earthy. I wonder what her cut was for a week's babyminding.'

'Do you mind telling me what you're talking about?' Young Jonathan looked, for once, out of his depth.

'I don't mind in the least. I'm talking about fraud, rather an ingenious one to fool sentimental old folks like me and con your hardboiled tabloid out of a considerable amount of cash. Poor old darling, what a soft touch you brilliant journalists are!'

'You mean . . .?'

'I mean Aunt Brenda was hired to put on a black mac with a dashing beret and remove the little boy from the mechanical donkey. Did you ever wonder why he went so quietly? Why he didn't cry or yell out? Because he knew he was safe with his dad's old auntie. She looked after him for a week, sometimes at her house, at least once or twice at her fortune shop. Then she dumped him in the squatters' garden as planned and made the call from a phone box in Swansdown Avenue.'

'But Sheena recognized your client's voice.'

'No, she didn't. That was all part of the plot to frame Thelma. Someone who is far easier to frame than a reproduction of "The Stag at Bay".'

'Why Thelma?'

'Sheena hates her. She'd been rude about Steve, called him a boring little company man and a dreary middle manager. That's why they chose Brenda, because she's got rust-coloured hair like Thelma's. And that's why they tricked Brenda out in Thelma's customary suit of solemn black.'

There was a pause while Jonathan Argent digested the information. Then he asked me if I could prove it.

'We'll see after I've finished cross-examining Sheena. What I *can* prove is that Thelma's innocent.'

'How?'

'She spent that week at a residential business course at a country house near Tunbridge Wells. She had lessons in salesmanship and competitive marketing. She went to school with a lot of ambitious reps and wore her name on a plastic label.'

'Did she tell you that?'

'Of course not. But we found it out, and we've got witnesses to prove it. Thelma's going to be furious when she hears the evidence.'

'Why?'

'Because it'll prove one thing. That she wants to become a

boring little middle manager just like Steve Constant. She's terribly ashamed of that. She'd rather be suspected of kidnapping than admit it. She even took the course under an assumed name. Luckily, one of the tutors recognized her photograph.'

'What did she call herself?'

'Tina Jones. Not Santos. Just the Christian name. It's odd that they all seem to have been jealous of Tina.'

The talkative journalist broke all records for a long and thoughtful silence. At last he said, 'If you tell that story in Court, it's going to make the *Trumpet* look rather foolish.'

'You can't make an omelette without breaking eggs.'

'And you can't expect us to pay you for holding us up to general ridicule.'

'That's why I advised you to save on the Dom Perignon. By the way, did you bring me the diva's leaving photograph?'

He said he had, but it seemed as though Claude's troubles no longer interested him greatly. Suddenly he was a very anxious young journalist.

'Of course,' I said, 'I could go and beard Lenny the Lion in his den and see if he'll drop the case.'

'Could you?' He couldn't help sounding eager.

'I could try.'

He thought it over and then said, 'Why do you call him Lenny the Lion?'

'Because he's such a fearsome prosecutor. Carnivorous, I'd call him. Still, I'm prepared to ask if he'll go quietly, and keep your name out of the papers. I imagine the *Sun* would rather make mincemeat of you.'

'Yes . . .' The thought clearly gave him no pleasure. 'Will you try to settle it?'

'On one condition.'

'You want money?'

'Strangely enough, I don't. But I want you to drop the story about Claude Erskine-Brown.'

'I think we can do that.'

'Anyway, it seems you've got the wrong chap.' I looked down at the photograph. It showed Katerina leaving the Galaxy with her appointment for the afternoon, the man she had no doubt embraced after her lunch with Claude. It was none other

than the huge, booming barrister who had organized her concert in the Outer Temple, Barrington McTear, Q.C., known to
me only as Cut Above.

'We've checked your client's alibi, Rumpole. I had a word with
the officer in charge of the case.'

'That was extremely brave of you. And . . .?'

'It appears to stand up.'

'That's right. It's not a baby any more. It's a big, strong
grown-up alibi.'

We were having coffee in the Old Bailey canteen before Mr
Justice Pick started work for the day. Around us, solicitors and
learned friends, plain-clothes officers of the law and accused
persons trying to look optimistic, were preparing to meet the
challenge of a day in Court. Lenny lowered his voice almost to
a whisper. 'I don't suppose the *Trumpet* wants to look foolish
in public.'

'No, Lenny. I don't believe it does.'

'The paper wouldn't welcome a prolonged investigation.'

'You might get rather a bad press if you go on.'

'Do you know, Rumpole, I've been thinking I might ask to
see the Judge.'

'You always were a brave prosecutor.'

'Tell him that, all things considered, the Prosecution aren't
offering any further evidence against your client.'

'I've always said you were a complete carnivore.'

'No need to subject the Constants and the paper to universal
derision.'

'No need at all.'

'It would serve no useful purpose.'

'None.'

'So I'll tell Pick I'm throwing in my hand.'

'It takes courage to do that.'

'Will that suit you, Rumpole?'

'It will suit me very well indeed.'

'So that's sorted then.'

'Yes.'

'Sorry we couldn't have had a fight.'

'So am I. In a way.'

'Never mind, Rumpole. There'll be other occasions.' He looked at me, I thought, quite gloomily.

'Yes, Lenny. I'm sure there will.'

That didn't seem to cheer him up at all.

It was all over. Thelma sniffed when she was discharged and told me that the whole thing had been a complete waste of her time. I got a little parcel from Jonathan Argent and took it to Claude Erskine-Brown in his room.

'Here's your picture back. And the negative.'

'They're not going to use it in the paper?'

'Don't worry. There'll be no scandal. And Soapy Sam Bollard won't throw you out of Chambers.'

'I might keep this photograph.' Claude took the record of his encounter out of its envelope and looked at it lovingly.

'I strongly advise you not to.'

'In my drawer? Here in Chambers?'

'Wherever you keep it, our Portia's going to find it some time.'

'Perhaps you're right.' He sighed heavily. 'But a memento of what might have been . . .'

'It's all in your mind, Claude. Keep it there.'

'I might have been famous as Katerina Regen's lover.' His voice was full of regret.

'You want me to take that picture round to the *Sun*?'

'Perhaps not. Let it go.' He handed me the package. 'Dispose of it how you will. But I shall think of her, Rumpole. I shall think of her quite often. When I'm alone.'

I took the package from him and looked at Claude with pity. Poor fool! He'd really wanted to get his name in the papers.

Rumpole and the Rights of Man

'A toast to Mr Rumpole, our fellow European.' The faces around me were pink and smiling encouragingly. Glasses of a colourless fluid were raised, which rushed down the throat like a hot wind, took your breath away and left you gasping and more than a little confused. Was I European? I supposed so, although I had never thought of it before.

If I think about it at all, I suppose I'm English. Not British. The Scots, the Irish and in particular the Welsh, although full of charm and excellent qualities, are undoubtedly foreign. I never talk about the U.K., an expression much favoured by politicians and management consultants who have retired to live on the Costa del Crime. Had I been mistaken all this time, I wondered, as the cold beer joined the eau de vie? Was I not just an Englishman abroad but a European who had stayed at home? I looked down at the huge plate of sour cabbage and boiled sausage (in England, I had been tempted to say, we don't boil sausages). The restaurant was in a street of huge, medieval, half-timbered houses, now sheltering boutiques and souvenir shops. We were in France but near that part of Germany where, so my hosts told me, the Rhine maidens and the dwarf and the giants lived through those endless operas Claude Erskine-Brown was so keen on, characters I found so much less interesting than the clients down the Old Bailey, or even my latest quarry, his Honour Judge Billy Bloxham, a new and unwelcome addition to the Judges entitled to try cases of alleged murder.

'And also to you, Mr Rumpole!' The toastmaster, a somewhat rimless man with rimless glasses perched on a long, narrow nose, who spoke with the pursed lips and squeezed vowels of a Nord, raised his glass to me: 'The defender of human rights'.

'Well,' I had to tell them, 'I'm not exactly that. I mean, I spend most of my time defending people.'

'Defending their rights.' Peter Fishlock, my instructing solicitor, who had travelled with me from England, was a great one for rights and for the Society for a Written Constitution, of which he was, as he kept telling me, 'chair'. During our long hours together, in English courts and on the bumpy ride across the sky to Strasburg, I realized how much I missed Bonny Bernard, who was less interested in human rights than in trying to find a decent bit of alibi evidence.

'I'm not so sure about that either.' We had gone through a good many toasts that evening, to the Community of Nations and the Irrelevance of Gender, Freedom from Torture combined with a Common Currency, and so much eau de vie had slipped down the red lane that my courage had become extremely Dutch. 'I'm defending their wrongs quite often. Their errors and foolish ways. I suppose I look on the law as a sort of disease, and I'm the doctor who tries to cure his patient of it as quickly as possible.'

'That is only your English modesty speaking there, Mr Rumpole.' A reassuring female voice sounded somewhere above my head. Betsi Hoprecht, tall and blonde, with a face as smooth and delicately brown as a new-laid egg, a young German lawyer with an encyclopaedic knowledge of the ways of the European Court, had appointed herself my helper, guardian, nurse and general protector for the purposes of the present proceedings. 'We all know how you English wish to conceal your finer feelings under all those layers of clothing you wear. But I think we know where Mr Rumpole's heart is, and I think it's in the right place.' Betsi's speech was in perfect English, although no one English would have made it.

'I propose a toast then.' Govan Welamson, the rimless Swede and Professor of International Law, had his slender glass refilled. 'To Mr Rumpole's heart.'

'Please,' I begged, 'couldn't we drink to something a little less embarrassing. Like the Common Agricultural Policy?'

'Come on, Rumpole. We all know you spend your time defending the underdog.' This came from Jeremy Jameson, Member of the European Parliament, who had a surprisingly young face stuck on the body of a sedentary and spreading politician. He had come with a half-smiling and mostly silent woman with a thin nose and a short upper lip. With her tight curls she had the appearance of an intelligent and attractive sheep. She wore a neat black suit with a few gold ornaments and smelled of the most expensive perfume in the duty free. The Euro M.P. had introduced her simply as Poppy.

Jameson stood, I seemed to remember, in the Liberal interest and had a huge constituency in the West of England, where no one was able to remember his name. He spoke, even when he was at his most polite, with a kind of contemptuous amusement: 'Defending the underdog brought you to Strasburg,' he said. 'To all these perfectly marvellous restaurants, with a side salad of human rights?'

'The great thing about underdogs,' I reminded him, 'is that they're usually on legal aid.'

'But you defend them,' Betsi told me firmly, 'for the sake of your principles.'

'I defend them,' I corrected her, 'for the sake of the rent of the mansion flat and my wife's effort to boost consumer spending every Saturday at Safeway's.'

'Don't know why we wanted to go into Europe anyway,' a deep-voiced woman, her grey hair tousled, her cheeks flushed, who had been chain-smoking over the choucroute, boomed at us. 'All a lot of bloody nonsense. They want us to grow square strawberries! They must be potty.' She had been introduced as Lady Mary Parsloe, the wife of Eddie Parsloe, the neat, pretty-faced man from the consular service who wore, whenever his wife was speaking, a smile of agonized patience. 'Mary,' he told us, 'is more of a gardener than a diplomat.'

'If you'd lost five great-uncles at Passchendaele and a father shot a week before V.E. Day, I don't think you'd be diplomatic, would you, Mr Rumpole?'

'And Mary's direct ancestor lost his leg at Waterloo, didn't he, dear?'

'That was a mere trifle.' She brushed her husband off as though he were a cloud of gnats bothering her weeding. 'Come on, Mr Rumpole, speak up. Don't you think it's potty?'

'I hadn't heard about the square strawberries.'

'Well, you've bloody well heard about them now. You can't be too happy about it.'

'Mr Rumpole is contented because he can enjoy a good dinner and also serve the cause of justice.' Betsi had also appointed herself my official spokesman. 'But there's someone over there who's not so happy, I'm just thinking.'

Our company turned to glance at the man sitting under an elaborate mural depicting an unfortunate and bloodstained moment during the Thirty Years War. I didn't turn. I had seen his Honour Billy Bloxham when he came in; he had stared past me as though he hoped I didn't exist.

'The Judge,' Peter Fishlock said with scarcely suppressed excitement, 'is looking as though he's waiting to be sentenced.'

At which point a waiter, who looked as though his day job was Euro Minister in charge of Strawberry Shapes, came up to point out that to *fumer* was *absolument défendu*.

'Eddie' – Lady Mary made what I felt was a rare appeal to her husband – 'can you tell me the French for piss off?'

It all started at the Bank Underground. It should seem a long time ago, for I have reached the age when every day must be savoured and cherished. In fact, the years flash by like stations at which the train doesn't stop, and the year which it took Amin Hashimi's case to reach the dizzy eminence of the European Court of Human Rights seemed to take up no time at all. I don't know how slowly it went for Mr Hashimi, but then he was in prison for life.

George Freeling was forty-three years old, with a wife and two children in Buckhurst Hill. He worked as a middle manager at Netherbank, a huge glass and concrete tower which dwarfed a Wren church not far from the Mansion House. Each night at approximately five forty-five Mr Freeling joined the population explosion which surged away from their computer screens and, leaving the world's markets to enrich or ruin their clients, struggled down the tube. On the evening in question the platform for the eastbound Central Line resembled the Black Hole of Calcutta. Most of the sufferers at least had a safe journey home but George Freeling, standing on the edge of the platform, fell in front of the train as it rattled out of the darkness on its way from St Paul's. He was found to have been shot in the back: a revolver with a silencer and a single blue glove made of polyester and wool were lying between the lines and beside his dead body.

This method of public assassination had, I later discovered, been copied from a detective story where it attracted less attention. Sandra Atherton, a secretary at Citibank, saw a young man of Middle-Eastern appearance apparently push Freeling in the back before he fell. She lost sight of him in the crowd, but then she saw him again, running towards the exit. She called to the guard, who gave chase, followed by some other passengers who also thought they'd seen Freeling pushed – among them Vernon Wynstanley, a young stockbroker, and Emily Brotherton, a tea-lady. For a very short time these witnesses lost sight of the supposed assassin in the tiled and echoing underground passages, but the guard managed to communicate with ground level. Amin Hashimi was stopped as he was leaving the station and the City police were sent for. The three named witnesses made a positive identification. Later, when Hashimi was examined forensically, fibres similar to those in the blue glove were found, in a microscopic quantity, under the fingernails of his right hand. Peter Fishlock got the case, thanks to a friend in the Magistrates Court, and, as I had just won a rather tricky affray and criminal damage for him, he was wise enough to instruct Horace Rumpole for the Defence. During the complicated course of the proceedings he got the idea of Rumpole as the champion of the underdog, or at least of a student of Middle-Eastern extraction, which led us to the choucroute and the eau de vie – and to my international acclaim in Strasburg.

The case came on before his Honour Judge Bloxham, a person who, I think, deliberately cultivated his likeness to a pallid bulldog. His skin was curiously white and his forehead was perpetually furrowed, as were his jowls. With these similar lines above and below, and his eyebrows matching his moustache, he had one of those faces which could make sense either way up, like the comical drawings that once appeared in children's books.

I can't say I had embarked on the Defence of Mr Hashimi
with any high hopes of success. I could only do my poor best,
although I have to say, in all modesty, that my poor best is
considerably better than the poorer best of such learned friends
as Claude Erskine-Brown and Soapy Sam Ballard, Q.C. The
most I could do, I thought, was to unsettle the identification
evidence, have a bit of harmless fun on the subject of wool and
polyester fibres, and point to the great weakness of the Prosecution case: the complete absence of any sort of motive for the
alleged assassination of George Freeling.

'You had never met this man Freeling?'
'Never. Never had I spoken to him.'
'Or seen him?'
'Perhaps. Travelling on that Underground line you see many
faces. Perhaps his was among them.'
'You use that line every day?'
'Back and forwards. To my college in Holborn, where I take
business studies and office management. I am reading during
the journey; I don't notice many people.'
'Did you know anything about Netherbank where Freeling
worked?'
'I have heard of it, of course. Not much more.' We were
sitting in the interview room in Brixton and I thought that Mr
Hashimi might appeal to the women on the Jury. He looked
young enough to be mothered and his large brown eyes gave
him an expression of injured innocence. He had long, pale
fingers and, even in the disinfected atmosphere of Brixton, he
seemed to give off a faint smell of sandalwood and spices. I
told him that I would do my best for him.
'We are in the hands of Allah the Compassionate and Merciful. He ordains life and death and has power over all things.'
'You pray to Allah?'
'Of course.'
'Well, ask him to be particularly compassionate and merciful
down the Old Bailey next week, why don't you?'
As the gates of the prison house closed behind us and we
squeezed into Peter Fishlock's small Japanese motor, I said,
'We have one bright spot in a rather gloomy prospect.'

'The absence of motive?'

'No. The presence of his Honour Judge Bloxham.'

'I thought Billy Bloxham disapproved of foreign students using the Health Service.'

'Better than that. He's allergic to any sort of alien. Visitors from what was once our far-flung empire bring him out in a nervous rash.'

'How's that going to help Amin?'

'Because if we can get Billy to show his hand, if we can needle the old darling into a quaint little display of racial prejudice, then we can present a bigoted Bloxham to the Jury and they might decline to obey orders. In fact, there's an outside chance, I say no more than that, my fine Fishlock, that we might just scrape home to victory!'

'Of course, their evidence on the fibres is very unconvincing.'

'The fibres are one thing. But Bloxham's prejudices are something else entirely. He never stops talking about being British and living in the U.K. He's a fellow who sings "Rule Britannia" in his bath and wants the Kingdom to be reserved strictly for Bloxham look-alikes, their lady wives and white children. If Allah the Compassionate wants a way for Amin Hashimi to walk, then Billy's going to lead him to it.'

'Miss Atherton. You say you saw a young man of Middle-Eastern appearance push the victim's back as the train was about to stop.'

'I saw the man in the dock do that.'

'That's what I'm trying to test, Miss Atherton. Just bear with me, will you? I suggest the first time you got a good look, face to face, at my client Mr Hashimi was when he was stopped on his way out of the station. You came up then and identified him?'

'I did, yes.'

'Are you quite sure that was the same Middle-Eastern gentleman you saw push the man on the platform?'

'Yes. I'm sure.'

'You had lost sight of him during the chase?'

'For a short while, yes.'

'And might not you and the others have ended up pursuing another Middle-Eastern young man?'

'I don't think so.'

'Come now, Miss Atherton. Don't all Middle-Eastern young men look rather similar to you? Are you sure you could have told the two of them apart?'

'Mr Rumpole.' I smiled towards the Bench, waiting for Billy to let his prejudices show. To my dismay he did nothing of the sort. 'Mr Rumpole,' he said, surprisingly gently, 'this Court is colour-blind! Where in the world this young man came from is a matter of no significance. He's fully entitled to the fair trial which I'm sure this jury is going to give him. I'm also sure that this very intelligent young lady can identify an assailant without going into racist characteristics. Isn't that so, Miss Atherton?'

'Of course I can.' Sandra Atherton was delighted to agree with the not so learned Judge.

'Very well, then. Let us continue, Mr Rumpole. And let us do so without reference to creed or colour.'

My heart sank. I could see the Jury, a mixed bag from the Hoxton area, looking at the pallid Bloxham and rather liking what they saw. He had decided, I now realized, to play a particularly mean trick on the Defence. He was going to give us a fair trial.

Vernon Wynstanley, the stockbroker, and Emily Brotherton were hardly less sure of their identification. Mrs Brotherton, the image of the jolly tea-lady about to be replaced by a mechanical dispenser, was particularly popular with the Jury. I let them both go as soon as possible, but spent a good deal of time cross-examining the fibre expert on the amount of wool and polyester mixture available in London, and the vast number of garments which might have left innocent traces under my client's fingernails. I stopped when I noticed that number three in the jury-box had dropped off to sleep.

In my final speech, given, I had to say, with even more than my usual eloquence, I dwelt on the uncertainty of identification evidence at the best of times, and particularly when the incident took place in an Underground station during the rush hour and must have been a horrific shock to all concerned. I gave the Jury at least twenty minutes on the absence of motive. What was my client, Amin Hashimi, meant to be? A criminal lunatic who killed at random just for kicks? Nothing in his history, his success at his studies and his hitherto unimpeachable behaviour could support such a theory. After I had imitated the Scales of Justice, and put in the ounce of reasonable doubt which would weigh them down on the side of the Defence, I sank into my seat, tired and sweating. I had done my best and I could only hope that Billy Bloxham would put his foot in it.

He didn't. He told the Jury that, although the Prosecution didn't have to supply a motive, they should take full account of all Mr Rumpole had said about the apparent purposelessness of the crime. He told them that identification evidence was often unreliable and they should approach it with great care, but whether they believed the secretary, the stockbroker and the tea-lady was a matter entirely for them. He said they should think about whether the fibres helped prove the case and that they mustn't convict unless they were quite sure. In fact, it was an appallingly fair summing-up.

I said goodbye to my client after Allah the Compassionate, the Merciful, had failed to come up trumps. Amin Hashimi, as calm as ever, thanked me politely and said, 'The hypocrites will not be forgiven. He does not guide the evildoers. And he has knowledge of all our actions. I have nothing to regret, Mr Rumpole, so please give my best wishes to your lady wife.' I had no doubt that, three or four weeks later, he would wake up to the reality of life imprisonment and his soft, brown eyes would fill with tears.

A few weeks later, however, the Compassionate one arranged something that might possibly provide an escape route for my imprisoned client. His Honour Judge Bloxham was invited to a rugby club dinner somewhere near his home in the Midlands, and he was asked to sing for his supper.

END IMMIGRATION TO END CRIME. JUDGE THANKFUL TO HAVE GOT ONE MORE ARAB STUDENT BEHIND BARS. So screamed the headline in Hilda's *Daily Telegraph* which I saw as we sat at breakfast in the mansion flat. 'Your Judge Bloxham,' she said, crunching toast, 'seems to have been rather a Silly Billy.'

'He seems to have said it all a bit too late.' I borrowed Hilda's paper. 'Anyway, he's not my Judge. I want no part of him.'

I suppose it was bad luck in a way. Billy Bloxham had no doubt expected the speech to be a private affair, and in this simple faith he must have let himself go with the pink gin, the claret, the brandy and the port. He stood up to address those used to scrumming down and tackling each other perilously low, and let the real Billy Bloxham bubble to the surface. He wasn't to know that some eager young rugby-playing reporter, fresh from the local *Echo* and anxious to make a name for himself in the world of journalism, was writing shorthand on the back of a menu and would communicate the highlights to the Press Association. The report in the *Daily Telegraph* of what Bloxham had said was fairly full:

A great many of these towel-headed gentry come here as so-called students to escape the tough laws of their own countries. No doubt they find a short stretch of community service greatly preferable to losing a hand if they're caught with their fingers in the till. No doubt they prefer our free Health Service to the attentions of the Medicine Man in the Medina. I don't know how much studying they do, but they certainly have time for plenty of extra-curricular activities. They take special courses in drug-dealing and the theft of quality cars.

Coming from a part of the world where scraps were always breaking out, they are easily drawn into violence. This is not so bad when they do it to each other, but not, repeat not, when a law-abiding subject of Her Majesty gets shot in the Underground. I have to tell you, gentlemen, that when my jury brought in a guilty verdict on the murderer Hashimi, I had a song in my heart. I retired to my room and invited my dear old usher, ex-Sergeant Major Wrigglesworth of the Blues and the Royals, to join me in a glass of sherry. 'Well done, sir,' Wrigglesworth said. 'You managed to pot the bastard.' 'One down,' I replied, 'and thousands left to go.'

When I got into Chambers Fishlock, the human rights solicitor, was already there, cradling a bundle of morning papers as though it were a long-lost child. 'Biased Judge,' he almost whooped for joy. 'Flagrantly biased! No doubt at all about that. So what do we do now?'

'We get whoever was the mole in the rugby club to swear an affidavit and troop off to the Court of Appeal.'

'To tell them the Judge was biased?'

'And has, with any luck, delivered himself into our hands.'

I am not an habitué of the Court of Appeal. It has none of the amenities I'm used to – such as witnesses to cross-examine and juries to persuade. One Judge is bad enough, but the Appeal Court comes equipped with three who bother you with unnecessary and impertinent questions which are not always easy to answer.

Lord Justice Percival Ponting, who presided over the Hashimi appeal, had hooded eyes and the distasteful look of a person who goes through life with a bad smell under his nose. He had never recovered from having achieved a double first at Cambridge and regarded Old Bailey hacks in general, and Horace Rumpole in particular, as ill-educated dimwits who couldn't read the Institutes of Justinian in Latin.

'Mr Rumpole' – the Lord of Appeal in Ordinary pronounced my name as though he regretted having stepped in it – 'will you be so good as to refer us to any passage in the transcript of the trial in which the learned Judge made any sort of biased remark to the Jury concerning your client, Mr Harashimi?'

'*Hashimi*, my Lord, as it so happens.'

'Oh, I'm so sorry. I do beg his pardon. Hashimi then. Well, Mr Rumpole, will you now refer us to the passages in the transcript.'

'In the transcript of the speech at the rugby club? The Judge couldn't have made his views more absolutely clear . . .'

'Do remind us, Mr Rumpole. The Jury wasn't empanelled to sit in judgement at the rugby club dinner, was it?'

'No, my Lord, but . . .'

'And by the time that event took place, the Jury had reached a verdict, after an unbiased summing-up, had they not?'

'His after-dinner diatribe, his post-prandial peroration, my Lord, shows exactly what the Judge had in mind.'

'Mr Rumpole. We all may have things on our minds. We may have views about the merits of this Appeal which it might be kinder not to express in public. You may have in mind a proper realization of the shallowness of your argument. It's what's said in Court that matters!'

'We don't live our entire lives in courtrooms. What's my client to think now? What's any reasonable man to think? That he was tried unfairly by a biased judge.'

'Is that your best point?'

'Indeed, it is!' I turned up the volume to show I was running out of patience with Ponting, alarming the ushers and causing the little Lord Justice on the left to open his eyes.

'No need to raise your voice, Mr Rumpole. You are perfectly audible. Your first point is that your client was tried by a Judge who successfully concealed his true feelings?'

'And secondly, that he did so deliberately to secure a conviction.'

'You were right, Mr Rumpole.' Percy Ponting smiled down at me from a great height and in a wintry fashion. 'Your first point was the best one.'

'"A great many of these towel-headed gentry came here as so-called students to escape the tough laws of their own countries ... when my jury brought in a guilty verdict on the murderer Hashimi I had a song in my heart." How can you possibly say that's not biased?'

'Words which he didn't utter at the trial?'

'Words which show exactly how he felt at the trial.'

'Mr Rumpole, I think we are now seized of your argument.'

'I don't think you are. I think you are about to ignore my argument.'

'If you have nothing more to add . . .'

'Oh, yes, I have. A great deal more to add.' I added it for another three-quarters of an hour, while Percy Ponting joined the little fellow on his left in carefully simulated sleep. It came as no surprise when we lost, and leave to appeal to the House of Lords was refused. Two days later that august and elevated body also refused leave.

'I'm afraid,' I had to tell Fishlock, 'it looks like the end of the line.'

'Not exactly.' He looked like a man possessed of a well-kept secret. 'What about Article Six of the European Convention on Human Rights?'

'A document,' I hastened to tell him, 'which is my constant bedtime reading.'

'Everyone is entitled to a fair hearing by an independent and impartial tribunal!'

'That is what I had in mind. So we're off to The Hague, are we?'

'*You* may be, Mr Rumpole. But the Court of Human Rights sits in Strasburg.'

'Of course! That's the one I meant. So you're going to brief me in Strasburg, are you? It'll make a change from the Uxbridge Magistrates Court.'

It was then that Peter Fishlock began to talk about Rumpole and human rights being as inseparable as Marks & Spencer, and I speculated on the possible generosity of Euro legal aid.

'I hear you're off to Europe, Rumpole.' Soapy Sam Ballard looked at me with incredulity and distaste, as though I had just won the National Lottery.

'Rather a bore, really.' I lit a small cigar in an offhand manner. The man had entered my room eagerly enough, but now covered his mouth with his fist and coughed as though I had set out to asphyxiate him. 'But you've got to be prepared to travel when you've got an international practice like mine.'

'I understand. And I'm perfectly prepared to travel, Rumpole.'

'Going far? We'll have to do our best to get along without you.'

'I'm coming with you, of course. In a case of this importance, you'll be in need of a leader. Preferably one from Chambers.'

'Oh, I don't think so, old darling. My instructing solicitor is prepared to leave it to me. The Rights of Man, you know, are rather my *spécialité de la maison*. I'm sure you've got enough landlord and tenant stuff to keep you fully occupied.' At which, I blew out smoke and the would-be leader, looking extremely miffed, simulated terminal bronchitis and withdrew from my presence.

So the long journey started which ended up over the choucroute and the water of life in the Grimms' fairytale Kammerzell House in Strasburg. There I was applauded for my devotion to justice by a fan club of Europeans and his Honour Judge Bloxham, looking extremely green about the gills, sat glowering at me with ill-concealed hostility from the corner of the room.

As Jeremy Jameson collected the bill to put in with his Euro expenses, I plodded off towards the facilities. As I stood in front of the porcelain, lit by a sudden and blinding white light, I was conscious of a shrunken figure at the far end of the row of stalls. Judge Bloxham turned to face me, zipping up his trousers; and, looking paler than ever, his eyes dead with despair, he uttered one word, pronounced like a curse from a dry throat, 'Rumpole', and shuffled away across the marble floor.

I gave him time to get away and then returned to the dining-room, only to discover that, as rare things will, all my newfound friends had vanished. Betsi Hoprecht and the rimless Professor of International Law (both of whom had met me at the airport), the Euro M.P., Poppy, the elegant sheep, and even my instructing solicitor had gone off into the night and the table was being cleared under the instruction of the Minister for Strawberries. At that moment I felt I was in Europe, a stranger and alone.

Walking back to the hotel in the moonlight, I looked at my watch. Almost eleven on a Saturday night. It seemed a long time since I and Peter Fishlock had been met at the airport by Betsi Hoprecht, who had stood tall and fair-haired above the smaller, darker inhabitants of Alsace-Lorraine waiting for their loved ones. She had taken us in charge, kept us going on a tour round the monuments, and arranged the dinner at the Kammerzell House at which we were to meet the gallant band who sat shoulder to shoulder, consuming choucroute and fighting for the Rights of Man. I had felt safe in Betsi's hands, relieved of the painful process of decision. Now I was on my own, crossing the cathedral square, and I decided to see the astronomical clock put on its hourly performance.

The shadowy cathedral was empty, the windows which Betsi had shown us glowing with coloured sunlight were now blind and black. Only a few candles, lit for the dead and the dying, flickered in the cloisters by the side-chapels. In the empty pews only a few heads, the anxious, the insomniac or old, were bowed in prayer and contemplation. I put in a coin and the clock towered above me in golden light with its minarets and huge dials, the signs of the Zodiac, the round sun in a bright blue sky dotted with stars, the columns of gold and black marble, and the figures of Christ and Death waiting for their hourly moment of confrontation.

As I looked up at these wonders, I was conscious of a tallish tourist standing beside me. I thought how badly his clothes went with the wonders of sixteenth-century science and architecture: a red plastic anorak with LES DROITS DE L'HOMME written on it, trousers that looked as though they'd been made in a computer, and a baseball cap which bore the insignia of the Common Market. Then eleven struck. The heavens began to whirr and move at the command of the master clockmaker, the Ages of Man passed in their chariots, the heavenly globe was lit up in front of the perpetual calendar with its statues of Diana and Apollo, and Christ, his hand held up in benediction, chased the skeleton Death. As the slow strokes died away, and all the devices on the clock shuddered to a standstill, a voice with which I was unfortunately familiar said, 'The continentals are clever fellows, aren't they?'

'Bollard! What on earth are you doing here?'

'What on earth? That's rather a good question, Rumpole. What are any of us doing on earth? Our duty, let us hope. To God and our country. And preparing ourselves for a better life *not* on earth. That's the hope we live with.'

'I have to tell you, Bollard, that if the hope you live with is infiltrating yourself into Monday's case as leading Counsel for Amin Hashimi, forget it. Your journey has been entirely unnecessary.'

'I shall be in the case on Monday, as you would know, Rumpole, if you were in the habit of reading your papers before going into Court. But I shall be appearing for a slightly more reputable client than your Mr Hashimi.'

'Oh, really. Who's that?'

'H.M.G., Rumpole.'

'Who's he, when he's at home?'

'Her Majesty's Government. I'm here to support Lord Justice Ponting's opinion in the Court of Appeal.'

'You mean you're for the H.M.G. of the U.K.?'

'Exactly so!' Of course Ballard failed to detect the note of sarcasm in my flight to the acronym.

'But you didn't do the case at the Bailey or in the Court of Appeal. Tubby Arthurian did it.'

'Quite right. But with the international importance this matter has now achieved, with the entire reputation of the U.K. judiciary at stake, it was thought by H.M.G. . . .'

'What was thought?'

'Well' – the man seemed embarrassed, as it turned out he had good cause to be – 'that Counsel should be chosen who would be likely to have some influence over you. To check what H.M.G. described, in a confidential memo to myself, as your worst excesses, Rumpole.'

'Why on earth would you have any influence over me?'

'Well, H.M.G. thought that as I am undoubtedly your Head of Chambers and therefore placed in some position of authority . . .'

'H.M.G. thought *that* might curb my excesses?'

'Naturally.'

'Then H.M.G. must be singularly ignorant of the inner working of our great legal system. H.M.G. should know by now that the sight of you, Bollard, causes my worst excesses to break out like the measles.'

'I had hoped' – Soapy Sam had the good sense not to sound particularly optimistic – 'that we might be able to reach some sort of common approach. We don't want to cause poor old Bloxham public embarrassment, do we?'

'Don't we? I've been looking forward to it for months.'

'Perhaps we could talk over a drink.'

'You can buy me a drink at any time,' I was kind enough to tell him.

'Thank you, Rumpole.' Ballard was now looking anxiously round the cathedral, and a note of fear had come into his voice, 'Hilda's not with you, is she?'

'Mrs Rumpole,' I told him, with some dignity, 'has gone to stay with her friend Dodo Mackintosh in Cornwall.'

'I wouldn't want Marguerite to hear that wives were allowed. I told her this was strictly no spouses.'

Marguerite, I remembered, was the ex-Matron of the Old Bailey, the person once in charge of aspirins and Elastoplast, whom the fearless Ballard had decided to marry. 'How did she take that?'

'Not too well, I'm afraid. But I told her that when you're appearing for H.M.G. confidential matters may arise.'

'Baloney!'

'Well, I have to confess, Rumpole, that the idea of being fancy-free on this agreeable little trip to the Continent did rather appeal to me. I thought I might stay on for a couple of days. I took the opportunity of buying some holiday gear this afternoon.' He looked down at his trousers with incomprehensible pride.

'You mean that rig-out? You look as though you were going in for a bicycle race.'

'You should learn to get with it, Rumpole. An old tweed jacket with leather patches' – the man had the ice-cold nerve to look critically at my attire – 'and grey flannel bags simply don't say *European.*'

'Unlike your plastic anorak? It doesn't seem to be able to stop talking about it.'

'Perhaps you should mix a little more with young people, Rumpole. Perhaps you should learn to approach the millennium. I've got to know some young people. Since I got here, I've got to know what you might call the international set.'

'You must be a quick worker.'

'What?'

'I said you must be a quick worker. Didn't you arrive today?'

'Oh, no. I've been here a few days. Getting used to the atmosphere. I must say, it's all been quite stimulating.'

'A few days?' I raised my eyebrows at a complacently smiling Ballard. 'I'm surprised that Marguerite let you off the leash for so long.'

'I have to confess' – Soapy Sam didn't look at all ashamed – 'I wasn't entirely candid about the date of our *cause célèbre.*'

'You mean you told her that Hashimi started last Wednesday?'

'Something like that, yes.'

'I bet they've got that written down, in the great charge-sheet in the sky.'

'The God I believe in,' he had the nerve to tell me, 'is deeply understanding of human frailty. You only flew over this morning, did you? That must be exhausting for you, at your age. I expect you're longing for your bed. Well, mustn't keep you.'

'So what are *you* going to do? Hang around until the clock strikes another hour?'

'Never you mind, Rumpole. There are better things to do in Strasburg than to wait for the clock to strike, I'm bound to tell you.'

As I left the cathedral, I saw, in the shadows of an empty pew, a fair head bent in prayer. To my surprise, Betsi Hoprecht was kneeling, no doubt interdenominationally calling on the God of the clock to ally Himself with the Merciful, the Compassionate, for the protection of Amin Hashimi.

It was a short walk to the Hôtel D'Ange Rouge, and from my bedroom I could still hear the odd calls of love from the backpackers who loitered round the cathedral or staggered home singing. I lay in bed reading the written brief to the Court of Human Rights, a somewhat long document prepared by Fishlock with an analysis of all the British cases on bias. The Judges were welcome to it. What I profoundly hoped would stir them out of their international coma would be the Rumpole address, the rallying cry against injustice, the devastating destruction of Billy Bloxham with which I expected to win the day. I heard the cathedral clock strike one and then I turned out my light.

It was a warm spring night and the window on to the little balcony that overlooked the square was open and the curtain flapping. The window of the next room must have been open also, and I heard the sound of a strong woman, who sounded very much like Betsi Hoprecht, laughing. The full and disturbing significance of this was not revealed to me until the next morning, however, when, setting out eagerly for breakfast, I saw none other than Soapy Sam Ballard emerge from the next-door room in question. He was shaved, bathed and, I had a shrewd suspicion, slightly perfumed. He was wearing his *Droits de l'Homme* anorak and looked like the cat that had got at the cream.

It was Sunday, a day of rest and respite before battle was joined between myself, a freelance, and the Government of Her Britannic Majesty, in the person of its improbable champion, Soapy Sam Ballard, Q.C. Breakfast was held in a small, hot room which I found to be crowded. Ballard was at a table in the corner with some unremarkable person I thought to be connected with H.M.G. The only seat I could find was at a table set for three at which the curly-headed Poppy was already installed, smiling vaguely and peeling an orange. I asked if I could sit down.

'Why not? Jeremy won't be here for hours. He's sleeping off the choucroute.'

I put in a request for ham and eggs and looked thoughtfully back towards my Head of Chambers. I tried to see him in a new light: Casanova Ballard, Soapy Don Juan, Lord Byron Ballard, bedroom Ballard, high in the list of the world's great lovers, and then the mind, I have to confess it, boggled. It also failed to come to terms with the idea of that slimmed-down Betsi Hoprecht on her way to Ballard's bed, even though she was kneeling, as though hoping for a miracle, in prayer as a necessary preliminary.

'Bloody Europe!'

I looked around for the source of this condemnation and decided it could only have come from the smiling Poppy, whose orange, by now, was neatly peeled and quartered.

'So you're a Euro-sceptic?' I thought she was, on the whole, preferable to that grumpy group of M.P.s who had appointed themselves the Prosecutors of the Common Market.

'Sceptic's not the word for it! Other people get taken to the Seychelles, or the Caribbean, or even Acapulco.'

'Other people?'

'Other people's girlfriends, I mean. When my daughter starts looking for a lover, I'll say I don't give a toss what he is doing, just so long as he's not a Euro M.P. I wouldn't even mind Jeremy being an M.P. if he took me out in England, but at home he's always at terrible black-tie dinners where we mustn't be seen together. He has to go on holiday with his wife and dear little Sebastian, who has to get postcards from everywhere and last-minute presents at the airport. All I see of the world is Brussels and Luxemburg and Strasburg, where there's nothing to do except eat until the brass buttons on your Chanel suit shoot off like bullets. You've left your wife at home?'

I had to admit it.

'I thought so! Everyone leaves their wives at home when they go to Strasburg. Jeremy's wife has taken little Sebastian to Brighton. God, how I envy them.'

'Aren't we going on a trip round the wine towns?'

'You haven't done that before?'

'No.'

'Jeremy and I've done it almost more times than we've had sex. Those little half-timbered buildings you wander round as though you were Hansel and bloody Gretel. And you know what the aim and object of the whole exercise is? Yes, you're right. A socking great lunch!'

At which point Betsi Hoprecht strode into the breakfast room, clapped her hands three times and announced that the bus would leave from the front entrance in exactly twenty-five minutes and would we make sure that we were on it. At her entrance, Ballard smiled in as sickly and ingratiating a manner as Malvolio in the play. Betsi returned this greeting with what I thought was an admirably contrived glare of non-recognition.

The Tokay d'Alsace tasted of grapes, a gentle flavour far removed from the chemical impact of Pommeroy's Reasonable White. The sun shone on the restaurant terrace, it glittered on the glasses and ice-bucket, and was warm on our faces. Around us the tops of the pinkish, plastered houses bulged like huge bosoms, kept in place by the ribbons of dark oak. Their steep tiled roofs were pierced with the eyes of numberless dormer windows. Flowers clambered round a well in the centre of the square and, on the slender, sand-coloured church steeple, the clock stood at half past one. We had filled the minibus and now occupied another long restaurant table. The rimless professor was there, as was the man in the consular service and his gardener wife. Jeremy Jameson was there, smiling with a mixture of defiance and guilt. He had come downstairs late, buttoning his shirt, which was not satisfactorily tucked into his crumpled linen trousers. Poppy was smiling, sipping Tokay, and reading the *Mail on Sunday*, hot from the morning plane and greeted by her like a missing child.

'Our whole team is here.' I was sitting next to Betsi and she was giving me her full and flattering attention. 'All of us are behind you, Mr Rumpole. Cheering you on!'

'Not that little chap from the consular service, surely? Isn't he on the side of H.M. Government?'

'Well, he should be, of course. That is where his duty lies. But his heart is with us, Mr Rumpole. He has read all of your memoirs, he tells me. Some of them twice over.'

'Is that really so?' I looked down the table at Eddie Parsloe with a new respect.

'"We must be free or die." He says the spirit of your poet Wordsworth breathes through you.'

'Well, that's remarkably civil of him.'

'And Lady Mary, she's what you would call a hoot, isn't she?'

'And do you know your Common Market's only going to allow us three varieties of bloody begonia?' Lady Mary Parsloe was hooting at the unfortunate Nordic professor. 'It's a disgrace. They'll be at our floribunda roses next.'

'What about Samuel Bollard, Q.C.? You didn't think of inviting him?'

'Mr *Ballard*, I have to correct you. Ballard is his name.'

'I know that perfectly well.'

'So why do you call him by the wrong name then?'

'I suppose in the hope of irritating him.'

'But he is a very nice man.' To my distress, a faraway look came into her pale blue eyes. She was wearing a crisp white dress, which showed off her brown arms to advantage. She smelt of clean linen and rustled like a hospital nurse. 'Also, he is your boss, I think.'

'You think wrong,' I had to tell her.

'He is Head of your Chambers?'

'Bollard has made himself responsible for the coffee machine and the paper clips. But I am a free spirit and a freelance advocate.'

'You are not afraid of him?'

'Of course not.' I felt full of courage, though I must confess that we had got through a number of bottles of Tokay with considerable help from me. 'An advocate can't afford to be afraid.'

'So' – Betsi gave me a display of blindingly white teeth – 'you are afraid of nothing or nobody?'

'Except sometimes,' I had to confess, 'She Who Must Be Obeyed.'

'Who is this she?'

'As a matter of fact, my wife, Hilda.'

'And you have to obey?'

'Well. No. Of course not.'

'So why do you call her that? Is it to irritate her?'

'It seems to describe her.'

'I feel it describes certain aspects of your character more. You are very English, Mr Rumpole. That's your characteristic, I think.'

I wanted to ask her if she found Soapy Sam Ballard was a good lover but my courage failed me. In any event we were interrupted by an even louder hoot from Lady Mary.

'That shower running Europe couldn't organize a village fête in Gloucestershire, I have to tell you.'

'You've got to admit, Lady Mary' – Peter Fishlock came galloping to the defence of Europe – 'The Common Market has kept peace in Europe.'

'Oh, yes? Didn't I read somewhere they're blowing each other up in Bosnia – or whatever you call it. Shooting children in playgrounds. Ethnic cleansing. But I suppose Yugoslavia's not in Europe. Where is it? China or somewhere?'

'Worse than that.' Poppy was reading a bit out of her *Mail on Sunday*. 'Saddam Hussein's buying stolen Russian nuclear weapons. We're all going to get blown up.'

There was a sudden, strangely uncomfortable silence, as though we had all been brought face to face with the ending of the world. And then Betsi leaned across the table and took the paper out of Poppy's hands. Poppy looked disappointed, as though deprived of a favourite toy, but said nothing.

'Neither Russia nor Iraq,' my instructing solicitor reminded us, 'is in the European Common Market.'

Poppy said, 'Lucky old them.' And Betsi, turning the pages of the paper, said, 'Here's some *really* important news. Your Princess Fergie is short of cash!' They all relaxed. The world crisis was clearly over, forgotten in the *important news*.

'You must have got to know Bollard before I arrived?' I said to Betsi.

'He is a very charming man.'

'Do you really think so? Charming in what sort of way exactly?'

'Perhaps' – Betsi was thoughtful – 'like all Englishmen, the charm lies in the innocence.'

'And you say you only got to know him a little?' I remembered the laughter from the bedroom with a certain pang.

'Quite enough to know that he will take a civilized attitude tomorrow. I think you will find him very reasonable.'

'He asked me to be reasonable too.'

'What did you say?'

'I said I had no intention of being reasonable. I intend to fight him with every weapon at my command.'

'You know' – Betsi looked at me thoughtfully – 'I asked Mr Fishlock why he didn't employ a more important barrister than you, a barrister of the same rank as Mr Ballard.'

'Oh, really?' I did my best to appear cool and hoped that I didn't sound envious of Soapy Sam. 'And what did Fishlock say?'

'He said he had every faith in you as a defender of human rights.'

It was at that point that the bill arrived and was grabbed by Jeremy Jameson, M.E.P., with a cry of 'I need this for my expenses.' He slapped his pocket and discovered that he'd left his credit cards in his other jacket and announced that he was writing out a cheque and could he borrow a pen from someone. I lent him mine and happened to see a cheque book of an unusual mauve variety. I also saw that our lunch was to be paid for by funds lodged in Netherbank of Queen Victoria Street, London.

Fresh air, Tokay and dislike of myself for feeling jealous of Soapy Sam Ballard ended in exhaustion as I sat in my room and tried to compose a rousing speech about the human rights of Amin Hashimi. I had decided to call it a day, sink into bed and rely in Court on the inspiration of the moment (such moments have rarely let me down), when the telephone rang and what sounded much like a voice from the tomb said, 'Is that you, Horace? This is Billy speaking. I say, could you spare me five minutes, old fellow? I'm in a bar quite near your hotel.'

It was this sudden use of Christian names that startled me about the beleaguered Judge. I didn't want to talk to him. I certainly didn't want to see him. Any contact between us at that moment could only lead to embarrassment. And yet I had to go and meet the old idiot. It was no longer a visit to a Judge; it was almost like the daily duty of a trip down the cells to cheer up an unsuccessful villain facing trial for a serious offence. I put my jacket on, stuffed my back pocket with a handful of francs, and went off to the tryst. I hadn't far to go, a small dark bar in the rue des Juifs close to the cathedral.

'It was good of you to come, Horace. I'd do the same for you, of course.'

'I hope you'll never have to.'

Billy was sitting in the company of a small espresso and a quartet of adolescents who were drinking rum and Coke and playing the fruit machine. Behind the bar a sleepy woman sat longing for us to go home. While Soapy Sam had gone desperately continental, Billy looked like the caricature of an English tourist, wearing a blazer with gold buttons, a Sheridan Club tie and hating being abroad.

'I was entrapped, Horace. You do realize that, don't you? I've complained to the Press Council. I didn't know that little runt of a journalist had sneaked into the rugger club. So far as I know journalists don't play rugger. It was pure bad luck. Could have happened to anybody.'

'Anybody wasn't a Judge who'd just sentenced a foreign student to life imprisonment.'

'I was giving voice to my private opinions. As I'm entitled to do. I didn't say any of that in Court, did I?'

'No, that's what I've really got against you.'

Billy Bloxham looked puzzled. Indeed, during our brief pretrial meeting he was either angry or puzzled, more often both at the same time.

'You think that might have helped you? If I'd said what I thought about foreigners?'

'I'm damn sure it would.'

'Horace, the very next time you're before me I'll do my best to help you. I'll say exactly what I think.' And then his voice began to break and his hand, lifting the dregs in the tiny coffee cup to his pallid lips, trembled. 'You think there may not be a next time?' he dared to ask.

'It's possible.'

'You mean they may sack me? The Lord Chancellor could do that, couldn't he? I'm not a High Court Judge.'

'I suppose it's on the cards.'

'Horace, you've got a wonderful reputation, down the Bailey, for being on the side of the underdog.'

'And you've become one?'

'In this particular instance, yes.'

'I don't know where everyone got the idea I only act for underdogs.'

Billy was sitting hunched, staring up at me with watery eyes. He looked as though he was prepared to do anything, even bark in a servile fashion and lick my hand. 'Horace, you won't put the case too strongly against me, will you, old boy?'

'I'll do my best,' I said, leaving him in doubt as to whether I was going to do my best to draw it strong or mild.

'You see' – Billy was putting every ounce of emotion into his final speech – 'I have to go on being a Judge. I'm really unfit for anything else.'

'I'm sure there are other things you could do.' I could not, however, imagine what they were.

'No. I know you're only trying to be kind. You see, I couldn't go back to what you chaps do. Arguing with each other. Catching out witnesses. Trying hard to win. I mean, would people give me any work, even if I was allowed back? Would they honestly?'

'I suppose they might.' It was an answer I wouldn't have given under oath.

'I don't believe it. Besides which, I've got used to a certain amount of respect. I like it when you fellows stand up and bow to me. I find that quite delightful. And when I go into the bank, the assistant manager sometimes pops over and says, "How can we help you, Judge?" And they ask me to say a few words at the Rotary and the rugby club dinners. Do you imagine they'd ask a sacked judge to speak at the rugger club?'

'Don't despair.' The sight of the man was beginning to pain me.

'You mean you'll go easy on me?' Billy cheered up a fraction.

'I mean, I may not win.'

'Why? Who's on the other side?'

'Samuel Ballard, Q.C.'

'He doesn't often win.' The Judge was back in the Slough of Despond.

'It's got to happen some time. Anyway, the Euro Judges may not want to upset the British Government.'

'But the British Government's always upsetting them. Do you happen to know who the Judges are?'

'I believe they come from a variety of countries.'

'Foreigners?'

'Bound to be. One's Irish.'

'All foreigners, then.'

'Oh, and one English. Because it's an English case.'

'Who've they got?'

'I think it's Thompson. Used to practise in the Chancery Division.'

'Tradders Thompson?' Billy looked seriously worried now. 'Didn't he marry an Indian?'

'I know nothing,' I assured him, 'about his domestic arrangements.'

'I feel sure I spotted him at an Inner Temple garden party' – Billy was now up to his neck in the Slough – 'with someone in a sari.'

'I've got to get to bed.' I yawned realistically and drained my cognac.

'Written your speech, have you? Couldn't you just water it down a bit, Horace? We Brits should stick together.'

'I haven't written anything.' As I said this, some faint hope returned to the desolate Judge. 'We drank rather a lot of wine at lunch and my eyes won't stay open.'

'Please,' he begged me, 'please have another drink.'

'Not possible.' I stood up then. I was fighting to keep awake. 'Goodnight, Billy. Remember, the trial isn't decided until it's over.' It was the poor crumb of comfort I always kept for my most hopeless of cases.

'I shall wear my Sheridan Club tie.' Billy was down to his last hope. 'Perhaps some of the Judges are members.'

'Oh, I expect so. Get a lot of Slovenes and chaps from Liechtenstein in there, do you?'

So I left him, conscious that my visit to the cells hadn't done much to cheer up the man who might go down in legal history as Lord Bloxham of Bias. I staggered out into the street and started on my way back to the hotel like a sleepwalker.

I hadn't gone far along the rue des Juifs when two things startled me into full wakefulness. First of all I saw an all too familiar red anorak and blue baseball cap moving, not altogether steadily, in the road in front of me. Then I heard the sudden acceleration of an engine behind me and I moved further from the edge of the pavement. An anonymous, dark-blue car thundered past and appeared to be aiming, like a heavy artillery shell, for Ballard's back. Just before it reached him, he skipped with hare-like agility on to the pavement, which the driver mounted. Luckily for Sam, there was a deeply recessed doorway into which he dived and the car, which had braked suddenly, couldn't follow him although he was lit, for a vivid moment, by its headlights, cowering as though from a fatal and expected blow. The car then reversed with a snort of the engine and vanished down the street. I emerged from the shadows as a second shock to my shaken Head of Chambers. 'My God, Rumpole!' he said. 'These continentals are the most terrible drivers!'

*

'I'm not sure about bad drivers, Bollard. It looked to me as if it might have been a deliberate mistake.'

I was ministering to the man, who was still in a state of shock, and I had shown my medical skill by activating the night porter to shuffle off in search of a bottle of eau de vie. I administered a dose of this to Ballard who was still complaining about Alsatian driving skills. 'I shall have to be careful,' he complained, 'now I'll be coming to Strasburg on a regular basis.'

'A regular basis?'

'I've been talking to Betsi.'

'So I understand.'

'And there's a need for Senior Counsel who understand the importance of human rights. She has told me that there will be a great deal of work for a skilled international lawyer who is prepared to stick up for liberty and so on.'

'And that's what you're going to stick up for? Liberty and so on?'

'That's what the work is. According to Betsi.'

'And does Betsi know about your long record as a persecutor? I mean, you're here to protect a biased Judge.'

'I think she knows as well as anyone, Rumpole, that I am an extremely fair man. With liberal opinions.'

'You made that clear to Betsi?'

'I think she knows that about me.'

'I expect she does. And on your future visits to Strasburg, will you be bringing your wife with you?'

'Marguerite is heavily engaged with her first aid classes to the Housewives' League in Waltham Cross.'

'That's all right then.' I poured out a further medicinal glass. 'Bollard, does it occur to you that what happened in the street wasn't an accident?'

'The car was out of control.'

'It seemed very much *in* control to me.'

'What do you mean?'

'Someone may not like you.'

'Who?' The possibility didn't seem to have occurred to the man.

'A jealous husband, perhaps. Or a boyfriend. Someone who took exception to your amorous adventures.'

'Rumpole! I have no idea what you're talking about.'

'Wasn't Betsi in your room rather late last night?'

'Of course she was.'

'Well, then.'

'We were discussing human rights.'

'I suppose that's another way of describing it.' I looked at the man without pleasure and emptied my glass.

It was Monday morning, the day dedicated to the rights of Amin Hashimi who had brought me to Europe and who, except for that moment when I had seen a cheque drawn on Netherbank, I had almost forgotten in a series of expensive and eventful meals.

I wasn't, I have to confess, feeling at my best on the day of the hearing. I have never tasted the bottom of a budgerigar's cage but I imagine it to be as dry as I felt that morning; added to which my head was stuffed with cotton wool penetrated, from time to time, with stabs of pain. Anxious supporters, interested speculators and the representatives of Her Majesty's Government, gathered in the sunshine outside the hotel and a fleet of taxis set off for the Cour Européenne des Droits de L'Homme.

I sat next to Betsi in the back of one taxi and told her that I hoped our driver was more reliable than the madman who nearly ran Ballard over the night before. 'There are some idiots in this town,' she said. 'I heard about that. It was absolutely unnecessary.'

'Unnecessary?'

'To drive so fast. Through the streets of the old town. The idiot was French, I have no doubt. They drive like madmen.'

The Court was a long, grey concrete erection beside a river, with two circular towers like gasworks sawn off crookedly. Inside, we had wandered, uncertain of the way, in what looked like the vast boiler-room of a ship, painted in nursery colours. We went up and down steel and wire staircases, and travelled in lifts whose glass sides let you see more of the journey than made you entirely comfortable. And then I was standing up at a desk in a huge courtroom. Across an expanse of blue carpet, so far away that I could hardly distinguish their features, sat the Judges in black gowns under a white ceiling perforated like a giant kitchen colander. Human rights, it seemed, like the scientific romances of H. G. Wells, had been set in the future and now the future had arrived with a rush and overtaken me before I was quite sure how to address it.

'Mr Rumpole' – the voice of the presiding Judge, a Dutchman, boomed electronically over the vasty hall of death – 'we have read the submission filed on behalf of your client. Would you now speak to your paper?'

'Speak to my paper?' It didn't sound much of an audience. I had been used to speaking to my Jury, so close that I could lower my voice, at dramatic moments, almost to a whisper. Now I was in contact only by microphone with the remote, international platoon of seven Judges: the Austrian, the Finn, the Slovene, the Hungarian, the British, the Irish and the Portuguese. In some glass case halfway between us, lit up like tropical fish, the translators were noiselessly mouthing my words in various languages which some of the Judges put on headphones to catch, and others, either superb linguists or premature adjudicators, didn't bother to fit over their ears.

'I haven't much to say to the paper, my Lords. But I have a point of the greatest importance to make to your Lordships.' I waited in silence for the maximum effect, and because I felt suddenly in need of a rest I leant on the desk in front of me for support. At long last the Irishman was good enough to say, 'And what is your point, Mr Rumpole?'

'My point is' – another stab of pain penetrated the cotton wool – 'that the learned Judge in this case was not only biased but bluffing. Not only prejudiced but perfidious. In fact, he might stand, if your Lordships will allow the phrase, as the personification of Perfidious Albion.'

For some reason I was rather pleased with this opening paragraph. I looked around and there, in an otherwise empty row at the back of the Court, I saw his Honour Judge Bloxham looking at me with ill-concealed hatred.

'Perfidious *what*, Mr Rumpole?' Some sort of panic had clearly affected the translator in the fish tank and the presiding Dutch Lordship asked for clarification.

'Albion, my Lord. An expression once popular on the

continent of Europe, in which you now sit. It described the hypocrisy and slyness of a certain class of Englishman.'

'You are using this expression to describe the learned Judge in this case?' The Finn's English was almost too perfect but he looked extremely interested.

'Indeed I am. We all know the Judge was prejudiced. He was as biased as a crooked roulette wheel. He'd picked up his so-called opinions in the back of a taxi. He hated all foreign students and he made that perfectly clear in his speech to the rugger buggers.' At this, I saw expressions of genuine despair in the fish tank and the presiding Hollander clearly couldn't believe his headphones.

'To the *what*?'

'To the rugby football players' annual dinner. You see, this is the point I wish to impress on your Lordships. We all have prejudices. You may have prejudices. So do I. I have always found, that is until I came here and sampled your excellent Tokay d'Alsace, that all discussions about the European Common Market were about ten points less interesting than watching paint dry. That was my prejudice and I freely and frankly admit it to your Lordships.' Here I looked down and saw the note Betsi Hoprecht had pushed on to my desk: CALL THEM THE COURT. WE DON'T HAVE LORDSHIPS IN EUROPE. 'But did the perfidious Judge admit his prejudices?' I boomed on. 'Did he come into Court and kick off with: "Members of the Jury, I personally cannot stick foreign students. The idea of a foreigner, particularly of the slightly tinted Middle-Eastern variety, makes my gorge rise to a dangerous level. I want that clearly understood. Now let's get on with it, shall we?"'

'And if he had said that?' Far, far away I heard the caressing voice of the Irish.

'If he had, we'd have all known where we were. The Jury could have marked its disapproval of such views by a not guilty verdict. I could have made considerable use of them in my final speech. Justice would not only have been done, but would clearly have been seen to have been done! But what did Judge Bloxham do?' I leant forward and whispered secretly to the Court through the microphone, in tones calculated to make its collective flesh creep. 'He decided to dissemble! He made up his mind to deceive. He set about to defraud. He very deliberately acted the part of a totally unbiased Judge, something which hardly exists in this imperfect world. And so, when he belatedly showed himself in his true colours, what was the unfortunate Mr Hashimi to think? What *could* he think? Except that his trial had been an elaborate charade performed by a Judge with the clear intention of deceiving the Jury, which was bad, and Counsel for the Defence which was, in my humble submission, unpardonable.'

My head had cleared and, as I spoke, I felt healthier, saner – even elated. I gave them my views on the perfidy of the Court of Appeal, only anxious to protect the reputation of a judge at the expense of justice. Peter Fishlock's résumé of the leading cases on bias came back to me and I took them through it. I even touched on the subject of human rights about which I had heard so much since I went into Europe. By the end of it, I thought that I had won over the Irish, although the Portuguese looked doubtful, and the Slovene had laid down his earphones and seemed to have fallen into a light doze. I turned up the volume of my peroration. 'Let us go on,' I told the seven, 'to a community of tolerance, a community which has shut the door on prejudice. To quote a great poet, who, like so many great poets, happened to write in English:

Forward, forward let us range,
Let the great world spin for ever down the ringing grooves of
    change.

Thro' the shadow of the globe we sweep into the younger day:
Better fifty years of Europe than a cycle of Cathay!

Then I sat down and applied the red-and-white spotted handkerchief to the slightly less fevered brow. Fishlock whispered, 'Well done!' Jameson gave me an admiring look and Betsi's eyes were glowing. And then Soapy Sam Ballard completely ruined my triumph by more or less throwing in the towel.

'Having heard Mr Rumpole,' the faint-heart representing Her Majesty's Government began, 'we cannot argue that the words spoken by the learned Judge at the rugby club dinner wouldn't be considered prejudiced by any reasonable man or woman. This must be borne in mind by the Court when considering if Amin Hashimi received a fair hearing by an impartial tribunal, within the terms of Article Six of the Convention for the protection of human rights . . .'

So there it was. I had taken a battering ram to the door of a castle which had been unlocked by its so-called defenders. It couldn't be called a famous victory. As we stood to bow and the Judges filed out, Betsi said we should get the result in three to six months and there was little doubt what it would be. On the other side of the Court the man from the consular service and Lady Mary were grouped round Billy Bloxham, as though he was the victim of a serious road accident. Sam Ballard, who had been looking gravely downcast, raised his eyes to smile across to Betsi. I noticed that she didn't smile back.

'So, Mr Rumpole. You have fought the good fight!'

'Too easy. Sam Ballard chucked in his hand.'

'He is very conscious of the importance we all attach to human rights. I told him that we need lawyers with such a fine record as you have, Mr Rumpole.'

'And did you tell him that a lot of European cases might come his way if he showed himself a good libertarian?'

Betsi Hoprecht and I were standing by a table in the airport bar. Jeremy Jameson was waiting in line to pay for the last round of European Court drinks, and Poppy had gone off shopping. Now Betsi gave me a smile which I can only describe as conspiratorial and put a brown hand on my arm, a touch so light I hardly felt it. 'He might have thought that. I don't know what went through his mind.'

'You had a good many little chats with Soapy Sam, didn't you?'

'It's always best' – Betsi was still smiling – 'to get to know the opposition.'

'You were in his room at night, weren't you? Painting a rosy picture of his future as an international lawyer.'

'We drank beer out of his refrigerator, certainly.'

'And Article Six of the Convention was your pillow talk?'

'Pillow talk? I think I don't know that phrase. Pillow talk?'

'Were you and Sam' – I put the question direct – 'in bed together?'

'Me and *Mr Ballard*? In bed together? What a ridiculous idea! You must be making a very big joke, Mr Rumpole.' Betsi wasn't just smiling then; she threw back her blonde hair and laughed loudly and clearly enough to scare the dwarf and startle the maidens on the other side of the Rhine. Jeremy Jameson was coming towards us with his hand round three eaux de vie and I felt an immediate need to slip off to the gents.

When I came back the bar was even fuller. I pushed my way towards the table in the corner and saw Betsi and Jameson with their heads together. My hearing isn't altogether what it was, and I can't be sure of this, but I think I heard the M.E.P. say, 'He won't talk now. He'll soon be on his way home.' Then they clinked their glasses together, drank and Betsi turned and saw me. I had the distinct feeling that I wasn't, at that moment, a welcome sight.

'Who won't talk now?' I asked her.

'Oh, no one you know, I think. We were discussing another case altogether.' And then she fell back, as she had with the unfortunate Ballard, on promises. 'But perhaps you will be asked to argue it for us. When the time comes.' Then the crackling, amplified voice of Europe announced that the flight to London Heathrow was boarding immediately from gate number three. I was, I must confess, quite relieved to hear it.

A bright spring turned into a long, wet summer and then, in September, pale sunshine returned. During those months Ballard complained that none of the promised briefs in international cases arrived on his desk, but I had almost forgotten the weekend in Europe until Peter Fishlock rang to say that we had won an almighty success in Strasburg, and Betsi and Jeremy and all our friends sent greetings and congratulations. I sat at breakfast that Saturday morning and felt curiously little elation. Was that because it all seemed so long ago and had none of the immediate excitement of a jury verdict on the last day of the trial? My *joie de vivre* was at a low level that weekend anyway as Hilda's old schoolfriend, Dodo

Mackintosh, was inhabiting the mansion flat in return for the hospitality she had shown to She Who Must in Cornwall during the Hashimi appeal.

'Dodo has suggested a trip to Kingslake, Rumpole. She says the garden has been thrown open to the public.'

'Sounds exciting. I'm sure you'll both have a rattling good time.' I saw a fine prospect of a solo lunch in the pub, and a snooze by the gas fire, opening before me.

'Of course you're coming too, Rumpole. It's about time you got a little fresh air into your lungs. And the herbaceous border at Kingslake will come as a nice change from all those squalid little criminals you spend your time with.'

'I don't suppose Rumpole can tell a mahonia from an azalea, can he, Hilda?' Dodo Mackintosh, with what I took to be an evil glint in her eye, piled on the agony.

'Dodo's going to drive us to Sussex, Rumpole. It's very good of her. So you'd better gulp down that coffee. We're going to make an early start.' I saw it was no time for argument. She has to be obeyed.

Always distrust people who have nicknames for their motor cars and, when my wife and her old schoolfriend were strapped into the front, and I had poured myself into the back, where I found precious little leg-room, Dodo switched on the engine which coughed, spluttered and started, my heart sank when she chirped, 'Buzzfuzz *is* in a good mood this morning.' It remained at a low level during the journey by reason of Dodo's habit of driving very slowly along clear and straight roads, and then accelerating wildly at intersections or dangerous corners.

When, after what seemed a lifetime of alternating bursts of boredom and terror, we got to Kingslake, it proved to be a greenish-grey Regency house in a poor state of repair – and full of draughts, I should imagine – with gumboots in the hallways. Dodo and Hilda had been gossiping about various mistresses and ex-pupils from their old school, and this less than fascinating conversation continued as we paid our duty call to the dahlias and chrysanthemums in the wide herbaceous border. It was around midday and the alcohol content in the Rumpole blood had fallen to a dangerous point. Muttering something about a search for the gents, I stole away through the rose garden and down the gravel paths between the greenhouses which looked in dire need of a lick of paint.

Round a corner I came to what I took to be a back door of the house. It was open and I had a view of a stone passageway, the regulation number of gumboots and pegs for tweed caps, battered panamas and some disintegrating macs. I also saw a wooden table with a tray-like top holding a welcoming collection of bottles, some glasses and a corkscrew. A desperate plan crossed my mind; I would pour myself a large snort, leave a more than adequate supply of money and retreat to a quiet refuge behind the cucumber frames. I had put my hand in my pocket and was advancing on the drinks table when a door opened further down the hallway and a voice boomed, 'The house is not, repeat not, open to the public!' It was Lady Mary Parsloe, looking windblown and armed with what I took to be an extra large gin-and-tonic. She narrowed her eyes, looked at me as though I were a serious blight on the roses and said, 'By God, it's you!'

'I'm sorry. Is this your house?'

'Eddie's house. His family house, as it so happens. He's in London, trying to assess the damage you've done.'

'Damage?'

'Peddling human rights. What human rights? The right to get us all blown up. I suppose that's your idea of freedom?'

'You're talking about the Hashimi case?'

'*And* I'm talking about your friends Fräulein Hoprecht and that dreadful fat Member of the European Parliament. I bet they're celebrating! Why aren't you with them, with your nose in the trough?'

'I thought they were your friends, too. You and your husband were at dinner . . .'

'Eddie was there to see what they were up to. He knew perfectly well, of course. Not that we'll ever prove anything now that your Mr Hashimi has walked away from us. With a life sentence in front of him, Eddie thinks he'd've talked eventually. Oh, you know what I'm talking about.'

'I'm afraid I don't.'

'The bloody great mess you've got us in!' She made an expansive gesture with her hand holding the glass, slopping some of the drink which settled the dust on the stairs of the hallway.

'Can I ask you a question?'

'I suppose so. I don't promise I'll answer it.'

'Can I have a drink?'

She stood looking at me, an old, untidy woman, swaying slightly like an unpruned shrub in a high wind. 'I'll pay for it,' I told her.

'Pay for it? You think that makes it all right, don't you? You think everything's all right if you pay. Or someone pays you. How much did they pay you? The gun-runners?'

'I got legal aid from the Court in Strasburg. Who were the gun-runners exactly?'

'Not guns, was it? Something much more than guns. You honestly don't know?'

'Honestly.'

'Then you should. You should know what you've done to the world.' She moved unsteadily to the table. 'What is it you want?'

'A brandy-and-soda,' I suggested, 'would be very welcome.' If I was going to be operated on, I needed an anaesthetic. I saw her pick up a bottle and wave it vaguely in the air. 'I'll pour it out,' I told her.

'You pour it out,' she said, 'and come into the kitchen. Don't let it go any further. Eddie would kill me, but I think you bloody well ought to know.'

A quarter of an hour later I walked across the garden alone. Should I have guessed? Were there moments that should have told me the truth? Betsi grabbing a newspaper? A car threatening Ballard – an incident Betsi Hoprecht said was 'unnecessary'? A few words overheard in the bar at Strasburg airport? Should these things have told me the truth, and was I getting too old to take the hint?

The sky had darkened as if in warning of a storm but the earth, the grass and the dahlias, golden chrysanthemums and blue Michaelmas daisies were still bright and stood out vividly against the gun-metal grey of the sky. Hilda and Dodo were walking towards me.

'Rumpole! Where on earth have you been?'

'Here and there. I had a look inside the house.'

'You've been drinking.'

'I've been listening.'

'Who to?'

'A woman who owns this garden. I met her when I was doing a case.'

'Oh, was it one you lost?'

'No, I won it. Unfortunately.'

'Dodo knows a place where we can have lunch in Haywards Heath.'

'They do homemade soups.' Dodo opened an unexciting prospect.

Whose fault was it that the truth never emerged and that deadly Russian weapons were still being traded to Iraq? Was it my fault, or Ballard's fault when he was tempted to show his libertarian principles in the hope of future briefs? Was it all because Billy Bloxham let his prejudices show at a rugby club dinner, or because a cub reporter heard what he said? Or because a new Court had been invented to take care of the Rights of Man? Who should I blame – or was I to blame myself?

These questions would never have occurred to me but for an encounter with a half-drunk woman who had thrown her garden open to the public. What she had told me were official secrets, and included the fact that the arms trade was being financed through Netherbank in London, and that George Freeling was an investigator reporting back to some modestly retiring Department of State. So my young Iraqi client, a servant of the arms dealers, among whom Betsi and Jameson were numbered, was chosen to silence him for ever. My job had been to get him out of prison before he decided to talk in exchange for parole. These important facts, like Billy Bloxham's racist opinions, never saw the light in the Old Bailey.

I put down my spoon in the restaurant, which was without a licence and served iced tea with the carrot soup and vegetarian quiche. 'It's Billy Bloxham's fault,' I said. 'He should never have developed a taste for rugby football.'

'*Do* stop thinking about your work, Rumpole,' Hilda rebuked me. 'Can't you enjoy a day out in the country?'

Quite honestly I couldn't. I was looking forward to Monday and a receiving of stolen fish at Acton. It had nothing to do with human rights at all.

Rumpole and the Angel of Death

I have, from time to time in these memoirs, had some harsh things to say about judges, utterances of mine which may, I'm afraid, have caused a degree of resentment among their assembled Lordships who like nothing less than being judged. To say that their profession makes them an easy prey to the terrible disease of judgeitis, a mysterious virus causing an often fatal degree of intolerance, pomposity and self-regard, is merely to state the obvious. Being continually bowed to and asked 'If your Lordship pleases?' is likely to unhinge the best-balanced legal brain; and I have never thought that those who were entirely sane would undertake the thankless task of judging their fellow human beings anyway. However, the exception to the above rule was old Chippy Chippenham, who managed to hold down the job of a senior circuit Judge, entitled to try murder cases somewhere in the wilds of Kent, and remain, whenever I had the luck to appear before him, not only sensible but quite remarkably polite.

Chippy had been a soldier before he was called to the Bar. He had a pink, outdoors sort of face, a small scourer of a grey moustache and bright eyes which made him look younger than he must have been. When I appeared before him I would invariably get a note from him saying, 'Horace, how about a jar when all this nonsense is over?' I would call round to his room and he would open a bottle of average claret (considerably better, that is, than my usual Château Thames Embankment), and we would discuss old times, which usually meant recalling the fatuous speeches of some more than usually tedious prosecutor.

In Court Chippy sat quietly. He summed up shortly and perfectly fairly (that I *did* object to – a fair summing-up is most likely to get the customer convicted). His sentences erred, if at all, on the side of clemency and were never accompanied by any sort of sermon or homily on the repulsive nature of the accused. I once defended a perfectly likeable old countryman, a gamekeeper turned poacher from somewhere south of Sevenoaks, who, on hearing that his wife was dying from a painful and inoperable cancer, took down his gun and shot her through the head. 'Deciding who will live and who will die,' Chippy told him, having more or less ordered the Jury to find manslaughter, 'is a task Almighty God approaches only with caution,' and he gave my rustic client a conditional discharge, presumably on the condition that he didn't shoot any more wives.

The last time I appeared before Chippy he had changed. He found it difficult to remember the name of the fraudster in the dock and whether he'd dealt in spurious loft conversions or non-existent caravans. He shouted at the usher for not supplying him with pencils when a box was on his desk, and quite forgot to invite me round for a jar. Later, I heard he had retired and gone to live with some relatives in London. Later still, such are the revenges brought in by the whirligig of time, he appeared in the curious case of *R*. v. *Dr Elizabeth Ireton*, as the victim of an alleged murder.

The Angel of Death no doubt appears in many guises. She may not always be palely beautiful and shrouded in black. In the particularly tricky case which called on my considerable skills and had a somewhat surprising result, the fell spirit appeared as a dumpy, grey-haired, bespectacled lady who wore sensible shoes, a shapeless tweed skirt, a dun-coloured cardigan and a cheerful smile. This last was hard to explain considering her position of peril in Number One Court at the Bailey. She was a Dr Elizabeth Ireton, known to her many patients and admirers as Dr Betty, and she carried on her practice from a chaotic surgery in Notting Hill Gate.

I'll admit I was rather distracted that breakfast time in the kitchen of our so-called mansion flat in the Gloucester Road. I was trying to gain as much strength as possible from a couple of eggs on a fried slice, pick up a smattering of the events of the day from the wireless and make notes in the case of Dr Ireton, with whom I had a conference booked for five o'clock. My usual calm detachment about that case was unsettled by the discovery that the corpse in question was that of Judge Chippy with whom I had shared so many a friendly jar. There was little time to spare before I had to set off for a banal matter of receiving a huge consignment of frozen oven-ready Thai dinners in Snaresbrook.

Accordingly, I stuffed the papers in my battered briefcase, placed my pen in the top pocket and submerged my dirty plate and cutlery in the washing-up bowl, in accordance with the law formulated by She Who Must Be Obeyed.

'Rumpole!' The voice of authority was particularly sharp that morning. 'Have you the remotest idea what you have done?'

'A remote idea, Hilda. I have prepared for work. I am going out into the harsh, unsympathetic world of a Crown Court for the sole purpose of keeping this leaky old mansion flat afloat and well-stocked with Fairy Liquid and suchlike luxuries . . .'

'Is this the way you usually prepare for work?'

'By consuming a light cooked breakfast and doing a bit of last-minute homework? How else?'

'And I suppose you intend to appear in Court with the butter knife sticking out of your top pocket, having thrown your fountain-pen into the sink.'

A glance at my top pocket told me that She Who Must Be Obeyed, forever eagle-eyed, had sized up the situation pretty accurately. 'A moment of confusion,' I agreed. 'My mind was on more serious subjects. Particularly it was on a Dr Ireton, up on a charge of wilful murder.'

'Dr Betty?' As usual Hilda was about four steps ahead of me. 'She's the most wonderful person. Truly wonderful!'

'You're not thinking of her as Quack By Appointment to the Rumpole household?' I asked with some apprehension. 'She's accused of doing in his Honour Charles Chippy Chippenham, a circuit Judge for whom I had an unusual affection.'

'She didn't do it, Rumpole!'

'My dear old thing, I'm sure you know best.'

'I was at school with her. She was a house monitor and we all simply adored her. I promised you'd get her off.'

'Hilda, I know you have enormous respect for me as a courtroom genius, but your good Dr Betty was apparently a leading light in Lethe, a society to promote the joys of euthanasia . . .'

'It's not a question of your being a genius, Rumpole. It's just that I told Betty Ireton that you'd have me to answer to if you didn't win her case. I know quite well she believes passionately' – and here I saw Hilda watching me closely as I dried the fountain-pen – 'that life shouldn't be needlessly prolonged. Not, at any rate, after old people have completely lost their senses.'

The case of the frozen Thai dinners wound remorselessly on and was finally adjourned to the next day. When I got back to Chambers I found my room inhabited by a tallish, thinnish man in a blue suit with hair just over his ears and the sort of moustache once worn by South American revolutionaries and now sported by those who travel the Home Counties trying to flog double-glazing to the natives. He had soft, brown eyes, a wristwatch with a heavy metallic strap which gleamed in imitation of gold, and all around him hung a deafening odour of aftershave. This intruder appeared to be measuring my room, and the top of my desk, with a long, wavering, metal tape.

'At long last,' I said, as I unloaded the antique briefcase. 'Bollard's got the decorators in.'

'It's Horace Rumpole, isn't it? I'm Vince.'

'Vince?'

'Vince Blewitt.'

'Glad to know you, Mr Blewitt, but you can't start rubbing down now. I'm about to have a conference.' I was a little puzzled; we'd had the decorators in more than once in the last half-century and none of them had introduced themselves so eagerly.

'Rubbing down?' The man seemed mystified.

'Preparing to paint.'

'Oh, that!' Vince was laughing, showing off a line of teeth which would have graced a television advertisement. 'No, I'm not here regarding the paint. I'm just measuring your work-space so I can see if it makes sense in terms of your personal through-put in the organization's overall workload. That's what I'm regarding. And I have to tell you, Horace, I'm going to have a job justifying your area in terms of your contribution to overall Chambers' market profitability.'

'I have no idea what you're talking about.' I sat down wearily in the workspace area and lit a small cigar. 'And I'm not sure I want to. But I assume you're only passing through?'

'Hasn't Sam Ballard told you? My appointment was con-firmed at the last Chambers' meeting.'

'I've given up Chambers' meetings,' I told him. 'I regard them as a serious health hazard.'

'I'm really going to enjoy this opportunity. That Dot Clap-ton. Am I going to enjoy working with her! Isn't she something else?'

'What *else* do you mean? She's our general typist and tel-ephone answerer.'

'And much more. That girl's got a big future in front of her!' Here, the man laughed in a curiously humourless way. 'Oh, and there's another thought I'd like to share with you.'

'Please. Don't share anything else with me.'

'Looking at your own workload, Horace, what strikes me is this: you fight all your cases. They go on far too long. Of course you get daily refreshers, don't you?'

'Whenever I can.' All I could think of at that moment was how refreshing it would be to get this bugger Blewitt out of my room.

'But the brief fee for the first day has far more profitability?'

'If you're trying to say it's worth more money, the answer is yes.'

'So why not accept the brief and bargain for a plea, what-ever you do? Then you'd be free to take another one the next day. And so on. Do I need to spell it out? That way you could increase market share on your personal achievement record.'

'And a lot of innocent people might end up in chokey. You say you've joined our Chambers? Are you a lawyer?'

'Good heavens, no!' Blewitt seemed to find the suggestion

mildly amusing. 'My experience was in business. Sam Ballard head-hunted me from catering.'

'Catering, eh?' I looked at him closely. He had, I thought, a distinctly fishy appearance. 'Frozen Thai dinners come into it at all, did they?'

'From time to time. Do you have an interest in oriental cuisine, Horace?'

'None at all. But I do have an interest in my conference in a murder case which is just about to arrive.'

'Likely to be a plea?' Blewitt appeared hopeful.

'Over my dead body.'

'Well, make sure it's a maximum contributor to Chambers' cashflow.'

'That's quite impossible,' I told him. 'If I don't do this case free, gratis and for nothing, I shall get into serious trouble with She Who Must Be Obeyed.'

'Whoever's that?'

'Be so good as to leave me, Blewitt. I see you have a great deal to learn about life in Equity Court. Things you'd never pick up in catering.'

He left me then, and I thought I wasn't only landed with the Defence of Dr Betty Ireton but the Defence of our Chambers against the death-dealing ministrations of Vincent Blewitt.

After our new legal administrator had left my presence, I refreshed my memory, from the papers in front of me, on the circumstances of old Chippy's death.

It seemed that he had a considerable private fortune passed down from some eighteenth-century Chippenham who had ransacked the Far East whilst working for the East India Company. He had lived with his wife Connie in a large Victorian house near Holland Park until she died of cancer. Chippy was heartbroken and began to show the early symptoms of the disease which led to his retirement from the Bench – Alzheimer's. This is a condition in which the mind atrophies, the patient becomes apparently infantile, incomprehensible and incontinent. Early symptoms are a certain vagueness and loss of memory (such as washing up your fountain-pen? Perish the thought!). After the complaint has taken hold, the victim remains physically healthy and may live on for many years to the distress, no doubt, of the relatives. Whether, although unable to express themselves in words, those with Alzheimer's may still enjoy moments of happiness must remain a mystery.

As he became increasingly helpless, Chippy's nephew Dickie and Dickie's wife, Ursula, moved in to look after him. They kept their ten-year-old son, Andrew, reasonably quiet and they devoted themselves to the old man. He was also cared for by a Nurse Pargeter, who came when the young Chippenhams went out in the evenings, and by Dr Betty, who, according to the witnesses' statements, got on like a house on fire with the old man.

In fact they were such good friends that Dr Betty used to call at least one or two times a week and sit with Chippy. They would drink a small whisky together and the old man had, in the doctor's presence, occasional moments of lucidity, when he would laugh at an old legal joke or weep like a child when remembering his wife. When she left, Dr Betty would, on her own admission, leave her patient a sleeping tablet, or even two, to see him through the night. So far, Dr Betty's behaviour couldn't be criticized, except for the fact that she thought it right to prescribe barbiturates. But, to be fair to her, she was told that these were the soporifics Chippy relied on in the days when he still had all his marbles.

One night the Chippenhams went out to dinner. Nurse Pargeter had been engaged with another patient and Dr Betty volunteered to sit with Chippy. (I couldn't help wondering if her kindness on that occasion included a release from this vale of tears.) When the Chippenhams arrived home Dr Betty told them that her patient was asleep and she left then. The old man died that night with a suddenness that the nurse, who found him in the morning, thought suspicious. In an autopsy his stomach was found to contain the residue of a massive overdose of the sleeping tablets Dr Betty had prescribed and also a considerable quantity of alcohol. Dr Betty was well known as a passionate supporter of euthanasia and she was charged with murder. She was given bail and her trial was due to start in three weeks' time.

'Of course I remember Hilda. She was such a quiet, shy girl

at school.' I looked at Dr Betty, sitting in my client's chair in Chambers, and came to the conclusion that here was a quite unreliable witness. The suggestion of a quiet and shy Hilda was not, on the face of it, one that would satisfy the burden of proof.

'She told me that you don't think life should be needlessly prolonged in certain circumstances. Is that right?'

'Oh, yes.' The doctor, I judged, was in her late sixties but her smile was that of an innocent; her eyes behind her spectacles were shining with as girlish an enthusiasm as when she led her mustard-keen team out on to the hockey field. 'Death is such a lovely thing when you're feeling really poorly,' she said. 'I don't know why we don't all give it a hearty welcome.'

'"The grave's a fine and private place,"' I reminded her, '"But none, I think, do there embrace."'

'How do we know, Mr Rumpole? How can we possibly know? Are you really sure there won't be any cuddles beyond the grave?'

'Cuddles? I hardly think so.'

'We're so prejudiced against the dead!' Dr Betty was almost giggling and her glasses were glinting. 'Rather like there used to be prejudice against women when I went in for medicine. There must be so many really nice dead people!'

'You believe in the afterlife?'

'Oh, I think so. But whatever sort of life goes on after death, I'd be out of a job there, wouldn't I? No one would need a doctor.'

'Or a barrister?' Or might there be some celestial tribunal at which a crafty advocate could get a sinner off hell? Plenty of briefs, of course, but my heart sank at the thought of eternal work before a jury of prejudiced saints. I decided to return to the business in hand. 'Do you think that sufferers from Alzheimer's disease are appropriate candidates for the Elysian Fields?'

'Of course they are! I'd fully decided to send old Chippy off there as soon as I judged the time was ripe.'

My heart sank further. The danger of having a conference with customers accused of murder is that they may tell you they did the deed and then, of course, the fight is over and you have no alternative but to stagger into Court with your hands up. That's why, during such conferences, it's much wiser to discuss the Maastricht Treaty or Whither the Deutschmark? than to refer directly to the crude facts of the charge. It was my error to have done so and now I had to tell Dr Betty that she had as good as pleaded guilty.

'No, I haven't,' she told me, still, it seemed, in a merry mood. 'I'm not guilty of anything.'

'You're not?'

'Of course not! It's true I was prepared to release old Chippy from this unsatisfactory world, when the time came.'

'And it had come the night he died?'

'No, it certainly had not! He was still having lucid intervals. I would have done it eventually, but not then.' I meant to rob the bank, Guv, but not on that particular occasion: it didn't sound much of a defence, but I was determined to make the most of it.

'So do you think' – I threw Dr Betty a lifeline – 'Chippy might have got depressed during the night and committed suicide?'

'Of course not!' I'd never had a client who was so cheerfully anxious to sink herself. 'He was an old soldier. He always told me that he regarded suicide as cowardice in the face of the enemy. He'd have battled on against all odds, until I decided to sound the retreat.'

It hadn't been an easy day and to go straight home to Froxbury Mansions without a therapeutic visit to Pommeroy's Wine Bar would have been like facing an operation without an anaesthetic. So, because my alcohol content had sunk to a dangerous low, I pushed open the glass door and made for the bar. I saw, on top of a stool, a crumpled figure slumped in deepest gloom and attacking what I thought was far from his first gin-and-Dubonnet. Closer examination proved him to be our learned clerk.

'Cheer up, Henry,' I said, when I had called upon Jack Pommeroy to pour a large Château Fleet Street and mark it up on the slate. 'It may never happen!'

'It *has* happened, Mr Rumpole. And I could manage another

of the same if you're ordering. Our new legal administrator has happened.'

'You mean the blighter Blewitt?'

'Tell me honestly, Mr Rumpole, have you ever seriously considered taking your own life?'

'No.' It was perfectly true. Even in the darkest days, even when I was put on trial for professional misconduct after a run-in with a hostile judge and when She Who Must Be Obeyed's disapproval of my way of life meant that there was not only an east wind blowing in Froxbury Mansions but a major hurricane, I could always find solace in a small cigar, a glass of Pommeroy's plonk, a stroll down to the Old Bailey in the autumn sunshine and the possibility of a new brief to test my forensic skills. 'I have never felt the slightest temptation to place my head in the gas oven.'

'Neither have I,' Henry told me and I congratulated him. 'We're all electric at home. But, I have to say, I'm tempted by a handful of aspirins.'

'Messy,' I told him. 'And, in my experience, not entirely dependable. But why this desperate remedy?'

'I have lost everything, Mr Rumpole.'

'Everything?'

'Everything I care about. Dot Clapton and I. Our relationship is over.'*

'Really? I didn't think it ever began.'

'Too right, Mr Rumpole. Too very right!' Our clerk laughed bitterly. 'And my job has gone. What's my future? Staying at home . . .'

'In Bexleyheath?'

'Exactly. Helping out with a bit of shopping. Decorating the bathroom. And my wife will lose all respect for me as a breadwinner.'

'Your wife, the Alderperson?'

'Chairman of Social Services. It gives her a lot of status.'

'You'll have a good deal of time for your amateur dramatics.'

'I have been offered the lead in *Laburnum Grove*. I turned it down.'

*See 'Rumpole on Trial' in *Rumpole on Trial*, Penguin Books, 1993.

'But why, Henry?'

'Because I'm losing my job, and I've got no heart left for taking on a leading role!'

Further inquiry revealed what I should have known if I'd had more of a taste for Chambers' meetings. The skinflint Bollard had decided to get rid of a decent old-fashioned barrister's clerk who got a percentage of our takings and to appoint a legal administrator, at what I was to discover was a ludicrously high salary. 'Vince takes over at the end of the month,' Henry told me.

'Vince?'

'He asked me to call him Vince. He said that for us two to be on first-name terms would "ease the process". And what makes me so bitter, Mr Rumpole, is I think he's got his eye on our Dot.' Mizz Clapton is so casually beautiful that I thought she must have many eyes on her, but I didn't think it would cheer up our soon to be ex-clerk to tell him that. Instead I gave him my considered opinion on what I took to be the heart or nub of the matter.

'This man, Blewitt,' I said, 'appears to be a considerable blot on the landscape.'

'You're not joking, Mr Rumpole.'

'One that must be removed for the general health of Chambers.'

'And of me in particular, Mr Rumpole, as your long-serving and faithful clerk.'

'Then all I can tell you, Henry, is that a way must be found.'

'Agreed, Mr Rumpole, but who is to find it?'

It seemed to me a somewhat dimwitted question, and one that Henry would never have asked had he been entirely sober. 'Who else?' I asked, purely rhetorically, 'but the learned Counsel who found a defence in the Penge Bungalow affair, which looked, at first sight, even blacker than the case of the blot Blewitt – or even the predicament of Dr Betty Ireton.'

'Then I'll leave it to you, Mr Rumpole.'

'Many doubtful characters have said those very words, Henry, and not been disappointed.'

'And I could do with another gin-and-Dubonnet, sir. Seeing as you're in the chair.'

So Jack Pommeroy added to the figure on the slate and Henry seemed to cheer up considerably. 'I just heard a really ripe one in here, Mr Rumpole, from old Jo Castor who clerks Mr Digby Tappit in Crown Office Row. Do you know, sir, the one about the sleeveless woman?'

'I do not know it, Henry. But I suppose I very soon shall.'

As a matter of fact I never did. My much-threatened clerk began to tell me this ripe anecdote which had an extremely lengthy build-up. Long before the delayed climax I shut off, being lost in my own thoughts. Did old Chippy Chippenham die in the course of nature or was he pushed? If he had been, would he have felt as merciful to Dr Betty as he had to my rustic client who shot his sick wife?

Had one long, confused afternoon arrived when Chippy muttered to himself, 'I have been half in love with easeful Death'? The sound of the words gave me a lift only otherwise to be had from Pommeroy's plonk and I intoned privately and without interrupting Henry's flow:

> 'Now more than ever seems it rich to die,
> To cease upon the midnight with no pain,
> While thou art pouring forth thy soul abroad
> In such an ecstasy!'

Then Henry laughed loudly; his story had apparently reached its triumphant and no doubt obscene conclusion. I joined in for the sake of manners, but now I was thinking that I had to win the case of Blewitt as well as that of Dr Betty, and I had no idea how I was to emerge triumphant from either.

'We don't call this a memorial service. We call it a joyful thanksgiving for the life of his Honour Judge Chippenham.' So said the Reverend Edgedale, the Temple's resident cleric. Sitting at the back of the congregation, I thought that old Chippy wasn't in a position to mind much what we called it, and wondered if some of the villains he'd felt it necessary to send away to chokey would call it a joyful thanksgiving for his death. Chippy was dead, a word we all shy away from nowadays when almost anything else goes. What would Mizz Liz Probert have said? Old Chippy had become a non-living person. And then I thought how glowingly Dr Betty had talked about Chippy's present position, happily unaware of the length of the sermon – 'Chippy was the name he rejoiced in since his first term at Charterhouse, but you and I can hardly think of anyone with less of a chip on his shoulder' – and the increasing hardness of the pews. I looked around at the assembled mourners, Mr Injustice Graves, and various circuit judges and practising hacks who were no doubt wondering how soon they might expect a joyful thanksgiving for their own lives. I peered up at the stained-glass windows in the old round church built for the Knights Templar, who had gone off to die in the Crusades without the benefit of a memorial service, and then I fell into a light doze.

I was woken up by a peal on the organ and old persons stumbling across my knees, anxious to get out of the place which gave rise to uncomfortable thoughts of mortality. And, when we joined in the general rush for the light of day, I heard a gentle voice, 'Mr Rumpole, how delighted Uncle Chippy would have been that you could join us.'

I focused on a pleasant-looking, youngish woman, pushing back loose hair which strayed across her forehead. Beside her stood an equally pleasant, tall man in his forties. Both of them smiled as though their natural cheerfulness could survive even this sad occasion.

'Dick and Ursula Chippenham,' the tall man bent down considerately to inform me. 'Uncle Chippy was always talking about you. Said you could be a devilish tricky customer in Court but he always enjoyed having you in for a jar when the battle was over.'

'Chippy was so fond of his jar. What he wanted was to ask all his real friends back to toast his memory,' Ursula told me. 'Do say you'll come!'

'I honestly don't think . . .' What I meant to say was that I already felt a little guilty for slipping in to the memorial service of a man when I was defending his possible murderer. Could I, in all conscience, accept even one jar from his bereaved family?

'It's thirty-one Dettingen Road, Holland Park.' Dick Chippenham smiled down on me from a great height. 'Chippy would have been so delighted if you were there to say goodbye.'

As I say, I felt guilty but I also had a strong desire to see what we old-fashioned hacks call the *locus in quo* – the scene of the crime.

It was an English spring, that is to say, dark clouds pressed down on London and produced a doleful weeping of rain. I splurged out on a taxi from the Temple to Dettingen Road and spent some time in it while the approach to number thirty-one was blocked by a huge, masticating rubbish lorry which gave out strangled cries such as 'This vehicle is reversing!' as it tried to extricate itself from a jam of parked cars. Whistling dustmen were collecting bins from the front entrance of sedate, white-stuccoed houses, pouring their contents into the jaws of the curiously articulate lorry and then returning the empty bins, together with a small pile of black plastic bags, given, by courtesy of the council, to their owners. I paid the immobile taxi off and took a brisk walk in the sifting rain towards number thirty-one. As I did so, I saw a solemn boy come down the steps of the house and, in a sudden, furtive motion, collect the black plastic bags from the top of the dustbin, stuff them under his school blazer and disappear into a side entrance of the house. I climbed up the front steps, rang the bell and was admitted by a butler-like person who I thought must have been specially hired for Chippy's send-off. Sounds of the usual high cocktail-party chatter with no particular note of grief in it were emerging from the sitting-room. The wake seemed to be a great deal more cheerful than the weather.

Ursula Chippenham bore down on me with a welcome glass of champagne. 'We're so glad you came.' She moved me into a corner and spoke confidentially, much more in sorrow than in anger. 'Dr Betty got on so terribly well with Chippy. We never thought for a moment that she'd do anything like that.'

'Perhaps she didn't.'

'Of course, Dick and I don't want anything terrible to happen to her.'

'Neither do I.'

'We know you'll do your very best for her. Chippy always

said you were quite brilliant with a jury on a good day, when you didn't go over the top and start spouting bits of poetry at them.'

'That was very civil of him.'

'And, of course, Dr Betty and Chippy became best friends. Towards the end, that was.'

'I suppose you know that she was against . . . Well, prolonging life?' Or in favour of killing people, I suppose I would have said, if I were appearing for the Prosecution.

'Of course. But I never dreamt she'd do anything . . . Well, without discussing it with the family. She seemed so utterly trustworthy! Of course we hadn't known her all that long. She only came to us when Chippy took against poor Dr Eames.'

'When was that exactly?'

'There are certain rules, Mr Rumpole. Certain traditions of the Bar which you might find it convenient to remember.' Chippy had said that to me in Court when I asked a witness who happened to work in advertising if that didn't mean he'd taken up lying as a career. In his room afterwards he'd said, 'Horace, sometimes I wish you'd stop being such an *original* barrister.' 'Is trying to squeeze information out of a prosecution witness while consuming her champagne at a family wake in the best traditions of the Bar?' he would have asked. 'Probably not, my Lord,' I would have told Chippy, 'but aren't you curious to know exactly how you met your death?'

'Only about six months ago.' Ursula answered my question willingly. 'Eames is a bit politically correct, as a matter of fact. He kept telling Chippy that at least his illness meant that his place on the Bench was available to a member of an ethnic minority.'

'Not much of a bedside manner, this quack Eames?'

'Oh, I don't think Chippy minded that so much. It was when Eames said, "No more claret and no more whisky to help you to go to sleep, for the rest of your life", that the poor chap had to go.'

'Understandable.'

'Dick thought so too.'

'And how did you happen to hear of Dr Betty Ireton?'

'Some friends of mine in Cambridge Terrace said she was an

absolute angel. Oh, there you are, Pargey! This is Nurse Pargeter, Mr Rumpole. Pargey was an angel to Chippy too.' The nurse who was wandering by had reddish hair, a long equine face and suddenly startled eyes. She wasn't in uniform, but was solemnly dressed in a plain black frock and white collar. I had already seen her, standing alone, taking care not to look at the other guests in case they turned and noticed her loneliness.

Ursula Chippenham drifted off to greet some late arrivals. 'Are you family?' the nurse asked in a surprisingly deep and unyielding voice, with a trace of a Scottish accent.

'No, I'm a barrister. An old friend of Chippy's . . '

'Mr Rumpole? I think I've heard him mention you.'

'I'm glad. And then, of course, I have the unenviable task of defending Dr Betty Ireton. Mrs Chippenham says she got on rather well with the old boy.'

'Defend her?' Nurse Pargeter suddenly looked as relentless as John Knox about to denounce the monstrous regiment of women. 'She cannot be defended. I warned the Chippenhams against her. They can't say I didn't warn them. I told them all about that dreadful Lethe.'

'Everyone *can* be defended,' I corrected her as gently as possible. 'Of course whether the Defence is successful is entirely another matter.'

'I prefer to remember the Ten Commandments on the subject. ' Pargey was clearly of a religious persuasion.

Those nicknames, I thought – Pargey and Chippy – you might as well be in a school dormitory or at a gathering of very old actors.

'Oh, the Ten Commandments.' I tried not to sound dismissive of this ancient code of desert law. 'Not too closely observed nowadays, are they? I mean adultery's about the only subject that seems to interest the newspapers, and coveting other people's oxen and asses is called leaving everything to market forces. And, as for worshipping graven images, think of the prices some of them fetch at Sotheby's. As for Thou shalt not kill – well, some people think that the terminally ill should be helped out of their misery.'

'And some people happen to believe in the sanctity of life.

And now, if you'll excuse me, Mr Rumpole, I have an important meeting to go to.'

As I watched her leave, I thought that I hadn't been a conspicuous success with Nurse Pargeter. Then a small boy piped up at my elbow, 'Would you like one of these, sir? I don't know what they are actually.' It was young Andrew Chippenham, with a plate of small brown envelope arrangements made of brittle pastry. I took one, bit into it and found, hardly to my delight, goat's cheese and some green, seaweed-like substance.

'You must be Andrew,' I said. The only genuine schoolboy around wasn't called Andy or Drew, or even Chippy, but kept his whole name, uncorrupted. 'And you go to Bolingbroke House?' I recognized the purple blazer with brass buttons. Bolingbroke was an expensive prep school in Kensington, which I thought must be so over-subscribed that the classrooms were used in a rota system and the unaccommodated pupils were sent out for walks in a crocodile formation, under the care of some bothered and junior teacher, round the streets of London. I had seen regiments of purple blazers marching dolefully as far as Gloucester Road; the exit from Bolingbroke House had a distinct look of the retreat from Moscow.

'How do you like being a waiter?' I asked Andrew, thinking it must be better than the daily urban trudge.

'Not much. I'd like to get back to my painting.'

'You're an artist?'

'Of course not.' He looked extremely serious. 'I mean painting my model aeroplanes.'

'How fascinating.' And then I lied as manfully as any unreliable witness. 'I was absolutely crazy about model aeroplanes when I was your age. Of course, that was a bit before Concorde.'

'Did you ever go in a Spitfire?' Andrew looked at me as though I had taken part in the Charge of the Light Brigade or was some old warrior from the dawn of time.

'Spitfires? I know all about Spitfires from my time in the R.A.F.' I forgot to tell him I was ground staff only. And then I said, 'I say, Andrew, I'd love to see your collection.' So he put down his plate of goat's cheese envelopes and we escaped from the party.

Andrew's room was on the third floor, at the back of the house. In the front, a door was open and I got a glimpse of a big, airy room with a bed stripped and the windows open. When I asked who slept there, he answered casually and without any particular emotion, 'That was Great-uncle Chippy's room. He's the one who died, you know.'

'I know. I suppose your parents' bedroom's on the floor below?' It wasn't the subtlest way of getting information.

'Oh, yes. I'm all alone up here now.' Andrew opened the door of his room which smelled strongly of glue and, I thought for a moment, was full of brightly coloured birds which, as I focused on them, became model aeroplanes swinging in the breeze from an open window. From what seemed to be every inch of the ceiling, a thread had been tied or tacked to hold up a fighter or an old-fashioned seaplane in full flight.

'That's the sort of Spitfire you piloted,' Andrew said, to my silent embarrassment. 'And that's a Wellington bomber like you had in the war.' I did remember the planes returning, when they were lucky, with a rear-gunner dead or wounded and the stink of blood and fear when the doors were opened. I had been young then, unbearably young, and I banished the memory for more immediate concerns.

'Are these all the models you've made?' I asked Andrew. 'Or have you got lots more packed away in black bin bags?'

'Bin bags?' He was fiddling with a half-painted Concorde on his desk. 'Why do you say that?'

'You know, the plastic bags the dustmen leave after they've taken away the rubbish. Don't you collect them? A lot of boys do.'

'Collect plastic bags? What a funny thing to do.' Andrew had his head down and was still fiddling with his model. 'That wouldn't interest me, I'm afraid. I haven't got any plastic bags at all.'

Back in Chambers that afternoon I found Dot Clapton alone in front of her typewriter, frowning as she looked over a brightly coloured brochure, on the cover of which a bikinied blonde was to be seen playing leapfrog with a younger, fitter version of Vincent Blewitt on a stretch of golden sand.

'I'm afraid Henry's just slipped out, Mr Rumpole. I don't know what it is. His heart doesn't seem to be in his work nowadays.' She looked up at me in genuine distress and I saw the perfectly oval face, sculptured eyelids and blonde curls that might have been painted by some such artistic old darling as Sandro Botticelli, and heard the accent which might have been learnt from the Timson family somewhere south of Brixton. I didn't tell her that not only Henry's heart, but our learned clerk himself, might not be in his work very soon. Instead I asked, 'Thinking of going on holiday, Dot?'

She handed me the brochure in silence. On the front of it was emblazoned THE FIVE S HOLIDAYS: SEA, SUN, SAND, SINGLES AND SEX ON THE COSTA DEL SOL. WHY NOT GO FOR IT? 'Quite honestly, is that your idea of a holiday, Mr Rumpole?'

'It sounds,' I had to tell her, 'like my idea of hell.'

'I've got to agree with you. I mean, if I want burger and chips with a pint of lager, I might as well stay in Streatham.'

'Very sensible.'

'If I'm going to be on holiday, I want something a bit romantic.'

'I understand. Sand and sex are as unappealing as sand in the sandwiches?'

'My boyfriend's planning to take me to the castles down the Rhine. Of course, I don't want to upset him.'

'Upset your boyfriend?'

'No. Upset Mr Blewitt.'

'Upsetting Mr Blewitt – I have to say this, Dot – is my idea of a perfect summer holiday.'

'Oh, don't say that, Mr Rumpole.' Dot Clapton looked nervously round the room as though the blot might be concealed behind the arras. 'He is my boss now, isn't he?'

'Not *my* boss, Dot. No one's my boss, and particularly not Blewitt.'

'He's mine then. And he told me these singles holidays are a whole lot of fun.'

'Did he now?' I felt that there was something in this fragment of information which might be of great value.

'I don't know, though. Vince . . . Well, he asked me to call him Vince.'

'And you agreed?'

'I didn't have much choice. Does he honestly think I haven't got a boyfriend?'

'If he thinks that, Dot, he can't be capable of organizing a piss-up in a brewery, let alone a barristers' Chambers.'

'Piss-up in a brewery!' Dot covered her mouth with her hand and giggled. 'How do you think of these things, Mr Rumpole?'

I didn't tell her that they'd been thought of and forgotten long before she was born, but took my leave of her, saying I was on my way to see Mr Ballard.

'Oh, he's busy.' Dot emerged from behind her hand. 'He said he wasn't to be disturbed.'

'Then it will be my pleasure and privilege to disturb him.'

'Have you "eaten on the insane root",' I asked the egregious Ballard, with what I hoped sounded like genuine concern, ' "That takes the reason prisoner?" '

'What *do* you mean, Rumpole?'

'I mean no one who has retained one single marble would dream of introducing the blight Blewitt into Equity Court.'

'I thought you'd come to me about that eventually.'

'Then you thought right.'

'If you had bothered to attend the Chambers' meeting you might have been privy to the selection of Vincent Blewitt.'

'I have only a few years of active life left to me,' I told the man with some dignity. 'And they are too precious to be wasted on Chambers' meetings. If I'd been there, I'd certainly have banned Blewitt.'

'Then you'd have been outvoted.'

'You mean those learned but idiotic friends decided to put their affairs in the hands of this second-rate, second-hand car salesman.'

'Catering.' Ballard smiled tolerantly.

'What?'

'Vincent Blewitt was in catering, not cars.'

'Then I wouldn't buy a second-hand cake off him.'

'Horace' – Soapy Sam Ballard rose and placed a considerate and totally unwelcome hand on my shoulder – 'we all know that you're a great old warhorse and that you've had a long, long career at the Bar. But you have to face it, my dear old Horace, you don't understand the modern world.'

'I understand it well enough to be able to tell a decent, honest, efficient, if rather over-amorous, clerk from the dubious flogger of suspect and probably mouldy canteen dinners.' I shrugged the unwelcome hand off my shoulder.

'The clerking system,' Ballard told me then, with a look of intolerable condescension, 'is out of date, Horace. We are moving towards the millennium.'

'You move towards it if you like. I prefer to stay where I am.'

'Why should we pay Henry a percentage when we can get an experienced businessman for a salary?'

'What sort of salary?'

'Vincent Blewitt was good enough to agree to a hundred, to be reviewed at the end of one year. The contract will be signed when the month's trial period is over.'

'A hundred pounds? Far too much!'

'A hundred thousand, Rumpole. It's far less than he would expect to earn in the private sector of industry.'

'Let him go back to the private sector then. If you want to be robbed, I could lend you one of the Timsons. They only deal in petty theft.'

'Vincent Blewitt has been very good to join us. At some personal financial sacrifice . . .'

'Did you check on what his screw was in the canteen?'

'I took his word for it.' Ballard looked only momentarily embarrassed.

'Famous last words of the fraudster's victim.'

'Vincent Blewitt isn't a fraudster, Rumpole. He's a businessman.'

'That's the polite word for it.'

'He says we must earn our keep by a rise in productivity.'

'How do you measure our productivity?'

'By the turnover in trials.'

'In your case, by the amazing turnover in defeats.' It was below the belt, I have to confess, but it didn't send Ballard staggering to the ropes. He came back, pluckily, I suppose. 'Business, Rumpole,' he told me, 'makes the world go round.' Later I discovered he'd got these words of wisdom from some ludicrous television advertisement.

'Rubbish. Justice might make the world go round. Or poetry. Or love. Or even God. *You* might think it's God, Bollard, as a founder member of the Lawyers As Christians Society.'

'As a Christian, Rumpole, I remember the parable of the talents. The Bible points out that you can't fight market forces.'

'Didn't the Bible also say something like Blessed are the poor? Or do you wish it hadn't said that?'

'I've got no time to trade texts with you, Rumpole.' Soapy Sam looked nettled.

I was suddenly tired, half in love, perhaps for a moment, with easeful death. 'Oh, let's stop arguing. Get rid of the blot, confirm Henry in the job and we need say no more about it.'

'I'm sure you'll find Vincent Blewitt a great asset to Chambers, Rumpole. He's a very human sort of person. He likes his joke, I understand. I'm sure you'll have plenty of laughs together.'

'If he stays . . .'

'He *is* staying . . .'

'Then I'll take a handful of pills, washed down with a glass of whisky, and cease upon the midnight with no pain.'

'If you wish to do that, Rumpole' – our learned Head of Chambers sat down at his desk and pretended to be busy with a set of papers – 'that is entirely a matter for you.'

That evening, before the news, Ballard's favourite commercial about business making the world go round came on. Later there were some pictures of a Pro-Life demonstration outside an abortion clinic in St John's Wood. Prominent among those present was a serious, long-faced woman with reddish hair. Nurse Pargey was waving a placard on which was written the words THOU SHALT NOT KILL.

★

'Alzheimer's isn't a killer in itself. Certainly the patient gets weaker and more forgetful. Helpless, in fact. But it would need something more to kill Chippy.'

'Like an overdose of sleeping pills, for instance?'

'Evidently that's what did it.' Dr Betty was one of those awkward clients, it seemed, who felt impelled to tell the truth. And what she went on to say wasn't particularly helpful. 'I might have given Chippy an overdose of something when the time came, but it hadn't come on the night he died. You must believe that, Horace.'

'Whether I believe it or not isn't exactly the point. What matters is whether the Jury believe it.'

'That's for them to decide, isn't it?'

'I'm afraid it is.' At which moment there was a rapid knock on the door which immediately opened to admit Blewitt's head. He took a quick look at the assembled company and said, 'Sorry folks! Mustn't interrupt the workers' productivity. Speak to you later, Horace.' At which, as rare things will, he vanished.

'Who on earth was that extraordinary man?' For the first time Dr Betty looked shaken.

'A temporary visitor,' I told her. 'Nothing for you to worry about. Now tell me about the sleeping pills.'

'I gave him two.'

'And you saw him drink his whisky?'

'A small whisky-and-soda. Yes.'

'And then . . .?'

'Well, I settled him down for the night.'

'Did he go to sleep?'

'He seemed tired and dreamy. He'd been quite contented that day, in fact. But incontinent, of course. Quite soon after he'd settled down, I heard the Chippenhams come home from their dinner-party, so I went downstairs to meet them.'

'What happened to the bottle of pills?'

'Well, that was kept in the house so that the Chippenhams or Nurse Pargeter could give Chippy his pills when I wasn't there.'

'Kept where in the house?'

'I put them back in the bathroom cupboard.'

'Are there two bathrooms?'

'Yes. The one next to the Judge's bedroom. You know the house?' Dr Betty looked surprised.

'I have a certain nodding acquaintance with it. And young Andrew?'

'His mother had sent him up to bed before they went out. But I'm afraid he hadn't gone to sleep.'

'How do you know that?'

'When I went to put the pills back in the bathroom, I saw his light on and his bedroom door open. He was still reading – or playing with his model aeroplanes more likely.'

'Quite likely, yes. Oh, one other thing. Had you ever spoken to Chippy about Lethe?'

'No, certainly not. I told you, Horace. The time had not come.'

'And was anyone else Chippy knew a member of Lethe? Any friends or his family?'

'Oh, no, I'm sure they weren't.'

'I think it might be just worth getting a statement from a Dr Eames.' I turned to Bonny Bernard, my instructing solicitor. 'Oh, and a few inquiries about the firm of Marcellus & Chippenham, house agents and surveyors.'

'David Eames?' Dr Betty looked doubtful.

'He treated Chippy before you came on the scene. He might know if he'd ever talked of suicide.'

Dr Betty once again spurned a line of defence. 'As I told you, I'm quite sure he never contemplated such a thing.'

'So if you didn't kill him, Dr Betty, who do you think did?'

She was looking at me, quite serious then, as she said, 'Well, that's not for me to say, is it?'

'Sorry to have intruded on your conference. Although it may be no bad thing for me to make spot checks on the human resource in the workplace.'

I had hardly recovered from the gloomy prospect of defending Dr Betty when the Blight was with me again. I sat, sunk in thought.

'Cheer up, Horace.' Vince's laugh was like a bath running out. 'It may never happen.' As he said that, I regretted having used the same fatuous words of encouragement to Henry, our condemned clerk. Most of the worst things in life are absolutely bound to happen, the trial of the cheerful doctor, for instance, or death itself.

'I wanted a word or two with you about formalizing staff holidays. You thinking of getting away to the sun yourself?'

'Hardly,' I told him, 'having glanced at the brochure you gave Dot Clapton.'

'Sea, sand and sex, Rumpole. You'd enjoy that. Very relaxing,' Vince gurgled.

'I'm hardly a single.'

'Well, send the wife on a tour of the Lake District or something, and you head off to the Costa del Sol. That's my advice. I mean, when you're invited to a gourmet dinner, why take a ham sandwich?'

I looked at Vincent Blewitt with a wild surmise. Was there no limit to the awfulness of the man? I could imagine no matrimonial situation, however grim, in which I could tell Hilda that she was a ham sandwich.

'I've rota'd Dot early July in the format,' Vince told me. 'I don't think she can wait to join me and assorted singles.'

I thought of telling him that Dot didn't even like the Costa del Sol. That she didn't think that sex and sand made a good mix. That she had a romantic nature and she wanted to drift past the castles on the Rhine listening to the Lorelei's mystic note. Some glimmering hope, a faint idea of a plan, led me to encourage the Blot. 'Considerable fun, these singles holidays, are they, Vincent?'

'You're not joking!' He had now sunk into my client's armchair and stuck out his legs in anticipation of delight. 'First day you get there, as soon as you've got checked in, it's down to the beach for games to break the ice.'

'Games?'

'I'll just tell you one. Whet your appetite.'

'Carry on.'

'The fellas get to blow up balloons inside the girls' bikini bottoms. And then the girls do it vice versa in our shorts. By the time we've played that, everyone's a swinger.'

I looked longingly at the door, thinking how restful the

forthcoming murder trial would be, compared with a quiet chat with our legal administrator.

'It sounds very tasteful.'

'I think you've got the message. I'll rota you for a couple of weeks then. After Dot and I have left the Costa, of course. I never knew you were a swinger, Horace.'

'Oh, we all have our joys and desires.'

'Don't we just!' Vincent looked at me, I thought, with unusual respect. 'Heard any good ones lately?'

'Ones?'

'You know. Jokes. You've got hidden talents, Horace. I bet you know about rib-ticklers.'

'You mean' – I looked at him seriously – 'like the one about the sleeveless woman?'

'Isn't that a *great* story?' Happily Vincent knew this anecdote and he gurgled again. 'Laughed like a drain when I first heard it. Whoever told you that one, Horace?'

I looked him straight in the eye and lied with complete conviction, 'Oh, Sam told me that. It's just his type of humour.'

'Sam?' Vincent was puzzled.

'You know, our learned Head of Chambers, Soapy Sam Ballard.'

I have often noticed that before any big and important cause or matter – and no one could doubt the size and importance of *R. v. Dr Betty* – a kind of peace descends on my legal business. In other words, I hit a slump. I had nothing in Court, not even the smallest spot of indecency at Uxbridge. I had no conferences booked and those scurrying about their business in the Temple, or waiting in the corridors of the Old Bailey, might well have come to the conclusion that old Rumpole had ceased upon the midnight hour with no pain. In fact I was docked in Froxbury Mansions with my ham – no, I will not be infected by Vince's vulgarity – with She Who Must Be Obeyed.

Needless to say, I had no wish to spend twenty-four hours a day closeted with Hilda, so I went on a number of errands to the newsagent in search of small cigars, to the off-licence at the other end of Gloucester Road to purchase plonk, stretch my legs and breathe in the petrol fumes.

I was walking, wrapped in thought, through Canning Place, when I saw the familiar sight of purple blazers marching towards me in strict battle formation, led by a sharp-faced young female wearing a tweed skirt and an anorak, who uttered words of command or turned to rebuke stragglers. I stood politely in the gutter to let them pass, raising my umbrella in a kind of salute when I saw, taking up the rearguard, Andrew Chippenham.

'Andrew!' I called out in my matiest tones, 'how are you, old boy? Marching up with your regiment to lay siege to the Albert Hall, are you? Or on the hunt for bin bags?'

It was not at all, I'm sure you'll agree, an alarming sally. I intended to be friendly and jocular, but when he heard my voice young Andrew stopped, apparently frozen, his head down. He raised it slowly and what I saw was a small, serious boy frozen in terror. Before I could speak again, he had turned and run off after his vanishing crocodile.

I was finding this enforced home leave so tedious that, a few days later, I took a trip on the tube back to my Chambers in the Temple, although I had no business engagements. I was sunk in the swing chair with my feet on the desktop workspace, trying to fathom out the depths of ingenuity to which the setter of *The Times* crossword puzzle might have sunk, when the Blot oozed through the door and defiled my carpet.

'I thought it might be rather appropriate,' he said in the sort of solemn voice people use when they're discussing funeral arrangements, 'if we gave a great party in Chambers to mark Henry's career change.'

'What's that called?' I asked him. 'Easing the passing?'

'At least give him a smashing send-off.'

'I suppose he can live on that as his retirement pension.'

'I'm sure Henry has got a bit put by.'

'He hasn't got a job put by. I happen to know that.' And then some sort of a plan began to take shape in my mind. 'Why does it have to be a *great* party?'

'Because' – and then Vince looked at me in a horribly

conspiratorial fashion as the penny dropped. 'Horace, you're not suggesting?'

'A bit of a singles do, why not?'

'Leave the ham sandwiches at home, eh?'

'Exactly!' I forced myself to say it, although it stuck in my throat.

'I mean, we'd ask Dot Clapton, wouldn't we?'

'Of course,' I reassured him.

'And some of the gorgeous bits that float around the Temple.'

'As many of them as you can cram in. We'll make it a real send-off for Henry.'

'Something he'll remember all his life.'

'Certainly.'

'Only one drawback, as far as I know.'

'What's that?'

'We'll have to ask permission from the Head of Chambers.' Vincent looked doubtful and disappointed.

'The Head of Chambers would be furious if he weren't included,' I assured him, and the gurgling laughter was turned on again.

'Of course. I remember what you told me about Sam Ballard. A bit of a swinger, didn't you indicate?'

'Bollard,' I said, remembering an old song of my middle age, '"swings as the pendulum do". Put the whole proposition to him, Vincent. Put it in detail, not forgetting the balloons blown up in the trousers, and then watch his eyes light up.'

'We're in for a good time, then?'

'I think so. At very long last.'

After the Blot had left me, suitably encouraged, I went home on the Underground. Emerging from Gloucester Road station, I saw the formation of purple blazers bearing down on me remorselessly on what must have been the last route-march of the day. I stood aside to let them pass, but the C.O. halted the column and looked at me, through a pair of horn-rimmed spectacles, with obvious distaste. 'Are you the person who spoke to Chippenham the other day, down at the end of the line?' she asked me. 'The boys told me he had spoken to somebody strange.'

'It just so happened' – I decided to overlook the description – 'that I know the family.'

'Whether you do or you don't' – she frowned severely – 'he was clearly upset by what you said to him. It's most unusual for people to speak to my Bolingbrokers in the street. He was obviously shocked, the other boys said so. Ever since he met you, Chippenham's been away sick.'

'But I honestly didn't say anything,' I started to explain but, before I could finish the sentence, the word of command had been given and the column quick-marched away from me.

When I got back to the seclusion of the mansion flat (there were times when I felt that our chilly matrimonial home was more a mausoleum than a mansion), I found Hilda had gone to her bridge club and left a message for me to ring my instructing solicitor and 'make sure neither of you slip up on Dr Betty's case'. When I got through to Bonny Bernard, he had news which interested me greatly. The puritanical Dr Eames had, it seemed, returned to care for the Chippenham family and, in particular, he was looking after young Andrew, who was suffering from some sort of nervous illness and was off school. As a witness, Bernard told me, Dr Eames was of the talkative variety and seemed to have something he was a strangely anxious to tell me. I hoped he would become even more talkative in the days before the trial.

I discovered that our case was to come before Mrs Justice Erskine-Brown, for so long the Portia of our Chambers and its acknowledged beauty (even now, when she is Dame Phillida and swathed in the scarlet and ermine of a High Court Judge, she is a figure that the unspeakable Vince might well have wanted to lure into a singles holiday on the Costa del Sand and Sex). I had known her since she had joined us as a tearful pupil;* we had been together and against each other, and I had taught her enough to turn her into a formidable opponent, in more trials than I care to remember. She was brave, tenacious, charming and provocative as compared with her husband

* See 'Rumpole and the Married Lady' in *Rumpole of the Bailey*, Penguin Books, 1978.

Claude who, upon his hind legs in any courtroom, could be counted upon to appear nervous, hesitant and unconvincing. I have a distinct fondness for Portia which I have reason to believe, because of the way she behaved during the many crises in Equity Court, is suitably returned. In short, we have a mutual regard, and I hoped she might feel some sympathy for a case which, in other hands, was likely to prove equally difficult for Dr Betty Ireton and Horace Rumpole. There, hopes were dashed quite early on in the proceedings.

'It may be argued on behalf of the Defence . . .' The Prosecutor was the beefy Q.C., Barrington McTear. He had played rugby football for Oxford and his courtroom tactics consisted of pushing, shoving, tackling low and covering his opponents, whenever possible, with mud. Although his name had a Highland ring to it, he spoke in an arrogant and earblasting Etonian accent and considered himself a cut above such middle-class, possibly overweight, and certainly unsporty barristers as myself. For this reason I had privately christened him Cut Above McTear.

Cut Above had massive shoulders, a large, pink face and small, gold half-glasses. They perched on him as inappropriately as a thin, gold necklace on a ham. Now, in a voice that could have been heard from one end of a football field to the other, he repeated what he thought would be my defence for the purpose of bringing it sprawling to the ground in a particularly unpleasant tackle. 'Your Ladyship may well think that Mr Rumpole's defence will be "This old gentleman was on his way out anyway, so Dr Ireton committed an act of mercy and not an act of murder" . . .'

'Such a defence will receive very little sympathy in this Court, Mr McTear.' Portia was clearly not in a mood to fuss about the quality of mercy. 'Murder is murder until Parliament chooses to pass a law permitting euthanasia.'

'Oh, I do so entirely agree with your Ladyship,' Cut Above informed the Bench and probably those assembled in the corridor and nearby Courts, 'so it will be interesting to discover if Mr Rumpole has a defence.'

'May I remind my learned friend' – I climbed to my feet and spoke, I think with admirable courtesy – 'that a prosecutor's job is to prove the charge and not to speculate about the nature of the Defence. If he wishes any further advice on how to conduct his case, I shall be available during the adjournment.'

'I hardly need advice on prosecuting from Mr Rumpole, who hasn't done any of it!' Cut Above bellowed.

'Gentlemen' – Portia's quiet call to order was always effective – 'perhaps we should get on with the evidence. No doubt we shall hear from Mr Rumpole in the fullness of time.'

So Cut Above turned to tell the Jury that they would find the evidence he was about to call entirely persuasive and leading to the inevitable verdict of guilty on Dr Ireton. A glance at Hilda, who had come to support her friend and make sure that I secured her deliverance from the dock, was enough to tell me that She Who Must Be Obeyed didn't think much of my performance so far.

Dick Chippenham was the sort of witness that Cut Above could understand and respect. They probably went to the same tailor and played the same games at the same sort of schools and universities. Dick even spoke in Cut Above's sort of voice, although with the volume turned down considerably. When he had finished his examination Cut Above said, 'I'm afraid I'll have to trouble you to wait there for a few minutes more,' as though there was an unfortunate deputation from the peasantry to trouble him, but it needn't detain him long.

'Mr Chippenham, I'm sure all of us at the Bar wish to sympathize with you in your bereavement.'

'Thank you.' I glanced at the Jury. They clearly liked my opening gambit, one that Cut Above hadn't troubled himself to think of.

'I have only a few questions. Up to six months before he died, your uncle was attended by Dr Eames?'

'That is so.'

'But, rightly or wrongly, your uncle took against Dr Eames?'

'I'm afraid so.'

'That doctor not being convinced of the therapeutic effects of whisky and claret?'

I got a ripple of laughter from the Jury and a smile of assurance from the witness. 'I believe that was the reason.'

'So you then engaged Dr Ireton. Why did you choose her?'

'She was a local doctor who had treated one of my wife's friends.'

'At the time when you transferred to Dr Ireton, did you know that she was a member of Lethe, a pro-euthanasia society?'

'Mr Rumpole admits that she was a member of Lethe.' Cut Above sprang to attention. 'I hope the Jury have noticed this admission by the Defence,' he bellowed.

'I'm sure you can't have helped noticing that,' I told the Jury. 'And I'm sure that, during any further speeches from my learned friend, earplugs will be provided for those not already hard of hearing.'

'Mr Rumpole!' Portia rebuked me from the Bench. 'This is a serious case and I wish to see it is tried seriously.'

'An admirable ambition, my Lady,' I told her. 'And tried quietly too, I hope.' And then I turned to the witness before Cut Above could trumpet any sort of protest.

'When you and your wife got back from the dinner party, it was about eleven o'clock?'

'Yes.'

'And apart from your uncle, the only people in the house were Dr Betty Ireton and your son?'

'That's right. Dr Betty met us in the hall and she said she'd given Chippy his pills and a drink of whisky.'

'At that time, would your uncle have remembered whether he'd taken his pills or not?'

'He probably would have remembered. Dr Betty said she'd given him his pills as usual.'

'When you got upstairs, you went in to see your uncle?'

'We did.'

'Was he asleep?'

'Yes.'

'Was he still breathing?'

'I'm sure he was. Otherwise we'd have called for help immediately.'

'You noticed the bottle of whisky. Was it empty?'

'It must have been, but I can't say I noticed it then.'

'So perhaps it wasn't empty?'

'I can't say for sure, but I suppose it must have been.'

'You can't say for sure. And the bottle of pills had been put away in the bathroom?'

'Yes, I believe it had . . . My wife will tell you.'

'So you can't be sure how many pills were left when you last saw your uncle alive?'

'In the morning I saw the bottle of pills empty.'

'And in the morning your uncle was dead?'

'Yes, he was.'

'Thank you very much, Mr Chippenham.' I sat down with what I hoped was a good deal more show of satisfaction than I felt.

'Dr Betty said she thinks you and that deafening McTear person are behaving like a couple of small boys in the school playground.'

I thought it was perhaps unfortunate that Dr Betty was allowed bail if she was going to abuse her freedom by criticizing my forensic skills. 'She only sees what happens on the surface. Tactics, Hilda. She's no idea of the plans that are forming at the back of my mind.'

'Have you any idea of them either, Rumpole? Be honest. Or have you forgotten that, in the way you forgot to turn out the bathroom light when you'd finished shaving?'

It was breakfast time once again in Froxbury Mansions. I felt a longing to get away from the sharp cut-and-thrust of domestic argument and be off to the gentler world of the Old Bailey. Hilda pressed home her advantage. 'I hope you realize that I am personally committed to your winning this case, Rumpole. I have given my word to Dr Betty.'

Then you'd better ask for it back again, was what I might have said, but lacked the bottle. Instead I told Hilda that Dr Eames was going to give us a full statement which I thought might be helpful. At which, I gathered up my traps, ready to hotfoot it down to the Old Bailey canteen where I had a date with the industrious Bernard.

'You certainly need help from somewhere, Rumpole. And, I don't know if you noticed, you've left me your briefcase and taken my *Daily Telegraph*.' As I made the changeover, he said, 'We've learnt a lot lately, haven't we, about the onset of Alzheimer's disease?'

Dr David Eames was a rare bird, a doctor who liked talking to lawyers. He was tall, bony, with large, capable hands and a lock of fair hair that fell over his eyes, and a serious, enthusiastic way of speaking as though he hadn't yet lost his boyish faith in human nature, the National Health Service and the practice of medicine. I don't usually have much feeling for those who seek to deprive their fellow beings of their claret, but I felt a strange liking for this youthful quack who seemed only anxious to discover the truth about the fatal events which had taken place that night in Dettingen Road.

As we sat with Bernard in the Old Bailey canteen, with coffee from a machine, and went through the medical evidence, I noticed he was strangely excited, as though he had something to communicate but was not sure when, or if indeed ever, to communicate it.

'I'm right in thinking Alzheimer's is not a killer in itself, although those who contract it usually die within ten years?'

'That's right,' Eames agreed. 'They contract bronchitis or have a stroke, or perhaps they just lose their wish to live.'

'There's no evidence of bronchitis or a stroke here?'

'Apparently not.'

'So it seems likely that death was hurried on in some way?'

There was a silence, then Dr Eames said, 'I think that must follow.'

'My old friend and opponent, Dr Ackerman of the morgue, the Home Office pathologist, estimates death as between ten p.m. and one a.m.'

'I read that.'

'At any rate, he was dead by seven-thirty a.m. when Nurse Pargeter came to look after him. Dick Chippenham says that Chippy was alive and sleeping well at around eleven the night before. If Dr Betty had just given him an overdose . . .'

'The pills might not have taken their effect until some time later.'

'I was afraid you'd say that.' I took a gulp from the machine's coffee, which is pretty indistinguishable from the machine's tea, or the machine's soup if it comes to that. 'When you stopped being the Chippenhams' doctor . . .'

'When I was sacked, you mean?'

'If you like. Had you had a row with Chippy? I mean, did *he* sack you?'

'Not really. As far as I remember, it was Mr Chippenham who told me his uncle wanted me to go.'

'There was no question of you having had a row with Chippy about drinking whisky?'

'No. I can't remember anything like that.' The doctor looked puzzled and I felt curiously encouraged and lit a small cigar.

'Tell me, Doctor, did you know Nurse Pargeter?'

'Only too well.'

'And did you like her?'

'Pro-Life nurses can be a menace. They seem to think of themselves as avenging angels.'

'And she didn't care for Dr Betty?'

'She hated her! I think she thought of her as a potential murderess.'

I wondered if that might be helpful. Then I said, 'One more thing, Dr Eames, now that I've got you here . . .'

'What are you up to *now*, Rumpole? Talking to potential witnesses? Is that in the best tradition of the Bar?' Wasn't Stentor some old Greek military man whose voice, on the battlefield, was louder than fifty men together? No doubt his direct descendant was the stentorian Cut Above, who now stood with his wig in his hand, his thick hair interrupted by a little tonsure of baldness so that he looked like a muscular monk.

'I am consulting with an expert witness. A doctor of medicine,' I told Cut Above. 'And for Counsel to see expert witnesses is certainly in the best tradition of the Bar.'

'I'm warning you. Just watch it, Rumpole. Watch it extremely carefully. I don't want to have to report you to her lovely Ladyship for unprofessional conduct.' My opponent gave a bellow of laughter which rattled the coffee cups and passed on with his myrmidons, a junior barrister and a wiry little scrum-half from the D.P.P.'s office.

'Who's that appalling bully?' Dr Eames appeared shocked.

'Cut Above, Q.C., Counsel for the Prosecution.'

'I've known surgeons like that. Full of themselves and care nothing for the patient. Doesn't he want me to talk to you?' I think it was Cut Above's appearance and interruption which persuaded Dr Eames to tell me all he eventually did.

'Probably not. I want to talk to you, though. Aren't you treating young Andrew? He seemed a charming boy!'

'I'm not sure what's the matter with him. Some sort of nervous trouble. Something's worrying him terribly.' Dr Eames also looked worried.

'I spoke to him in the street, and a schoolmistress ticked me off for it. But that couldn't have had anything to do with his illness, could it?'

'I'm afraid you reminded him of something.' I felt a prickle of excitement. Dr Eames was about to reveal some evidence of great importance.

'What exactly?'

'I think I know. It was something you'd said before, when you came to the house. It reminded him of his dream.'

At a nearby table Cut Above was yelling orders to his junior. If Dr Eames hadn't taken such an instant dislike to my opponent he might never have told me about young Andrew's dream.

Without doubt, the Jury took strongly to Ursula Chippenham and I have to say that I also liked her. Standing in the box with her honey-coloured hair a little untidy, a scarf floating about her neck, her gentle voice sounding touchingly brave, yet clearly audible, she was the perfect prosecution witness. She showed no hatred of Dr Betty; she spoke glowingly of her care and friendship for the old Judge; and she was only saddened by what the doctor's principles had led her to do. 'I'm quite sure that Dr Betty was only doing what she thought was right and merciful,' she said. Having got this perfect, and unhappily convincing, answer, even Cut Above had the good sense to shut up and sit down.

If I'd wanted to lose Dr Betty's case I'd've gone in to the attack on Ursula with my guns blazing. Of course I didn't. I started by roaring as gently as any sucking dove, showing the Jury how much more polite and considerate I could be than Cut Above at his most gentlemanly.

'Mrs Chippenham, I hope it won't offend you if I call the deceased Judge, Chippy?'

'Not at all, Mr Rumpole.' Ursula's smile could win all hearts. 'We both knew and loved him, I know. I'm sure he would have liked us to call him that.'

'And that's how he was affectionately known at the Bar,' Portia added to the warmth of the occasion.

'And Chippy was extremely ill?'

'Yes, he was.'

'And, entirely to your credit, you and your husband looked after him? With medical help?'

'We did our best. Yes.'

'He was unlikely to recover?'

'He wasn't going to recover. I don't think there's a cure for Alzheimer's.'

'Can we come to the time when Dr Betty started to treat Chippy? Was Nurse Pargeter coming in then?'

'Yes, she was.'

'And Nurse Pargeter strongly disapproved of Dr Betty's support for legalizing euthanasia?'

'She warned us about Dr Betty, yes.'

'And you discussed the matter with your husband?'

'Oh, yes. We thought about it very carefully. And then I had a talk about it with Dr Betty.'

'Did you?' I looked mildly, ever so mildly, surprised. 'Was your husband present?'

'No, I didn't want it to be too formal. We just chatted over coffee, and Dr Betty promised me she wouldn't give Chippy ... Well, give him anything to stop keeping him alive, without discussing it with the family.'

I looked around at the dock where Dr Betty was shaking her head decisively. So I was put in the embarrassing position of having to call the witness a liar.

'Mrs Chippenham, I have to remind you that you said nothing about this conversation with Dr Betty in your original statement to the police.'

'Didn't I? I'm afraid I was upset and rather flustered at that time.' Ursula turned to the Judge, 'I do hope you can understand?'

'Of course,' Portia understood, 'but can I just ask you this, Mrs Chippenham? If Dr Ireton had come to you and recommended ending Chippy's life what would you have said?'

'Neither Dick nor I would have agreed to it. Not in any circumstances. We may not go to church very much, but we do believe that life is sacred.'

'"We do believe that life is sacred.",' Portia repeated as she wrote the words down, and we all waited in respectful silence. 'Yes, Mr Rumpole?'

'We've heard that it was Nurse Pargeter who found Chippy dead.'

'Yes, she called for me and I joined her.'

'And it was Nurse Pargeter who reported the circumstances of Chippy's death to the police?'

'She insisted on doing so.'

'And you agreed?'

'I think I was too upset to agree or disagree.'

'I see. Now, that morning, when the nurse found Chippy dead, the whisky bottle was almost empty and the bottle of sleeping pills empty. You don't know how that came about?'

'I assumed that Dr Betty gave Chippy the overdose and the whisky.'

'You assumed that because she's a well-known supporter of euthanasia?'

'Well, yes, I suppose so.' Ursula frowned a little then and looked puzzled, but as attractive as ever.

'Because she believes in euthanasia, she's the most likely suspect?'

'Isn't that obvious, Mr Rumpole?' Portia answered the question for the witness.

'And because she was the most likely suspect, is that why you decided to ask her to look after Chippy?' I asked Ursula the first hostile question with my usual charm.

'I'm not sure I understand what you mean?' Ursula smiled in a puzzled sort of way at the Jury, and they looked entirely sympathetic.

'I'm not sure I understand either.' Portia sounded distinctly unfriendly to Counsel for the Defence.

'I'll come back to it later, if I may. Mrs Chippenham, we've got a copy of Chippy's will. Nurse Pargeter does quite well out of it, doesn't she? She gets a substantial legacy.'

'Twenty thousand pounds. She did a great deal for Chippy.'

'And let me ask you this. Your husband's in business as an estate agent, is he not?'

'Marcellus & Chippenham, yes.'

'It's going through a pretty difficult time, isn't it?'

'I think the housing market is having a lot of difficulty, yes.'

'As we all know, Mr Rumpole.' The Erskine-Browns were trying to get rid of a house in Islington and move into central London, so the learned Judge spoke from the heart.

'Let's say that the freehold of the house in Dettingen Road and the residue of Chippy's estate might solve a good many of your problems. Isn't that right?'

The Jury looked at me as though I had suggested that Mother Theresa was only in it for the money and Ursula gave exactly the right answer. 'We were both extremely grateful for what Chippy decided to do for us.' Then she spoilt it a little by adding, 'When he made that will, he understood it perfectly.'

'And I am sure he was conscious of all you and your husband were doing for *him*?' Portia was firmly on Ursula's side.

'Thank you, my Lady.' Ursula didn't bob a curtsey, but it seemed, for a moment, as if she was tempted to do so.

'Mrs Chippenham, you know the way the Lethe organization recommends helping sufferers out of this wicked world?'

'I'm afraid I don't.'

'Are you sure? Didn't Nurse Pargeter give you a pamphlet like this when she was trying to persuade you not to engage Dr Betty?' I handed her the Lethe pamphlet which Bonny Bernard had got me and it was made Defence Exhibit One. Then I asked the witness to turn to page three where a recipe for easeful death was set out. I read it aloud: '"The method recommended is a large dose of sleeping pills which are readily obtainable on prescription and a strong alcoholic drink such as whisky or brandy. When the patient is asleep, a long plastic bin-liner is placed over the head and pulled over the shoulders.

Being deprived of air, the sleep is gentle, painless and permanent." Did you read that when Nurse Pargeter gave you the pamphlet?'

There was a silence and the courtroom seemed to have become suddenly chilly. Then Ursula answered, more quietly than before, 'I may have glanced at it.'

'*You* may have glanced at it. But I suggest that someone in your house remembered it quite clearly when old Chippy was helped out of this troubled world.'

Of course there was an immediate hullabaloo. Cut Above trumpeted that there was no basis at all for that perfectly outrageous suggestion, and Portia, in more measured tones, asked me to make it clear what my suggestion was. I said I was perfectly prepared to do so.

'I suggest someone woke Chippy up, around midnight. He hadn't remembered taking his pills, of course, so he was given a liberal overdose, washed down with a large whisky. One of the long black bin-liners that your dustmen provide so generously was then made use of.'

Ursula was silent, but Counsel for the Prosecution wasn't. 'I hope, my Lady, that Mr Rumpole will be calling evidence to support this extraordinary charge?'

I didn't answer him, but asked the witness, 'Your son Andrew hasn't been well lately?'

'I'm afraid not.' Ursula recovered her voice, thinking I'd passed to another subject.

'Mr Rumpole' – Portia was clearly displeased – 'the Court would also like to know if you are going to call evidence to support the charge you have made.'

'I'm happy to deal with that, my Lady, when I've asked a few more questions.' I turned back to the witness. 'Is Dr Eames treating young Andrew?'

'Yes, Dr Eames has come back to us.'

'Is Andrew's illness of a nervous nature? I mean, has he become worried about something?'

'I don't know. He's had sick headaches and we've kept him out of school. Dr Eames isn't sure what the trouble is exactly.'

'Is Andrew worried by something he might have seen the night Chippy died? Remember, he sleeps with his door open and Chippy's room is immediately opposite. He saw something that night which has worried him ever since. Perhaps that's why he collects the plastic bags from the dustbins and hides them away. Is it because he knows bin bags can cause accidents?'

Ursula's voice slid upwards and became shrill as she asked, 'You say he saw . . . What did he see?'

'He thought it was a dream. But it wasn't a dream, was it?'

'My Lady, are we really being asked to sit here while Mr Rumpole trots out the dreams of a ten-year-old child?' Cut Above boomed, but I interrupted his cannonade.

'I'm not discussing dreams! I'm discussing facts. And the fact is' – I turned to Ursula – 'that you were coming out of Chippy's room that night, perhaps to take the empty bottle of pills back to the bathroom. It was then Andrew saw Chippy propped up on the pillows. Shrouded, Mrs Chippenham. Suffocated, Mrs Chippenham, with a black plastic bag pulled down over his head.'

The Court was cold now, and silent. Ursula looked at the Judge who said nothing, and at the Jury who said nothing either. Her beauty had gone as she became desperate, like a trapped animal. I saw Hilda watching and she appeared triumphant. I saw Dr Betty lean forward as though concerned for a patient who had taken a turn for the worse. When Ursula spoke, her voice was hoarse and hopeless. She said, 'You're not going to bring Andrew here to say that about the plastic bag, are you?'

I hated my job then. Chippy was dying anyway, so why should either Dr Betty, or this suffering woman, be cursed for ever by his death? I felt tired and longed to shut up and sit down, but if I had to choose between Ursula and Dr Betty, I knew I had to protect my client. So I took in a deep breath and said, 'That entirely depends, Mrs Chippenham, on whether you're going to tell us the truth.'

To her credit she didn't hesitate. She was determined to spare her son, so she turned to Portia and said quietly, 'I don't think he suffered and he would have died anyway. When I thought of doing it, I got Dr Ireton to treat Chippy so she would be blamed. That's all I have got to say.' Then she stood, stunned, like the victim of an accident, as though she didn't yet understand the consequences of any of the things she'd done or said.

When I came out of Court, I felt no elation. Cut Above, almost, for him, pianissimo, had offered no further evidence after Ursula's admission, and the case was over very quickly. I had notched a win, but I felt no triumph. I saw the Inspector in charge of the case talking to Dick and Ursula, and when I thought of their future, and Andrew's, I hated what I had done. The merciful tide of forgetfulness which engulfs disastrous days in Court, sinking them in fresh briefs and newer troubles, would be slow to come. Then I saw Hilda embrace Dr Betty and give her one of She Who Must Be Obeyed's rare kisses. My wife turned to me with a look of approval which was also rare; it was as though I were some sort of domestic appliance, a food blender perhaps, or an electric blanket, she had lent to an old friend and which, for once, worked satisfactorily. They asked me to join them for coffee and went away as happy as they must have been when young Betty Ireton led the school team to another victory. Bonny Bernard went about his business and I stood alone, outside the empty Court.

'Rumpole, a word with you, if you please, in a matter of urgency.'

Soapy Sam Ballard had paused, wigged and gowned, in full flight to another Court. He looked pale and agitated to such an extent that I was about to greet him with a quotation I thought might be appropriate: 'The devil damn thee black, thou cream-fac'd loon! Where gott'st thou that goose look?' Before I could speak, however, Soapy Sam started to burble. 'Bad news, I'm afraid. Very bad news indeed. We shall not be entering into a contract of service with Vincent Blewitt.'

I managed to restrain my tears. 'But Bollard,' I protested, 'didn't you think he was the very man for the job?'

'I did. Until he came to me with an idea for a Chambers' party. Did you know anything about this, Rumpole?' The man was suddenly suspicious.

'He told me he wanted to give Henry some kind of a send-off. I thought it was rather generous of him.'

'But did he tell you exactly what sort of send-off he had in mind?'

'A Chambers' party, I think he said. I can't remember the details.'

'He described it as a singles party. At first, I thought he was suggesting tennis.'

'A natural assumption.'

'And then he asked me to leave my ham sandwich at home – I wondered what on earth the man was talking about. I mean, it's never been my custom to bring any sort of sandwich to a Chambers' party. Your wife's friend, Dodo Mackintosh, usually provides the nibbles.'

'Have you any idea, Ballard' – I looked suitably mystified – 'what he meant?'

'I have now. He was talking about my wife Marguerite.'

'Marguerite, who once held the responsible position of matron at the Old Bailey?'

'That is exactly whom he meant.'

'Who was known, even to the red judges, as Matey?'

'Marguerite got on very well with the Judiciary. She treated many of them.'

'Can I believe my ears? Vincent Blewitt called your Marguerite a ham sandwich?' I was incredulous.

'I can't imagine what she would have to say if she ever got wind of it.'

'All hell would break loose?'

'Indeed it would!' Ballard nodded sadly and went on, 'He said we'd all have more fun if I left her at home. And the same applied to your Hilda.'

'Ballard, I can see why you're concerned.' I sounded most reasonable. 'It was a serious error of judgement on Blewitt's part, but if that was the only thing . . .'

'It was not the only thing, Rumpole.'

'You mean there's worse to come?'

'Considerably worse!' Ballard looked around nervously to make sure he wasn't overheard. 'He suggested that the party should start . . . I don't know how to tell you this, Rumpole.'

'Just take it slowly. I understand that it must be distressing.'

'It is, Rumpole. It certainly is. He thought the party should start . . .' Soapy Sam paused and then the words came tumbling out. '. . . By the male Members of Chambers and the girl guests blowing up balloons inside each other's underclothes. Rumpole, can you imagine what Marguerite would have said to that?'

'I thought Marguerite was to be left at home.'

'There is that, of course. But he wanted Mrs Justice Erskine-Brown to come. What would she have said if Blewitt had approached her with a balloon?'

'She'd have jailed him for contempt.'

'Quite right too! And then to top it all . . .'

'He topped that?'

'He said he knew I liked a good story, and wasn't that a great joke about the sleeveless woman?'

'What on earth was he talking about?' I looked suitably mystified.

'I have no idea. Do you know any story about a sleeveless woman?'

'Certainly not!' I replied with absolute truth.

'So then he told me about a legless nun. It was clearly obscene but I'm afraid, Rumpole, the point escaped me.'

'Probably just as well.'

'I'm afraid I shall have to tell Chambers. I'm informing you first as a senior member. We shall not be employing Vincent Blewitt or indeed any legal administrator in the foreseeable future.'

'It will be a disappointment, perhaps. But I'm sure we'll all understand.'

'Henry may have had his faults, Rumpole. But he calls me Sir and not Sam. And I don't believe he knows any jokes at all.'

'Of course not. No, indeed.'

The case of *R.* v. *Ireton* had not, so far as I was concerned, ended happily. *Rumpole* v. *Blewitt*, on the other hand, was an undoubted victory. Win a few, lose a few. That is all you can say about life at the Bar.

Henry decided, in his considerable relief, that he should have a Chambers' party to celebrate his not leaving. All the wives came. Hilda's old schoolfriend Dodo Mackintosh provided the cheesey bits and, perhaps because he had a vague idea of what I had been able to do for him, our clerk laid on a couple of dozen of the Château Thames Embankment of which I drank fairly deep. The day after this jamboree, I was detained in bed with a ferocious headache and a distinct unsteadiness in the leg department.

In a brief period of troubled sleep about midday, I heard voices from the living-room and then the door opened quietly and the Angel of Death was at my bedside. 'Mr Rumpole,' she smiled and her glasses twinkled, 'I hear you're not feeling very well this morning.'

'Really?' I muttered with sudden alarm. 'Whatever gave you that idea? I'm feeling on top of the world, in absolutely' – and here I winced at a sudden stabbing pain across the temples – 'tiptop condition.'

'And Hilda tells me the dear old mind's not what it was?' Dr Betty smiled understandingly. 'The butter knife in the top pocket, is that what she told me? Dear Mr Rumpole, do remember I'm here to help you. There's no need for you to suffer. The way out is always open, and I can steer you gently and quite painlessly towards it.'

'I'm afraid I must ask you to leave now,' I told the Angel of Death. 'Got to get up. Late for work already. As I told you, I never felt better. Full of beans, Dr Betty, and raring to go.'

God knows how I ever managed to climb into the striped trousers, or button the collar, but when I was decently clad I hotfooted it for the Temple. There, I sat in my room suffering, my head in my hands, determined at all costs to keep myself alive.

READ MORE IN PENGUIN

In every corner of the world, on every subject under the sun, Penguin represents quality and variety – the very best in publishing today.

For complete information about books available from Penguin – including Puffins, Penguin Classics and Arkana – and how to order them, write to us at the appropriate address below. Please note that for copyright reasons the selection of books varies from country to country.

In the United Kingdom: Please write to *Dept. EP, Penguin Books Ltd, Bath Road, Harmondsworth, West Drayton, Middlesex UB7 ODA*

In the United States: Please write to *Consumer Sales, Penguin USA, P.O. Box 999, Dept. 17109, Bergenfield, New Jersey 07621-0120*. VISA and MasterCard holders call 1-800-253-6476 to order Penguin titles

In Canada: Please write to *Penguin Books Canada Ltd, 10 Alcorn Avenue, Suite 300, Toronto, Ontario M4V 3B2*

In Australia: Please write to *Penguin Books Australia Ltd, P.O. Box 257, Ringwood, Victoria 3134*

In New Zealand: Please write to *Penguin Books (NZ) Ltd, Private Bag 102902, North Shore Mail Centre, Auckland 10*

In India: Please write to *Penguin Books India Pvt Ltd, 706 Eros Apartments, 56 Nehru Place, New Delhi 110 019*

In the Netherlands: Please write to *Penguin Books Netherlands bv, Postbus 3507, NL-1001 AH Amsterdam*

In Germany: Please write to *Penguin Books Deutschland GmbH, Metzlerstrasse 26, 60594 Frankfurt am Main*

In Spain: Please write to *Penguin Books S. A., Bravo Murillo 19, 1° B, 28015 Madrid*

In Italy: Please write to *Penguin Italia s.r.l., Via Felice Casati 20, I–20124 Milano*

In France: Please write to *Penguin France S. A., 17 rue Lejeune, F–31000 Toulouse*

In Japan: Please write to *Penguin Books Japan, Ishikiribashi Building, 2–5–4, Suido, Bunkyo-ku, Tokyo 112*

In South Africa: Please write to *Longman Penguin Southern Africa (Pty) Ltd, Private Bag X08, Bertsham 2013*

BY THE SAME AUTHOR

THE RUMPOLE BOOKS

'Rumpole is simply one of the great fictional characters of modern English literature' – Marcel Berlins in the *Sunday Times*

The First Rumpole Omnibus

Horace Rumpole's legal triumphs, plundering sorties into the *Oxford Book of English Verse* and less-than-salubrious hat are celebrated in this volume. It contains *Rumpole of the Bailey*, *The Trials of Rumpole* and *Rumpole's Return*.

'I thank heaven for small mercies. The first of these is Rumpole' – Clive James in the *Observer*

The Second Rumpole Omnibus

Here is Horace Rumpole turning down yet another invitation to exchange the joys and sorrows of life as an Old Bailey hack for the delights of the sunshine state, where Senior Citizens loll on beaches and the sarcastic tones of the Mad Bull (Judge Roger Bullingham) are heard no more. He settles instead for the beaded bubbles of Château Pommeroy's ordinary claret, the domestic chill emanating from She Who Must Be Obeyed, and his role *extraordinaire* as Defender of the Faith: 'Never plead guilty'. This volume contains *Rumpole for the Defence*, *Rumpole and the Golden Thread* and *Rumpole's Last Case*.

'Rumpole has been an inspired stroke of good fortune for us all' – Lynda Lee-Potter in the *Daily Mail*

and

Rumpole and the Age of Miracles
Rumpole á la Carte
Rumpole on Trial
The Best of Rumpole

Rumpole and the Angel of Death is also available as a Penguin Audiobook, read by Leo McKern